Dear Love, I hate you...

ELIAH
GREENWOOD

www.eliahgreenwood.com

This book is a work of fiction. Any references to historical events, real people, or real places are used fictitiously. Other names, characters, places, and events are products of the author's imagination, and any resemblance to actual events or places or persons, living or dead, is entirely coincidental.

Warning: This book contains topics which may be triggering to some readers (talks of suicide, undescriptive sexual assault, foul language, and graphic mature scenes) Helpful hotlines will be listed at the end of the book. Please proceed with caution.

ISBN: 978-1-7776223-0-5
Editing by One Love Editing
First printing edition 2021
Reality Survivor Publishing (Eliah Greenwood)

For anyone with dirty little secrets...

May you find someone who deserves your confession.

Playlist

- Secrets And Lies - Ruelle

- River – Bishop Briggs

- I Need You To Hate Me – JC Stewart

- Out of My League – Fitz And The Tantrum

- A little Bit Yours – JP Saxe

Please note that mistakes in the prologue were made intentionally.

* * *

Dear Ms. Callahan...

You're an asshole.

Knew it from the first time I walked into your class at the beginning of senior year. There. I said it. You. Are. An. Asshole. And not the "she's nice once you get to know her" asshole. You're the human equivalent of stepping into a puddle with socks on.

I wouldn't be surprised if you spent your evenings bathing in hell fire, trying to come up with new ways to make your students suffer. Seriously, what's your thought process like?

"Twenty pages on poetry? Great idea! Giving high schoolers less than forty-eight hours to read the book and turn the paper in? Even better!"

Now, before I proceed with my rant, I'd like to apologize (not really) for any mistake I might make in this letter that your never going to get. Can't really be bothered with grammar right now.

You see, I'm in a bit of a time crunch between trying to graduate high school, score a once in a life time scholarship so I can get the F out of this town, playing chauffeur to my prodigy sibling and being a full-time disappointment to my mom.

Oh, and don't forget the twenty pages.

Who needs sleep, right?

Sure, "technically", I'm to blame for getting stuck with this poetry book, but how the heck was I supposed to know the one time I'd get sick and miss English lit would be the time you'd let us pick the book for the essay that's worth fifty percent?

Granted, I would've been stuck with a boring book

either way, (You didn't exactly have thrilling options lined up) but you didn't have to do us dirty like that.

You must think I'm crazy. I promise you I'm not. I'm actually a pretty decent person when I'm not calling middle-aged women Satan. In my defense, my therapist says writing down my feelings will help me cope.

So, what if I called u an asshole? So, what if I'm sitting here, in the library, wasting my time writing a hate letter to a teacher who can never remember my name when I'm already running late? It's not like anyone is ever going to read this anyway.

I'm realizing this letter is a bit all over the place, so let me summarize it for you.

Dear Ms. Callahan,

Sincerely,

From the bottom of my heart,

Go fuck yourself.

-L

1

Aveena

"Aveena Harper D'Amour?" Mr. Lowen, my sixty-year-old math teacher, shouts over complete chaos, and I feel a twinge of pity for him—no one ever said taking attendance in the middle of a raging thunderstorm was easy.

"Here!" I yell once.

Twice.

Three times.

No luck.

Mr. Lowen spots me in the crowd a minute later, bows his head in acknowledgement, and inches his list closer to mark me down as present. How did I get here, you ask? Out in the pouring rain? Freezing my ass off on my school's front lawn with Easton High's entire student body?

Not. A. Fucking. Clue.

"Vee, thank God!" Someone yanks on my sleeve, spinning me around so fast that I lose my footing. It takes me a solid second to steady myself and recognize my best friend, Diamond, through the torrent. She's completely soaked, her signature black curls now straight as an arrow.

"I've been looking all over for you!" Dia blurts as she traps me into a hug so tight the oxygen is squeezed out of me. The only class Dia and I don't have together is math, so, *of course*, that's when the whole school had to be evacuated.

"What on earth is going on? Teachers won't tell us anything." I break away from her. "Is there really a fire?"

"Has to be." She shrugs. "Why else would the fire alarm go off?"

I give her a slight nod, scanning the small building that's Easton High School for a sign of a fire. I've got zilch to go on here—no smoke, no fire smell, absolutely *nothing* to pin to blame on.

Thunder booms in the distance, and I yelp, gripping my best friend's arm like a wuss. The sky is a dark, cloudy nightmare, Mother Nature's way of letting us know she's just getting started.

"You think it's a drill?" I ask Dia.

A mocking scoff keeps her from answering. We flip our heads to see a messy-haired, drenched Theodore Cox. He goes by Theo, and, piece of advice, don't ever call him by his full name.

He bites.

Theo, like many of his basketball teammates, is your typical quick-witted, popular asshole. You know, the "more handsome than he deserves" type. He's tall, arrogant, unfamiliar with the concept of being wrong, and to my great misery…

Someone I have to hang out with on a daily basis.

"Something you want to share with the class, Cox?" Dia sighs.

"'No fucking way that's a drill," Theo scoffs. "We already had one this year. Plus, they wouldn't do it during this end-of-the-world shit." Theo gestures to take a look around.

So, I do.

The school's front lawn is damn near bursting with students.

We're all freezing.

Soaked from head to toe.

The idiot has a point.

They wouldn't just throw a fire drill smack-dab in the middle of the apocalypse. And, as crazy as it might sound, Theodore Cox isn't *completely* deprived of brain functions.

You see, I went years assuming jocks had the intelligence of a doormat, and was perfectly content adhering to the stereotype. Then my best friend had to go and fall for one of the cool kids…

Finley Richards. Star basketball player, notorious flirt, and, as of late, Dia's favorite bad decision. Bottom line: we hang out with Finn's crowd this year. *What?* Dia's my only friend, so it's either that or I eat alone until graduation.

It all started last summer when Dia got herself a job as the Richardses' house sitter. Finn's filthy-rich father spends every summer up in Santa Monica and didn't trust his son to take care of the house one bit—did I say house? I meant *mansion.*

Golden boy didn't take his father's lack of faith in him very well and unleashed his wrath on Dia. Made her life a living hell, crossing every line imaginable to get her to quit, but she was determined to see things through.

Long story short, they hated each other.

Until… their genitals didn't.

Thus began the most confusing love/hate relationship to ever exist. Why? Because Dia and Finn aren't dating. *Not really*. They like to say they're "friends with benefits," but anyone with half a brain knows that's a load of crap. Everything a couple does, they do. Sex, PDA, exclusivity, nauseating nicknames.

The list goes on and on.

It's so painfully obvious that they have it bad, but you will never hear them refer to each other as boyfriend and girlfriend. If you ask me, their so-called "casual" relationship is a big, fat disaster just waiting to happen.

Two fire trucks branded ***Silver Springs Fire Dept*** and a police car come charging into the school's lot before Dia and Theo can argue further.

"How's that for a drill, *Finn's girl*?" Theo snarks.

"Shut up, Cox," Dia grumbles, grabbing a handful of her black, curly hair and squeezing the water out. The deluge has decreased into a drizzle. It's about time. I don't know how much longer they could've left us out in the pouring rain.

"Speaking of, where *is* Finn?" Dia pushes to her tiptoes, searching for her *not*-boyfriend. She's right. He should be here by now—these two are like magnets. Plus, it must've taken five minutes tops for kids to disobey their teachers and go find their friends.

"How should I know where your boyfriend is?" Theo drawls, his phone pinging with a text. He plucks it out of his pocket, his jaw going slack when he skims through the message on his screen. "You have *got* to be kidding me."

"What?" Dia asks.

"These crazy sons of bitches. They actually did it," he says, more to himself than us.

"The hell you talking about?" Dia pushes.

"It's—" Theo stops talking abruptly, eyes dead set on something in the distance. And it's not just him. The entire student body has gone quiet.

Dia and I track Theo's gaze to the school's main entrance, more specifically to the two six-foot-something morons being escorted out of the building by the sheriff.

The first person I see is Finn.

Then I see him.

Xavier Emery.

Finn's brother—I'd say best friends, but these two are practically family. They literally wear matching chains for Pete's sake. Xavier is a lot of things: popular, captain of the basketball team, so beautiful it's almost painful, but to me? He's the asshole little boy who cut off one of my pigtails when we were kids.

Dia loses it. "Cox, so help me God, if you don't tell me what's going on right now, I'll—"

"Chill." Theo caves. "I heard them talking about some prank after practice yesterday. Thought it was just locker room talk. I didn't think they were serious."

Is that why we were evacuated?

The basketball team's star players pulling a *prank*?

What could they have done that was so bad they had to pull the fire alarm and evacuate the whole school?'

"What sort of prank?" Dia's voice wavers with worry.

Theo shrugs. "Something about stink bombs, I think?"

Dia squeezes her eyes shut and exhales a long, exasperated sigh. Worst part is, she doesn't even look surprised. Finn Richards has *always* been the troublemaker.

That impulsive, reckless kid who, if it weren't for his rich daddy, would have been expelled many moons ago. But, hey, *what can you do*? Easton High needs the funding, and just like Xavier, Finn is one of the team's most valuable players, so they sweep his behavior under the rug.

Objectively, Finn is a no-brainer. It's the Xavier part of it all that makes no sense to me. Dude hasn't so much as *breathed* wrong since freshman year, so to take part in a prank like this? I don't get it.

"Wait, isn't setting off a stink bomb illegal?" I realize.

"Sure is. Jesus, what are they, dense? This could cost them the rest of the season." Theo *tsks.*

I haul my attention back to the boys. Finn seems to realize just how horribly he messed up when he catches sight of the six hundred kids standing in the rain. Meanwhile, Xavier doesn't give a *semblance* of a fuck.

Not one.

It's the droop of his shoulders, the way his eyes glaze over the crowd with boredom. Even his walk feels like a statement. If I didn't know any better, I'd say Xavier and Finn switched bodies in the world's worst remake of *Freaky Friday*.

A police officer pulls Principal Emery aside—yep, Xavier's mom is the principal. Might come in handy right about now, but the cherry on top? Xavier's dad is also employed at Easton High. He's our PE teacher. The one we love to hate.

I get Silver Springs is a small town and all, but they could've at least *tried* to branch out.

The cop tells Principal Emery something we can't hear, to which she replies with a "Do what you have to do" nod. That's the universe's cue to drop the entire Pacific Ocean on our heads. The rain picks up again, harder than it was moments prior, and I can't help watching Dumb and Dumber get dragged toward the cop car out front.

Remember when I said Xavier Emery was so beautiful it's almost painful? The way he looks right now… *that's* what I'm talking about. Even soaked, about to get his ass thrown in the back of a cop car, with his shirt sticking to his hard, sculpted body and his light brown hair dripping down his forehead, he's every girl's wet dream—pun intended.

Granted, the guy was an asswipe when he disappeared from

my life at age eight, but I can appreciate the blue-eyed Adonis just as much as the next girl.

"Never a dull moment in Silver Springs, huh?" Theo remarks as Xavier and Finn are shoved into the back seat and the police car takes off at full speed. "Man, I hope this means we have the day off tomorrow. I haven't even started Ms. Callahan's paper yet."

Memories slam into me.

I landed a job at the school library this year—which, fun fact, also operates as Silver Springs' public library—and I had a shift yesterday before I went to pick up my sister from her singing lesson.

Ended up writing some stupid letter to my English teacher to vent. I couldn't find the poetry book in my bag this morning.

I left it there, didn't I?

I left the book at the library.

With the letter inside.

For crying out loud, Vee, how dumb can you possibly be?

It's one thing to be having a really bad day and take it out on your ball-busting teacher in a hate letter. It's another to be so stupid you forget the letter at the library for anyone to find.

I can already see it. The school ringing up my mom to let her know her least favorite daughter got suspended for, quote, "accusing her teacher of bathing in hellfire."

My dad's voice pops into my head before panic wins me over.

Slow down, take a breath, and find the bright side.

Well, it doesn't hurt that I left the letter inside an old, dusty book that hasn't been checked out in over ten years. Odds are I'll be off to college with a bun in the oven by the time someone finds it. And even if someone did happen upon it, what's to say they'd trace it back to me?

Shit, I think I mentioned my musical genius of a sister.

And my potential scholarship.

Fine, maybe they could trace it back to me if they put in the research. But that's not going to happen. I'm not going to let it. Mr. Lowen tells us we have the rest of the day off, and all thoughts of Xavier Emery vanish from my mind.

There's only one thought left in there.

One mission.

One plan.

I have to get my hands on that letter before someone else does.

2

Xavier

"Do you two shit-for-brains have *any* idea what you just did?" Hank, Finn's dad, grits out in that low, whispery voice that's ten times scarier than when he yells in your face.

I should probably be quaking in my boots right now, reflecting on my "immature and reckless actions"—Hank's words. Better yet, I should be trying to come up with an excuse to justify what I did, but all I can think about as the man I consider to be my second father grills me is…

Man, that is one big-ass forehead vein.

Has the vein on Hank's forehead always been this big?

He's so pissed it looks like it's about to pop.

Why do I kind of *want* it to pop?

Please pop, vein.

Part of me was hoping Sheriff Daniel had only driven us to the police station for show. After all, I've spent *years* watching Finn pull pranks like this and get off without so much as a warning. My hopes went up in smoke when they threw our delinquent asses into an interrogation room and told us to take a seat. Then the sheriff and Finn's dad took turns yelling at us for three hours.

"Xav?" Hank urges.

I snap out of it. "Mm?"

"You waiting for the grass to grow? Answer the goddamn question."

Shit.

Note to self: you might want to try listening when people talk.

"I—"

Finn cuts in, "No, of course we didn't think they were going to evacuate the school, Dad. It was just one little stink bomb."

I make eye contact with my best friend.

Finn smirks.

Thanks for the save, dickhead.

"Oh, cry me a fucking river. That 'one little stink bomb'—" Hank makes air quotes with his fingers, "—smelled so bad your poor teacher thought it was some sort of gas leak. You knew what you were doing, Finley. Don't you get it? You're in deep shit. And I don't know if I can get you out of it this time."

Hank inhales a deep breath to keep himself in check.

"How does a three week suspension sound, huh? What about senior year without basketball? And prom? I sure hope you weren't planning on going because there's no way in fucking hell that's happening now."

Helpless, Finn smacks his mouth shut, sagging back into his

seat. To be fair, while it did smell like something died in that classroom, I have no idea how our substitute teacher could confuse "hot garbage and fart" with "gas."

I was sitting at the back of the class and set off the stink bomb when she stepped out for a bit. The lady panicked as soon as the smell hit and notified the school's front office of a "disgusting, toxic smell" through the intercom.

They set off the fire alarm and got us out of the building in record time. Makes sense, they couldn't risk that many kids' safety. What if it really had been a leak?

I still can't believe how quickly we got caught.

All thanks to their so-called "video."

That's the first thing they said when they came to extract Finn and me from the crowd after the school gathered outside. They hit us with "*Don't bother, we've got it on video. You're busted*" before dragging us back inside to wait for the cops.

I have no idea how they managed to catch it on video in a classroom with no surveillance camera, but I can't think about that right now.

"You've got to learn to think before you act, son." Hank knocks on Finn's forehead like he's making sure there's a brain in there. "Fucking *think*."

I remember finding Hank so cool for cursing when I was a kid. I paid attention when he talked because of it. And, trust me, that means a lot coming from the two second attention span, little shit that I was. Then the accident happened, and he started dropping the f-bomb every two words.

Eventually, it lost its impact.

But then again… I'd curse, too, if I'd lost the love of my life.

"As for you." Hank glares straight through my skull. "Consider yourself lucky this is your first time pulling this kind of crap. Unlike *someone*—" He eyes Finn, "—you should be able to finish the season. Maybe get a few weeks of detention. And that's only because we've got the sheriff on our side. If you two clowns were *any* other kids, you could be facing criminal fucking charges right now, do you get that?"

Finn and I nod. My best friend's eyes are packed with regret. That's downright torture for him. Ball is our whole lives. And I know how much he wanted to land team captain.

He didn't smile for days when I got it.

Ah, shit, I can't let them do this.

"He had nothing to do with it," I blurt out.

Arms folded over his chest, Hank doesn't say a word for the longest of seconds. I can tell he doesn't buy it one bit, but if there's the tiniest chance that I could save his kid's senior year, he has to hear me out.

Finn widens his eyes at me. "Xav, what are you—"

"Let him talk, son." Hank gestures for me to go ahead with a flick of his chin.

"He wasn't a part of it. *I* came up with it. *I* brought the stupid thing to school. *I* set it off. It was all me," I lie.

"Nice try, but I saw the video. Hell, I'm willing to bet your whole school's seen it by now. You showed him the stink bomb in your backpack a minute before it went off."

I swallow the urge to ask him about that damn video they keep referring to.

Not the time, Xav.

"Exactly, I *showed* it to him. How does that prove anything? Doesn't mean he knew about it beforehand. Or that he was involved in any way."

In response, Hank starts pacing around the room, rubbing his temples as though he genuinely believes it'll help him think better. Then, five painful seconds later, he says it.

"I don't believe you."

There goes my hero moment.

"You're not that type of kid, Xav. You're a good kid. Eighteen years I've known you and you haven't let my son talk you into his bad ideas *once*, so no, I don't believe you pulled this off all by yourself."

Defeated, I look down at my feet.

"But…" Hank surprises me by adding. My head jerks up. "If that's the story you want to go with. If you want to shoulder the blame to save your buddy, I can't stop you."

I peek at Finn from the corner of my eye. Finn, who for *once* in his life, wasn't the mastermind behind a prank. I might've been lying when I said he had nothing to do with it, but this part is true: it was my idea. *Mine.* If anything, I'm the one who talked him into it.

"I'm not covering for him. That's what happened."

I can practically see the weight of the world lifting off Finn's shoulders when the words escape my mouth.

"If you say so." Hank nods, a small smile tugging at his lips.

I read him crystal clear.

That's a "*thank you*" right there.

"All right. We'll pass the message along to the school, let them handle your punishment. Sheriff wants to talk to you again, then you'll both be free to go." Hank trails toward the door, but seconds before he exits the room, he stops, eyeing me over his shoulder. "I just have one question."

I wait for him to lay it on me.

"Why now?" he asks.

"Not following?" I reply.

"Why are you acting out all of a sudden? This isn't you, kid."

If I told you, you'd never look at me the same way again.

"No reason."

* * *

"What on earth were you thinking?" my mother belts, her voice sounding like nails on a chalkboard.

Shut up.

Just shut up.

"Xavier Emery! I'm talking to you!" she screeches.

I don't flinch.

If she thinks "full-naming" me is going to do shit, she's got another thing coming. I sink deeper into the passenger seat, watching the only town I've ever known roll by through the car window.

The woman's been hounding me with questions since she picked me up from the police station thirty minutes ago. I haven't answered her once, but it's become more than obvious that "*giving up*" isn't a part of her vocabulary.

Between us… she's also unfamiliar with the term "*fidelity.*"

"Xavier, did you hear me?" She grows impatient.

"I heard you," I drone.

Satisfied, she continues to yell. "Do you even realize how lucky you are that Hank is close friends with Sheriff Daniel? He's the only reason, and I mean the *only* reason, you were able to walk free today. Best I could've done is beg the sheriff not to charge you."

I snort out a laugh.

Well, it sure wouldn't be the first time you got down on your knees in front of another man this week, would it, Mom?

"I told you this Finn kid is a bad influence. Just like his older brother." She checks herself out in the rearview mirror at a red light, wiping a smidge of lipstick from her mouth with her index. "I don't care how long you've known each other. Or that your father and his are old friends. That family's trouble. I wish the two of you would just cut ties with these people already."

I bite down on my tongue so hard not to talk back I draw

blood. A metallic taste floods my mouth, and I ball up my fists in an attempt *not* to blow the passenger door open and jump out of the car.

You really have no idea, do you?

I know what you did.

I know everything.

Hank's question has been gnawing at me since I left the police station. *Why are you acting out all of a sudden? This isn't you.* Maybe, subconsciously, I convinced myself that starting shit in my mom's place of work was the next best thing to getting revenge on her.

To hurt her for what I saw.

But then… why do I still want to punch a hole through her windshield? Why can't I stomach the thought of looking into my dad's eyes? And why, *fucking why*, can't I bring myself to tell him?

Mom tries forcing small talk for five more minutes before taking a hint. The remainder of the drive home is uneventful except for my phone pinging with a text from Finn just as we're pulling into the driveway.

Finn: Thanks for what you did back there, man. I owe you one. Oh, and, just a heads up… You might want to check your girlfriend's snapchat story.

Aveena

Three days later

"Brie's Snapchat story?" A laugh shoots out of me as I shadow my best friend up the stairs leading up to her room. "No way?"

"*Yes way.*" Dia sneers. "It's all everyone's been talking about. I can't believe you haven't seen it yet." Dia pushes the door to her closet bedroom and launches herself onto the single bed shoved into a corner. I'm not making fun of her room, it *literally* used to be a closet.

Dia comes from a family of six, and her dads ran out of room when they adopted their youngest last year, so they had to improvise. We'll all be leaving for college in a few months, hence Dia giving her parents the green light to move her into this shoebox until then.

"Five bucks says Xavier dumps Brie for this." Dia pats the empty space on her bed. "Get your ass over here."

I oblige, sitting cross-legged on my best friend's bed while she pulls out her phone and opens the Camera Roll.

"I screen-recorded her story before it disappeared," Dia explains, scrolling through pictures of her and Finn smiling, hugging, kissing—mind you, these two are *still* claiming to be just friends. It takes her a moment to find it amongst all the cute couple shit.

"Gotcha," she says and enlarges the video.

Brielle Randall, cheerleader, student council president, and expert mean girl, pops up on the screen, flaunting the Snapchat puppy filter. This has to have been taken when the teacher stepped out. Pouting, Brie fluffs her long, fiery red hair with one hand and puckers her lips to the camera with the caption:

#IHaveNoSelfieControl

I don't see it at first—neither did Brie, ironically.

Until Dia plays it again.

And I spot them in the background.

Xavier and Finn.

Completely unaware of the phone pointed at them, the boys exchange knowing looks as Xavier points to the backpack at his feet and kicks it closer to Finn so he can peek inside.

They are so obviously up to something it's no wonder the school put two and two together in minus ten seconds. Xavier inspects his surroundings for witnesses—not thoroughly enough, obviously—and plunges a hand inside his backpack. The video cuts just as he's pulling out the stink bomb.

Yep. That'll do it.

Good luck proving your innocence, bud.

I know I shouldn't find humor in other people's misery, but the irony of His Majesty Xavier Emery getting his ass exposed on social media by his own girlfriend is unreal.

"What happened? Did they get suspended?" I bite back a grin.

"You didn't hear?" She sounds shocked.

I scoff. "I'm sorry, do you *not* know who you're talking to?"

Dia knows damn well I can't keep up with school gossip. This girl is the reason I know anything these days.

"Right." She chuckles. "Xavier took the fall. Swore Finn had nothing to do with it. That's the official story, anyway."

"He did? Why?" I can't conceal my surprise.

"I'm guessing to save his buddy?" She shrugs. "Finn said they were going to cut him from the team, so Xav stepped up. That's *so* Xavier."

I abstain from telling her what I really think of Mr. Nice Guy. It's like the whole school—*the whole town, really*—shares an undying passion for blowing smoke up Xavier Emery's ass.

Understandably so.

They don't know him like I do.

As far as anyone can tell, Xavier is this great, stand-up kid. He's faithful to his girl, wields just as much talent on the court as he does in the classroom, doesn't go around stirring up trouble—*well, until now.*

Xavier spends all his time with Finn and Theo, the two of whom have pretty much slept their way through the entire cheer squad, and yet… Xavier's been in a serious relationship with Brie for over a year now.

Everybody knows Finn and Theo eat this shit up: the parties, the whole town following every game like a religion, the groupies. In the ladies' defense, Silver Springs, North Carolina, isn't exactly "hot guy central"—downside of living in a town with a population of 5,658. If you ever find yourself lucky enough to spot a fine specimen roaming freely, you can bet your ass twenty other girls saw him, too.

But Xavier?

He actually seems a little… *bored.* Bored with the easy victories, the after-game ragers, the eyelash-batting girls. To the world, Finn is that jock who tackles a kid in the hall, and Xavier is the jock who helps the kid to his feet.

But I don't buy it.

Not for a single second.

Just because Xavier's slightly less awful than the rest of his friends doesn't make him a saint in my book. In fact, I must not know the same guy as the rest of the world because Xavier Emery's never been anything other than a royal ass to me. Sure, we were eight the last time we interacted, but *potayto, potahto.*

Finn, Xavier, and I used to be sort of friends when we were eight. We'd have playdates at Finn's house every Sunday morning during my sister's singing lessons, eat brunch, annoy the fuck out of each other while our moms gossiped.

And by annoy the fuck out of each other, I mean Xavier and Finn annoyed *me*. RIP to all the Barbies they tossed into the barbecue that summer.

Of course, that was back when our moms could still stand each other. Turns out the only thing my mom and Delilah Emery, Xavier's mom, ever had in common was their friendship with Nora Richards. So, when Finn's mom died in a tragic boating accident that summer, the trio fell apart.

Then everything changed.

There were no more brunches, no more playdates, no more suffering at the hands of evil little boys. Then Xavier and Finn transferred elementary schools, and I never gave them another thought. Until I saw them waltz into Easton High like they owned the place freshman year.

Okay, that's a *lie*.

I did think about Xavier a little after he evaporated from my life. But, only because of what happened at the park the last time we played together. To think we had no idea Ms. Richards would meet a tragic fate twenty-four hours later.

Right before her son's eyes, no less.

I was hiding under the big slide in tears, choking on my snot with blood gushing out of my knee after Xavier pushed me down the jungle gym. That has to be the first and only time I've ever seen real emotion in this boy's eyes.

And the emotion in his eyes was guilt.

A lot of it.

"I'm sorry. Please stop crying," he begged. I think he was afraid of getting in trouble. It was one thing to tease me, another to literally *hurt* me. "I swear I didn't mean to. I'm sorry. Please, don't tell my dad."

This was also the first time he'd ever been *semi*-nice to me.

When I didn't stop weeping, he panicked and added, "What do you want me to do? Just tell me. Want me to kiss it better?"

I remember looking at him like he was mental for suggesting to kiss my bloody knee, and he laughed at the realization. Then he grabbed my face, wiped a tear rolling down my cheek…

And kissed *me* instead.

Believe me when I say that shut me right up.

Xavier Emery was my first kiss.

But he's still an asshole.

"—heard he and Brie got into a big fight about it. She deleted some of their pics from Instagram, too."

I snap back to reality, nodding along to my best friend's story and wondering how she knows everything about everything. It's barely been three days since the guys' prank.

The weekend isn't even over yet.

They gave us the day off on Friday. Had the fire department go around the school to make sure the boys didn't leave us any more… *surprises.* I've never been this impatient to go back to school in my life.

Two words: Hate letter.

I've been obsessing over getting that stupid piece of paper back since they sent us home on Thursday. Thanks to the boys' stunt, the library was closed all weekend, which meant no work for me, and no opportunity to burn the damn thing.

I'm probably overreacting. The odds of someone finding the letter before I do are next to zero. Ms. Callahan made it known she owns copies of all essay books to help her grading process, so she definitely won't go looking for it, but I'm still terrified of getting caught.

"So, what's Xavier's punishment?" I ask. "If he took the fall, it's got to be serious."

"*Eh*, I don't know yet." Dia shrugs. "I don't even think Xav knows. But since he's a first offender and all, probably detention?" Dia's phone chimes with a text, and she checks the screen quickly. "There's this thing at Theo's later. His parents are gone for the night. You in?"

"Let me think about it." I pause. "*Pass.*"

"That wasn't thinking about it," Dia scolds.

"I'm a very fast thinker," I tease, and she heaves a discouraged sigh. "What happened to hanging out just the two of us tonight?"

She nibbles on her bottom lip. "Vee, you know I love you, but… we've spent *three years* hanging out just the two of us. It's our senior year. Don't you want to make sure we live it?"

Deep down, I always suspected Dia wanted more.

More popularity, more parties, more flings. And, if I'm being honest, part of me has been dreading the inevitable day where "more" would want her back.

Waiting for the day Easton's airhead boys would wake up and realize my best friend is drop-dead gorgeous. Dia is of Spanish and Indonesian origins. The tan, dark-haired beauty who'd have no problem racking up millions of followers on Instagram if she just tried.

I don't mean this in an envious way.

I'm confident enough to say that I'm no dog myself. On my good days, I even like how I look—my butt-length, wavy, caramel-brown hair, my hazel eyes with flecks of green, even the freckles I used to cover up, but I'm nowhere near as comfortable in my skin as Dia is.

I don't do shorts, crop tops, or bikinis. I'm a turtleneck, one-size-too-big mom jeans kind of gal, and as much as I like my wallflower style, sometimes I think it's gifted me with the power of invisibility. As far as the male population is concerned, anyway.

Meh. It's probably for the best.

My papa used to say Silver Springs was a dead-end town. Called it a "Loserfest." He was *this* close to convincing Mom to get the hell out before he died. He'd roll over in his grave if he saw his little girl focusing on anything other than her dreams. Right now, the only thing that matters is getting a scholarship.

"Earth to Vee?" Dia waves a hand in my face.

"Sorry. Look, if you want to go see Finn, just say so, it's

okay."

"I don't," she says, and I arch an "are you for real" eyebrow at her. "Okay, fine, I haven't seen him all weekend, but I want to hang out with you, too."

"It's cool, D. We'll just reschedule. I've got to pick up Ashley in half an hour anyway." I haven't even taken a step before Dia's leaping off her bed and holding me back.

"Vee, do you know how many people at school would *kill* to be invited to these things?" She grips my shoulders as if to drill the words into my brain. "In a few months, high school will be over. Done. *Forever.* If you don't at least try to enjoy what's left of it, future-you will regret it."

Hesitant, I chew on the inside of my cheek.

"Come on, we're just going to play pool, have a few drinks. It'll be low-key. Just us and the guys. *Pleaseee.*" She joins her hands together, shamelessly begging.

"Jesus Christ, fine," I relent. "I'll stop by after I've picked up Ashley, but if it sucks, I'm gone."

Squealing, Dia traps me into a hug. "It won't suck, promise."

Withdrawing from the hug, I say my goodbyes and make my way out of the Mitchells' house.

* * *

"Ashley Camilla Harper!" I shout from the bottom of my lungs the moment I step foot inside my house. "Would it kill you to text me when rehearsal gets canceled?"

No reply.

Her shoes are here, which means she is, too. In a fury, I dump my keys into the bowl by the door and take the stairs two at a time in direction of my sister's bedroom.

"I waited for you for two hours. *Two hours*!" I yell over the music emanating from her closed door. The closer I get, the louder the chorus of "River" by Bishop Briggs roars. Gripping the knob, I slam her door open and…

Regret it instantly.

First thing I see is my sister half-naked on her bed.

Second thing I see is the shirtless guy on top of her.

Funny enough, the sight of my seventeen-year-old sister getting down and dirty is not what does it for me. What sends my heart straight to my stomach is the boy with his tongue shoved down her throat.

What in heaven's name is *he* doing here?

The music is so loud they didn't even hear me come in. They probably didn't hear me yell on my way up either. Douchebag's hand snakes around my sister's back to unclasp her bra, and I break into a mini panic attack. I'd rather she didn't have her breasts out when I yelled at her, *thank you very much.*

In a moment of panic, I unplug my sister's phone from her portable speaker and let out the loudest "What the fuck?" I can muster. The two culprits jump, backing away from each other as fast as humanly possible. Ashley's jaw plummets to the ground as she pats the bed for her shirt.

"Vee! W-What are you doing home so early?" She crushes her T-shirt against her chest.

"Early? It's past six."

"It is?" Ashley pounces off her bed, throwing her T-shirt back on like the time on the clock is a much bigger deal than her getting caught in bed with *him*.

"You left me stranded at the academy for two hours!"

"Shit, shit, shit." She begins roaming around her room like a maniac. "I…. Please don't tell Mom. I'm so sorry, Vee. I was going to meet you at my school so you could pick me up, but then… I guess we lost track of time and—"

"Wait a second," I cut in, "What do you mean you were going to *meet* me at the school so I could pick you up? As in you weren't there to begin with?"

The face she makes next says it all. That wasn't supposed to come out, was it?

She winces, "Okay, don't be mad, but… I might've sort of made up the Sunday rehearsals."

"*Excuse me*?"

She covers her face with her French manicured hands. "I know, I'm sorry. Please don't hate me. I just wanted to have some free time. Mom is driving me insane."

"So, you're telling me I've been going out of my way to pick you up from a place you didn't even *have* to go to every Sunday for three months?"

As if it weren't bad enough that I have to pick her up from her singing lessons at her fancy-pants music academy every day of the week.

"You know damn well if I hadn't come up with the rehearsals, Mom would have scheduled me like five lessons on Sundays, on top of Saturdays, and I barely have time to breathe as is. I'm sorry you have to play chauffeur. I told Mom I'd grab the bus so she wouldn't make you pick me up, but she insisted you had nothing better to d—"

"Ash." I exhale. "It's fine. I get it."

As much as I want to be mad at her, I can't.

Can't blame her for wanting to live a little.

Can't blame her for being so ridiculously talented she won *Rising Voices*, a huge televised singing competition, when she was six years old. And I *especially* can't blame her for paying a good part of our bills with said competition's winning prize and her YouTube channel ever since.

Eleven-year-old Aveena used to yearn for this shit. There was a time where I would've killed to be my mom's shining star. To be the center of her universe, to take Ashley's place.

Not anymore.

Now I understand how lucky I was to be born ordinary.

My mother became my sister's "momager" from the moment she realized Ashley could carry a tune. Ash couldn't have been older than four the first time Mom looked at her with dollar signs in her eyes. And if there's one thing I've learned, watching Ashley exhaust herself trying to build a career since kindergarten, it's that being special comes at a price very few are brave enough to pay.

"Are you going to tell Mom?" Ashley stresses her bottom lip.

I pretend to think about it, when, in fact, my answer is already set in stone.

"No," I say, and her shoulders drop with relief.

"Thanks, Vee. You're the best."

"But you're getting your ass home by cab from now on. I don't care where you go during the day, as long as we're both home at the same time, Mom doesn't have to know."

Without a word, she traps me into a hug, which I return halfheartedly. I want to hate her. I did for a long time, but it didn't last. Because no matter how talented she is, no matter how many hits her original songs get on YouTube, my little sister is a genuinely nice person.

I might not agree with my mom on many things, but she was right to insist Ashley graduate high school in Silver Springs before moving to LA and giving this superstar thing a shot. It kept her grounded…

For the most part.

Fine, Ash can have a bit of an inflated ego at times, thinks the world revolves around her, and doesn't realize how blessed she is to have all this at seventeen, but she's a good soul at her core… Which is more than I can say for the piece of trash in her bed.

"Oh, and this—" I point to her ex-boyfriend, "—has to stop. Mom will kill you."

Ashley's bad decision gives me a slow body scan.

"Long time, Vee." His smirk sends shivers of disgust oozing through my entire body.

"Logan." I don't so much as glance his way, focusing on Ashley. "Since when are you two back together?"

"Just happened, actually," my sister says, a big, dopey smile on her face, and my chest aches.

"I thought you left town," I tell Logan, directing every ounce of my energy into hiding my disdain for him.

Bastard, you promised.

You promised you'd never come back after what we did.

"I know, but I changed my mind. What can I say? I missed my girl." He looks me dead in the eyes as he says it, the innuendo so painfully clear I want to dig myself into a hole and hide from my demons.

Hide from my shame.

Ashley's phone rings seconds before it gets awkward.

"Shit, it's Rob." She flips the screen and shows me her manager's name. Mom likes to think she's in control, but we all know Ash gets her opportunities elsewhere. "I have to take it."

She exits the room, leaving me alone with the person I like least on this earth. Her footsteps rumbling down the stairs are Logan's cue to make his move.

"Missed me?" he has the audacity to ask.

"Not for a fucking second."

Unfazed, he stalks toward me.

"Well, that's too bad. Because I missed you, *Vee-card.*"

Disgust coils in my throat.

Is that what he's been calling me?

My nickname when he talks to his friends?

"Get it? *Vee*-card? Because your name's Aveena, and, well… I don't need to explain the rest, do I?"

"L-Let me make myself perfectly clear: you two were over. You'd been broken up for months." I try my best to sound confident, but my voice is barely above a whisper. "And you said you'd never come back. You and I… it meant nothing. *Nothing*, got it?"

"Okay."

At first, I'm surprised. Surprised by how easy it was. Surprised that he genuinely seemed to get the message. Until he nudges the door closed and traps me into the tight corner by Ashley's desk.

I could puke.

Because he's hard.

Because I'm a horrible person.

But most of all, I'm a horrible sister. I hate that the one wild thing I ever did turned out to be my biggest mistake. Well, actually, it wasn't *that* big… if you know what I mean.

"But that doesn't mean we can't do it again, does it, Vee-card?" Logan's thumb brushes down the side of my face, and I recoil. "Hell, if Ash is up for it, what do you say we make it a threesome?"

The worst part is, I don't think he's kidding.

"Get the fuck off me!" I shove him away.

"Such a dirty little mouth. I liked it better when it was wrapped around my—"

I slap him so hard even I'm shocked. His jaw goes slack, his eyes as dark as his soul as he takes a threatening step forward.

"You bitch," he says through clenched teeth, stopping dead when Ashley's voice climbs in volume. She's on her way back, still on the phone. "Look, sissy's coming back. What do you think? Bad time to present the threesome idea?"

Fear must be written all over my face because he cracks a spiteful laugh. Ashley and I just got our relationship back in a good place. She can never know about what happened.

Ever.

"Oh, don't pout, Vee-card. Your secret's safe with me." Logan retreats to the bed where my sister left him. Tears prickling at my eyes, I swing the door open, but two seconds before I book it down the hall, Logan adds,

"For now."

4

Aveena

It's a quarter to seven when I park my car into Theodore Cox's driveway and kill the engine. On any other day, I would've gone through every excuse in the book to skip this party, or "small gathering"—or whatever the hell they're calling it—but I had to get out of my house.

Away from Ash and Logan.

Especially after my mom invited the psycho over for dinner.

It's crazy to me how easily Logan can flip his "nice guy" switch on. It's been well over a year since he and Ashley broke up, and the bastard still slid back into character without blinking.

He's got his kiss-ass persona down to a T: the shy smiles, the *please's* and *thank you's*, the bogus compliments to my mom who wants nothing more than to believe she looks half her age.

Could've fooled me—hell, he *did* fool me. Fooled me into trusting him, fooled me into opening up, fooled me into betraying my own blood.

Theo's driveway is packed with cars, one of them Dia's lime-green bug car. Sauntering toward Theo's single-story house, I pull out my phone to text my best friend a quick "I'm here."

Crickets.

I've been to Theo's place once before, for the back-to-school party Dia dragged me to at the beginning of senior year. I knock on the door five times before ditching my manners and walking in uninvited. Theo's kitchen is desert, although every flat surface is covered in empty beer cans and red cups.

"Dia?" I call, craning my neck to peek into the living room.

Not a soul in sight.

That's when a high-pitched scream slices through the air, accompanied by a loud splash and distant laughter. I tail the noises to the backyard and slide the glass door open to find Easton High's elite in the pool.

Well, technically, only Finn, Dia, and Theo are in the pool. Brielle and cheer captain, Lacey Mattson, are lying out on yellow sun loungers in their bikinis while Axel Fletcher, a guy from the basketball team, eyes them like they're racks of lamb.

I venture out of the house, anxiety stirring up in my stomach. Dia is yelling at Finn for pushing her into the water all dressed, splashing him, calling him names, but Finn's smile doesn't waver one bit as he swims toward her. He scoops her up into his arms to kiss her and she practically melts into his hands.

No one's seen me yet.

I couldn't fit in less if I tried. *Yep, that's my cue.* I backtrack slowly, hoping to retreat to my car before they notice m—

"Vee?" I recognize Dia's voice.

Shit.

"Oh, hey." I wave awkwardly.

All eyes are on me.

"Were you leaving?" my best friend worries.

"What? No, I was just… going to get myself a drink. Inside. Because I'm hot." I fan myself.

Real smooth, dumbass.

"Can't argue with that." Axel Fletcher lowers his sunglasses as if to inspect the merchandise.

Classy.

I've got to give it to him, the guy sure lives up to his reputation. To think he'd be a solid eight if he didn't sexualize everything with a heartbeat.

Dia hurries out of the pool, making a beeline for the red cooler by the barbecue. Her drenched shorts and tank top fit her like a second skin, her thick black hair a tangled, curly mess. Finn got her *good.*

"What do you want? Beer? Iced tea? We got everything."

"Iced tea's good."

"Here you go." She hands me a can of Arizona Iced Tea. "Shoot, you didn't bring your bathing suit, did you?"

I shake my head.

"Did *you*?" I gesture to her attire, and she laughs.

"Yeah, I was about to put it on before my dumbass of a boyf—" She clears her throat, "Before *Finn* tossed me in the pool."

There it is. I've been waiting for her to slip up for a while now, to validate my suspicions.

Their nonexclusive relationship isn't Dia's idea. It never was. It's Finn. *He's* the one pushing this "friends with benefits" nonsense. Dia would've locked it down ages ago. She already sees him as her boyfriend.

This is so not going to end well.

"I'm going to go change into my swimsuit real quick. Go mingle." She motions to her shiny, newer-model friends.

I nod, but internally, I'm begging her not to leave me alone with them. Dia takes off in the direction of the house, then stops, shoulder-checking me. "Oh, and Vee?"

"Yeah?"

"I'm really glad you came."

I crack a small smile.

"Me too," I lie.

I make my way over to the pool as Dia retreats inside Theo's house. I consider mixing with the girls for a second, then realize I'd rather gouge my eyes out with a pitchfork than make small talk with Brielle Randall.

We went to middle school together, and I swear Brie and her minions got off on making my life miserable. She actually took a few jabs at me the first time we hung out with the jocks at school.

Lucky for me, Finn shut her down faster than a speeding

bullet. Told her anyone important to Dia was important to him and she could either shut the fuck up or leave. Finn might be a scared-of-commitment little bitch, but even I've got to admit the guy is fiercely loyal.

"Hey, Aveena!" Lacey waves as I close in on the pool.

"Hey." I smile, and surprisingly, it's genuine.

Sometimes I wonder why Lacey hangs out with Brielle. Sure, they're both cheerleaders, gorgeous, popular, but personality-wise, they're worlds apart.

I did a science project with Lacey once—let's try that again: I did a science project all by myself while Lacey *watched* once, and she was nice. She might not be the brightest crayon in the box, but for the captain of the cheerleading team, she's… surprisingly decent.

I sit by the pool, rolling the hem of my jeans as high as I can and kicking off my fake Toms to dip my feet into the water.

"Vee, hey. Glad you could make it," Finn says to be polite. It's as obvious as Brie's fake-tan that he's only being nice to me because I'm his girl's best friend, but I appreciate it nonetheless.

Theo snorts. "Aveena, is it? Anyone ever tell you your name sounds like a hand cream?"

I'm about to reply when Theo's eyes light up.

"There he is," Theo cheers. "About fucking time."

"Where'd you go, princess? Got held up at the hair salon?" Finn laughs.

I whisk my head back to see none other than Xavier Emery

walking out of Theo's house in all his sexy good-boy glory—I'd say *bad boy*, but according to the entire flipping town, the guy can do no wrong. He's in shabby jeans and a black T-shirt. Looks like he didn't get the pool party memo either.

"Babyyy!" Brie leaps off her lounge chair, strolling toward him and flinging her arms around his shoulders to plaster a kiss to his cheek. Xavier doesn't even *look* at her before untangling her arms from his neck one by one.

Ouch.

Then he ambles over to the pool to give some sort of handshake to Finn and Theo. *It's a guy thing, don't ask.* Brie stands there, eyes widened, jaw hanging.

"You can't be fucking serious. You're still mad?" she whines.

As cool as a freaking cucumber, Xavier swivels around, looks her dead in the eyes, and says, "I'm not mad. We're just over."

The backyard is so quiet I can hear my own breathing.

"*Daaamn, son*!" Theo presses his fist to his mouth.

Remember when I said Theodore Cox wasn't that stupid?

Never mind.

"I meant what I said last night, Brie. We're done. You need to stop hanging around my friends." Xavier finishes her.

Any normal person would be devastated in this situation, but the most prominent emotion on Brie's face isn't sadness. It's *rage*. She looks like she's wondering how to get away with cutting Xavier up into a million tiny pieces.

"Whatever. Not like I ever loved you anyway," she spits,

turning to leave. "Lace, you coming? We're not welcome here."

"Actually," Finn chimes in. "Lacey came over because Dia invited her, unlike your stalker ass who decided to tag along and invite herself, so she can stay, and you can scram. How's that?"

Brie's bruised ego peeks through her poker face for a fraction of a second.

"Lacey?" she insists.

Lacey avoids Brie's glare. "Actually, I… I think I'm going to stick around for a bit."

I almost feel bad for Brie.

Almost.

Then I remember the time she superglued my chair in the third grade and I had to strip off my pants to get up.

Dia pads out of the house in her bikini just as Brie's telling Xavier, "Just so you know, if anyone asks, you've got a micro dick."

On that note, she flips him off and exits the Coxes' property. Her car roars down the street seconds later.

"What the… What'd I miss?" Dia asks.

"Brie just got dumped. That's what. Get your cute ass in that pool," Finn commands, and Dia complies, joining her *friend* pronto. Finn draws her into his chest, scattering kisses all over her neck and cheek as she giggles.

Wow, I'm so single.

"Lace, come on!" Dia yells, and Lacey wastes no time diving into the pool. When did these two become friends? Right. What did I expect? *Dia's popular now*. I'm convinced I couldn't possibly feel more out of place than I do in this very moment.

Until he proves me wrong.

"What the fuck is *she* doing here?"

I don't need to look at him to know he's talking about me. My head whisks up, and I meet the most vibrant pair of aqua-blue eyes I've ever seen. I've been quiet, near invisible up until this point, but there's no hiding now.

"I thought we said close friends only." Xavier stares at me in sheer disgust.

"Don't be a dick, man. She's Dia's best friend." Finn comes to my rescue.

"So fucking what? She's no friend of mine."

"There's the bully I remember." The words fall out before I can stop them. Xavier's eyebrows shoot upward at my response. I'm guessing he didn't think I'd talk back since I never did before.

Well, we're not eight anymore.

His eyes won't leave me, a million questions stirring beneath his gaze. Only then do I understand I've got it all wrong. He's not surprised that I talked back. He's confused.

He doesn't remember me.

"Fuck you, Xavier," Dia snaps. "She's staying."

"You know, guys, if we're going to hang out with the less fortunate from now on, at least tell me so I can add that shit to my resume." Xavier huffs a sarcastic laugh and ambles back inside Theo's house.

I'm stunned.

"Sorry about that. It's not you." Finn breaks the silence as soon as his buddy's out of range. "'He's shitty to everyone these days. Just going through a bit of a rough patch."

I nod, knowing damn well he's lying. It *is* me. Xavier was always like this in my presence, but I guess I'd deluded myself into thinking he might have changed over the past ten years.

The kids at school got at least one thing right.

Xavier Emery isn't like his friends.

He's *worse.*

* * *

"You didn't answer my question earlier. Your name... where's it from? Shampoo or hand cream?" Theo leans over the pool table to take the first shot and break up the balls. I roll my eyes at his question, a hint of a smile on my lips. We're on our fourth game.

It turns out Theodore Cox isn't the worst conversationalist when he's not making bad jokes about my name. He's been chatting me up since we all relocated to the living room.

Axel left twenty minutes ago. *Good riddance.* I couldn't bend over to play without feeling his eyes on me. As for Xavier, he never came back after he stormed off. Finn tried texting him, but it seems I repulse him so much the poor guy couldn't take another second of being in my presence.

"Wait, isn't your sister famous or something?" Theo asks when I don't respond to his teasing.

"Maybe. Why? You want an autograph?" I mock, knocking down three balls at once.

Theo cracks a smile. "Sorry. Must suck getting asked about her all the time."

I'm tempted to tell him he's actually the first to bring her up in a hot minute. Ashley was so young when she won *Rising Voices*, the people who remember her are usually older, parents and grandparents for the most part. I'm always a pinch surprised when someone our age knows Ashley from her TV days.

Not to mention my sister is pretty low key.

She goes to her private music school two towns over, keeps away from parties and the Silver Springs youth. She's also not a bragger. You'd never be able to tell when meeting her that she's approaching two million subscribers on YouTube, or that she was loaded by age six.

"My mom's obsessed with those damn talent shows," Theo elaborates. "She's watching reruns of her favorites right now. Not a single episode goes by that she doesn't talk my ears off about that winner who was born and raised here. Ashley, is it?"

I nod.

"I looked her up. She's good."

Believe me, she *knows.*

"She's also hot. Like very." Theo smirks.

She knows that, too.

Yes, Ashley's got the whole package: the voice of an angel, tanned, slim with all the right curves, amber eyes, long honey hair. People used to refer to her as "the beauty of the family," which, naturally, made me feel like the ugly duckling. But my dad liked to say we were equally beautiful.

Only different *kinds* of beautiful.

Took me years to understand what he meant by that.

I know now that my sister is not as much prettier than me as she is *flashier*. She's a bit like Dia in that sense. Ash is the very definition of femininity. She wears flattering dresses, the right makeup to accentuate her God-given beauty, spends thousands on a hair mask for her golden locks to be just the perfect amount of shiny.

She *wants* people to be looking at her.

Me? Not so much.

I felt so overshadowed by my sister as a child that I eventually embraced my "Casper the Ghost" status and committed to being invisible. I wore oversized sweatshirts and boyish jeans for most of my childhood. I still do to this day. I didn't bother with my hair, let alone pretty dresses.

What's the point? It's not like anyone's going to notice.

"She single?" Theo shoots his shot.

I bite back a smile.

"I'd get you a date with her, but she's not doing charity this time of year."

Finn, Dia, and Lacey snicker at my comeback, and I feel like that proud kid who made the whole class laugh. This has to be the first time, since the day Dia told me we'd be eating with the jocks moving forward, that I've felt I might *sort of* belong with these people.

I mostly stood by and kept my mouth shut before, but with wicked Brie gone, and Xavier-the-bully missing in action, I'm starting to realize I don't entirely hate their company.

"Hot damn, Vee. Didn't know you had it in you." Finn holds his hand up for me. "Up top."

I laugh, high-fiving him seconds before Dia loops her right arm around my neck and pulls me in for a side-hug.

"You're ballsy, Harper. I respect that," Theo says as he sweeps his dark, almost black hair away from his emerald-green eyes.

"But…?" I anticipate.

"I'd respect you even more if you gave me your sister's number."

I scoff. "Nice try, lover boy."

Theo and Ashley together wouldn't last a day. Theo loves the ladies too much, and Ashley's way too smart to be seduced by a guy like him—although I suspect from her current and past boyfriends that a fit, green-eyed hottie like Theo would be exactly her type.

We play for thirty more minutes before I excuse myself to the bathroom. My phone rings as I'm washing my hands, and I step out into the kitchen to check the caller ID.

Mom.

I also have three unopened texts from her.

Mom: Where are you?

Mom: Ashley has to be at school at seven a.m. sharp tomorrow. Early lesson. And you're driving her. She can't be late.

Mom: Aveena???

It's barely eight.

I stay out later than usual *once* and she's all over my case, terrified that I'll disrupt her perfect schedule. I'm sending the call to voicemail when the back door swings open and Xavier bursts into Theo's kitchen.

By no means am I excusing his behavior earlier tonight, but Finn wasn't lying. Xavier *does* look like he's having a grand time navigating life right now—note the sarcasm.

I wonder why he came back. Strike that—I wonder why he *left* at the mere sight of me. Last I checked, I'm not the one who dumped paint balloons on his white dress when we were kids, nor did I butcher his entire family with an axe, so I'd appreciate if he took the hostility down a notch.

"Still here?" he drawls when he notices me.

"Still a presumptuous asshole?" I snap back.

I expect him to double down on the nasty replies, to crush me with spite, so you can imagine my surprise when he clamps his mouth shut, the corners of his lips twitching into a small smile. His pale eyes rake over my face for a second too long, and I squirm under his undivided attention.

Why, oh why, does he have to look like that?

Low blow, Life, low blow.

Oddly enough, I get the feeling that he's never taken the time to look at me before. He *sees* me every day at school, yes. *Sees* my face in the crowd. *Sees* me around the lunch table somewhere in his herd of groupies. But does he *look* at me?

Nah.

Not like this.

Not like he's discovering something new.

He seems like he's debating on whether this "new" thing is good or bad. When his half-grin evolves into a full-blown smirk, I know he made up his mind, but I don't have the means to translate the verdict in his eyes.

"What did you say your name was again?" He squints, an indicator of some serious brain racking.

My blood starts boiling.

The asshole took my first kiss and he can't even place me!

"Aveena?" I say, hoping it will ring a bell.

He continues to assess me as though he can't quite put his finger on it.

"I know you, don't I?"

I scoff out a laugh.

Is this guy for real?

"We go to the same school? Not to mention hang out with the same people every day?"

He shakes his head. "No, that's not it. I know you from somewhere. That's what you meant earlier, right?"

I chastise myself for opening my big mouth. I should've left well enough alone.

"You said you remembered me as a bully," he clarifies. "Did we use to hang out or something?"

I consider denying it out of self-respect. I can't lie, I'm a tad offended that he didn't connect the dots sooner. I get that we were eight, but even Finn brought it up once. If Finn Richards, the biggest airhead I know, not to mention a guy who, unlike Xavier, didn't steal my first kiss, remembers me, why the hell can't he?

"I have no idea what you're talking about." I spin to leave.

"No fucking way." It clicks in his mind. "Little Vee?"

Here he is.

"You're that girl Finn and I used to…" He doesn't complete his sentence, but I know all too well what he was going to say.

"Annoy? Tease? Torture? Why, *yes,* that would be me. Did you seriously just figure that out? A bit slow, are we?" I snark.

My outburst only seems to amuse him.

"Look, in my defense, your mom only ever called you '*Vee.*'

I thought it was short for Vicky or Vivian or something. And it was ten years ago. I can't even remember what I had for dinner last night."

"Whatever." I shrug.

"Shit, I've got to say, Vee." He gives me a once-over. "Puberty did you a solid."

My cheeks combust.

"Wish I could say the same about you," I lie through my teeth.

Xavier smiles at my failed attempt to deny the undeniable. Let's not pretend like puberty didn't do *every* female on earth a solid when Xavier Emery went from "cute" to "sinfully hot" in the span of a summer.

"I think you mispronounced *thank you*." He flashes a smug grin that makes me want to knee him where it hurts.

And yet… my heart beats a hair faster when he proceeds toward me. He's intimidating, and in the most annoying way. The "unintentional" way. He's not even *trying* to get to me. He just has this presence to him, this charisma that's hard to ignore. I wish I didn't notice how tall he is, how bright his eyes are.

I wish I didn't see the kid I used to know.

"Surprised you remember what I looked like then. You know, Alzheimer's and all," I fire back.

"Aw, are you offended that I didn't remember you, *Little Vee*?" he teases, and it irks me.

Because he's right.

It shouldn't bother me, but it does. I never let myself admit it, but I think "Little Vee" might've developed an itty-bitty crush on the blue-eyed boy who kissed her under the slide that day. How unfortunate that said boy grew up to be a conceited tool.

Finn, Dia, Theo, and Lacey all come tumbling into the kitchen before I can answer.

"Told you I heard him," Theo tells Finn.

"Xav, you're back." Finn states the obvious.

"Thanks, Einstein." Theo snorts, and Finn elbows him in the stomach.

"Where'd you go earlier, man?" Finn snakes his arm around Dia's neck to draw her closer.

"Got detention on Sundays now, dipshit. I told you yesterday," Xavier explains. "I remembered they started tonight right after I got there."

That explains it.

"Right. I'm sorry, man. For… everything." Finn's voice is dripping with guilt. I'm guessing the school board went twice as hard on Xavier for claiming to be the only brain behind the stink bomb operation.

Xavier might as well pack his shit and move into the detention center now. Fat chance he'll be spending his time anywhere else this month.

"I didn't even know weekend detentions were a thing." Theo crinkles his nose.

"Yeah, well… you also didn't know *condoms* were a thing.

Isn't that right, Lacey?" Xavier says with a shit-eating grin.

Everybody laughs, minus Lacey and Theo. It's practically common knowledge that Theo and Lacey had a pregnancy scare a while back.

"Go fuck yourself with a cactus, good sir," Theo deadpans.

Word is, these two were actively sleeping together all of junior year. Until Lacey found out she was late. It was a false alarm, but real enough for Theo to end it. He must've been scared shitless to dump his side piece altogether.

It's no secret that Lacey's been hoping to pick up where they left off ever since. She's been obsessed with Theo since the third grade. If only he still wanted her when the sun comes up.

The remainder of the evening is fun—I know, *crazy*, right? We laugh, play more pool, and while he doesn't say another word to me all night, Xavier doesn't seem to completely loathe my existence.

Baby steps.

Dia hugs me tight when I call it a night shortly after ten.

"I'm so glad you gave…" *Hiccup.* "Gave them a chance," she slurs in my ear, her speech a bit jumbled from all the vodka sodas she's had, and I play along. But don't think I believe we'll all be one big happy family from now on.

I know, come Monday, I'll go back to keeping quiet at lunch, and they'll go back to being Easton High royalty. I'll pick up a shift at the library while Xavier, Theo, and Finn pick up a basketball. Tomorrow, everything will go back to normal.

Tomorrow, I'll get to burn the letter that could ruin my life…

Assuming someone else doesn't find it first.

5

Aveena

They say when it rains, it pours.

I've always thought of it as a fancy way of saying, "When life sucks… it really *fucking* sucks." Although I must admit I'd never quite understood what that meant until now.

The letter is gone.

G-o-n-e, *gone.*

Translation: my life is over.

Pretty sure I flatlined for a second when I stopped by the school library at lunch and realized the poetry book wasn't where it was supposed to be.

We only have one copy in stock, and I'm absolutely positive I didn't misplace it. Aisle six is the book's designated spot. I would know—I reorganized the books in alphabetical order myself.

It's got to be some sort of mistake, I thought. I had to ask Lucille, the librarian and my coworker, if she remembered who borrowed it. She didn't, but she also frequently searches for her glasses while wearing them, so I took it with a pinch of salt.

I considered asking her if I could pop behind the counter and check our systems myself but decided against it. I'm off the clock. What could be *so* important I'd need to use the computer during the day when I'm already working tonight after school?

My first guess was that the sheet of paper somehow fell out of the book when it got picked up, but the letter wasn't anywhere in the library.

It's like it just disappeared from the face of the earth.

Poof!

I turned in my twenty pages to Ms. Callahan fifth period but couldn't listen to a single word coming out of her mouth for the rest of the class. I was too busy obsessing over who borrowed the poetry book.

Consumed by anxiety, I crush my phone into my palm and maneuver around the crowd on my way to the library. I work until six every day after school, then drive straight to the music academy to pick up Ashley from her private singing lessons.

I haven't been called to Principal Emery's office yet, which is a good sign, but my anxiety won't let me off the hook until I get my hands on that letter and rip it to shreds. I pull up social media as I dart down the hall and tap my Instagram notifications to get my mind off the letter disaster.

Three notifications.

@The_Axel_Fletcher followed you.

@The_Axel_Fletcher liked your picture.

@The_Axel_Fletcher liked your picture.

I cringe, careful not to follow him back. Remember when I said everything would go back to normal after I went to Theo's place yesterday?

That might not have been *entirely* true.

Finn and Theo greeted me with a nod in the hall this morning. And *get this,* Dia wasn't with me. These two have never acknowledged me unless she was around. I didn't nod back. Thought maybe they were looking at someone else and I'd be the idiot thinking it was meant for me.

After all, Xavier was with them, too, and he looked right through me. Then Theo flipped his head back and yelled, "Hey, Harper! Still waiting for your sister's phone number. Get on that."

There isn't a single person in the hall who didn't stare at me.

"You're going to be waiting a while," I hollered back, and Theo cracked a laugh before dissipating into the crowd with the guys. *Weird*, I thought.

Then lunch rolled around.

I was more than thrilled to learn Brie wouldn't be eating with us anymore, having just been dumped by the captain of the basketball team and all. And, to my great surprise, the cool kids didn't flat out ignore me the way they usually do.

It's almost as if yesterday opened their eyes to my existence.

Axel hit on me a few times. I politely turned him down, but

if his name in my Instagram DMs is anything to go by, it didn't stick. Theo bugged me about Ashley some more. I had to tell him she was taken. Poor guy turned his attention over to Lacey as soon as I crushed his dreams. Then Finn asked Dia and me if *we* were going to the game on Friday.

Being addressed directly, rather than treated like an inanimate object, felt weird.

A good weird.

I also couldn't help noticing that Xavier looked like he'd rather be watching paint dry than be there. He barely ate. Barely talked. He didn't laugh when everybody else did.

I've been hanging out with the jocks for months now, and while Xavier isn't as chatty as his buddies, he's also never *this* quiet. He usually talks back, entertains Finn and Theo's rubbish, but not today.

Finn was worried about him, I could tell. He kept glancing at his best friend as though he wanted to say something, but never did. All in all, I've decided to cut the lot of them some slack. Maybe they're not so bad.

Nudging the door to the library open, I slip my phone into my back pocket. Lucille stands behind the computer, ruffling through her purse. Her shift is over, and she looks ready to get the hell out.

Good.

We exchange pleasantries before she feeds me a run through of all that is left to do tonight. I nod along to her list, so desperate for her to leave I mentally count down the seconds until she's out the door.

The minute she's gone, I study the library, which is now deserted with the exception of me, and enter my access code into the system to search our catalogue. I type in the name of the poetry book, and the loading circle pops up on the screen.

Come on, you dinosaur.

Get a move on!

The computer gives me what I want three excruciating minutes later. For the first time since Thursday, it feels like I can breathe again. Like my shoulders have shed the weight of the world in a single second.

The book is in stock.

It was returned today. After I came searching for it, obviously. But by who? I take my investigation further, seeking the book's borrows history.

"Mr. Tate?" I think out loud.

Why in the ever-loving hell would my science teacher check out a poetry book? I notice he borrowed nine other books along with it and frown at the date.

Sunday.

Wait, what?

But the library was closed on Sunday.

He must've worked something out with the school to get the books. That's the only explanation. I don't overthink it for a moment longer, speed-walking to aisle six to grab the book and hopefully my letter to Ms. Callahan.

Please be there.

Please be there.

Please be there.

I could sob tears of joy when I spot the crumbled sheet of paper. It's still there. Same pag—

Wait.

At first, I think I'm imagining things.

Then I see them. The scribbles, the words, the comments. Someone replied to me. Even worse, someone *corrected* me.

Now, before I proceed with my rant, I'd like to apologize (not really) for any mistake I might make in this letter that ~~your~~ never going to get*

***Your is the possessive adjective, you're is you are. Jesus, it's not THAT hard.**

I can't believe what I'm seeing. Who the heck does he think he is? I say *he* because the handwriting looks like a boy's.

*I'm in a bit of a time crunch between trying to graduate high school, score a ~~once in a life time~~*scholarship*

***Once-in-a-lifetime. NEEDS HYPHENS. My eyes are burning**

So what if I called ~~it~~ an asshole*

* ***For fuck's sake. Two more letters. How hard was it to add TWO LETTERS?***

It's not like anyone is ever going to to read this anyway.

Well, this is awkward...

Sincerely,

From the bottom of my heart,

Go fuck yourself

- L

L, huh? I wonder what your real name is. Oh, I know! L...earn how to fucking spell? ☺

And now he's mocking my "name."

I shouldn't have signed the letter in the first place. I only did it out of habit. Chose *L*, short for *Love*, off the top of my head. I guess you could say the nickname "Love" has sentimental value for me, which is something this dickwad couldn't even begin to understand.

Did he not see the part where I clarify I wouldn't correct my mistakes? No, screw that, did he not see how vulnerable I was in that letter? I'd had enough that day, so naturally this butthead thought to himself, "Huh, I should roast the hell out of this stranger."

Just when I think I've seen it all, I flip the page and find a note in the same handwriting.

That was fun. Piece of advice: drop the victim act. Nobody likes a crybaby. I'd also stop with the hate letters, angry chick. Imagine if your teacher found it. You wouldn't want to give her a stroke from laughing too hard at your grammar.

What the *fuck* did I just read?

Who could be such a gigantic asshole?

Mr. Tate?

He did borrow the book, after all. *No way*. The man wouldn't hurt a fly let alone bulldoze someone's self-esteem, and this handwriting is somewhat understandable. Mr. Tate's was always a killer headache to read on my science tests.

This is someone else.

Fuming, I dump the poetry book on the nearest table, rip the letter into a thousand pieces, and toss it deep into the trash. Then I go grab a pen and paper from the front desk.

I'm well aware that slipping another letter inside the book is a royal waste of time. There's little to no chance my answer will ever make it back to the original bully, but I couldn't care less right now.

You think you saw me angry, troll?

Just wait.

* * *

I begin concocting an escape route from the moment I unlock the front door to my house. *Just get to the stairs before she sees you. You can do it.* My mom is in the kitchen, on the phone with someone.

"Absolutely not. What part isn't registering? We've been over this. *My* daughter will be free to leave town when and only when she's graduated. Not a day before!"

I take it she's arguing with Robert, Ashley's manager. She's been doing that a lot lately. Throwing a fit every time she feels herself losing control of her precious Ashley. Ash is slowly slipping through her fingers, and my mom knows it.

She *feels* it coming, creeping up on her with each passing day.

The impending moment where Ashley turns eighteen and leaves her. Mom will no longer be able to hold, "*As long as you are a minor and living under my roof,*" over Ashley's head. And I think—no, I know—she's poured so much energy into Ash's career, she's terrified she won't know what to do with herself once the gifted daughter leaves the nest.

Rob's been patiently waiting for the day he can make Ashley

a real star, and he won't have to wait much longer. Next year, Ash will be graduating from her prestigious music school, and my mom's reign will end once and for all. I wouldn't be surprised if she sold the house and followed Ashley halfway across the world to keep it going.

As quiet as can be, I push the front door closed with my palm and tiptoe toward the stairs. I'm not in the mood to talk to—

"Aveena? Is that you?"

Damn it.

"Who else would it be?" I mumble.

"Perfect, you're home." My mom turns the corner. "Did you pick up Ashley from—"

"Yes, I picked her up from her singing lesson." I know the drill by now.

"And did you drive her to the ten-year reunion for—"

"Yes, Mom," I repeat.

"Good girl." Mom nods in satisfaction.

We found out a few days back that the producers of *Rising Voices* were interested in taping a ten-year reunion with Ashley. Technically, it's been *eleven* years, but I'm guessing it didn't sound as catchy. They were so eager their team even made the trip to North Carolina.

They'll be throwing a quick interview with Ashley at the end of next week's episode in a "Where are they now?" type thing. I'm not surprised. Ashley is one of the only winners from the competition to actually build a career and online presence from the show's exposure.

I still remember it like it was yesterday.

It couldn't have been more than two days since Ashley had won first place. Dad, Ashley, Mom, and I were about to leave California, where the show was taped, and waiting for our delayed flight in a ridiculously expensive suite—courtesy of the show's network.

That's when Mom pulled out her brand-new camcorder and told my sister to sing something. My mom's name should've been Esther *Overachiever* Harper because it took her under ten minutes to create Ashley's YouTube channel and post a video of six-year-old Ash nailing "No One" by Alicia Keys.

Twenty-four hours later, she had ten thousand subscribers.

Forty-eight hours later, fifty thousand.

On day three, one hundred thousand.

Then, ironically, by the time Ashley's seventh birthday rolled around, she had seven hundred.

Mom pulls out her phone to order dinner. She doesn't cook anymore. Says she's too busy since she made assisting Ashley in her musical career a full-time job. She now spends her days locked in her "office", aka my dad's old trophy room, on her computer doing only heaven knows what.

I can't recall the last time we were allowed in there while she worked. She's kept the door locked since Dad left us.

Ashley has never so much as batted an eye at Mom living on the *Rising Voices* million-dollar prize and her YouTube channel ad revenue and sponsors. I asked my sister about it once, and she said she could only be grateful Mom believed in her so much she quit her job as an accountant.

"What time do I have to pick her up again?" I ask before exiting the room.

"Rob will be giving her a ride home tonight," Mom says, eyes glued to her phone. "He flew into town this morning to accompany her."

"Okay." I swivel to leave but…

Something keeps me in place.

A long-forgotten memory.

At least, by everyone but me.

"Mom?" I glance at her over my shoulder.

"Yes, honey?" She continues to scroll on her phone.

"D-Do you know what today is?" I falter.

She pauses to think. "Monday?"

She could rip my heart out and it would *still* hurt less than what she just said. Anything would hurt less than her ignorance.

"No, the date," I choke out.

It's as if the heater broke down when the words trickle out of my mouth. The room grows cool, the air as frisky as the heart I'm not sure she has. I'm the tiniest bit relieved at the streak of pain ripping across her gaze.

She *knows.*

Even if she'd rather die than talk about it.

She clears her throat. "I picked up some of your clothes from the dry cleaner. Put them on your bed."

I didn't know it was humanly possible to be this disappointed. I want to scream, "That's it? We're going to go *one more year* pretending like nothing happened? One more year acting like our world didn't end on this day nine years ago?"

But I can't find the courage. So, instead, I storm out of the house, climb inside my car, and sink my teeth into my bottom lip to keep the tears at bay. I'm almost out of gas, but I don't care. I have to do this.

For him.

For *me*.

I have to celebrate his life.

Lacking the guts to drive to the springs,—the town had to get its name somewhere—I drive aimlessly until thirty minutes becomes forty-five. I once read that experiencing a traumatic event at a young age was better than experiencing it when older. Something about children locking up their most disturbing moments into the remotest corner of their memory, therefore allowing themselves to move past the unthinkable.

While that may be true for some… I wasn't so lucky.

I was nine when I found him—not exactly a child but not old enough to be considered a teenager.

But I still remember everything.

Every detail.

Every noise.

But what I remember most vividly is the smell.

Booze, cigarette…

Death.

My father committed suicide in the garage the day after my ninth birthday. Ashley, Mom, and I had gone to a benefit concert for leukemia where Ash was set to sing. We'd made a girls' day out of it, dropped by the hair salon, then to the mall to snag the perfect dress for Ashley's big performance. Mom had even agreed, very reluctantly, to let me get the tips of my hair dyed dark pink while my sister got blonde highlights.

It was the perfect day.

Until it *wasn't.*

I'd run inside the house ahead of Mom and Ashley to go find Dad. I just couldn't wait to show him my hair. Ashley was always a mommy's girl, but I was my father's daughter all the way. Curtis D'Amour was more than my papa.

He was my best friend and the only person in my life who I felt saw me just as clearly as he saw my sister. The only person who made me feel like *I* was his favorite. He had a special nickname for me and me only.

Love.

One silly little name.

That's all I've got left from him.

When he was nowhere to be found, I'd made my way to the garage. I knew he liked to hang out in there since the crash. I couldn't understand why, though. *Doesn't it remind him of what he's lost?* Nine-year-old Aveena asked herself. *Doesn't it make him think about how he'll never drive one of those fast cars again?*

My dad was a race car driver, and a damn good one at that. He loved it more than anything in the world.

Even his family, apparently.

One wrong turn and it was over.

He lost use of his legs, his career, his dream. He landed in a wheelchair and became a completely different person. He went from world's best dad to shell of a human being overnight. Then he fell into a depression so dark, no one, not even my mom, could pull him out.

And she tried. Lord, did she try. She loved my father more than she ever loved any of us, even Ashley. She forced him to get help. But two years of constant therapy later, here we were.

In a cold, dusty garage that reeked of goodbyes.

He was sitting in an old swinging chair when I came in. At first, I shook his arm. I asked, *screamed* for him to wake up until my voice was no more. My child brain couldn't comprehend what the empty bottle of pills in his hand meant.

There was a letter, too.

One my mom refused to let us read.

She claimed it contained the rambles of a broken man and we were too young and fragile to be exposed to such tragedy. She swore it was for the best and the only important thing was that he said he loved us and he was sorry. I cried, begged her for a chance to read it.

She burned the letter a few days later.

Then she never spoke of him again.

She sent Ashley and me to therapy so we could talk about him to professionals but *never* to her directly—I still go from time to time. She was in complete denial then, and she's in complete denial now. It's like she shut down after she had to rip me away from his body. She was closer with Ashley than with me long before my dad passed, but she grew even more distant after that night.

I gather the courage to drive to the springs two hours later. Dad used to take me there whenever I was sad as a kid. The springs were our spot. Our favorite place in town, in the whole wide world, really. We'd sit by the stream, listen to nature and the water rumbling in the distance.

It always cheered me up.

Now it just makes me sad.

I park my car in the designated area. You can see and hear the springs without getting out of your car from here. Funny enough, the springs' parking lot is never packed. The locals have grown bored with the town's wonders and leave visiting honors to the tourists now. Oh, and the couples looking for a hookup spot.

Halfheartedly, I open my car's glove compartment and pull out a pen and paper. I come prepared every year. I'll never say it out loud, but I hate my mother for what she did to his final words.

And since I never got to read his letter…

I thought maybe he could read mine.

Every year, I come here, put on music as I bawl my eyes out, and write him a letter. Tell him everything he's missed. It's probably pointless, but I do it anyway.

I used to throw the letter into the water and watch it sink to the bottom, but I figured that wasn't good for the environment, so now I just shred it to pieces and let the breeze blow them away.

It's probably still not good for the environment, but hey, I tried.

I turn the radio on to dampen the sound of my breakdown and let it all out. I cry until I can't breathe. My letter isn't lengthy, but then again, neither was his.

It was one page.

One short page to say goodbye. I sign off the letter with "*Love*," his nickname for me, and reverse out of the parking lot. As I'm rolling down my window to let the wind take my words to my dad, I dare hope that one day…

"*Love*" will stand for something good.

Xavier

Brie: Come to your senses yet?

Brie: I said I was sorry about the snapchat story. What else do you want from me?

Brie: Stop being such a fucking baby and come over. I need some… loving ;)

Scrolling through my ex's texts, I hop out of my truck and toss my gym bag strap over my shoulder. The girl's been blowing up my phone since I told her we were over.

I text back quickly.

Xavier: I'm good. Thanks.

She replies in a nanosecond.

Brie: How about now?

Brie attached a picture.

My eyes pop out of their socket at the picture on my screen. The lighting's shit but just bright enough for me to discern a topless Brie lying in bed in her panties with nothing but lollipop emojis covering her nipples.

I'm not above a "please take me back" nude, but I'm also not looking to date her again. *Eh, what the hell*, maybe I'll stop by her place after detention. I don't need to date her to fuck her.

I text back for the first time in days.

Xavier: You should be careful who you send these to.

I dated the girl for a year. She can rest easy knowing I'd never do anything with her nudes, but there are guys at Easton who'd make that shit viral in a heartbeat.

My phone pings once.

Brie: Is it another girl?

Twice.

Brie: Xavier?

Then comes the threat.

Brie: Mark my words, if you're fucking someone else, I don't care who she is, I'll rip her apart.

Annd that's enough of that.

I don't give her tantrum another thought and toss my phone into my open gym bag. I catch a whiff of sweat as I stroll toward my house. *Jesus, is that me?* I really need to hit the shower before detention. Practice was brutal.

Hank's car sits in the driveway.

So does my dad's.

I almost forgot. Tonight's poker night. Poker Tuesdays are practically a ritual around here. Finn and I might be good friends, but our dads? They're as tight as you can get without being blood related. What's that saying again? You can choose your friends but not your family?

My friendship with Finley Richards wasn't as much of a choice as it was fate. Thanks to our old men, we grew up together, played ball together, went to school together. What else was there for us to do except follow our dads' lead and become ride or dies?

I spot the white roses scattered across the countertops the second I enter the kitchen. There's a card tucked inside one of the bouquets. I make my way over to snatch the piece of paper.

For Delilah,

Here's to twenty-years together.

I love you more than life itself.

- Ray

My eyes sweep over the note and my father's clumsy handwriting. *Right*, tomorrow is my parents' twentieth wedding anniversary. Dad prides himself in organizing something special for Mom to come home to every year, but he really overdid it this time. There's got to be at least twenty bouquets in here.

Let me guess, twenty bouquets for twenty years together?

Please excuse me while I hurl.

He cares so much it makes me sick. It'd be so much easier if he didn't take her on romantic getaways. So much easier if he didn't do every fucking thing imaginable to keep the spark alive. If he didn't love her, I'd have no problem shitting on their parade. No issue watching their marriage go up in flames.

Just say the word and I'll bring the matches.

Fine, I'm a coward. I talk a big game, but I'm too much of a pussy to tell him. Either way, it's my mom's mess to clean up. Only she can be the one to confess what she did.

What she's been doing for years now. Maybe if it'd just

happened once with some rando, maybe my dad could find it in himself to forgive her.

But she made her bed when she chose *him.*

Footsteps echo down the hall, and I swivel to see my dad pad into the kitchen with Hank on his tail. They're probably on their way out to meet a few other guys for poker night.

"Why aren't you at practice?" my dad asks.

Hi to you, too, Father.

"Coach let us off early. I figured I'd grab a shower and change before detention."

"Who you trying to smell good for, hotshot? That Brie girl, perhaps? You two going on a date?" Hank pokes fun at me. "Fingers crossed that doesn't end up on the internet, too."

"It's called hygiene, old man," I counter, and Hank lets out a throaty laugh. Crazy how I'd never have the balls to say that to my own dad but can say it to Finn's without blinking.

Hank has always been a much better sport than my dad. He's the cool dad who laughs at his own jokes—you know the one. But don't think for a second he won't kick your ass to Mars and back if you fuck up. *Police station, anyone?*

Overall, when he's not yelling at you with that freaky ass vein bulging out of his forehead, he's pretty worry free. Might have something to do with the fact that he's loaded and set for life.

My dad is the polar opposite.

Raymond Emery is the frigid, uncomfortable with affection Dad who hides under the pretense of only wanting what's best for his kid without ever *listening* to said kid. It's one of the many reasons why he and Hank balance each other out so well. Finn's pops reminds mine to take a breath every once in a while.

I snort thinking about what Hank said earlier.

One thing is for sure: I am *not* trying to smell good for this Mr. Tate motherfucker. I knew these after-school detentions were going to be a pain in the ass when I saw my old science teacher waltz into the detention center last Sunday.

The guy hates Finn, Theo, and me with a burning passion for stirring up trouble in his classroom freshman year. I thought surely, he couldn't still be holding a grudge after all this time, but the way he looked at me?

I swear I saw a smile.

The bad kind.

I could practically hear him thinking, *Karma, bitch.*

He also looked like he'd rather be sipping on a jizz smoothie than monitoring detention, so there's that. There were ten of us in that room. And the son of a bitch had to give *me* the thickest poetry book in history to copy for the next two weeks.

Coincidence?

I think the fuck not.

Little did he know I'd find something in there to entertain myself. Highly doubt I'll be lucky enough to snag another letter from that angry chick, but it was fun while it lasted.

"You ready for the game on Friday?" Dad pesters me about basketball.

"Always." I turn to walk away. Detention starts in forty-five minutes, and I smell like hot garbage. Thank fuck I only have detention on Sunday, Tuesday, and Thursday for the next two weeks or I'd lose my marbles.

"Your coach's new plays any good? What about practice?" he hounds me. "You get enough hours in with all that detention crap? What's that I hear about your coach letting you off early?"

Mom says that's my dad's way of showing me he cares, but I think that's *all* he cares about. To think my dad was next in line for the coaching job at Easton. He only took the leftover PE job in the hope that he'd get a shot at coaching if he stuck around. I thank my lucky stars he didn't get it on the daily.

"Dad, I'm going to be late. Mind if we pick this up later?"

His lips pinch in disapproval. He didn't get nearly enough info to satisfy his hunger. "I'll hold you to that." Dad trails to the front door. "Your mom should be home soon. Tell her I wish I'd been there to see her reaction." He gestures to the flowers.

"You got it."

"See you later, punk." Hank lifts a hand to his forehead in a salute before tracking my dad out of the house.

* * *

Someone pinch me.

There's another letter.

There's. Another. Letter.

I spent the evening convincing myself that getting a reply was a long shot, but here it is. Neatly tucked between two pages. First, I dodge my dad's interrogation, and now this?

Today must be my lucky day.

I steal a glance toward Mr. Tate, sitting at the front desk grading papers. I have no idea how this is even possible. How this angry chick managed to access the book in the forty-eight hour window it was gone, but I don't give a rat's ass. I'm just glad to have something to do other than copying poetry for the next ten minutes.

I unfold the letter carefully and start reading.

Dear Grammar Police,

I hope you get hit by a car.

Don't get me wrong, I don't want you to die. You see, unlike you, I am a GOOD person. And a good person doesn't go around bullying people for no reason.

But I still wish you'd get hit by a car.

Maybe break a rib or two.

Or twenty-four.

Maybe you could use your time of remission to ask yourself why you're such an asshole. Think real hard about what could've made you this way. Tough childhood? Absent parents?

What was it, troll?
I'd love to know.

I know you'll probably never read this, but in case it wasn't clear enough, I didn't need your corrections or nasty input on my letter which, by the way, was supposed to stay PRIVATE.

And for the record, YOU DON'T KNOW ME. I am the furthest thing from a crybaby. Or an "angry chick." Actually, how can you be so sure that I'm a girl at all?

I could be a seven-foot-tall dude with a mean right hook for all you know. So, here's an idea, asshole. Let's play a game of fuck off.

You go first.

-L

I should be offended, shocked by the mouth on this girl, but all I can do, as I devour the letter for the third time, is smile until my cheeks sting.

Angry chick has a temper.

Score.

I have to remind myself to wipe that dopey smirk off my face not to draw suspicion from the detention warden. I can barely believe it, but I'm pretty damn entertained right now—maybe even weirdly aroused?

So, I grab a pen, flip the letter over…

And get to work.

* * *

Aveena

The book was borrowed again on Tuesday.

What's even crazier? It was by Mr. Tate.

Again.

He checked out the same ten books, too, which is odd, but I couldn't be bothered to think twice about it. Maybe he just really likes boring books? But then again, he doesn't seem to be reading them or he'd have found my letters by now.

That's probably borderline unrealistic on my part, but the only thing plaguing my mind when I found out the book was MIA was… Will I get an answer again?

Then I mocked myself.

Dream on, Vee.

Waving goodbye at Lucille, I impatiently await the sound of the door closing before typing the name of the book into the library catalogue.

Loading.

Loading.

Loading.

The book's status pops up on the screen.

I stop breathing.

In stock.

What the…

I can't rip my eyes away from these two little words. The library is a ghost town except for a granny and her husband, and I'm confident I can get away with sneaking a peek inside the book while they're browsing.

Hesitant, I tiptoe toward aisle six like a criminal, relieved to find the book tucked away on the bottom shelf.

Here goes nothing.

My letter rests between two pages, untouched.

No corrections.

No mean comments.

Zero.

Then I turn the letter over.

Well, I'll be damned.

Dear Angry Chick,

First, thanks for the good laugh. I needed that. Second, you shouldn't be so easily triggered. Takes the fun right out of it.

To answer your question, I know you're a girl from your girly handwriting. (You might want to ditch the hearts on the i's.) Oh, and how you played victim in your first letter to Ms. Callahan. Remember when you were all like "Poor me, my mommy doesn't love me and I have to write a paper"?

Boo-fucking-hoo.

We all have our problems.

You also asked me why I'm an asshole. The truth is, I'm not. Not in real life, anyway. I'm actually a nice enough guy when you get to know me. Although not nearly as nice as I'm guessing you are. I act out when life sucks balls. But you, angry chick? You seem like someone who takes it and says thank you.

Kudos to you for not becoming homicidal.

And you say you're a good person. (Almighty on your good-girl throne with your pure, untainted soul.) How about I be the judge of that? You see, I happen to think we're only as good as the worst thing we've ever done.

So, tell me, angry girl,

What's the worst thing you've ever done?

- Zac

***P. S. :** Here's a fake name so you don't have to keep calling me "Grammar Police." You're welcome.*

I could choke him.

If this "Zac" boy genuinely thinks I'm dim enough to spill my darkest secrets to a stranger, he's in for a surprise. I make quick work of studying the library, zeroing in on the elderly couple scouring the psychology section, and debate on giving this troll any more of my time. Do I answer? Or trash the letter and end this once and for all?

Five minutes later, I settle on "Eh, what do I have to lose?"

He wants a confession?

A confession he'll get.

Aveena

Dear Zac,

(What a basic name, by the way. You could've chosen any name. ANY name. *Shaking my head*)

Congrats, you caught me. I'm a girl. Too bad it's the only thing you got right. I said I was a good person. I NEVER said I was "untainted" or "pure."

In fact, not that it's any of your business, but I stole twenty dollars from my parents to buy a Jonas Brothers' album when I was eleven.

So technically, I'm a criminal.

Also, "technically", your theory is trash.

Who says you can't fuck up and still be a good person? Screw this "you're only as good as the worst thing you've ever done" mentality. How about "you're only as bad as your lack of remorse"?

It doesn't end with someone fucking up. There's so much more to life than that. It's not all black and white. Sometimes it's gray. Confusing, inconclusive gray. And at the end of the day, it all comes down to one question...

Do you regret it?

If the answer is yes, then there's hope for you. It means you see the error of your ways and can do better. You can change.

People's mistakes don't define them, Zac.
It's the decisions they make moving forward.

- L

P. S. : *what's the worst thing YOU'VE ever done?*

P. S. 2 : *Your theory is still trash.*

* * *

Dear L,

THAT'S IT?

A TWENTY-BUCKS THEFT?

THAT'S the worst thing you've ever done? Jesus, I'm embarrassed for you. Oh, and nice speech you delivered there. Five stars. Almost teared up.

So, you want to know what my darkest sins are? Don't hold your breath. I only give as much as I get, and your pathetic excuse for a confession doesn't even make up for the calories I'm burning writing this.

Such a shame. I was about to pull out the big guns and give you la crème de la crème (I'm talking jaw-dropping stories), but now I'm not sure you deserve the good stuff.

So, brace yourself, angry chick.

Kindergarten-level confessions coming up.

Worst thing I ever did #1: I accidentally knocked a girl's front teeth with a football when I was ten. Her parents couldn't afford to get them fixed, so she called me out on it (hoping my parents would vomit cash) and I denied it like the little shit that I was. She walked around without front teeth for three years and got heavily teased for it. Still feel guilty about it to this day.

Worst thing I ever did #2: My buddy and I stole his dad's car before we got our license and crashed it into a pole. We freaked out, drove the car to the middle of nowhere, hoping his dad would report it as stolen and never find out. Long story short, they found the car in two hours and we worked for his company for free all summer.

Thanks, traffic cams.

That's enough for today. Like I said, I got stories WAY crazier than this. Unfortunately, you haven't proved yourself worthy. But since I'm in a good mood, I'll give you another chance. Tell me something crazy.

Maybe I'll reconsider...

- Zac

***P. S.**: Calling you "angry chick" is getting old. You got a name?*

I fold his letter in two and take it out of the book before detaching a sheet of paper from my notebook to reply. The library has been closed to the public for ten minutes now. Ten minutes, and I'm still here "working" overtime just so I can write a letter to a complete stranger.

We had such a busy night, typical for a Friday, I didn't get a chance to write back until now. That's it, I must've gone bonkers, because as I craft out the perfect reply, I catch myself having fun. Real, *genuine* fun. This Zac character is giving me a run for my money, that's for sure.

Once I'm done, I slip the letter back between two pages and wind up in aisle six to stash the book back where I found it. Hopefully, Mr. Tate checks it out again next week. My phone buzzes with a text from Dia just as I'm locking up.

Dia: We're hanging out at Finn's tonight after the game. Just the gang. Interested?

I text back with one hand, patting my pocket in search for my keys as I tread to my car. I'm usually halfway to Ashley's school by now. Mom's going to stick my head on a pike and hang it above the fireplace if my sister gets home late.

Aveena: D, you know you don't have to invite me everywhere, right? You can totally go party and see your boyfriend without me tagging along.

It's bad enough that she insisted we go to tonight's basketball game together. The last thing I want is for her to feel obligated to lug me around because we're best friends. Dia's life is different now, and I understand that, but I'd gladly skip the pity invites.

She texts back instantly.

Dia: First, he is not my boyfriend. Second, Finn wanted me to invite you. (Although I would've done it anyway)

Dia: And Theo asked if you were coming.

Dia: With your sister, but still.

Dia: Looks like you're growing on them, Vee ;)

I can't stop a big, fat grin from stretching across my face. I did feel the dynamic shift between the guys and me this week.

Dia: Sooo? Are you coming? And if you're thinking of saying no, there's a new way to spell it now.

Aveena: What's that?

Dia: Y-E-S.

A chuckle escapes me.

Aveena: I'll be there.

Dia: VICTORY! Want to get ready together before the game?

Aveena: Sure. Be at your place as soon as I drop off Ashley.

* * *

We won.

Now, I'm not going to lie and pretend I had the time of my life in that gym, but saying I didn't enjoy sweaty, muscled Xavier, Finn, and Theo running around in black and white jerseys would be a travesty.

I'd never gone to a game or seen Xavier in action before. I knew he was good. He didn't land team captain of the Stallions for nothing, but I didn't know he was this good.

No, I didn't know he was *the* best.

The real kicker? He doesn't even seem like he tries that hard. The boy plays as though it's in his blood. He nailed what Dia called a "slam dunk" without batting an eye. You'd think he was already playing back in the womb or something.

Finn is a close second. Not far behind is Theo, although it's plain as day that he doesn't take basketball as seriously as his friends do.

I'm not sure what it is about Xavier that makes him a hair faster and more agile than his teammates. Maybe it's the fact that he has a good inch on Finn, making him a whopping six foot three, but then again, Theo is the exact same height as Xavier and he didn't take the winning shot like Xav did tonight.

The clock on my dashboard shows 11:18 by the time Dia and I pull into Finn's endless driveway. I'm not exaggerating, the path to his house is longer than a freaking airport runway.

We're late. The party started at ten, but Dia and I went back to her house to hang out after the Stallions defeated their opponents with flying colors. I had to ask my mom if I could sleep over at Dia's place, and she reluctantly agreed to give her errand girl the night off.

But not before calling Dia's dads to authenticate my story first. Gaten and Dave covered for me because technically, it wasn't a lie—I *am* sleeping at the Mitchells' house tonight. I just didn't tell my mom what I'd be doing before the actual sleeping part.

"Seriously?" Dia sighs at something on her phone.

"What?" I glance at her in my passenger seat.

"Well, that didn't take long," Dia grumbles, shoving a hand into her handbag and pulling out a hairbrush to…

Wait, what?

Why the fuck is she drinking from her hairbrush?

I do a double take, pumping the brakes to make sure I'm not hallucinating. I thought I'd imagined it, but no. Homegirl really uncapped the bottom and started drinking straight from her hairbrush like it was normal.

Noticing the question marks in my eyes, Dia laughs. "Just found out we're going to be spending all night with Brie. Excuse me for needing a fucking drink."

I blink at her, my brain short-circuiting.

"Did you just… drink from your hairbrush?"

She laughs. "It's a secret flask, Vee. Could hardly see myself driving around with a bottle of tequila in my purse. Want some?" She guides the "hairbrush" closer to my face, and I decline, victim to the nostalgia creeping into my chest.

Just last year, Dia and I had never had beer, let alone strong liquor, and now? She's chugging tequila like it's water. I guess I'd never truly stopped to think about how much she's changed since last summer.

Since Finn.

I'm not shaming her. She has every right to want to live her life and experience new things, but we used to be twins, soul sisters. Dia was always the first to praise my decision to keep away from alcohol. I could never stomach the smell after I found my dad that night.

Bourbon.

It was all I could smell while I cried on his lap. Could that have something to do with my vow of sobriety? My therapist certainly thought so. Blamed it on my brain having associated the smell of booze with the worst night of my life.

"Wait. We're going to be spending the night with Brie?" I ask.

Dia nods. "I saw her and Xav sucking face in the hot tub on Lacey's Instagram story. Looks like they're back together."

I cringe and park my car by the water fountain.

Finn's square shaped mansion sits on top of the hill, flaunting ginormous windows that overlook the first and second floor, three garages, and one of those ridiculous circular driveways you don't need to back out of. Because everybody knows the rich never go backward. *Only forward.*

To think this is where it all started for Finn and Dia. I can't help wondering if my best friend would still be the shy, anti-alcohol virgin I used to know if she hadn't stepped through that door last summer.

"They're out back. Come on." Dia gestures to follow her as

she rounds the house. My stomach twists into a tight knot. Why am I such a nervous wreck? Is it Brie? Am I dreading her nasty comments?

Nah, that's not it.

I've already made my peace with the unpleasant evening awaiting me. Then what's to blame for the pit in my gut?

It comes to me.

It's this place.

Finn's house.

I have very vivid memories of Finn's backyard. The perfectly trimmed hedges, the glass-walled pool and nightmare of a trampoline—almost broke my ankle falling off that thing when I was eight. Just days before they had the safety net installed, too.

Yes, I'm lucky like that.

The last time I was here was ten years ago. Back when Finn's mom was still alive. Back when *my* dad was still alive. Everything is so different now. Well, everything except the backyard itself. It hasn't changed one bit, exactly the same as it was a decade ago.

My heart picks up the pace when the gang comes into view.

A small part of me expected this gathering to evolve into a rager party. The Stallions did just win their third game in a row, but Finn stayed true to his word. I only see Xavier, Theo, Axel, Lacey and Brie here.

The six of them are spread across Finn's trampoline,

laughing, drinking, passing a joint around. The closer we get, the more apparent it becomes that Easton High's cool kids are higher than the Empire State Building.

"Ladies, just in time," Axel quips at the sight of us. His comment earns us the attention of everyone there, except for Brie and Lacey. The girls are too busy whispering in each other's ears and giggling for no reason.

Finn bites the inside of his cheek the second he sees Dia, wasting no time in meeting us by the pool. At first, I think maybe he's mad at her. Then I realize I couldn't be more wrong.

It's not anger I see in his eyes.

It's desire.

Carnal, shameless desire.

Finn stops an inch away from her, leaning forward to whisper something in her ear, and Dia swallows hard. I assume he asked her a question from the way he pulls back and stares at her in expectation. Flushed, my best friend casts a conflicted look in my direction.

"Go," I say with a grin.

Dia cracks a thankful smile and nods at her almost boyfriend, who doesn't miss a beat grabbing her hand and setting out toward his house.

"Real fucking subtle," Xavier hollers, and Theo and Axel snort out a laugh. Even I can't repress a smile. As for Brie and Lacey, they're still too high to function.

"Wasn't trying to be," Finn hollers right back.

"Hey, dickhead?" Xavier calls.

Finn shoulder-checks his best friend.

"Don't pull a Theo. Use protection."

Finn smirks before disappearing inside the house with Dia. I eye Theo sitting on Xavier's right and wait for a comeback of some sort. Theo opts for the good old finger, flipping Xavier off before dragging a hit from the joint in his hand. You know Theodore Cox is *stupid* high when he doesn't bother arguing.

Silence ensues, and I become overly aware of the awkward situation I've been dumped in. I'm alone with a bunch of high jocks, one of whom makes my pulse rise in a way I don't like, and two cheerleaders who have been laughing at the same joke for five minutes straight.

And I can't even hold it against Dia. She might've just left me alone with them less than five seconds after we got here, but she's in love.

"What are you waiting for, babe? Get in here." Axel pats the spot next to him on the trampoline, and I cringe so hard at the pet name it physically hurts. Timidly, I make my way over to the trampoline and crawl inside through the safety net door, only to be met with a dilemma…

Where do I sit?

My eyes scour the vicinity. There's stuff everywhere—beer packs, the boys' basketball jackets, Brie and Lacey's purses—leaving only one spot next to creepy Axel, which is eyeing me with a vicious smirk and clear expectation.

Over. My. Dead. Fucking. Body.

I study my surroundings again in a desperate attempt to find another seat and randomly lock eyes with Xavier.

His eyes aren't red or small.

In fact, he doesn't look high at all.

I'm guessing he turned down the joint tonight. His light brown hair is a damp, sexy mess from the hot tub, and I curse my body's reactions to his good looks. For crying out loud, I can practically *feel* my pupils dilating.

Silent, Xavier holds my gaze.

Then he moves his leg.

It's almost nothing, but it opens up a spot by his side.

Did he just…

I don't let myself think twice about how rude he was to me at Theo's, plopping down next to him and inwardly yelling, "Are you shitting me?" at the universe when the wind smacks me in the face with a whiff of his cologne.

News flash: Xavier Emery smells good.

Of course he does.

Fuck you, wind.

"You pussies down to play or what?" Axel plucks a deck of card from his pocket.

"Jesus, Fletcher, you still on that?" Xavier drawls. "Will you drop it already? We're not playing Suck and Blow."

"Why the hell not? There's three of us and three of them." Axel points to comatose Brie and Lacey. "What else are we supposed to do while Finn and Dia are off bumping uglies?"

"I'll play." Lacey chooses *now* to returns to the land of the living. I connect the dots when she sneaks a not-so-discreet peek at her longtime crush.

Theo's sitting on her left, completely smashed and obviously more interested in the joint in his hand than the conversation happening around him. *Ah.* If we were to play, Lacey would have to pass the card to him.

With her mouth.

Enough said.

"Me too." Brie sits up. "This party sucks."

"*Not* a party, prom queen," Theo gibes.

"Whatever," Brie huffs.

"Cox, you playing?" Axel asks.

Theo snorts. "Not in this lifetime."

I drink him in. With his squinty, bloodshot green eyes and tousled dark hair, the guy looks higher than Brie *and* Lacey combined.

"What? But you have to play." Lacey pouts.

"Way to be obvious, Lace," Xavier mocks under his breath, his voice so low and hoarse no one hears him but me. I bite back a closed-mouthed smile at his remark.

"Just one round, for me. Please." Lacey bats her eyelashes at Theo in a "I'll make it worth your while" way and he sighs.

"One. That's it," he caves.

"Xav?" Brie turns to her boyfriend.

"Yeah, whatever," Xavier drones, barely listening, and kicks Theo's foot to get his attention. "Give it." He straightens out his hand, and Theo passes him the joint.

I assume I was wrong about Xavier laying off the sauce, until he wets the tip of his fingers with his tongue and puts out the joint without a warning.

"The fuck?" Theo screeches, but Xavier's already crushed the doobie with his shoe.

"You're like a hit away from not being able to tell the difference between Lacey and your right hand. Thank me later," Xavier says unapologetically, and the group laughs.

Theo blows out an annoyed "Fuck you, man."

Axel commands Lacey to sit between Theo and Xavier to avoid the boys having to "Suck and Blow" each other—yes, I am aware of how dirty that sounds—and wraps it up with, "Everyone know the rules?"

"I've never played, actually." I speak for the first time since I joined them.

That's Brie's cue.

"*Ugh.* Forgot she was here. How's your sister, Vee? Still better than you at literally everything?" Brie cackles.

I wish I had the perfect comeback to shut her venom-spewing mouth, but all I can do is sit there and take it. Let her walk all over me. By all means, spit in my face.

Story of my fucking life.

"Oh, I'm sorry, where are my manners. Is it too bright for

you here? We can turn off the patio light if you want. You must be used to the dark. You know, living in her shadow," Brie adds.

I usually don't give a flying shit about Brie's comments, but right now, I feel like she's scrabbling at the few strings still holding me together. It's one thing to tell yourself you're the family's reject, and another to have a professional bully dig up your insecurities and weaponize them against you.

"What about mommy dearest? She send you back for a refund yet—"

"Oh, fuck off, Brie."

We all stop breathing, trading glances that essentially say, "What. Just. Happened?"

Then it hits me.

Xavier.

Xavier happened.

"Excuse me?" Brie spits.

"Did I stutter? Stop talking shit to her."

Stunned, I blink at my childhood bully. *Did I just get transported into a parallel universe where Xavier Emery is a good person?*

Meanwhile, Brie is staring daggers at me.

Not her boyfriend, who just put her in her place.

Me.

As though *I'm* the one she's blaming for this.

"Why the fuck are you defending her?" she hisses.

"Dia's one of us now, which means she is, too. End of story."

A beat of silence.

I'm dumbfounded by Xavier's chivalry.

"Are we fucking playing or not?" Brie snaps, her glossy red lips curling with rage as she reclines against the safety net.

"Vee still doesn't know the rules," Theo points out.

"Right." Axel turns to me. "It's easy. You suck in air so the card sticks to your lips, then pass to whoever's sitting next to you by blowing. Sound good, babe?"

"And if we drop the card?" I skirt his flirting.

"Both you and the person next to you drink, then you rip parts of the card so there's more lip action. Ready?"

There are two things I want to say in that moment.

First thing being that I don't drink, and I'm not about to start for some moronic drinking game. The second being that I might have a heart attack just *thinking* of going anywhere near Xavier's mouth. But I can't tell them any of that.

So, I just nod.

And hope to God I don't drop the card.

"I'll start," Lacey volunteers—gee, I wonder why. And Axel tosses her the deck of cards. She's passing the card to Theo a heartbeat later and "accidentally" dropping it once their mouths are touching.

The others laugh as Lacey goes in for the kiss. Theo doesn't reject nor welcome her lips. Just lets her kiss him for a short moment, then pulls away and throws back his beer, which is exactly what he's supposed to do in that scenario. Don't think I miss the disappointment flashing through Lacey's gaze.

I feel bad for her.

She so desperately wants to rekindle something between them, but Theo only sees her as a pregnancy scare. Theo rips the card a bit, and my anxiety shoots off the charts. If there's no card left by the time it gets to me and I have to semi-kiss Xavier, I'm dying on the spot.

Theo passes the card to Brie without a hitch, and she turns to Axel to do the same. Except she drops the card at the last second and starts full-on *sucking face* with him instead.

She's punishing Xavier.

Not a doubt in my mind. This is her trying to hurt him for defending me. And she's not shy about it either. She grips Axel's hair and goes to town. Axel doesn't even pretend to fight her, kissing her back in an instant. It's all tongue and teeth, and Brie's fake moans, and I did *not* need that visual.

My focus drifts to Xavier.

He doesn't even bat an eye at his girlfriend cheating on him. He doesn't look hurt, jealous, or mad. In fact, if I didn't know any better, I'd say he seems uninterested. Didn't Dia say they were back together?

Why doesn't he care?

Brie throws him a side look to catch his reaction, quickly realizes she missed the mark, and propels Axel off her. Her mouth is swollen, her lipstick smeared. And Axel? He's in shock.

"Xav, bro, I…" Axel realizes how awkward this is.

"It's cool, man." Xavier shrugs. "She's fair game."

So… they're not back together?

Axel doesn't insist and takes a sip of beer as stated by the rules. Brie follows his lead, tears of rage amassing in her eyes over her failed manipulation. Alex rips the card again, and my stomach drops.

I'm next.

I couldn't care less about Axel passing me the card. Especially considering what he just did. There's no way he'll try anything after eating Brie's face off in front of her ex. But then why…

Why am I so nervous about passing it to Xavier?

I inhale a breath and inch closer to Axel, who transfers the card from his mouth to mine. The card is so small now it's impossible for our lips not to touch in the process, and a shiver of disgust ripples through me.

That's when I turn to Xavier.

And suddenly, there's not enough air in the universe.

It's his eyes.

One look and I'm back to hiding under the slide, crying my heart out with the little boy who stole my first kiss.

Vee, it's just some stupid game, snap out of it!

Not nearly as conflicted as I am, Xavier leans closer.

And closer.

And clos—

"I have to go to the bathroom," I word-vomit.

Then I'm running inside the house.

* * *

I sit in Finn's bathroom for thirty minutes after that. And before you ask, *no*, I'm not taking the dump of the century. I just couldn't imagine showing my face outside again after I ran for the hills. At least, not without Dia. Dia who hasn't even replied to *one* of my million texts asking if she'd be mad at me for bailing.

Technically, I could've left ages ago. I drove my car here, but I'm supposed to be taking Dia home and sleeping at her place tonight. That's the only reason I'm not in bed right now.

On the bright side, I could hear from the cracked open window in the bathroom that my escape left the gang unfazed. They kept playing, bickering, laughing without a second thought about my disappearing act.

Made me realize that my escape probably seemed a lot more humiliating in my head than it did in real life. As far as they're concerned, I was just hit by the violent urge to pee and that's that. They don't have the slightest clue as to what I was thinking in that moment. And if we're being honest…

I'm not even sure what I was thinking.

I've always known I was attracted to Xavier Emery—join the fucking club—but I didn't know it was to the point of running away at the mere thought of kissing him. I don't understand the effect he has on me, which is why I only have one option: stay the hell away from him until we leave for college and never see each other again.

Easy enough, right? I sigh in relief when my phone lights up with a text from Dia.

Dia: I need to get the hell out of here.

Dia: Wait for me by the door.

My best friend radar goes off instantly, deafening sirens blaring in my head. Something's wrong.

Aveena: Everything okay?

No reply.

I'm quick to follow her instructions and tiptoe out of the bathroom. I doubt she's already there, but I don't mind waiting for her. As long as I don't run into Xav—

"So that's where you've been hiding?"

Are you fucking kidding me?

He's right there.

Leaning against the kitchen island, arms folded over his chest, pale eyes set on me. How did I not see him?

"I-I wasn't hiding," I stammer.

He glances at the bathroom door, biting back a grin.

Oh my God.

It sounds like I've been taking a shit this whole time, doesn't it?

"Not that I was… you know," I sputter. "I wasn't. I actually didn't even have to go, I…"

Stop.

Fucking.

Talking.

I clear my throat. "What are you doing in here? Looking for a shoulder to cry on?"

Xavier arches an eyebrow. "What makes you think I need one?"

"Gee, I don't know, maybe because your girlfriend just made out with another dude in front of you? Forgive me for thinking you'd care. Won't ask again."

"Why did you? You worried about me, Harper?" he taunts, a devilish smile tugging at his lips. "Or were you hoping *you* could be my shoulder to cry on?"

"I'd rather set myself on fire," I deadpan.

"You sure? Position's still open," he teases, pushing off the kitchen island and stalking toward me.

Is he… flirting with me?

Nah, don't be ridiculous, Vee.

He's just bored.

"Positive." I back away, refusing to let his charms get to me.

"Eh, it's just as well," he concludes. "Pretty sure I'd have to be sad to actually need your shoulder."

"And you're not?"

"Why would I be? We're not dating."

"Why invite her here if you're not dating?"

He rubs at the back of his neck. "Fuck if I know. Moment of weakness, I guess? She's so persistent I told her I'd think about giving it another go if everything went fine tonight. And well… we all know how *that* turned out."

I have a feeling Brie's stunt with Axel just sealed the deal. He's not taking her sorry ass back anytime soon.

"So, you're really done with her?"

He scoffs. "I'm not getting back together with her if that's what you're wondering."

Neither of us speak for a few seconds.

"What about you, Little Vee? You talking to anyone?" he asks.

I pause.

"Nope."

He breaks into a grin. "I saw that."

"What?"

"You hesitated."

"I did not," I blurt.

Okay, maybe I did. I hate myself for it but the first person that popped into my mind is this Zac idiot.

"Lies. Who's the guy? Do I know him?"

Hell, *I* don't even know him.

He's just a mean stranger who writes me letters. There's no way we'll ever meet, and I definitely *don't* like him, but he's the only guy I've interacted with lately.

"You don't know him because he doesn't exist." I hop on one of the stools around the kitchen island. "I don't exactly have boys banging down my door, in case you hadn't noticed."

"Yeah, but that's because you're hard to approach," Xavier says like it's obvious, resting his forearms flat against the counter.

"Excuse me?" I'm taken aback.

"You heard me. You're intimidating as shit."

"What?" I'm stunned by his bluntness. "That's not true. I'm very approachable."

He snorts. "Sure you are."

"Fine. Enlighten me, then." I rise off my stool. "How am I intimidating?"

If Mr. All-Star knows why I've been a boy repellent my whole life, you bet I'm going to make him tell me.

"You really want to know?" He drags out the suspense.

"Yes." I grow restless. "Spill."

"Well, for starters… most guys our age aren't looking to date." He elaborates. "They just want to fuck around. And those who do want to date are only looking for a girl to make them feel good about themselves."

"Meaning?"

"Meaning they want her to laugh at their jokes, stroke their egos, give good head and… that's pretty much it." He draws a small smile out of me. "So, when guys like that see a girl like *you,* a girl who doesn't look easy or desperate, they get intimidated. Label her high-maintenance and run like hell. You're beauty and brains, Vee. You're an immature high school boy's worst nightmare."

I can't form a sentence. I expected something along the lines of "You're so closed off" or "You don't smile enough," but this? Nothing, absolutely *nothing,* prepared me for this.

"But hey, that's just my two cents." He pushes off the counter.

Heat spreads to my cheeks. I suck in a breath, crossing the space between us—don't ask me where I got this courage from, I have no idea. We're not even that close and I feel like every nerve in my body is on high alert.

"And you?" I surprise myself by saying.

I dare another step forward and think I see his throat bob.

"Me what?" he asks, his voice a bit husky.

"Do you find me intimidating?"

I hold my breath as he gazes down my face for long seconds. He looks like he's trying to decide whether or not to tell me.

Finally, he makes up his mind.

"Always have, Vee."

Slow the fuck down, pulse.

"I—"

"Dia, wait!" Finn's panicked voice echoes all the way from the second floor the next second.

My stomach plummets to my feet.

This isn't good.

My best friend comes bursting into the kitchen the next second, teary eyes burning with rage and tan cheeks stained by mascara. Her once perfectly defined curls are now a wild, tangled mess. They definitely weren't playing Tic Tac Toe up there.

"Vee. Car. *Now*!" Dia orders.

Confused, I glance over at Xavier, who seems just as clueless as I am, and sprint to Dia's side. We storm out of the house with Finn on our tail, and I understand Dia isn't messing around when she takes off running toward my car. You best believe if my best friend is running away from a boy, *I'm running, too.*

"Dia!" Finn yells, chasing after us, and he sounds so desperate I almost feel bad for him.

I unlock the door with the remote, and Dia climbs into my passenger side in a hurry. I get in a second later, stuff the key into the ignition, and lock the doors. Dia can't hold it together a second longer.

"Get me out of here." She bursts into sobs, crying so hard she can barely breathe, and I consider running Finn over for whatever he did to her. Until he *literally* throws himself in front of my car, and I realize I'd look awful in a prison jumpsuit.

"Dia, please." He looks straight at her through the dashboard. My window is open a crack, allowing us to hear him loud and clear. "Don't fucking do this. Just listen to me."

"Drive," she pleads, and I push the gear into reverse, hoping I won't crash into a gold fountain or some expensive shit on my way out. But Finn isn't having it. The car hasn't moved an inch before he's rushing to the passenger-seat window, smacking his palm to the glass.

"Dia, look at me. Just fucking look at me. Please." He begs for her attention, but she refuses to acknowledge him, covering her face like a world-renowned pop star denying paparazzi a picture. Finn's sharp jaw flexes with pain, his dark brown hair dangling in front of those devastating hazel eyes.

I'll admit, Finley Richards looks good.

Just like Xavier.

Just like Theo.

But… when he's about to cry, his charms are damn near devastating. I repeat, *Finn Richards*, the guy I spent years thinking had a block of ice where his heart should be, is about to cry.

Real tears.

Real. Human. Tears.

Does Dia have a magic pussy or something?

How the fuck did she do that?

"Diamond, I love you," he croaks.

Only then does she look at him. Judging by the shock in her eyes, this is the first time Finn's ever said that to her. And this is definitely a moment I shouldn't have been here to witness.

"I fucking love you, Dia. I do. Just give me a chance to explain. Just… *Please.*"

She doesn't make a sound, doubt floating around her glassy eyes, and dabs at her tear-soaked cheeks with her sleeve. He looks so beautifully damaged, standing there, begging her with tears in his eyes, I almost think she's going to change her mind.

Hell, I'd *change my mind.*

Until she belts, "Tell that to your whore!" at the top of her lungs, and I realize she has every reason not to take him back. *Ever.* And I'd rather risk killing Finn than put Dia through one more second of this.

I shut my eyes, grip the wheel so tight my knuckles scream at me, and step on the gas. If Finn wants to live, he'll move out of my way. Thankfully, he does. And as I speed away from the mansion with my heartbroken best friend in the passenger seat, I contemplate how wrong I was.

Maybe Xavier isn't the big bad wolf after all…

8

Dear Zac,

Screw you.

That twenty-dollar theft haunted me for the best part of sixth grade! I thought the police were going to show up at my house at any moment and send me to kid jail.

I'm like 99 percent sure I'm going to regret this, but you got me intrigued with all this talk of "crazier stories", so I'm going to take you up on your offer. My crazy story in exchange for yours.

Game on.

I accidentally put on a sex tape while babysitting a little girl when I was fourteen. The family wasn't much into technology and only had a VCR player with one Disney movie in VHS. The cassette stopped working right at the beginning of my shift and the kid threw such a massive tantrum, I panicked and searched EVERYWHERE for another movie.

Almost shed tears of joy when I found the Little Mermaid.

Except it was really called the Little "Spermaid."

And the characters were her parents.

Thank God I stopped it before she saw anything

(I still see the dad's hairy butt every time I close my eyes.)

Does that earn me one of the good stories?

Tell you what, make the next one REALLY good, and I'll tell you my name. (Fake, obviously. Wouldn't want you to find out who I am…)

-L

* * *

Dear L,

Not bad. I'd even go as far as to say your story was decent. Yes, I just gave you a compliment. No, I'm not on drugs. Looks like I owe you a confession, doesn't it?

I desperately needed a car after I crashed mine a year back (don't ask), so I grabbed a batch of brownies my mom'd just made and sold them at my best friend's birthday party for $30 a pop. No one ever asked if there was weed in them. They just assumed there was.

Hint: there wasn't.

Bottom line, I made $1,000 in a half hour.

Correct me if I'm wrong, but I think that earns me your name—your fake name, but still. Not that I'd ever try to figure out who you are. (Can you imagine the fucking horror of realizing we know each other?)

Your move, angry girl.

- *Zac*

* * *

Dear Zac,

I can't wait to tell you what "L" means just so you stop calling me that god-awful nickname. How many times am I going to have to tell you? I am NOT an angry girl.

If anything, you should call me "quiet girl" or "passive-aggressive girl." Better yet, "you'll never even know I'm mad girl." You got it right the first time. When life sucks, I don't say a word and take it… Wait, that didn't come off nearly as flattering as I thought it would.

Ahem, let's just get straight into the story, shall we?

Sometimes, I'll purposefully hide my best friend's phone when I'm over at her house (like put it in my bag or under her mattress) so that she can't get invited to places and disrupt our plans for the night. It's not that I don't want her to have a social life, it's just we were perfectly fine hanging out the two of us before, and now she's all about parties and boys.

I know, I know. This one was pretty tame. But not

everyone's had tons of crazy things happen to them. My life, for one, is very boring. Plus, I can't tell you too much or you'll end up figuring out who I am.

Let's even things out.

Next time, you tell me a boring story.

- Love

P. S. : *I was thinking, why don't we make a pact? Neither of us can EVER try to find out who we're talking to. And we can't tell anyone about the letters.*

P. S. 2 : *With that said, I'd like to know I'm not talking to a 13-year-old boy. How old are you?*

* * *

Dear Love,

Nice name. A bit cheesy, but I can roll with it. And shit,

you're right. I hadn't even thought of that. I'm a senior at Easton. What about you?

You're not just pretending to be older when you're really the one who's twelve, are you?

About what you said, you're wrong. Your life isn't boring. You're just not giving me the good stuff. (I'm talking the dark, twisted shit.) And I can't even blame you. I've barely scratched the surface myself. It's about time I give you a real confession, don't you think?

My real confession: I just found out my best friend fucked my ex-girlfriend. And the worst part? I don't care. I know, as a matter of principle, I should be pissed or want to beat the shit out of him, but I haven't even bothered telling him that I know.

I'm not perfect either and he already has a lot going on (he's always had his fair share of demons). If you knew his backstory, you'd probably want to give him a pass, too.

I'm not sure I'll ever tell him because I value our friendship a lot more than I ever valued any moment spent with my ex.

That real enough for you, L?

Just so you know, I will be expecting a confession that's on the same level of fucked-up, thanks.

- Zac

P. S.: *Yes to the anonymity pact. Again, I would've never tried to figure out who you are, but if it helps you sleep at night, you have yourself a deal.*

* * *

Dear Love,

Where'd you go?

Did my last confession scare you away?

Or is it that I saw right through your lies and you really are a thirteen-year-old imposter? I sincerely hope the answer to both these questions is no.

I'd be lying if I said I wasn't bummed out to find no reply from you today. Don't go getting a big head, but I've kind of been looking forward to your letters lately. They're like a nice little break from reality.

Write to you later?

- Zac

* * *

Dear Zac,

Can't live without me, can you?

The school was closed on Wednesday, remember? For some holiday?

I couldn't access the book. Although I must say I take

great pleasure in you acting like a needy teenage girl. To address your concerns, no, I'm not twelve. I'm a senior, too.

Do you realize there's a good chance we've encountered each other at least once this year? For all we know, we could be running into each other every single day. *Gasps*

Your last confession made my jaw drop so hard I had to pick it off the floor and glue it back on. I'm surprised you'd trust me with such a massive secret, but I do admire the leap of faith.

Might even return the favor if you promise to be there for the next letter.

And the letter after that.

And the one after that.

(It's my turn to be needy.)

Your mini freak-out made me realize this pen pal thing has an expiration date, and I'd rather not spill my guts to someone who could stop answering at any moment.

So, tell me, Z, are you going to stop?

- Love

9

Aveena

Dear Love,

The irony of you asking me how much longer this is going to last is unbelievable… You guessed it, this is my last letter.

It's been real, L, but I'm not going to be able to answer you through the book anymore. I'd tell you why, but that would kind of defeat the purpose of our anonymity pact.

I have to say, two weeks ago, I would've done anything to never see this damn book again, but now? I'm not so sure. You brought life to mind-numbingly dull moments, angry girl.

Thank you.

"That's it?" I screech, single-handedly causing two heart attacks at once. The middle-aged women reading by aisle six both jump an inch in the air, one of them clutching at her chest, while her friend glares at me, eyebrows tight with disapproval.

"Sorry," I mouth.

They have every right to be pissed. There is a spectacular irony to me, *the librarian*, being the loudest in the library, but I couldn't help myself. You mean to tell me I thought about Zac's reply all weekend, tossed and turned, impatiently awaiting my Monday shift for *this*?

Seriously? That's the best he could do? He couldn't even sign his name, and it's three letters. I don't know what I expected. It was always going to end this way. *My bad for getting invested.*

I'm plucking the letter out of the book, ready to throw away our last correspondence, when a fleeting "what if" crosses my mind. What if… there's more?

Wouldn't be the first time he wrote on the back. Willing myself not to get my hopes up, I flip the letter over and feel my heart swell with relief at the familiar handwriting.

There's a phone number.

Next to the number is a challenge.

Text me if you dare.

- Zac

* * *

"Are we ever going to talk about it?" I bug Dia as we march down the hall toward our last class of the day. I hate gym class. Our PE teacher, Mr. Emery, is far from a delight, to put it mildly. He's that teacher who tells girls their killer period cramps aren't a big deal and to suck it up. Xavier deserves a fucking award for dealing with this man every day.

"Dia?" I urge, irritated by her lack of a response.

"What?" she drones, eyes locked on her phone. Heaven only knows which of her rebound guys she's texting this time.

"Are we ever going to talk about your breakup?"

"Can't break up with someone you never dated." She misses the point by a mile.

She's been like this since last Friday.

Closed off, dismissive.

Dia's locked herself in a tower of denial, where no soul can reach her. She didn't utter a word about Finn after I nearly ran him over with my car. She didn't vent, didn't pour her heart out. She just cried in my arms. All night. Sobbed until she had no strength or tears left in her.

She strictly refuses to tell me anything except the bare minimum, that Finn fucked some bitch. She won't tell me who, or when it happened, or how she found out.

All she said is she needs to move on.

So far, Dia's been doing a pretty solid job of pretending like she's fine, but you know who can't pretend for shit?

Finley Richards.

He showed up at Dia's house at 7:00 a.m. on Saturday morning and pulled us out of bed, begging her to hear him out. It took both Dia's dads *and* her older brother, Jesse, to get him off the property. I wish I was kidding.

He hasn't been at school since.

That's how bad this is.

I glance at Dia, who's immersed in her text conversation with her boy toy of the day, and grab my own phone. I scroll through my contact list and tap the number I added five days ago.

Zac's.

I've been staring at these damn digits all week, trying to gather the courage to text him. But I can't bring myself to do it. There's something rather… *personal* about texting someone.

Something more dangerous.

The risk was manageable when we were just writing letters, but giving him my number? Isn't that just *begging* him to try and uncover my identity? What if he asks around?

Many people in this school have my number. Dia, Lacey, even Finn, just to name a few. Zac could easily trace it back to me. With that said, he did promise that he'd never try to find me.

The question is…

Do I trust him?

"Who's Z?" Dia's voice startles me.

"What? Oh, it's nothing. I mean, h-he's no one." I put my phone away before she can blink.

Dia's eyes widen. "*He*?"

Shit.

"Aveena Harper D'Amour, are you talking to a boy?" She completely butchers my French name, pointing an accusing finger at me. "Is that why you're always searching for someone in the halls lately? Because you're seeing some guy?"

And here I thought I was being so slick.

It's true that I've been playing detective around school this past week. I can't stop myself. Every time I see a guy from the senior class, I wonder if I'm looking at Zac.

Every. Single. Time.

This whole pen pal thing is screwing with my mind. I want nothing more than to tell Dia about the letters, but I'm a firm believer that once you let a secret out into the universe, word will spread. Might not be tomorrow, might not be next week, but it *will* get out one way or another.

The only way to make sure something truly remains secret is to keep it to yourself.

I make up an excuse. "Don't be ridiculous. That's just an old number. Been going through my contacts. Deleting a bunch."

Guilt sweeps over her.

"Vee, you know you can still talk to me about these things, right? Just because my love life is a pile of dog shit doesn't mean yours has to be, too. I'm here for you. Always."

Right.

Except when you're *not.*

Which is often lately.

"I'm telling you, there's no guy."

I'm met with a puzzled look. She's not falling for it.

"Okay. Well, say there *was* a guy, I'd tell you to go for it. Who knows? You could be missing out on the hottest, most epic love story of your life."

Highly doubt it.

Turning the corner, we charge toward the locker room down the hall. Dia spots her new best friend barely two steps inside the changing room.

"Lacey!" Dia is off to meet my replacement in a heartbeat. We cut all ties with Finn and his buddies since the cheating disaster, but Lacey and Dia are still the best of friends. *Yay!*

Dia might've lost Finn, but she definitely didn't lose her popularity. The numerous guys sliding into her DMs post-breakup made that clear. I pick a locker at random, shove my things inside, and pad into the first stall I can find to change into my gym clothes.

Dia's words eat away at me.

You could be missing out on the hottest, most epic love story of your life.

While I don't see Zac like that, she does have a point. I've missed out on a lot in my life. My dad, a relationship with my mom, boy stuff.

No more.

Collecting my courage, I unlock my phone, select his number, and begin to type.

Love: Hey, it's L.

* * *

He never texted back.

It's been hours.

Hours.

He's probably going all over town asking everyone if they have my number registered as we speak. Why did I have to send that stupid text? Also, why is Ashley taking so long to come out of her school? Her lesson should be over by now.

And why—

Ding!

I jerk in surprise.

He answered?

Zac: L who?

The moving dots pop at the bottom of the screen.

Zac: Lydia, Leonard? I'm going to need a bit more than that.

I wish I was the kind of girl to make a boy wait twice the time it took him to text her back, but it turns out I'm a *reply-in-a-microsecond* kind of gal.

Love: It's Love, dumbass.

Love: Also, bet you don't even know a guy named Leonard.

To my pleasant surprise, he texts back as quickly as I did.

Zac: I could.

Love: But you don't.

Zac: But I could.

Love: Still don't.

Zac: Fine, I don't.

Zac: But at least I'm not an awful texter.

I can't contain a smile.

Shots fired.

Love: Yeah… sorry about that.

Zac: About time, L. I was growing old over here.

Love: Aw, were you hurt that I didn't text you?

Zac: Hell no. With that said, I may have gone and checked if you'd left another letter in the book this week…

I crack a laugh.

I went and checked the book, too. What can I say? I got used to our banter over the past two weeks.

Love: Want to know a secret?

Zac: Shoot.

Love: I almost didn't text you.

Zac: Why?

Love: It's going to sound stupid, but I was scared you were going to ask around about my number. Like try to figure out if people have it in their phones to trace it back to me.

A few minutes pass.

Zac: Damn, I hadn't even thought of that.

Zac: Thanks for the tip. Will do.

It's official. I'm a self-sabotaging idiot.

Love: ZAC!

Zac: Relax, I'm kidding. I won't ask around about you… if you tell me what you look like.

Love: You wish.

Zac: Come onnn. I'm not asking for a picture here. I just want a vague idea of who I'm talking to.

Love: Well, I'm a girl. And I'm eighteen.

Zac: Boring. I knew that already. Give me something new.

Love: Sucks to be you then, because that's all you're going to get. Anonymity pact remember?

Zac: BOO!

I'm about to text back when my phone pings with a message from Dia.

Dia: Party at Theo's tonight. You're coming.

Aveena: Isn't Finn going to be there?

Dia: Don't know, don't care. I'm not going to hide from his cheating ass for the rest of senior year.

Dia: Oh, and Lacey invited us over to her place for the pre-drink. What time should I pick you up?

Aveena: I don't know if I'm in the mood.

Dia: What? But you HAVE to come. I need you for moral support. That's like the number one rule of the best friend code.

I wrestle with playing supportive friend for the night or letting her down easy. She did just get her heart broken. And I *did* say I wasn't going to miss out on anything anymore.

Fuck it, why not?

Aveena: Pick me up at 9.

Xavier

"You told Lacey to do *what*?" Finn shouts over the deafening music, glowering at Theo as though he's debating on letting him keep his balls. Being an unpleasant asshole is Finn's MO these days, courtesy of his broken heart, but *drunk* Finn?

Theo is in for a treat.

"Look, man, I fucked up." Theo holds his hands up. "I shouldn't have told Lacey to invite whoever she wanted, but how was I supposed to know she'd invite Dia?"

"Gee, that's a tough one. Maybe try using your fucking *brain*?" Finn leaps to his feet, crowding every inch of Theo's space. "You know they're friends. What the hell were you thinking?"

Theo's fists contract, and he inhales noisily to keep his rage in line. "I said I was fucking sorry. What else do you want me to do, Richards? Uninvite them?"

Axel and I swap "*should we intervene*" glances from across the packed living room. Finn and Theo are equal in strength, our half drunk arm-wrestling tournaments last month can attest to that. I'd rather not see them in a fight. That shit would last for hours.

"Damn it, Cox, I don't need my old plaything lurking around while I'm recruiting new pussy!" Finn snarls.

I almost laugh.

Fucker isn't fooling anyone.

Finn's been such a wreck over Dia this past week everyone and their grandma know the only pussy he could ever want to "recruit" is hers. He thinks he's so smooth, pretending like he doesn't want her here, but I'd be willing to bet he was actually *hoping* Theo would invite her tonight.

He's the one who asked Theo to host the party in the first place. Dia will definitely have him begging for a second chance before the party's over. The guy's completely whipped, but he'd rather slam his meat in a car door than admit it. I've never, in the many years I've known him, seen Finn want to chase a girl like this. Key word: *want* to, because he's not letting himself do it.

Of course not.

Too much pride up in this bitch.

He showed up at Dia's house last weekend, and she turned him down. Any normal guy would keep trying after that but not Finley Richards. *Nope.* Finn thought it'd be a better idea to start avoiding her like the plague.

Call it a bruised ego or complete incapacity to deal with basic emotions. Whatever it is, it's got Finn trying to convince himself that he never cared about her anyway.

He won't even tell Dia that he didn't cheat on her. He swore it on his life, and normally I'd call BS, but the look on his face after she left with Vee that night? I believe him.

Although I can't blame Dia for thinking otherwise.

The evidence *is* pretty damning.

Every time I ask him why he won't just get over himself and tell her the truth, he spins me a bunch of crap about how he had his fun with Dia, but he's bored of her now. It's like he thinks needing her, or *anyone*, is above him or some shit.

But I know my dickhead of a best friend, and while I'm sure in Finn's trauma-plagued little world there's a good explanation for this, he's going to have to grow up and start acting like a normal person soon.

Before he loses the only girl who can put up with him.

"Fan-fucking-tastic." Finn fumes at something in the distance.

My head jerks back.

I spot Dia, Lacey, and Aveena stumbling through the front door clutching vodka bottles. They already look wasted, well, except for Vee. Girl looks painfully sober.

As always.

"Yep, I'm out." Finn collects his liquor bottle off the couch, throws back a long sip, and dissolves into the crowd of party animals. Doubt we'll be seeing him much tonight.

As soon as hurricane Finn's cleared, Axel ditches the girl he was hitting on by the spiked punch and makes his way over to snatch Finn's seat. Theo mirrors his actions, plopping down on the leather couch. He feels shitty about the Dia thing, I can tell.

"He'll get over it," I tell him.

Theo gives a small nod, not convinced.

"Quick question. When did Aveena Harper get this fucking hot?" Axel erupts, hungry eyes shadowing someone around the party. I track his stare to Vee and her friends chatting by the stereo. The answer pops in my head, flickering to life like a broken neon sign.

She was always this hot.

She's just a professional at hiding it.

The girl walks around with hunched shoulders in her loose sweaters and torn jeans, terrified to let someone see her. It's like she feels bad for taking up space or something.

But not tonight.

Tonight, she's different.

She went all out—makeup, hair, the whole shebang. This has to be the first time I've ever seen Aveena wear something remotely tight. *Thank God for leggings.*

"Turn around, baby. Come on." Axel cranes his neck for a peek of Vee's ass, which is facing away from us. "Show me what I'm working with."

As if they heard him, the girls spin on their heels, heading for the kitchen where a few guys from the team are playing Flip Cup. I'm not going to lie and pretend I didn't check out Aveena's ass as she walked.

Because I did.

Very much so.

Hey, at least I'm not a staring pig like Axel.

"Jesus Christ, where has she been hiding that body?" Axel is on a roll. "I'd fuck her in the ass so hard she wouldn't be able to walk for a mont—"

I smack him in the back of the head. *Hard.* He blinks at me in shock. But no one's nearly as shocked as I am.

Why the hell did I just do that?

"Classy, bro," I try and justify it.

"Don't act like you wouldn't hit that," Axel accuses.

I'd hit you.

In the face.

With a brick.

Does that count?

"You should see her sister," Theo chimes in. "Good genes in this family, I'm telling you."

The conversation shifts toward Vee's sister, and I stop paying attention, fidgeting with my phone. I have five unopened texts from Brie, asking when we can meet up to fuck.

And none from Love.

She never texted me back after I asked her to tell me something about herself. Maybe she felt pressured?

Maybe I shouldn't have said that?

I snort.

Look at you.

Getting all bent out of shape over some girl you'll never meet.

I study Theo's jam-packed living room and wonder what Love is doing right now. If she's as bored as I am. If she's home alone or stuck at a party, too. All my questions dwindle into oblivion when the front door swings open and a familiar voice carries through the house.

"Is it just me, or are Theodore Cox's parties not what they used to be?"

My entire body tenses.

No.

Not him.

Not now.

Theo and Axel don't waste a second springing to their feet and greeting the bastard by the door. A month ago, I would've been right behind them. But now? I can barely stand to be in the same room as this motherfucker.

I keep my ass drilled to the couch, chugging the drink in my hand in one go. I crush the red cup with all my strength, milking every last drop and wishing it was a certain backstabber's skull. Then I unlock my phone and pretend to be in the middle of a fascinating conversation with no one.

The only acknowledgement this guy is going to get from me is a meeting with my fist.

"Brody fucking Richards, as I live and breathe." Theo hypes up Finn's big brother like the kiss-ass that he is. Understandable. We've barely seen Brody since he went away for college.

"You son of a bitch, you said you weren't going to make it." Theo gives Brody a quick bro hug. "What changed your mind?"

"Oh, you know, I got back into town early. Had some… *commitments* to attend to, if you catch my drift," Brody brags, and the guys laugh like two well-bred groupies.

Make no mistake, I used to be one of them.

Grew up admiring the waste of space that's Brody Richards. He taught me and Finn to play ball, showed us how to score, and I'm not talking about basketball. He got us into clubs way before our time, too. I looked up to him since he's two years older. Considered him a "mentor."

He was the big brother I never had.

Until I saw him for who he really is.

"How long you staying?" Axel continues. "The pussy at Duke not missing you too much?"

Brody laughs. "Just for the weekend. And you know how it is. Pussy follows everywhere I go."

"Read you loud and clear, my man. See anything you like?" Axel asks, and Brody pretends to scan the living room.

"*Meh.* Too young for my taste."

"So, you're into cougars, huh?" Axel elbows him jokingly.

"Something like that." Brody smirks.

Rage fuels my body, the urge to dislocate his jaw itching in my veins like sandpaper. If the bastard so much as looks in my direction, I swear to G—

"Earth to Xavier Emery?"

Seriously?

"Your mama didn't teach you it's rude to ignore people?" Brody nags. I pretend I didn't hear him, keeping my eyes fixated on my phone. "Dude, you've been staring at that phone for like twenty minutes. There better be some fucking nudes on there."

Theo and Axel laugh at their master's joke. Their balls should get vacuumed back inside their bodies any minute now.

I squeeze my fist so tight the blood drains from my knuckles and I have to remind myself that he's still Finn's brother. Not to mention my dad's best friend's son, but man… if he was *anyone* else, he'd be in desperate need of a dentist appointment right now.

"Nah, man, just bored," I mumble, as cold as can be.

He doesn't think twice about my tone, picking up where he left off with the guys. I think I'm rid of him until…

"Hey, asshole, have you seen my brother?" Brody pesters.

Nope, mission aborted.

I can't take another second of pretending like I don't want to kick his face in. Not even for my dad.

Or Finn.

I need to get out of here.

"No." I rise off Theo's couch and shoulder my way through the crowd, heading for the front door.

"Where you going?" Theo asks when I edge around them and fling the front door open.

I dig through my wallet, presenting him my fake ID and a lie. "Just going to get more booze."

Theo frowns. "What? But the fridge is ful—"

I'm already gone.

* * *

Aveena

I've always prided myself in knowing my best friend. I mean, *duh*. What best friend doesn't? Diamond Mitchell has been my non-biological sister since we met at the town's annual carnival the summer before freshman year.

Dia's family had just relocated to Silver Springs for her dad's work, and I'd gotten a new job monitoring the children's games for the weekend. And by "monitoring" I mean making sure kids didn't get trampled in the bouncy house.

I spent my high school years considering Dia a part of me. Scratch that, a *reflection* of me. A different, more confident version, but a reflection nonetheless.

But lately?

The reflection's become foggy.

Distorted.

And the girl I'm looking at now? The one who's doing shots with the cheer captain and inhaling weed gummies? She's a reflection I don't recognize. A picture I'm not sure I want to keep.

I wasn't looking to get peer pressured tonight—I wasn't looking to get peer pressured *ever,* but somehow, I was stupid enough to believe Dia needed me for moral support.

I let her talk me into attending this drug fest, lied to my mom so she'd let me go, and now I'm considering never saying yes to anything ever again.

I stopped counting the times Dia's new bestie tried pressuring me to "live a little." *Come on, just one gummy*, Lacey urged. *You'll feel amazing.* I bet she didn't think I'd hear her call me a "Prudy Trudy" under her breath either.

Who am I kidding?

Dia doesn't need me to tend to her wounds. She found her cure at the bottom of a red cup just fine. I thought that, with Finn's bad influence out of her life, she'd stop chasing the next high, cut back a little, slow down. I was wrong. If anything, it's been worse since she and Finn called it quits. It's like she's on a marathon to destruction.

Desperate to outrun the pain.

Too bad you can't run in heels.

Spread across Theo's leather couch with the girls, I examine Theo's living room and the drunk basketball players wrecking it. There are drugs everywhere. On the living room table. In the kitchen. Oh, and I'm pretty sure the cheer squad is snorting lines in the bathroom.

I fall back down to earth at the sound of Xavier's name, my focus shifting to the conversation I've been ignoring for twenty minutes.

"Xavier? Really?" Dia cringes. "Didn't he *just* dump Brie?"

Lacey rolls her eyes. "Oh, give me a break. They weren't together when we did it."

My eyes bulge out of their sockets.

Wait… Xavier slept with Lacey?

His ex's best friend?

So much for him being the "nice" jock, huh?

"When did you even have time to screw him?" Dia questions.

"That night at Theo's," Lacey admits.

Shit… He'd *literally* just dumped Brie a few hours prior.

Lacey winces at Dia's sheer disapproval. "Don't look at me like that, D. We were both wasted, and I was sad, and… I don't know, I kissed him, and things escalated."

"Girl, you are *so* dead if Brie finds out." Dia speaks my mind.

"Who gives a shit at this point?" Lacey shrugs. "It would've been one thing to fuck him when we were friends, but Brie and I barely talk anymore. Plus, like I said, he's single. Fair's fair."

"I thought you weren't over Theo?" Dia reminds her.

"I'm not, *not even close*, but what else am I going to do? I can't get the guy's attention to save my life. A girl's got to eat."

Dia cracks a small laugh, tossing a thousandth weed gummy

into her mouth. She's been at it since she spotted Finn by the beer pong table earlier. She didn't flinch, didn't cry, didn't let *one* drop of emotion bleed through her facade, but I know from the way she downed two vodka shots back-to-back that she took it hard.

"Why him, though? Out of all the dudes at school?" Dia asks.

"Don't get me wrong, Theo's a fucking dreamboat," Lacey elaborates. "He's hot, funny, a good lay, the whole package, but I always thought Xavier had this sort of…" She pauses. "*Mystery* to him, you know? He's like an enigma. I can't tell what he's thinking most of the time. Oh, and hello? He's drop-dead gorgeous."

I have to agree with her on the enigma part.

Xavier always looks miles away. Like he's somewhere in his head, looking out onto a world of idiots and thinking to himself, *I fucking hate it here*. The boy seems unimpressed with the crap folks his age rave about.

And I've never related to anything more.

"What? It's true," Lacey insists when Dia snickers. "He's unattainable. It's like he doesn't give a shit about being popular. The guy is too cool for the cool kids."

She's right.

Xavier *is* too cool for the cool kids.

Why?

He never wanted the title in the first place.

"Don't ask me why, but that's a huge turn-on," Lacey says

unapologetically. "And between us… He's an amazing fuck. I came four times. *Four.*" She squeals, and I cringe at the visual. Lacey cranes her neck, sifting through the area. "Speaking of Xav, have you seen him? I wouldn't say no to round two."

"Not since earlier." Dia mimics Lacey's actions, her gaze combing the room. "I think I heard Theo say he went out to get some booze."

The girls resume with their gossiping, and I pluck my phone out of my pocket, selecting my conversation with Zac. I never texted him back after he tried to coax me into sharing more info about myself. Ashley climbed inside my car before I could reply. I hadn't realized I'd left him on Read until now.

I peek toward Lacey and Dia choking on shots of raspberry vodka, then back at my phone.

Should I text him?

Better late than never, right?

What if he doesn't text back?

What if he's asleep?

It *is* past midnight.

Shut up and do it.

I grab my courage by the vagina, —that's right, balls are sensitive. Vaginas are the rightful winners here—and compose an answer.

Love: I have a tattoo on my left shoulder.

Seven minutes elapse.

No reply.

Then comes the blow to my ego.

Read at 12:30 a.m.

Okay, I deserved that.

But I'm not giving up just yet.

Love: You wanted to know something new about me, didn't you?

He reads the message as soon as it delivers.

Five minutes later, he still hasn't replied.

Oh, well.

Got to learn when to admit defeat.

I begin to put my phone awa—

Zac: What is it?

A big, silly grin creeps onto my lips.

Love: Can't tell you. It'd be WAY too dangerous if you ever saw me in real life.

His response comes through right away.

Zac: At least tell me why you got it.

I debate on letting him in on my tragic backstory for a minute but quickly come to my senses. No one on this earth knows why I got a caterpillar tattoo on my shoulder.

Hell, until a minute ago, no one on this earth knew I had a tattoo *at all.* Well, except Dia, who saw it once at a sleepover, but my mom has no idea. You'd be surprised what you can hide when you don't do tank tops and revealing outfits.

The tattoo's meaning is a secret I'll take to my grave.

I'm not giving that up to a stranger.

Love: Can't tell you that either.

No response.

Six minutes later, I worry he's grown bored of my deflecting.

Until my phone dings again.

Zac: Whatever. Bet it's a typical girl thing like a rose.

Love: *Buzzer sound* WRONG!

Zac: A butterfly then.

Love: Wrong again. Also, why the hell are butterflies SO overrated? They don't do any of the work. It's all caterpillars. And they don't get nearly enough credit. I'm pissed.

Zac: Yeah, but butterflies are much cooler.

Love: Agree to disagree.

Zac: Did I strike a nerve?

Love: Nah. Just having a shit night. Sorry.

Zac: You too?

Love: You have no idea.

Zac: What happened?

Love: You go first.

Zac: Just been stuck at some lame-ass party and debating on drowning myself in the punch bowl. You?

My breath hitches, scraping at the back of my throat.

A party?

As in… *this* party?

Love: Theodore Cox's party?

Please say no.

Zac: Yeah. How'd you know?

Fuck.

Love: Because I'm here, too.

He stops replying for a bit, and it doesn't take a genius to know he's probably just as freaked-out as I am. We're closer to each other than anticipated.

Much closer.

And here I thought this anonymity pact would be child's play.

Zac: So, we run in the same circle then?

Love: Looks like it.

Zac: I didn't know you were popular, L.

Love: Who says that I am?

Zac: Don't bother. You got invited to the cool kids' party. The jig is up.

Love: So? Maybe I snuck in through the back door.

Zac: You mean the locked back door? Fat chance.

Love: How do you know it's locked?

Zac: Tried to take a piss outside earlier. Backyard's off limits.

Damn it.

For what it's worth, his presence here most likely means he's part of the basketball team or friends with a player. Whatever it is, he's got to be popular—even if it's just by association. Or maybe he's a stoner? I wouldn't put it past Theo. I know he tends to invite whoever can keep the grass coming.

Before I can text back, Zac tops it off with an emoji of two hands high fiving each other.

Love: What was that?

Zac: Just me high fiving myself.

Love: For what?

Zac: For being right. I had a feeling you were attractive.

I bite back a chuckle.

Love: Or so you think!!! I could be quasimodo for all you know.

Zac: Not possible. I know these guys. They wouldn't invite a girl they'd regret waking up to the next day. You're hot, L. Just deal with it.

I scoff.

I find great irony in the fact that technically, Theo didn't personally invite me and Lacey is the only reason I'm here. Zac's so certain of his claims, he never stopped to think that I could be the only *non-popular* person in this house.

Zac: Don't take this the wrong way but I wish you'd stayed home. Now I'm going to spend all fucking night thinking about you.

He's right.

I messed up. I didn't have to tell him I was here. Sure, the party is *crawling* with girls, making it hard for him to find me, but I could've just kept my big mouth shut instead of digging myself into a massive hole.

Now, I'm going to wonder if every guy I see is him. At least, until Dia agrees to leave, which is probably not happening until four, five a.m. What the hell was I thinking letting her drive me? Did I seriously expect my heartbroken friend to stay sober at a party when her hot mess of a cheating ex is on the guest list?

I study the living room, my heart pounding every time I spot a guy on his phone. The first candidate is Axel, standing by the fireplace, arm wrapped around a brunette's shoulders, staring at his phone screen with a lazy grin on his fuckboy face.

Oh, God no.

Please no.

On his right is Theo, also on his phone, although he seems to be scrolling on social media rather than texting.

Vee, knock it off!

If you go into detective mode every time you see a guy on his phone, we'll be here until graduation.

My phone chimes, reminding me that I left my texting buddy on hold.

Zac: I give it a week, tops.

Love: What?

Zac: Our anonymity pact.

Zac: One week. Two, if we're lucky.

Love: Okay, Negative Nancy.

Zac: What? Someone had to say it. I'm telling you something will happen and we'll find out without meaning to. No way we can keep this up if we're friends with the same people.

His gloomy prediction weighs me down.

But the worst part is the realization that comes next.

Shit, I have to ghost him, don't I?

The universe seems dead set on throwing us in each other's way. We connected through some old poetry book, exchanged anonymous letters for two weeks—what are the odds, seriously—and now we're at the same party?

Drop it, Universe, I'm not playing your games.

I stop replying, shoving my phone into my back pocket.

"Dia, Axel's got the magic mushrooms," Lacey says, and my head snaps up. "Let's go."

Lacey's request seems to remind Dia of my existence because my best friend's bloodshot eyes jump to mine.

She's worried.

But it's not about me.

It's my *reaction* she's scared of.

She knows damn well if she stands off that couch… she's breaking her promise. The one she made me at the back-to-school party months ago. I'd caught her popping a molly and pulled her aside. Told her I didn't recognize my best friend anymore.

She promised never to touch the hard stuff again, then fed me a bunch of excuses about feeling peer pressured and losing herself trying to fit into Finn's world.

I bought every word.

But she can't pull the Finn card anymore.

If she goes with Lacey, it's on her.

"Dia, move your ass, will you?" Lacey tugs on Dia's sleeve. "We have like five minutes before Axel gives the shrooms to Finn's brother."

Dia doesn't budge.

Annoyed, Lacey whines a squeaky "D, come on! It was your idea!"

Then Dia rises off the couch.

And my heart cracks a little. It's one thing to get dragged into Lacey's whack plans. It's another to literally *come up* with the plan.

As if she can sense my disappointment, Dia stops in her tracks, and I rejoice, foolish enough to believe that she might be having second thoughts. That the Dia who used to pick me up from work every summer before I got a car just because she felt like it is still somewhere in there.

"Vee, I…" Dia stares at me with the same guilt-ridden eyes as she did the night I confronted her about drugs.

"It's fine, I'm leaving anyway." I push to my feet.

"Vee, wait," she calls, but I'm already tearing through the crowd. I'm storming out of Theo's house a minute later, my throat throbbing with pain, and booking it down the sidewalk by foot. I don't have the slightest idea of how I'm going to get home.

My mom thinks I'm crashing at Dia's. I *could* just tell her we had a fight, but I'd have to call and wake her up at 1:00 a.m. so she can come pick me up from the party I lied about.

Any good deals on caskets this time of year?

Seeing as my house is in a completely different part of town, I pull up my phone's GPS and enter my home address to check the distance from here.

Twenty-five minutes.

My chest inflates with relief.

Then I realize I'm looking at the time by car.

And the time by foot is nowhere near as reassuring.

Two hours and fifty-eight minutes.

Great.

Defeated, I shamble down the street, cursing my stupid small town for neglecting to host a cab company. Hopefully, I don't get kidnapped. All lights are off, except for Theo's house, and apart from the faint music emanating from the party, there isn't a sound to be heard. Worry grips me when I spot a truck parked down the street.

Someone's inside.

Just sitting in the dark.

Alone.

At one in the morning.

Lovely.

My pulse jolts, but I don't halt my pace, approaching the car with quick, hurried strides. The truck sits across the street from me, and the closer I get, the more apparent it becomes that the stranger is a male.

He's also on his phone, the pale blue light illuminating half his face. A heartbeat later, I reach the vehicle's level and the guy's head lifts up. We make eye contact at the same time, and my shoulders release all tension.

Is that Xavier?

His chiseled features light up in recognition, and he frowns, battling a confusion I reciprocate. I can tell he's wondering what the hell I'm doing out at night, and I could ask him the same question. Why is he not inside enjoying the party?

Or… enjoying Lacey?

I know the guys were looking for him earlier.

Is that where he's been all night?

Holed up in his car?

Reminding myself to mind my own business, I carry on down the street. Then I hear his car start. I turn to check and see him speed down the street. He's probably going home. I keep walking, squeezing my phone for reassurance as if I expect to get jumped at any moment.

A honk pierces through the night, and I yelp, releasing hold of my phone and dropping it facedown on the sidewalk. I'm about to pick it up when a car slows down next to me.

Don't let it be some creep.

Don't let it be some creep.

Xavier just left, which means there'd be no witnesses.

"Are you trying to get killed?" a deep voice startles me.

I flick my head to see Xavier staring at me through his rolled-down window. *I thought he left?* I scan the vicinity over my shoulder and realize he probably just drove further down the street to turn his car around since he was on the wrong side of the road.

I don't reply right away, picking up my phone and wincing at the cracked screen.

"Want to tell me what the hell you're doing walking alone in the middle of the night?" he asks.

"Dia's in no shape to drive me, and I have no other way to get home, so… walking it is." With that, I resume down the sidewalk. I expect Xavier to call it a night and take off, but he doesn't, driving extra slow next to me.

"How far do you live?" he tries again.

"Like twenty-fives minutes away," I tell him.

Technically, it's not a lie.

"By car or by foot?" He sees right through my game.

"Car," I mumble.

"Get in." He's not asking. "I'll drive you."

Thank you, Jesus.

"Are you sure?" I pretend to hesitate when inside I'm weeping tears of joy. I couldn't care less that he banged his girl's best friend the day they broke up right now. I'm way too scared of the things that go bump in the night to turn down his offer.

Truth is, this isn't the best part of town. Theo's house is the nicest, most decent home on the block. Granted, we live in a relatively safe place, but the little crime that happens in Silver Springs usually happens around here.

"Vee, I'm not waking up to the news that your body was found in a dumpster. Get in the damn truck." When I don't reply fast enough, Xavier adds, "Unless you want me driving next to you like this the entire time."

A chuckle rips from my throat.

As crazy as it may sound, I don't think he's bluffing.

He'd actually do it.

"Thanks." I crack a shy smile and use the truck's step to climb into his passenger seat.

"Where to?" He pumps the gas as soon as I've buckled up.

I give him my address, and he nods, knowing what part of town I'm referring to. We drive in silence for over ten minutes. The memory of Dia saying Xavier had gone out to get booze crosses my mind halfway to my house, and I search the car for evidence.

Nothing in the front.

Nothing in the back.

Maybe it's in the trunk?

Might as well make conversation.

"Didn't you go buy booze?" I ask.

"Nah." He shrugs. "I just said that to get out of there. I needed a break."

The fact that he'd prefer sitting in his car by himself than partying with his friends makes me think he didn't read the jock manual correctly.

"What about you? What's your excuse for leaving so early?"

"More like what's my excuse for coming *at all*," I mutter.

He nods in understanding. "Not your scene, huh?"

"What are you talking about? I throw ragers like these every weekend," I joke, and his lips tip into a smile.

"And you never invited me?" He gasps.

I swallow a chuckle.

"*I would*, but I'm scared you'd just end up hiding in your car the whole time."

He laughs.

It's just a laugh. Like so many other laughs. I've heard guys laugh a million times before. But *his* laugh feels warm. Like a soft blanket. It resonates through my body, fuels that thing in my chest, gives it an extra beat. A squeeze. I may dislike a few things about Xavier Emery…

But I love his laugh.

If there was a laugh competition, he'd win.

Okay, moving on from the laugh thing, it's getting weird.

"Why'd you hide?" I don't expect him to confide in me but push my luck anyway. "I thought parties were supposed to be a jock's happy place."

"Is that really what you think?" he mocks. "That every jock on earth just loves getting wasted? Like we're the same person copied and pasted or something?"

"No, of course not," I backtrack. "It's just… have you *met* your friends?"

He grins, getting my point.

"Yeah, well, they're all talk. Between you and me, Finn only showed up tonight because he was hoping to see Dia, and Theo just threw the stupid thing because Finn asked him to."

That would explain why it was so last-minute.

"He's wasting his time, you know," I comment.

"Who is?"

"Finn. He can throw all the parties he wants, Dia's never taking his ass back." I'm annoyed with myself. Dia just flat out told me *drugs* were more important to her than our friendship, and I'm still rooting for her happiness.

"I wouldn't be so sure about that, Harper."

"You're kidding, right? Finn cheated on her. He *cheated.* Sure, they were both too chicken to admit they were ever dating in the first place, but you don't come back from cheating."

"He didn't, though," Xav corrects me.

My jaw drops.

"What?"

"He didn't cheat on her. Dia just thinks he did."

I'm about to swamp him with questions when loud, piercing sirens split my ears in two. Xavier and I jump, our gazes darting to the rearview mirror and the red and blue lights flickering behind us.

Cops.

We're getting pulled over.

"You've got to be fucking kidding me," Xavier huffs before parking his truck on the side of the road. My anxiety spikes.

What if my mom finds out about this?

What if we get brought back to the station?

And what the hell are they even stopping us for? Xavier wasn't driving recklessly. Maybe we went a bit over the speed limit but nothing crazy. If my mom discovers I was in a car with a boy, getting a ride home from a party, to make matters worse, I'll be confined to my room until graduation.

She'll make me quit my job, too.

She made it clear she thinks I'm wasting my time working at the library. "*It's not like you need the money anyway*," she said once, gesturing to look around the three-story house my sister paid for. I'll become the real-life version of Cinderella, only allowed out of the house for school and to run Ash's errands.

At least, I still have Dia.

It hits me.

No, you don't.

She left you, too, remember?

"Vee?" Xavier's voice halts my downward spiral.

I snap back to reality, looking up to meet a set of gorgeous, aqua eyes. Only then do I notice how fast I'm breathing. My chest is raising up and down, my hands shaking like leaves.

Not. Enough. Air.

"Vee, what's going on?" he asks again when I don't reply.

Not because I don't want to.

Because I *can't.*

The words on my tongue explode into tiny fragments, lodging themselves deep inside my throat. That's when I understand that I'm having an anxiety attack. And I need to get a grip before the police officer reaches the car.

I open my mouth once more, wanting to tell him, "*My mom can't know about this*" but barely managing a squeaky, "M-My mom." Thankfully, that seems to be enough explanation for him because Xavier nods, glancing at the cop car pulling up behind us in the mirror.

We're running out of time.

Then he says the last thing I expected.

"Breathe with me."

I blink at him, my poor heart doing a whole-ass backflip when he reaches for my trembling fingers and takes my hand. His hand feels warm. Reassuring. It's big, too. Much bigger than mine.

But I still can't fucking breathe.

This can't be happening.

Here I thought my anxiety attacks were over. I haven't had one this bad since my dad's birthday last year.

"Vee, look at me, I'm here." Xavier tilts my chin up with his index. "You're not alone."

He has no idea how wrong he is about that.

No idea.

"Just breathe with me, all right?" he instructs and inhales deeply.

Slowly.

It takes everything in me to match his tempo, but after a few minutes, I manage to pull a miracle out of nowhere and discipline my speedy pulse.

I breathe in.

Breathe out.

Over and over again.

Until, finally, I regain a semblance of calm.

"You going to be okay?" Xavier worries. "Just say the word and we'll work something out." The way he says it causes an unknown, gut-wrenching feeling to stir in my chest.

I never, in a million years, would've suspected that there was such kindness in this boy. It's hard to believe this is the same guy who's been bedding cheerleaders left and right.

"I mean it, Vee. I'll just tell him you're having an anxiety attack or something. We—"

"Xav, I'm okay," I choke out. "I'm fine."

He doesn't seem convinced but reluctantly nods, squeezing my fingers one last time before unlinking his hand from mine.

I miss the warmth instantly.

The sheriff comes knocking on the driver's-side window the next second, and Xavier rolls down the glass, flashing his best suck-up smile to the man on the other side.

"Sheriff Daniel, what can I do for you?"

The forty-something man seems taken aback by Xavier's attitude but quickly schools his expression. I'm guessing the kids he arrests at 1:00 a.m. aren't all this merry.

"Well, well, Xavier Emery." The sheriff pushes to his tiptoes to see further inside the truck. He spots me in the passenger seat and stifles a scoff like he's not surprised to find a girl in there. "Where you two coming from so late?"

"A friend's house." Xavier doesn't miss a beat.

"You mean the party at the Coxes you lot think we don't know about?" Sheriff Daniel's lips twist into a crooked smile.

"That would be the one." Xav doesn't bother lying.

"Have you been drinking?" Here comes the obvious question.

"No, sir."

I'm willing to bet that's a lie and Xavier's had at least *one* drink tonight, but the truth could cost him his license. Plus, if he did have a few drinks, it doesn't reflect in his behavior or driving.

The man arches an eyebrow. "You sure about that?"

"Positive."

"Where you off to?" The questions pile up.

"Just taking her home."

"Are you now?" The sheriff grins, his words heavy with innuendo. Neither me, nor Xavier, waste our breath denying it. He's already made up his mind. The questions drag on for eternity, until finally, Sheriff Daniel surrenders to the facts.

Everything checks out.

He's got no reason to hold us.

"All right, well, you've got a burned-out taillight in the back, son. You need to get that fixed right away."

I can't believe it.

That's what this is about.

I had a panic attack for a broken headlight.

"I'm giving you three days to take care of that. Not one more. Are we clear?"

"Crystal," Xavier assures him.

The sheriff proceeds to give Xavier a notice to fix the violation and requests his license and registration. Xavier doesn't put up a fight, pulling out his wallet and handing it over. Sheriff Daniel pauses when checking Xavier's license.

"That really you?" He squints.

"Unfortunately. Old picture, you know how it is," Xavier says.

Sheriff Daniel inches the license closer to his wrinkly face.

"How old were you on this?"

"Sixteen, sir." Xavier cringes. "I'd just gotten my license."

I can't help the smile tugging at my lips.

The photo wasn't taken this long ago. There's no way he looks *that* different. I knew him when he was sixteen and he was still good-looking. He just wasn't as buff back then. The sheriff gives a wheezy, smoker laugh before handing Xavier his license and papers back.

"You should get a more recent one taken," he suggests.

"Will do, sir." Xavier nods.

"All right. Drive safe, kids" are the sheriff's parting words and Xavier's cue to toss his license facedown in the cup holder of his car and start the engine.

The rest of the ride home is uneventful and quiet, to my relief. I wasn't particularly looking forward to addressing my freak-out earlier. But when Xavier comes to a slow stop in front of my house and kills the ignition rather than keep the car running, I know he's about to venture down a path I don't like.

"About earlier," he says quietly.

"Don't. *Please.*"

I can tell he wants to ask me what that was about, but he doesn't push it.

"Thank you," I whisper. "For what you did."

His eyes lift to my face. "The ride or the intervention?"

"Both," I admit. "But more so for the intervention."

"You're welcome. Leave me a review on Yelp," he jokes, and

I snort out an embarrassing pig laugh. It's one of those ridiculous *oink* snorts. The kind that's impossible to miss, and Xavier is trying so hard not to laugh he looks like he's in pain.

Our eyes lock.

His blues ask, "*Are we just going to ignore that?*" My cheeks burn with embarrassment. So, not only did I go through a solid anxiety attack in front of this guy, I also have to laugh like a pig when he's around?

Oh hell no.

Running on impulse, I snatch his license from the cup holder.

"What do we have here?" I turn the tables on him.

His smile fades instantly.

Not laughing anymore, are we?

"Don't you dare," he warns, but his tone is playful. It takes me back to our countless games of tag in Finn's backyard when we were kids. The never-ending banter. Makes me think that maybe… the only thing that's changed between now and then is we're ten years older.

"Let's see that picture, shall we?" I threaten, and he stretches his arm out to try and steal it back from me. I shriek in between laughter, dodging his hand just in time. I tilt my body toward the passenger door, but before I can get a good look at his license, I hear him unbuckle his seat belt.

Oh, he's not messing around.

His long, brawny arm reaches all the way to my side, and he

swipes the license from my hands without blinking.

Just like that.

Like taking candy from a baby.

Not that I'm shocked. He's taller than me. He's stronger, too. I know I don't stand a chance, but that doesn't stop me from unfastening *my* seat belt and pouncing to retrieve the license. He won't let go of it, fighting me off with a disarming smile that would probably leave me dazed in any other situation.

We wrestle until Xavier accidentally crushes the steering wheel with his elbow and a piercing honk roars through the night. I'd go off on him for risking to wake up my mom if I weren't laughing so hard.

Wait. That's not a bad idea.

"Shit, you woke up my mom," I blurt, and he falls for it, just like I knew he would, lowering his guard and glancing toward my house. I jump at the chance to pluck the license from his fingers and take a good look.

If victory had a taste, it would be sweet.

So why does this taste so sour?

Why do I feel like I'm going to be sick all over his leather seats? It's not the picture's fault. Sixteen-year-old Xavier looks adorable, as expected. No, what flips my stomach upside down and clogs my throat with panic…

Is his middle name.

The name I never saw coming.

Xavier Zachary Emery.

Aveena

Most moms tell their daughters "Good morning" or "Did you sleep well?" first thing on a Saturday morning. Most moms ask you what you want for breakfast, or what you've got planned for the day…

But my mom…

My mom gives me my to-do list.

Sometimes, it's picking up Ash's clothes from the dry cleaner. Other times, it's driving Ashley to an early photo shoot. This time, it's going into town to fetch her fancy mineral water, because Mom says tap water is no good, and Ash needs to stay hydrated during her private dance lesson.

My mom insisted being a good singer doesn't mean squat if you can't dance, and Ashley needs to become a "real performer" to stand a chance in LA.

And so, here I am, waiting in line at our local grocery store with five bottles of Fiji Water dumped into a cart. Unfortunately for me, the entire population of Silver Springs decided to hit the grocery store at the same time, and the line stretches for miles on end. After a few minutes of drumming my fingers on the cart's handle, I pluck my phone out of my hoodie and select my text conversation with Zac.

I'm supposed to be ghosting him. I should've deleted his number the second I hopped out of Xavier's truck last night. But I didn't.

I couldn't.

Instead, I spent seven hours fussing in bed, replaying Xavier's full name on repeat and trying to debunk my own theories.

Xavier. Zachary. Emery.

Zachary as in… *Zac*?

No, this has to be a coincidence. Xavier *can't* be Zac. He just can't. And even if he was, it wouldn't matter, because I'm never texting him again and—

My phone pings with a message.

Zac: I didn't end up drowning myself in the punch bowl last night… Just in case you were wondering.

I'm mad at myself for smiling at that.

And I'm *furious* at myself for answering when I just promised I'd never talk to him again.

Love: I wasn't, but thanks.

His reply comes through ten minutes later.

Zac: Not a morning person, are we?

Love: Just surprised you're still texting me.

Zac: Why wouldn't I be?

Love: Gee, I don't know, maybe because you said our anonymity pact was destined to fail?

Zac: So? Everything in life is.

Love: What's that supposed to mean?

Zac: Think about it. Our lives literally end because our hearts and bodies fail at some point. Doesn't mean we shouldn't enjoy it while it lasts.

Love: Thanks, Dr. Phil.

Zac: I aim to please.

Love: So, you're saying you're not nervous about me

finding out who you are? Like at all?

Zac: Not really, no.

Love: Even with all the personal things you've told me?

Zac: Nope. If it's meant to happen, it will. Nothing I can do about it.

He says if I'm meant to find out, I will.

But the nagging voice in my head screams…

What if I already have?

The line begins to pick up, and I estimate that I should be at the front in less than five minutes.

Zac: I mean, I could always stop texting you. If that's what you want.

Do you want *him to stop texting you?*

Be honest, Vee.

Do you?

No.

No, I don't.

Love: I'm just saying we shouldn't tell each other where we are from now on. I think last night was WAY too close.

Zac: Ditto.

Love: And no more sharing specific stuff like tattoos. It makes it too easy to find out who we're talking to and we made a pact for a reason.

Zac: Yes, ma'am.

"Miss?" The cashier calls for my attention, and I jerk, realizing that I'm up next. I squeeze my phone inside my jeans pocket without answering and dump the water bottles on the checkout counter.

* * *

Dia's lime-green car has never been what one would call "subtle." I could always spot it from a distance, day or night, no matter the weather, but I still come to doubt my own eyes when I drive down the cul-de-sac leading to my house and make out her Beetle in my driveway.

I blink one time.

Two times.

She's really here.

At my house.

At 10:30 a.m. on a Saturday morning.

I fill the last available parking space in the lot before stretching my arm out to grab the reusable grocery bags in the back seat. Try as I may, I can't seem to come up with a feasible explanation to justify her presence here. Could it be that she forgot something at my house the last time we hung out?

Her loyalty, perhaps?

I proceed to the front door, my attempts at containing my nerves falling flat, and cross the threshold. At first sight, the kitchen is empty, but I flip my head to find Dia sitting on our velvet entryway bench.

A basket of mini muffins rests on her laps.

I wonder what to make of her visit until the familiar scent of apple pecan muffins tips me off as to her intentions. She got my favorites—wild guess: she's here to apologize.

"Hey." She jolts to her feet, her full lips shaped into a timid smile.

"Hey?"

"Your mom let me in," she explains. "Then she had to go monitor Ashley's dance lesson." She points to the ceiling, more specifically to the upstairs studio where Ash's lessons take place every weekend.

Beyoncé's "Partition" echoes throughout the house, all the way down to the kitchen, and I roll my eyes to another dimension.

That's so my mom.

God forbid the pricey, professional dance teacher she

hired—the woman literally choreographed for some of the industry's biggest names—be trusted to do her job correctly.

"I just thought I'd bring you muffins." Dia gestures to the gift basket—her version of a white flag.

I stare blankly at her.

"What are you really doing here, Diamond?" I cut to the chase.

She cringes at my usage of her full name, bracing the basket on the bench behind her, then letting out a pained "Trying not to lose my only friend."

I drink her in.

Wearing sweatpants, an old cardigan, and a messed-up bun, she looks like she hasn't slept a wink in at least twenty-four hours. On second thought, I'm positive parts of the dark spots under her eyes are remnants from last night's makeup.

Has she been crying?

"I'm not your only friend. You have Lacey, remember?"

She heaves a scoff. "Not anymore."

I want to ask what she means by that. To ask her what happened after I left. If only my wounds weren't so painfully fresh.

"I'm so sorry, Vee. I've been an awful friend." Her eyes glimmer with regret. "And I'm not just talking about last night. I'm talking about all of senior year."

I can't maintain the eye contact, but it feels like a three-thousand-ton skyscraper has just been lifted off my shoulders.

Maybe there's hope for us yet.

"If I'm being honest with myself, I've been an awful friend since the moment I stepped into Finn's house last summer. I've changed. I know I have."

She's right.

She *has.*

Ever since the day she dropped by my place and broke the news that she was seeing Finn Richards, I've been trying to convince myself that I was crazy. That by being reluctant to embrace Dia's new world, I was standing in the way of change.

Change is normal, I told myself.

Change is a part of life.

Change is to be welcomed.

I just wish our friendship didn't have to change, too.

"I got so wrapped up in it. I wanted to get a taste of that *teenage experience* everybody talks about, to try new things and I…" She pauses. "I love you so much, Vee, but I've always felt like I had to hide this part of myself from you. The part that wants to make mistakes, kiss the wrong boys. The part that wants to go wild every once in a while."

"Is it something I did?" I drop the act.

"No, it's just… you're always so composed. You don't like the attention, you're not boy-crazy, you want nothing to do with popularity. And the alcohol thing because of your dad…" She winces as though the words left a sour taste in her mouth. "I can't help feeling like a monster for wanting all those things. And when I started seeing Finn…" She flinches at his name.

The player really did a number on her.

"He made me feel like it was okay to give in to my impulses. Being with him was like a high I'd never experienced before. But then the high ended. And I tried to get that feeling elsewhere, tried to keep it going for as long as I could… no matter the cost."

She starts tearing up.

That's why she wanted to try magic mushrooms.

To keep it going.

"Until you walked out last night. And I realized that the high isn't worth it if you don't have anyone to come down to."

It's my turn to tear up.

"I told Lacey I wasn't going through with it, then we got into a fight and she blocked me on Snapchat, so… I guess that's the end of that." She chuckles.

"That sucks, D. I'm sorry."

To my own disbelief, I mean it. Resisting the peer pressure couldn't have been easy, and I'm proud of her.

She shrugs. "Whatever. Lacey was a fun party friend. She's not the friend you call at 4:00 a.m. crying, or the friend you make lasting memories with. Let's be honest, she's not even the friend you keep in touch with after high school. Us, this… we're for life, Vee. I'm not losing a forever friend over a *temporary* one."

I'm full-on crying at this point.

"Are we good?" Dia asks, the wretched plea muffling her

voice.

"Why do you think I'm crying, dummy?" I sniff and open my arms for a hug. She laughs, advancing straight into my embrace.

I think back to Xavier's words right then.

You're not alone.

And for the first time in a long time…

I agree.

* * *

"She did what?" I screech so loud I startle myself. When Dia suggested we go up to my room and munch our way through her mini-muffins basket, I had no idea she'd tell me a story so shocking it'd make me want to rip Finn's balls off his body. "She showed up at the party? *The* girl?"

"Yep." Dia indulges in another gummy bear from our last sleepover—without weed, this time. "Bastard has the audacity to trap me in a corner, begging me to listen to him, then the bitch just waltzes into the party with her friends like she owns the place."

"You're fucking with me? Finn *invited* her? Are you sure it wasn't Theo?"

"I don't care if the queen of freaking England invited her. Point is, she was there."

"What did Finn do when he saw her?"

"He left me there." Her voice is weak.

"*What*?"

"You heard me. The asshole actually left me to go talk to her. Then I didn't see either of them again for the rest of the night."

"You don't think he…" I can't even say it.

"I mean… One plus one equals two," Dia croaks, failing to keep her misery at bay.

"This guy is unbelievable!"

I can't fathom Finn's behavior. After everything he's done, he should consider himself lucky Dia is willing to even *look* at him. If he really does want her back as much as Xavier says he does, he has a hell of a funny way of showing it.

Xavier.

His name zaps through my memory, rehashing my last conversation with him. Last night, he said Finn didn't cheat on Dia. I personally don't believe it, but Dia should be able to make that decision for herself.

"Xavier told me something last night, and I think you should know."

Worry darkens her features. "What is it?"

"It came from the mouth of someone who'd do anything for Finn, so take it with a grain of salt, but… Xav said Finn didn't cheat."

Dia's face doesn't twist with shock. Her eyebrows don't shoot up to her hairline. In fact, her expression remains blank.

Indecipherable.

"I know," she simply says.

"You do?"

"Don't worry, not buying it for a second, but Finn tried to sell me the same bullshit last night."

"And would it change anything… if he *hadn't*?"

Undecisive, Dia nibbles on her bottom lip.

"It doesn't matter because he did. End of story." She writes off the possibility, and I get the sense that she'd prefer we left it at that. I think we're done discussing Easton High's playboys when Dia's almond-shaped eyes flash in realization.

"Hold on a second, when were you with Xavier last night? He disappeared like halfway through the party."

Crap.

"Is that where he was the whole time? With you?" Her high-pitched, excited tone tells me everything I need to know. She's seeing romance where there was nothing but polite chitchat and human decency.

"Whatever you're thinking, *un*think it. He just gave me a ride. I couldn't get home since you were…" I stop short.

The smile is instantly slapped off her face.

"Vee, I'm… I'm so sorry about that. Did I say I was sorry? God, I could slap myself. Do you want me to slap myself? Because I will."

A chuckle leaves my mouth.

"It's fine. Ancient history."

"So, did you ask Xavier for a ride, or did he offer?" she nags.

"What difference does it make?"

"All the difference in the world." Dia gives my shoulder a slight shake as if to knock some sense into me. "So?"

I give in. "He offered."

This earns me a smirk and a very suggestive "I see."

"Shut up." I flush, and Dia laughs.

"Tell me everything."

"There's nothing to tell. He just gave me a ride home. He didn't ask for my hand in marriage."

Although he did *hold* my hand.

Squeezed it when I was losing my shit.

And it didn't feel… awful.

"You mean to tell me that absolutely nothing worth telling happened during this ride home?"

My brain says, *Well, except for the fact that we got pulled over and I burst into the most inconvenient anxiety attack of all time*, but my mouth blurts, "Yes. Just let it go, okay?"

"Fine. I should get going anyway. I'm babysitting Charlie tonight." Dia leaps off the bed. "It's my turn to explain to him that we can't get rid of Dad to have a dog."

I snort out a laugh.

Charlie, Dia's younger brother, has to be the most endearing little monster you'll ever meet. Gaten, one of Dia's dads, is allergic to dogs, so, naturally, Charlie's solution was to suggest Daddy sleeps outside from now on.

Dia halts at the door, glancing at me one last time. "Oh, and, just so you know… I may hate Finn, but I'd totally support it if Xavier gave you another ride and you wanted to…" She pauses for dramatic effect. "*Learn to drive stick*."

The innuendo isn't lost on me.

"Get out of here." I lob a pillow at her with a laugh, and she shoots me a dramatic wink before scurrying down the stairs.

* * *

I don't hear a peep from Zac until ten that night.

Zac: How was your day?

I glance down at my oversized pajamas and the bag of sweet-and-salty popcorn nudged between my legs. I'm lying in bed, stuffing my face and rewatching my favorite shows to cope with the fact that Mom and Ashley went out to dinner and a movie without me.

Again.

They do it every Sunday night.

I shouldn't be hurt. Chances are, I'd decline the invitation anyway. But it'd be nice if they asked. Chasing these depressing thoughts away, I pause my show to text back.

Love: I've had better. You?

His response comes quickly.

Zac: What's wrong?

What's wrong is my own family would rather bathe in strangers' toenails than spend time with me.

Love: Nothing. Just a lot on my plate. And you didn't answer the question. How was your day?

Zac: Passable.

Love: Passable?

Zac: Yeah.

Love: What's wrong?

Zac: I asked first.

Love: I already answered.

Zac: No, you didn't. You dodged like you always do. Let's try that again. What's wrong?

Zac: Does it have something to do with your prodigy sibling?

I'm shocked by the memory on this guy.

Zac: You mentioned you played chauffeur to your prodigy sibling in your first letter. The one to Ms. Callahan.

Love: How on earth do you remember that?

Zac: There's this magical thing called paying attention.

I heave a chuckle.

Love: It's about my mom, actually.

Zac: What'd she do?

Love: It's what she doesn't do. Like remember that I exist.

Zac: Ouch. I'm sorry.

Love: Not your fault.

Zac: I know. But I'm sorry anyway.

A small smile tickles the corner of my mouth.

Zac: Look, if it makes you feel any better, my mom is a cheating liar who screws everything with a heartbeat. Is your sibling older than you?

I'm baffled by his ability to throw such a massive bombshell into the conversation, then keep talking like nothing happened.

Love: Slow down. Your mom is cheating on your dad?

Zac: Yup.

Love: That really sucks. I'm sorry.

Zac: Don't be. I was just trying to make you feel better about yourself. I don't need your pity.

Love: I know. But I'm sorry anyway.

Zac: Using my own words against me. Well played.

Love: **Bows** Thank you, thank you.

I feel a yawn coming on, fighting the urge to doze off.

Love: I'm tired. Might go to bed soon.

His reply is instant.

Zac: Don't. Please.

Zac: I need you to distract me right now.

Love: From what?

He stops replying.

I spend the next fifteen minutes overthinking. Shit… am I actually *worried* about him? My fingers type out a second message before I know it.

Love: Zac, what's going on?

Zac: I can hear them.

I don't put the pieces together at first.

Until the obvious explanation reveals itself to me. He just said his mom screwed everything with a heartbeat. Is that what he's hearing? His mom with… someone else?

Oh my God.

Love: Holy shit. Your mom?

Five more minutes elapse before he texts back.

Love: Zac???

Zac: Sorry, I was projectile-vomiting.

Love: That's awful. I don't know what else to say.

Zac: Just say you'll stay.

Love: I'm staying.

The image of Zac slash possibly *Xavier* locked in his room, trying to drown out the sound of his mother cheating on his dad, is sickening to me. I'm dying to ask him why she'd bang some loser with her kid in the house, but abstain in fear of pouring salt into his wounds.

Only explanation I see is, she doesn't know Zac is home.

Love: I wish I could hug you right now.

Zac: Fair warning, if you hugged me, another part of me would probably hug you…

I snort.

Boys, I swear.

How they can be discussing serious topics one second, then talking about sex the next, I'll never understand. Although something tells me he's just deflecting. Desperate to think about a sexual scenario that *doesn't* include his mother.

Love: DOWN, BOY.

Love: You don't even know what I look like, remember?

Zac: We've been over this. I'm like 99% sure that you're my type, L.

My chest tightens as images of Xavier's driver's license flash before my eyes. Well, if Zac is who I think he is…

He's definitely my type, too.

I hate that I want to rip open his soul and deep dive into the darkest corners of his mind. Figure him out. Understand what makes him tick. I'm not supposed to be this curious. We literally made a pact promising not to be curious.

Love: Have you ever had people close to you die?

Ten seconds go by.

Zac: Is this how you talk dirty? If so, we might need to work on that.

I'm embarrassed by how loud I laugh at his message.

Love: I'm serious, dork.

Zac: No one says dork anymore

Love: Who are you? The dork police?

Zac: I should. That sounds fun.

Love: I asked you a question, dork.

Zac: Stop calling me that. And I lost my grandpa when I was five. You?

Love: My dad.

Zac: What happened?

Love: He was sick.

What? It's true. *He was sick of life.* The bubbles pop on my screen as he texts back, but I don't want to discuss this further, so I text him again with a topic change.

Love: Do you believe in fate?

Zac: Like destiny?

Love: Yes.

Zac: Not really.

Love: So, you've never had something happen to you that's so crazy the odds are almost unreal? Something that makes you believe that maybe everything does happen for a reason?

Zac: Such as?

Love: I don't know. Like not getting on a plane because you missed your flight and it crashes?

Zac: Nope, can't say that I've ever had something this

freaky happen to me.

Love: You do realize that the only reason we're talking to each other right now is because I wrote a hate letter to my teacher and accidentally left it in a book?

Zac: Doesn't prove anything.

Love: Okay, what about the fact that the timing perfectly aligned and we were able to keep exchanging letters and confessions through the book for weeks?

Zac: Fine, that was weird, I'll give you that.

Love: Do you ever miss it? Writing the letters?

Zac: I haven't really thought about it since we stopped. Why?

Love: Because I do.

I'm startled by my own honesty.

Startled, but truthful nonetheless.

I miss writing him letters. Not having the slightest idea of who's on the receiving end. I miss being able to look at my childhood crush without wondering if he's my secret pen pal.

I miss when Zac was just Zac.

Love: Don't get me wrong, I like the texting, but I can't help feeling like everything was so much easier when we were just two kids writing stupid confessions in a book.

It takes him ten minutes to reply.

Zac: Then let's keep doing it.

Love: Are you serious?

Zac: As a heart attack.

Love: So, what? We each leave one confession in the book a week?

Zac: Why the fuck not?

Love: What if someone finds them?

Zac: They won't. We'll take our dirty little secrets out of the book as we go.

Zac: But no more PG-13 shit. I want the good stuff. Go big or go home, L. What do you say?

I weigh the pros and cons for over five minutes. Providing him with more information about myself is the definition of insanity. We're already walking a fine line here. Playing with fire every time we press Send.

One wrong move and all our good intentions could crumble, along with our anonymity pact. I might as well give him my social security number while I'm at it.

You promised, Vee.

You promised you'd stop being scared.

It starts now.

Love: You're on.

Aveena

THEN

My daddy once told me some things in life happen in slow motion. Like that short moment where you make eye contact with your soul mate for the first time. Or that split second before you cross the street too soon and someone holds you back.

He'd go and on about how rare it was.

He said he hoped I'd get to experience the legendary "*slow-mo*" for myself one day. Same way he had when he'd won his first car race—better yet, when he'd seen Mommy walk down the aisle on their wedding day.

My dad's "slow motions" were amazing.

Mine, on the other hand…

Throw in a tall glass of grape juice, my sister's favorite white dress, a television show set to air all over the country, and there you have it.

An invisible, seven-year-old girl's nightmare.

I can still hear my mother's screams when I tripped over my own feet and the glass slipped out of my hands. Visualize the stain as purple liquid bled right through Ashley's dress. Feel the sting of pain when I cut my finger trying to pick up the glass—it's almost as though my child brain thought cleaning up my mess would *un*ruin the thousand-dollar dress.

It all happened in slow motion, yes, but it's the resentment in my mom's eyes, the disappointment, the *shame* of having a world-class klutz for a daughter that lasted forever. The hatred in her voice when she'd insinuated I'd done it on purpose.

"I didn't mean to, I swear," I croaked after thirty minutes of Mommy dearest raining hell down on me, and rushed out of the house in tears.

I was barefoot, but I couldn't feel a thing as my little feet thumped toward the red maple tree behind the shed in the backyard. Not the wet grass under my toes. Not the open cut. Not the blood trickling down my hand.

Nothing.

I liked to go there—correction: I liked to *hide* there—whenever Mom put me through the wringer for being anything less than perfect. The old tree was my safe haven. It was a place to cry in peace, a sanctuary where Mom never found me.

Where no one ever would.

Or so I thought.

"Love?" My father's voice sounded far at first, until I heard the branches crackling on my right and realized my hiding spot wasn't as infallible as I'd thought. I tried silencing my erratic breathing so that he wouldn't find me, puffy eyes burning with unshed emotions.

"Love? *Chérie, où es-tu?*" he called again, this time in his native language. I loved when Dad spoke French. I never understood why Mom insisted he kept it to a minimum in public. Looking back, I realize she was probably scared it would make him stand out. And everybody knows Silver Springs, North Carolina, is a judgmental, cookie-cutter town filled with cookie-cutter people.

I didn't answer him, nuzzling my head into the crook between my legs to muffle my breakdown. Branches and leaves ruffled next to me. And while I never *saw* him sit down by my side, I knew he was there.

I felt him.

Felt his warm, loving presence.

One touch and the tightness in my chest exploded. All he did was place a comforting hand on my back, but it blew the water gates wide open and left me sobbing pathetically.

"I'm so sorry, Daddy. I didn't mean to stain her dress. You have to believe me," I barely said through my snot and dared to look in his direction. He was smiling.

Smiling.

It was a real smile, too, but it was sprinkled with distant sadness. I'd seen my dad fake smile before—like when he had to explain to ignorant people why he wanted to spend the rest of his life driving fast cars around a loop. Only his real smiles could cause the wrinkles near his green eyes.

It made no sense to me.

What was there to smile about?

"I believe you're telling the truth," was all he said, and an outpour of relief seeped through my bones.

Until he added, "About being sorry, that is."

"What?" I asked.

"We both know this wasn't an accident, Love." His smile didn't falter one bit. He wasn't mad, or pointing fingers. He was stating the facts. Saying things as they were. My sadness morphed into anger, rage spreading inside me like a tumor.

"You think I did this on purpose?" I spat. How could he think this low of me? How could he think me so evil I'd *want* to ruin my sister's big night?

Daddy was usually on my side.

He was the *only* one on my side.

"Okay, let's put it this way," he rephrased. "Do you think maybe… it's possible that you tripped without meaning to, but you also didn't try to hold yourself back as much as you could've?" He arched an eyebrow at me, and I blinked at him in what I wish I could say was confusion, but a buried, unassumed part of me read him crystal clear.

"No." I muttered as I ripped out grass that was still wet from the rain, leaving bald spots at my feet.

"You're saying there's not even a minuscule chance that I might be right? Not even *this* small?" He pinched two fingers together to illustrate his question, and I half-smiled.

But no smile could've ever eased my guilt.

Because he *was* right.

Don't get me wrong, it wasn't like I'd planned to spill my drink on her and operation "wreck the dress" was premeditated, but when my foot had gotten caught in the carpet and the opportunity presented itself…

I'd made the split-second decision to take it.

Maybe, subconsciously, I wanted her dress ruined.

Wanted her to feel the way I did on a daily basis.

Damaged.

Shabby.

In need of fixing.

I could've denied it, but I'd never lied to my papa before, and I sure wasn't about to start now.

"Maybe just *this* small." I'd mimicked his pinching gesture, and he'd nodded at my admission, his thumb sweeping the tears off my cheek gently.

"Aveena, love." He sighed. "You know Mommy loves you, right?"

It's the way he said it.

Like he was trying to convince me that Santa was real, which, at seven years old, I knew he wasn't. Some tool named Chad had been more than happy to burst my bubble at recess.

He was right, in a sad, disappointing way. Mommy did love me… but like she would a fake Picasso painting she bought on sale and hung up on her wall.

She was really excited about it, at first.

Until she could afford to buy the real thing. Never got around to taking down the first painting, though.

Now, it was just… *there.*

Collecting dust.

"Are you going to tell her?" I cut to the chase. "That it wasn't an accident?"

Dad sucked in a breath. "I should. This is not the person I want you to be, Aveena. You will never be happy, never be at peace holding so much resentment in your heart." He'd tapped the left side of my chest where a cavity filled with black goo would one day appear if I wasn't careful. "But no, I won't tell her."

I'd blinked at him in shock.

"Why not?"

"Because the only thing you're guilty of here is trying to remind your mother that she has two daughters. And I can never blame you for that, Love."

I didn't ask him to elaborate, but this simple comment revived the glimmer of hope I'd almost let die.

He was on my side.

Still.

"But you have to apologize to your sister. Can you do that for me?" He'd arched an eyebrow.

"Yes, Papa, anything." I'd stopped short. "But what about

Mommy?"

"I'll deal with her."

On that note, I threw myself into my papa's arms, holding on to him so tightly I most definitely cut off his airways. He didn't flinch, extending his arm around my shoulders and squeezing me to his chest as though his life depended on it.

Then he let me cry for what felt like an eternity.

He rubbed my back the whole way through, played with my hair until my cheeks were dry, and I was ready to function like a human being again. Dad and I agreed to leave the safety of the tree five minutes later.

That's when I belted a scream so piercing it sent the neighbor's Doberman into a barking fit.

"What is it, baby?" Dad asked right away.

"*Ew!*" I'd shrieked, pointing at the wormy thing crawling up the cherry tree. "Kill it, Daddy!"

The last thing I expected was for Dad's deep laugh to cut through the air. *What's so funny?* I thought. *And why is Dad bending down on one knee?* I near gasped in horror when he nudged the green worm off the trunk of the tree into his cupped hands.

"Do you know what this is?" Dad inched his hands in my direction, and I recoiled, backing away. "It's okay, honey, I promise. Come, take a look."

Inhaling a shaky breath, I obliged, eyeing the hairy insect inside my father's palm with the utmost attention.

I'd seen these before.

"That's a caterpillar," I recalled.

"It sure is, but I'm not going to hurt it."

"Why not? It's so… weird. And look how slow it's going." I racked my brain for an explanation as to how this green thing was *any* different from the giant spiders and mosquitos Dad crushed without a second thought when we went camping.

"What about the butterfly we saw last week?" Dad questioned. "Was *it* weird?"

I pictured the gorgeous white-and-yellow butterfly I'd seen when playing with Dad at the park. He had this warm, golden aura to him. Was probably just the sun reflecting on his wings, but I'd still spent the ride home daydreaming about seeing it again.

"No." I smiled in recollection. "He was beautiful. Like a shining star."

"You're wrong," Dad shocked me by saying. "This little guy right here—" He gestured to the striped insect with his chin. "—*he's* the real star. *He's* the one with all the merit. *He's* the one who puts in the work. And yes, he's slow. Yes, it can take him a while to get to where he's supposed to be, but he keeps going anyway. So, that one day… he can become a butterfly, too."

Fascinated, I'd kneeled down in the damped grass by his side, consuming every last drop of my father's knowledge

"You see, without the *weird phase*. Without the work, the struggle, there'd be no victory. Without the ugliness, there'd be no beauty."

"So… the only way to get *there—*" I pointed at the blue sky where butterflies all over the world spread their wings, then at the fuzzy caterpillar squirming in my papa's hands. "—is to start *here*?"

"That's right." Dad nodded in satisfaction before presenting me with an unexpected gift—the caterpillar itself. First, he'd eased my contracted fist open, and then he'd transferred the fragile little guy over from his palm to mine.

Looking at him then, he wasn't weird anymore.

Or gross.

He was a fighter.

Here to remind us that it's okay to struggle and fall.

Because if you didn't… then how would you ever fly?

"So, tell me, Love," Dad asked as I stared at my new friend with beady eyes. "What kind of person do you want to be in life? A butterfly?" He paused. "*Or a caterpillar*?"

NOW

Three things I've learned in my two years of employment at Easton High: *One*: if you're a librarian, people will automatically assume you're a book nerd. There's nothing you can do about it. In their eyes, you breathe, live, and eat books. *Two:* the job doesn't require nearly as much "*shushing*" as society thinks it does. And *three*: when your grumpy sixty-year-old coworker looks like someone took a dump in her coffee, you're in for a *long* night.

I knew Lucille was in a bad mood from the moment I stepped foot inside the library twenty minutes ago. She has those crazy eyes. The one she makes when someone pissed her off.

My money is on the jocks.

Nothing gets good old Luce riled up like the "punks" of Easton. I'm not sure what they did to deserve such wrath, but I do know every time she encounters one of them, I turn into her emotional punching bag for the rest of the week.

Usually, I can take it, but I'm not in the mood to listen to her "*kids these days*" monologue right now.

Especially after the text I just got.

My phone chimed with a message from Zac just as I was walking out of sixth period.

Zac: Page 31.

At first, I was confused.

Then I remembered the conversation we had on Saturday. He's telling me where to find his first confession.

That has to be it.

"You should've seen the bums in here earlier. Bunch of troublemakers." Lucille *tsks* under her breath. "They shouldn't even be allowed in the library, if you ask me. It's not like any of them has ever voluntarily read a book in their life. They should just stick to that stupid game of theirs."

I nod along to her story, grabbing a random book from the return pile to check our alphabetical system and put it back where it belongs.

Aisle six, the screen reads.

Got to love the coincidence.

This is perfect. I'll just put this novel back and sneak a peek at the poetry book when she's not looking. Confident with my plan, I make my way to aisle six and squeeze the book on the right shelf while Lucille continues her yapping.

"But that's not even the half of it." Lucille laughs bitterly, her pinched eyebrows adding wrinkles to her crowded forehead. "That Emery kid keeps coming for Emily Dickinson's poetry book at lunch. *A poetry book*! Can you believe this? Bet he thinks he's hilarious. A disgrace, these kids, I tell you."

Every hair on my body stands on end.

I replay Lucille's words in my head, the realization of what she just said sinking into me like a thirty-thousand-pound anchor.

Did she just…

No.

I was right?

Think about it, Vee. Zac texted me how much he hated Theo's party, while Xavier was hiding in his truck, also hating the party. Holy shit, he was also in detention for two weeks, which would explain how he answered me.

Then there's his middle name. And all the things he said

about his best friend fucking his ex… Just when Dia found out about Finn cheating. Wait, Finn fucked Brie? No, it wasn't Brie. Dia said it was some random girl. *Back to the point, Vee.*

"R-Really?" I can't seem to conceal the tremor in my voice.

"Positive. I should go through the book just in case he stashed some drugs in it or whatever it is punks like him do." Lucille rounds the counter, her intentions as clear as they are terrifying. She thinks he used the book for some sort of drug deal. *She can't open that book.*

"I got it." I hold my hand up like it's a stop sign.

"Are you sure?" She slows down.

"Don't be ridiculous. I'm already here, I'll do it."

"All right, then." Lucille nods, unsuspecting, but doesn't retreat to the front desk. I tread down the aisle, pull the poetry book from the lower shelf, and skip straight to page thirty-one.

The confession is exactly where he said it would be.

Written on a sticky-note.

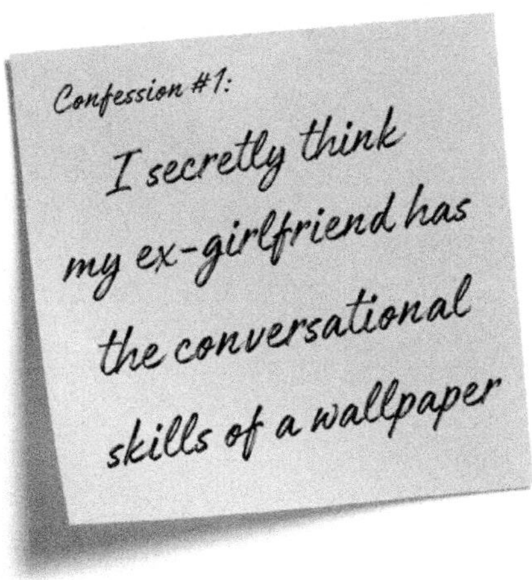

I bite back an inconvenient grin, overly aware that Lucille is watching me like a hawk, and angle my body to the right so she can't see me slide the sticky note out of the book and shove it into my pocket.

"So?" Lucille asks impatiently.

"Nothing. Looks like he genuinely likes poetry," I lie through my teeth and amble back to the front desk to resume sorting through the return pile as though nothing happened.

As though everything isn't different now.

As though I didn't break our anonymity pact.

I hate it.

I hate it more than words can say.

But there's no running from the truth anymore.

Zac is Xavier Emery.

13

Aveena

Love: I thought we said go big or go home. That last confession was pretty weak, Z.

Staring at the unanswered message on my screen, I anxiously bounce my leg and consider deleting Zac's—or should I say, Xavier's—number from my phone.

We've never heard that one before.

I keep saying I'm going to ghost him, but my idiotic brain seems to have a hard time differentiating the words "ghost" and "text." In my defense, I've been sitting in my car, waiting for Ashley to come out of her fancy music school, for over an hour. I figured I'd spare myself the boring wait.

Did you hear that?

Sounds like excuses.

Finally, my phone pings with a reply.

But the sender isn't who I'd hoped for.

It's Dia.

Dia: Senior prank night tonight, don't forget. I'll pick you up at midnight.

Love: Gotcha.

I could pat myself in the back for my lack of resistance. Aveena Harper, going to a social event willingly? Tell the aliens the abduction went wrong. *She likes people now.*

Dia and I have been talking about senior prank night since sophomore year when Dia's older brother, Jesse, started raving about it. He'd ramble on about how he and Finn's older brother superglued Mr. Tate's desk shut.

Dia made me promise we'd join in on the fun when the time came, and I agreed partly because it felt so far into the future.

But here we are now, months away from graduation.

Truth be told, I'd gladly pass on the whole, "vandalizing your school" trend, but I know how important these experiences are to Dia. Especially now that she's cut all ties with Finn and Lacey. She wouldn't have anyone to go with, so, long story short, I decided to get over myself and go superglue shit with my best friend for one night.

My phone chimes, and I pull up my conversation with Dia, certain she's to blame for the notification.

Only… she's not.

The culprit is Zac.

Zac: You didn't see it, did you?

I frown.

Love: See what?

His response doesn't come until five minutes later.

Zac: Turn it over.

Confused, I slip a hand inside my jeans pocket, pull out the wrinkly sticky note I squeezed in there earlier and flip it over.

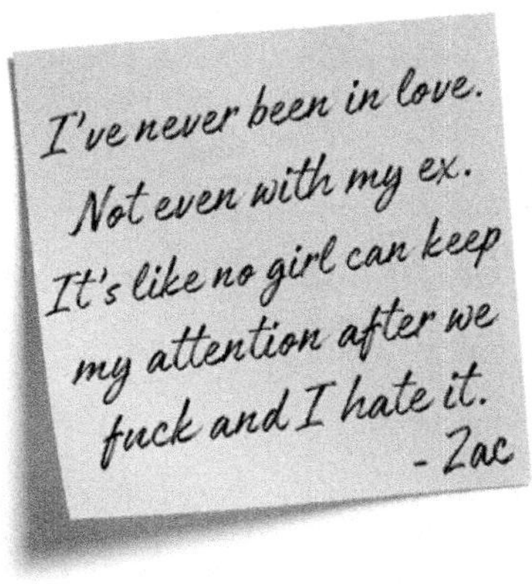

It quickly becomes apparent that the first confession was just his attempt at making me laugh.

A joke.

But the second one…

It's everything but.

He did warn me he wouldn't hold back. So, why do I feel so… disappointed? If Brielle fucking Randall—we're talking double D's, stick-thin waist, shiny red hair, and Kylie Jenner lips—can't keep his attention, little old me doesn't stand a chance. Unleashing my unrealistic hopes back into the universe, I face my wake-up call head on…

And delete our conversation.

* * *

Senior prank night was a bust.

Literally. We got busted two hours in—okay, maybe that's not entirely true. *I* didn't get busted just yet, but if my current situation is anything to go by, it shouldn't be long now.

I never would've imagined, when I first agreed to this awful tradition that I'd wind up here, huddled up in a dark classroom with Theo and my *not so anonymous* pen pal.

Dia and I were halfway through TPing the gym with a dozen seniors when Axel came bursting through the door, yelling that the cops were here and to get the fuck out.

While I'm not sure what the consequences for partaking in senior prank night are, I know this: there is no world, no universe, no *galaxy* in which getting caught wrapping your school in TP ends well.

Dia hasn't answered one of my texts since I lost her in the

crowd of frantic seniors. I blinked once and she was gone. I found myself alone before I knew it. Stranded in the main hallway while the cops raided the school from every entrance.

I was considering bolting to the exit by the cafeteria when I heard the sheriff and a few deputies talking in the distance. They were headed straight toward me, and I knew for a fact I couldn't access the exit without exposing myself.

That's when the door to the chemistry lab flew open.

He was standing on the other side, hot as ever—*what's new*—gesturing for me to get in before it was too late.

Xavier.

Of course, it had to be him. Why *wouldn't* I get rescued by the one guy I didn't want to see tonight?

Xavier or not, I couldn't afford to get caught, so I welcomed the help. It was either get in that classroom with him or have my mom trade me for a new daughter on the black market. Seriously, she'd sell my organs if she knew I snuck out in the middle of the night.

Footsteps come rushing down the hall, and Theo warns us with a threatening "Everyone, shut the fuck up." Terrified to make a sound, I cradle my knees against my chest. The three of us are sitting with our backs pressed to the wall in the furthest corner of the classroom.

"*Fucking kids.*" I recognize Sheriff Daniel's voice from the night Xavier and I got pulled over. "Because that's where I want to be at two in the morning."

"They're long gone, Joe. We got most of them. Why don't we just call it a night?" An unidentified officer yawns.

"Not yet," the sheriff objects.

The footsteps stop dead in front of the chem lab.

They're right here.

On the other side of the door.

One sound, just *one*, and we're toast.

"Did we check this classroom?"

"Don't think we did, boss," Cop Number Two responds.

I tense up when one of them shines a flashlight into the classroom through the small rectangular window in the door. They can't see us from this angle, but if they just open the door an inch, we're done for.

Panic overtakes me.

My breathing grows heavy, erratic.

Shit, not now.

"Did you hear that?" Sheriff Daniel asks.

Fuck, fuck, fuck.

"Hear what?"

I smack my palm flat against my mouth in an unsuccessful attempt to muffle my panic. It's not changing squat—on the contrary, it's making breathing an even more difficult task.

I can feel Xavier's eyes on me.

I expect him to be annoyed.

Angry, even.

After all, this will be the *second* time I've lost my shit around him now, but to my disbelief… there isn't so much as an ounce of resentment in his gaze. Only worry. The same worry he displayed the night he held my hand in his car.

"Breathe," Xavier mouths in the dark, and I'm faced with the cold hard truth.

No one's going to save me this time.

No one's going to hold my hand, walk me through breathing exercises. It's up to me to kill this anxiety attack before it kills *me*. I close my eyes, focus every bit of my energy into filling my lungs to the brim with air.

Nothing else.

I just breathe.

Slower and slower each time, until I'm in control again, until I don't feel like I'm dying.

A few seconds elapse.

"What, Joe?" the second officer snaps.

"Forget it. Just thought I heard something."

"So, we going in or not?"

"Yeah, let's check this one, then we're out."

The knob begins to turn, and I clutch my phone so tightly against my chest my knuckles burn.

This is it.

Game over.

The door starts to ope—

"I need backup on the second floor, room B-2506. Got over a dozen kids up in the library," calls a masculine voice over the radio, and my joints relax, restoring blood flow to my limbs.

"On it," Sheriff Daniel replies and shuts the door.

The two men charge down the hall the next second. The moment their footsteps fade out of range, Xavier, Theo, and I let out the longest, deepest sigh of relief I've ever heard.

"Holy fuck, that was close." Theo speaks my mind.

The three of us rise to our feet.

"Now's our chance. I say we get the hell out while they're upstairs," Theo suggests.

"Are you crazy?" I oppose. "There could still be a million of them walking the halls."

"So?" Theo shrugs. "Running sounds a hell of a lot better than staying put, just waiting to get busted."

"She's right, dude," Xavier chimes in. "The school is crawling with cops. I think we should just wait it out."

"Fuck this, we'll be here all night," Theo opposes.

"It won't get to that. They're clearing out soon," Xavier says.

"Suit yourselves. I'm not spending another fucking second in here." Theo advances toward the door, opens it quietly, and shoulder-checks us. "*Later, losers.*"

He's gone before I know it.

Silence descends upon the chemistry lab. Neither Xavier nor I say a word for a minute, paying close attention to the nonexistent noises outside of the classroom. It sure doesn't sound like Theo's getting chased or handcuffed out there.

I take it that's a good sign?

I meet Xavier's gaze and come to the conclusion that *yes*, his eyes are just as mesmerizing in the dark, and *yes*, I still have a very inconvenient crush on him.

"Maybe he's right and we should book it," I whisper.

He gives a weak nod.

"Okay, but you go first." He gestures to the door.

The look on my face must be priceless because Xavier stifles a laugh at my expression.

"Relax, it's just in case shit goes wrong. I'll hold them off."

"B-but what about you?" I worry.

"Aveena, listen to me." He moves closer to me, the sound of my name rolling off his tongue weirdly intoxicating, and I try my best to school my racing heart.

Now is *so* not the time, heart.

"I set off a stink bomb inside the school, *a stink bomb,* and all I got was two weeks of detention," he points out. "That's a fucking joke for what I did. My mom's the principal, and I'm team captain. I'll be fine, Vee. You won't."

I'm forced to admit he has a point.

"All right," I give in.

"On three?" Xavier asks.

"On three." I nod.

"*One*," we say together.

I tiptoe toward the door.

"*Two*."

My hand reaches for the knob.

"*Thre*—"

I haven't even opened the door an inch before Xavier's pulling me behind the massive filing cabinet beside us. Not a single word or warning escapes his lips. He just traps me into an isolated corner, his tall, towering frame swallowing my five-foot-seven body whole.

He's hiding me.

But from what?

"What the hell are you doin—"

His index finger cuts to my lips, shutting me right up.

Then I hear them.

The voices, the running footsteps outside of the classroom. "*We got another one. Back door. Chasing him now,*" I hear an officer shout on the radio, his words shrouded by static.

My mouth drops in realization, and I look up at my pen pal, only to find him already staring at me. It doesn't take a degree to figure out who they're referring to.

It's Theo.

He got caught.

And if it weren't for Xav stopping me, we'd be the ones getting chased. If he hadn't heard them first and dragged me away from the door, the cops would've seen us through the window.

A door slams in the distance, and I jump, clutching Xavier's varsity jacket instinctively. I think I see a smirk forming on the corner of his lips, and my cheeks blaze with embarrassment.

Jesus Christ, how does he smell this good?

Is it his cologne?

His fabric softener?

Makes me want to sniff him.

Don't you dare sniff him.

We remain in this position, with my face level to his torso and my fingers squeezing the fabric of his jacket, until the noises subside. I let go of him with a gulp, giving him the green light to back away from me, which he does too soon.

Too fast.

As he moves back, I catch myself yearning for more. More of his nice-smelling fabric softener. More of his infuriatingly toned body on mine. More of that feeling I get when he stands this close. But "more" wasn't made for girls like me…

Especially not with the captain of the basketball team.

Plus, it's not like I ever had a real shot with him anyway. The guy doesn't do love. His last confession made that clear. I beg my emotions to take a beat. Beg my composure to return to me, but the stupid butterflies in my stomach are having a hard-core party, and they're not going home anytime soon.

"I… Thanks for the save."

"Anytime." Xavier clears his throat, rubbing at the back of his neck, and for a fragment of a second, I wonder if he felt whatever *that* was, too.

"So… what do we do now?"

"The only thing we can do." He shrugs. "*Wait.*"

I watch as Xavier plops down on the floor, back against the wall, and braces his forearms on top of his knees. A silence as thick as they come enfolds us. For the first time since I stepped into the classroom, it occurs to me that my texting buddy is right there.

My snarky pen pal.

Right. Fucking. There.

Xavier is Zac.

Zac is Xavier.

Why won't it register?

"Sit down, Vee. We're going to be here a while." Xav gestures to the spot next to him, and I swallow hard. He's right. This isn't over yet. Might as well get comfortable.

Flustered, I sink down by his side and press my bent knees to my chest. Xavier pulls out his phone to check his locked screen once. Twice. Then a third time less than five seconds later.

I can't believe how quickly this night turned into a load of shit. But what I definitely can't wrap my head around? How quickly Xavier suggested that I go first. Dude didn't even hesitate. He just agreed to take the fall if he had to, no questions asked.

Oh Xavier, what the hell were you thinking?

"What do you mean?"

My breath catches in my throat at his response.

I whisk my head to see him staring at me curiously.

Shit, I said that out loud, didn't I?

"Don't take this the wrong way, but you *just* got in trouble for a prank not even a month ago."

"And?" He arches an eyebrow.

"And you're *here*," I say like it's obvious. "On senior prank night, practically begging to get in trouble again. Either you're really careless or really dumb. No offense."

He grins. "Damn, Harper. You're kind of blunt. *No offense*."

He's avoiding the question.

"But am I wrong?"

"Look." He sighs. "I wasn't even planning on coming, but Finn and I have been talking about this night since freshman year, and I…" He pauses. "I guess I'd rather be anywhere than at home these days."

The pit in my gut evolves into a stomachache. Every detail "Zac" told me about his mom through text crashes over me in slow, gradual waves. How she's cheating on his dad.

How he heard her while she…

The thought makes me nauseous.

"Want to talk about it?" I ask, the guilt gnawing at my conscience. I hate having to pretend like I have no idea what he's referring to. I feel like an impostor, digging around a "stranger's" world, collecting jars of secrets I don't deserve.

"Not even a little," he says without a fuck given.

I'll have to ask him how he does that.

Say no so easily.

So confidently.

"What about you? Why'd you show up?" He turns the tables on me. "I thought events like these weren't your thing."

"They're not, but Dia needed someone to go with. You know, since she's single."

Xavier scoffs. "Take it from me, she won't be single much longer."

"What do you mean?"

"I saw Finn drag her into a maintenance closet earlier."

All the lights come on in my head. So, *that's* where she disappeared to. It would also explain why she didn't answer my gazillion texts.

"What do you think they're doing right now?" I realize how stupid the question sounds as soon as it escapes my lips.

"Probably just talking," Xavier deadpans.

We trade glances.

And we both start laughing.

"*Right*." I sneer.

My best guess is they're having scandalous closet sex as we speak. Maybe Finn finally managed to convince her he didn't cheat? There's no way she wouldn't have answered my texts by now. Not unless she was… *busy*.

Our laughter dies down at the same time, and we make eye contact, equally breathless and exhausted. It's a quarter to three in the morning at this point.

He doesn't look away.

I don't either.

"At least some of us are having fun right now." I chuckle.

"Hey." He bumps his knee against mine, and I shiver like an unexperienced virgin who's never been touched by a man in her life. "I'm not… *not* having fun."

Don't blush.

Don't blush.

"Are you blushing?" he asks.

Fucking hell.

"No," I say a bit more defensively than intended. "And you don't have to pretend like you're actually having fun. I'm not stupid."

"No pretending needed," he assures me.

"Aw. Pity compliments. My favorites."

He laughs. "It's true. You're not the worst company I've ever had, Harper. The most uptight maybe, but not the worst."

"Thanks…" I half-smile. "*I think*?"

We don't speak again for a few minutes, and I can't help noticing, as I absentmindedly scroll down my social media feed, that he's still checking his phone screen constantly.

He's definitely waiting for a text.

But from who?

Brie?

Lacey?

Or could it be…

Love?

"I have to warn you, if you check your phone one more time, it might break," I tease, and he flashes an adorable, guilty grin. I'm talking the kind that could melt through steel and nurse a broken heart back to health.

"That obvious, huh?"

"A little bit."

His grin morphs into a full-blown smile. "Busted."

"Who's the girl?"

"Just a friend."

A friend. I'm not dumb. I know damn well what the word "*friend*" means in a jock's vocabulary.

"Let me guess, Brie?" I try to cover up the disappointment in my voice with a cackle so fake it makes my skin crawl. "You two back together?"

"Fuck no." He cringes.

I can't wipe the smile off my face.

Be more obvious, Vee, seriously.

"Who, then? Anyone I know?"

He scoffs. "A bit ironic talking about girls with you, don't you think?"

I'm not sure if it's just my sleep deprived brain gradually shutting off or if I'm missing something here, but I can't seem to decipher the innuendos plaguing his words.

"How is that ironic?"

"Oh, come on, Vee." He arches an eyebrow, shooting me an unconvinced look. "*You know.*"

"Know what?" I ask.

"You going to make me say it? Really? Not cool, Harper." He throws his head back, a sexy, lazy smirk plastered to his lips, and that sight alone is enough to melt my insides.

"I'm too tired for this shit. Just tell me already."

"I liked you, Vee."

My airways nearly close up.

"As a kid, I had the biggest fucking crush on you."

I expected everything,

Everything but *this.*

"Very funny." I let the joke roll right off my back.

"Not trying to be." He looks me dead in the eyes.

Holy crap… he's serious.

"*Excuse me*?" I screech.

"I said what I said."

"But you were so mean!" I rack my brain, fishing for one memory, just *one* moment where Xavier seemed even remotely interested in me. Well, he did kiss me that day at the park, but I always assumed he was just *that* desperate to keep me from ratting him out.

"And you're surprised *why*? I was a little shit to everybody."

"Yeah, but you were extra shitty to me!"

He holds his hands up in surrender. "In my defense, I had no clue how to act around girls, and the only time my parents ever communicated back then was when they were saying hurtful shit to each other. I guess, I thought… that's how it worked, or something?"

There it is.

The root of all that is wrong with this toxic, "you're mean to people you like" mentality.

Kids have to learn it somewhere.

"I thought you knew." He seems genuinely shocked.

"You're right, I'm sorry. I should've known to take you tossing my dolls into the barbecue as a sign of affection."

"I accept your apology." He can barely get through that short sentence without smiling. It's more than obvious he's just trying to get a rise out of me.

And it's working.

"Screw you, I loved those dolls!" I swat him in the shoulder, and he laughs. We both do. A bit louder than acceptable when trapped in the school's chemistry lab at three in the morning. We spend the next ten minutes discussing the crazy, borderline cruel pranks Finn and Xavier put me through that summer.

"That was a good summer, admit it," he reminisces.

"Speak for yourself, evil one."

His grin doesn't waver one bit.

Silence ensues. But it's the good kind. The kind where your stomach hurts from laughing too hard and you need a beat to catch your breath.

"They were all your ideas, weren't they? The pranks?"

"Yep," he says shamelessly.

"So, Finn didn't even come up with *one*?"

"No, but he was more than happy to join."

"God, I hate you," I say in between chuckles.

He pauses, eyeing me suspiciously.

"Can I ask you a question?"

I nod.

"Why do girls say shit they don't mean?"

"What makes you so sure we don't mean it?" I counter.

"Brie used to say she hated me all the time when she clearly didn't. It's a thing you girls do. Say I hate you to guys you don't."

Damn it, ladies. Who the hell let him in on our secret?

We had a deal.

"So, what?" I scoff. "*I hate you* means *I love you* now, is that it?"

"Pretty much, yeah."

"So, according to your theory, I just told you I loved you?"

"Sure did." He nods. "You see, whenever you tell me I hate you from now on, it'll mean the opposite. I don't make the rules," he declares, smirking like the cocky bastard that he is, and I flush, propping the side of my forehead against the ice-cold classroom wall.

"You're ridiculous, you know that?" I whisper, my closing eyes clouded by heavy lids.

"Thanks, I try."

We stare at each other in silence.

I overanalyze his features.

His blade-sharp jaw, his strong cheekbones. And that light

brown hair… *Good Lord, don't even get me started on his hair.* The guy could pull off the stylishly messy look in his sleep. The tension in the air thickens faster than should be legal, and I seek an escape from the aqua eyes boring into my soul.

It's too quiet.

Too intimate.

If this were a movie, one of us would be going in for the kiss. And in a perfect world, it'd be him. But in this one? I sever the eye contact, hoping to disrupt the magnetic pull drawing me closer to him. My eagerness to outrun my feelings leads me to notice a piece of silly string tangled in his hair.

I smile.

"Did you get sprayed with silly string tonight by any chance?"

"Might've had a silly string battle in the locker room. Why?" His voice is raspy, sleepy. He's barely keeping himself awake as it is, and I'm not doing much better.

"It's in your hair." I release a quiet chuckle. "Hold on."

I scoot over until I'm close enough to pick the tiny silly string off the top of his head and dangle it in front of his eyes to show him. Only issue is… it's not the string he's looking at.

It's me.

Just me.

He stares down my face intently.

Attempting to decode what this guy is thinking feels like trying to translate a long-forgotten language. I should back away, retreat to an acceptable distance before I embarrass myself, but

I can't move a muscle. My throat feels clogged, my lips so dry I instinctively wet them with the tip of my tongue.

Xavier's eyes shadow the motion.

He's looking at my mouth now.

Hard.

Holy. Fucking. Cheese-balls.

Then he leans forward.

And my heart does that thing where it slams against my rib cage so violently I wonder if it's going to carve a hole through my chest just to prove it can. It's almost nothing. A gesture so small I don't even think it qualifies as "making a move." Xavier just angles his head toward me a few inches. Barely, but enough to make me wonder if I'm crazy.

But the move he makes next…

Is one I *can't* overthink.

His fist closes around mine, and I become very aware that I'm still holding the piece of string at his eyes' level. I've been holding it this whole time. Without a word, he lowers my hand.

Slowly.

To get it out of the way.

He doesn't make another move for long seconds.

I'm screaming so loud internally I'll be lucky not to wake up with a headache tomorrow.

Our breaths mix.

Just an inch.

Just one and we'd be kissing.

He leans forward again, our lips almost touch—

"Rise and shine, motherfuckers," a masculine voice blurts.

It takes me a second to realize Finn and Dia just waltzed into the classroom. Xav and I back away from each other at the speed of light. Seriously, if there's some sort of world record for quickest withdrawal from a kiss, we just beat it, but it's no use.

They saw us.

At least, Finn did.

Dia came in a second too late.

"We interrupting something?" Finn doesn't even bother trying to conceal his smirk. I open my mouth, only to realize that I have no fucking clue how to answer his question.

Thankfully, Xavier takes one for the team and lets out a bored, "Nope" before rising to his feet. I blink at him, baffled by his carelessness. I'm a complete mess over here, and he's just… okay?

Unaffected?

I hate boys.

"I'm guessing the cops are gone?" Xav drawls.

"Yep. Axel saw them pull out of the lot through the cafeteria window. We should get the fuck out of here, preferably before first period rolls around," Finn jokes.

Dia pads toward me, holding out her hand and helping me to my feet. Her lipstick is smeared, her clothes wrinkled and her gorgeous black hair a wild, curly mess.

We were right.

They weren't talking.

But she still looks… *sad?*

There's this twinkle of pain flickering in the back of her eyes.

Are they back together?

My gut feeling says no.

My best friend tangles her arm with mine, setting out for the exit, and as we walk side by side, it registers that I almost kissed Xavier. I, Aveena Harper, almost kissed Xavier Emery, slash my secret pen pal, slash texting buddy, slash the guy who poured his heart out to me on a sticky note mere hours ago.

And the real kicker?

He wanted to kiss me, too.

* * *

The clock shows 4:05 a.m. by the time I garner the courage to text him. It only took an hour of tossing and turning in bed, thirty minutes of trying to make peace with the fact that sleep would not be an option tonight, then another thirty wondering if it'd be okay for me to change my mind and *un*ghost "Zac."

Love: You still up?

The message doesn't deliver for five minutes. And

when it *does* deliver, it doesn't get the "Read" receipt it usually does—not exactly a shocker. Xavier probably passed out as soon as he got home. I've just put my phone down, willing to give sleep another go when it vibrates on my desk.

Zac: Maybe.

I break into a smile.

Love: Can't sleep?

Zac: No.

Love: Me neither.

He stops replying, and I get the sense that he's mad at me for something. To be fair, I've been ghosting him since I found his confession earlier today. Left him on Read for hours. It's got to suck opening up to a stranger, only to get bailed on.

Love: I'm sorry for taking so long to reply. That was really shitty of me. I saw your confession and I just freaked.

Zac: Why?

Love: I think it got too real for me? I realized my next confession would have to measure up, and I'm scared that I'm going to scare you away with all of my baggage.

Zac: I just told you I'm emotionally fucked up, L. It's me who should be worried about scaring you away.

Love: Tell you what, I'm going to leave my confession in the book tomorrow. Then we can revisit the "who's more fucked-up" debate.

Zac: Deal.

Love: What'd you do tonight?

Zac: Nothing much. Went to senior prank night, too. Got stuck in a classroom with a girl from my childhood. You?

Love: What do you mean "too"?

Zac: I'm assuming that's why you're still up? Because you were there?

Warning signs flash in my head.

Do I tell him the truth?

What if he figures it out?

No, I can't risk it.

Love: I didn't go. Just stayed in, watched movies. How'd you end up stuck in a classroom with a girl?

Zac: Cops showed up and she was going to get caught. We let her hide with us.

Love: Oooh, is she pretty?

What? I had to ask. Anxiety stirring in my gut, I stare at my screen, waiting for his reply, which takes forever and a day to come. Twenty minutes later, my screen lights up with a new message.

Zac: Very.

I probably shouldn't be this happy. Just like I shouldn't be giggling like a twelve-year-old girl, but I can't help myself.

Then he texts me again.

And the smile evaporates from my face.

Zac: But in an unassuming, unconfident way.

Is that really what he thinks of me?

That I'm insecure?

Self-effacing?

I mean… he's not wrong.

Shut up, Inner Vee.

Love: And is that your type? Girls who hide?

Five minutes go by before he answers.

Zac: No.

My stomach sinks faster than a herd of elephants walking on thin ice.

Zac: At least, not usually.

Not usually?

I don't get the chance to ask before he adds,

Zac: It's going to sound batshit crazy but I realized

something tonight.

Love: What?

Zac: Remember when I said no girl could ever keep my attention?

Love: Yeah?

My heart flutters with anticipation.

Zac: I think I was wrong.

Week 1

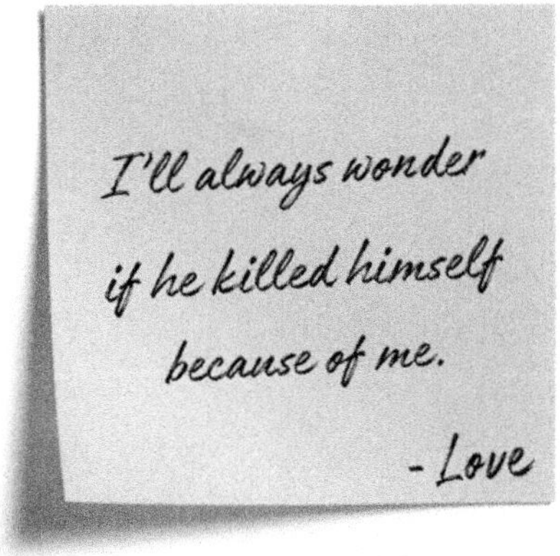

* * *

Zac: Damn, L... I was not expecting that.

Love: Told you I was fucked-up.

Zac: Find me one fucking person who isn't.

Zac: You don't have to answer me, but can I ask who

you're talking about?

Love: I'd prefer if you didn't.

Zac: Well, whoever it is, I'm sorry. I really am.

Love: Don't be. You ready for your confession next week?

Zac: Was born ready.

Week 2

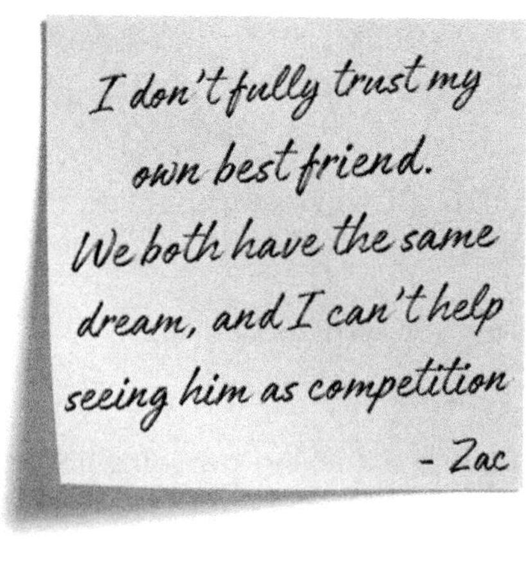

* * *

Love: Just saw your confession. Are we talking about the same best friend who slept with your ex?

Zac: That would be the one.

Love: And you're still friends with him becauseee?

Zac: He's a good person. Just deep, deep, deep down.

Love: Hate to break it to you, but no one's that deep.

Zac: So, you're saying you've never slept with someone you shouldn't have before?

Love: Fine, point taken.

Zac: Wait, really? Who'd you sleep with?

Love: I'm not telling you.

Zac: How about writing it?

Zac: Say in tomorrow's confession perhaps?

Love: I'll think about it.

* * *

* * *

Zac: Holy shit, L. You're wild.

Love: You think I'm a horrible person, don't you?

Zac: Do you regret it?

Love: Every day.

Zac: Then no, you're not a horrible person.

Love: How can you be so sure?

Zac: Well, this girl I wrote letters to once told me you're only as bad as your lack of remorse. She said people's mistakes don't define them. I'd like to think she's right.

Love: Thanks, dork.

Zac: Don't call me that.

Week 3

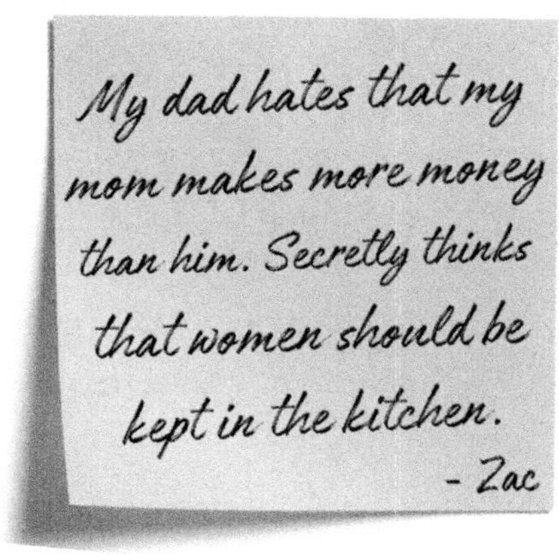

* * *

Deep down, I'm terrified
that I'll never be good
enough...
P.S. : Flip this over for
another confession.

I wish she died
instead of him.
- Love

* * *

Zac: Two for one, huh?

Love: Yeah, the first one was pretty soft, so I thought I'd throw in the second one to make it worth your while.

Zac: Want to talk about that last one...?

Love: Nope.

Zac: At the risk of repeating myself, I'm so fucking sorry this happened to you.

Love: Thanks, dork.

Zac: Don't call me that.

Zac: Anything I can do?

Love: There is.

Love: You can make next week's confession so epic it takes my mind off it.

Zac: I'll do you one better and give you two.

Week 4

Came home to my mom
sucking off one of my
friends... Found out
they started fucking years
ago. The worst part?
He was a minor.
- Zac

Oh, and I may or may
not have poured extra
strenght laxatives into
every bottle of booze in
his trunk. Ooops.
- Zac

* * *

Love: WHAT. THE. FUCK.

Love: You can't just drop this on me with no follow-up! What happened afterward? Did you confront them?

Zac: I couldn't bring myself to. They still have no idea that I saw them that day.

Love: So, she's been cheating on your dad with one of your friends this whole time?

Zac: Yep. Well, him and the neighbor. And the plumber.

Love: THERE'S THREE OF THEM?

Zac: Afraid so.

Love: I'm so sorry. I don't know what else to say.

Zac: Take a shot every time one of us says sorry in this conversation.

Love: R.I.P to our livers.

Zac: Did it work? My confession, I mean? Did it take your mind off it?

Love: Take my mind off what?

Zac: Ah. I see what you did there.

Love: Jesus, Zac. Talk about a tough act to follow. My next confession is going to suck compared to this.

Zac: Just give me two then. Like I did.

Love: On it.

* * *

* * *

Aveena

I've barely stepped foot inside my bedroom after a long day at school before my phone chimes with Zac's response to my last confession.

Zac: Excuse me, ma'am. That was only one confession. I believe you owe me two.

Love: Sorry, I chickened out. Figured the first one made me look bad enough already.

Zac: You think that's bad? Did you forget the part where my mom hands out free blowies to my buddies?

Love: Yeah, but it's your mom who looks bad here. Not you.

Zac: What difference does it make?

Love: A HUGE difference. Think about it. Almost all your confessions are about other people. Your best friend, your mom, your dad. MY confessions are mostly about shit I did. You look like a fucking saint next to me, Z.

Zac: A saint who can't love. Or get attached to anyone. Saint my ass.

Love: What about the girl you got stuck with on senior prank night? You said she made you reconsider.

Zac: I was wrong.

Zac: Just got caught up in the moment.

An unexpected twinge of pain skitters through my chest.

Zac: Not that it matters anyway. She's been avoiding me like the fucking plague since then.

Maybe if he was lying, I'd have a right to be mad. To feel disappointed. Hurt. But he's right. *I* did this. It was all me. Me who ripped out the roots before the tree could grow.

I've been texting "Zac" for weeks but avoiding *Xavier* in the halls. It's like I need the virtual Xav but can't handle him in real life. Truth is, I'm scared. *Petrified* by the possibility of him looking me in the eyes one day and figuring it all out.

Realizing it's been me all along.

Something changed between us after our almost kiss a month ago. Xavier started stealing glances my way during lunch. I would've had to be blind not to notice those sharp blue eyes lingering on me. It's almost as though the hours we spent stuck together flipped a switch. *Made him notice me.* It even seemed like I might have a chance with the Stallions' star shooting guard for a second there. And by "me"… I don't mean Love.

I mean *Aveena.*

But I couldn't be both girls to him, so I had to choose. Choose whether I wanted to be Vee—real, vulnerable, scared of getting hurt. Or Love—safe, predictable, just a name on a screen.

I chose Love.

Love: I don't buy it. That confession had to be a lie. There has to have been at least ONE girl that meant something to you.

Zac: It wasn't a lie. At the time.

Zac: But it is now.

Wait…

So, he didn't like anyone then, but he does now?

Love: What does that mean?

It takes him twenty minutes to reply.

Zac: I think you know exactly what it means.

My cheeks combust.

I stare at the screen, my heart rattling against my rib cage. Is he saying what I think he's saying? What if he's not even talking about me and I've got this all wrong? Inhaling a deep breath, I think up a response, but nanoseconds before my thumb can hit Send, my screen flashes with a text from my best friend.

Dia: I'm outside.

Already?

Love: I'm so sorry, I have to go. Promised my best friend I'd go with her to get a piercing tonight.

His reply comes through in a heartbeat.

Zac: Back the fuck up. YOU'RE getting a piercing? Who are you and what have you done to Love?

Love: Dork.

Zac: Don't call me that.

Love: What are you, the dork police?

Zac: You're never going to let this one go, are you?

Love: Not a chance.

Love: I'm not getting a piercing, just accompanying her. Although she'll probably try and convince me otherwise. Talk later?

Zac: You betcha. Don't do anything stupid.

Love: I won't.

* * *

The next day

Love: So… I did something stupid.

Zac: You didn't.

Love: I did.

Zac: Not falling for it.

Love: Honest to god.

Zac: So… you're too chicken to tell me who you are, but you're cool with a three-inch needle puncturing your skin? Bullshit.

Love: I know it sounds crazy but my best friend was hyping me up and I've always wanted one. Plus, I can't remember the last time I did something just for me. So, I thought fuck it and did it.

Zac: I'm afraid I'm going to need some proof of this alleged piercing.

I go back and forth with myself for thirty minutes, only to come to the conclusion that a little picture never killed anybody. As long as he doesn't see my face, it should be fine…

Right?

I create a fake Snapchat account—before my better judgment can try reasoning with the reckless person these new piercings have made of me—and send him a screenshot of my username.

Love: Add me.

An invite from @TheDorkPolice pops on my screen a minute later. I snort out a laugh and accept his request with trembling fingers. I slip out of my long-sleeve, tossing it onto my bed next to me. I'm wearing a tank top underneath and no bra. I took the torture device off the second I got home from my shift at the library.

I spend the next half hour taking pictures and deleting them. Another five minutes wondering if I should send a picture at all. This isn't like me—the piercing, the semi-provocative picture. None of this is like me, but hey… neither was spilling my darkest secrets to a stranger in a book, so, safe to say people change?

Zac: Can't believe I made a whole ass snapchat account just to get a picture of your belly button.

Zac: You've got me wrapped around your fucking pinky, you know that?

My mouth stretches with a devilish grin as I skim through my camera roll, searching for the perfect shot. I set the picture's timer at four seconds. Then I send it, topping it off with a text that reads "**Who said anything about my belly button?**"

The picture shows a faceless, braless Aveena lying in bed in a thin tank top, the glass of ice water on my nightstand visible in the background. But the real focal points are the outlines of my tight, pierced nipples peeking through the fabric.

Even I have to admit the gold barbell piercings make my girls look damn good—almost makes up for me passing out when the needle went through.

He opens the Snapchat right away.

I can't move a muscle, holding my breath to the point of light-headedness. We were platonic pen pals up until this point, but this… *It could make us rated X.*

The three bubbles pop on my screen as he texts back, and the air feels scarce in my lungs, thinning dangerously with each breath.

Zac: Holy fucking shit, L.

Zac: Give a guy a warning, I almost dropped my phone.

I stifle a laugh with my palm.

Love: Sorry?

Zac: It's fine, just don't send me a picture like that

again.

Embarrassment paints my cheeks bright red.

He wasn't into it.

Talk. About. Awkward.

Love: I'm so sorry if I made you feel uncomfortable.

He texts back before I can blink.

Zac: Uncomfortable? L, the only thing uncomfortable about the picture you just sent are the fucking blue balls it gave me.

Heat stirs up in my stomach.

Well… *There goes our platonic relationship.*

Love: then why don't you want me to send pictures again?

Zac: Because if you do, I'm going to break our pact and scour the entire fucking planet until I find you.

I can't comprehend how hot and bothered his threat makes me. Temptation overrides his warning, and I set out to push his limits to the absolute max, see how far I can go before he breaks his promise. All I need is for him to take the bait.

Love: Does that mean you can't send me pictures of you...

And he does.

Without hesitation.

Zac: You mean pictures like this?

@TheDorkPolice sent you a Snapchat.

Gulp.

I tap his picture, the blood in my veins boiling like lava as I drink in the scene. I can't see his face—shocker—but he's standing in a gloomy room, a faint light fitting his naked, ridiculously toned chest with a defined V.

Oh, and abs I'd like to lick ice cream off.

I've always known, from the way his clothes mold bulging biceps and rock-hard pecs, that Xav was hiding a glorious body. But seeing it with my own eyes? He's got me feeling like a horny jersey chaser. I'm drooling over him like a groupie wishing the captain of the basketball team would "*drive it through her hoop.*"

Love: Not fair. If I can't send them, you can't either.

I strip off my tank top, throw on a lace, black bralette as soon as the message delivers and send him a more revealing shot of my nearly exposed cleavage and bare stomach.

Love: Oops. Finger slipped.

He opens it twice as fast.

Zac: Fuck, L.

Zac: This is torture.

Zac: You can't fucking do this to me, then tell me I can't know who you are.

Love: Or what?

Love: What are you going to do?

I expect him to send me another picture. Another message. But my phone ringing and the caller ID spelling out his name?

That… I *didn't* expect.

Zac: Pick up the phone and find out.

The phone rings once.

Twice.

Four times.

Oh.

My.

God.

For a sliver of a second, I let myself consider it.

Imagine what would happen if I picked up.

Talked to him.

Let him hear my voice.

I wonder if we'd stand a chance in the real world. Or if he'd never forgive me for lying to him about uncovering his identity from the start. Wonder if I did the right thing by hiding behind this "Love" persona.

Instead of being me.

Aveena.

All of my hopes and dreams spiral out of control before colliding with the cold brick wall they call reality.

We can never be more than confessions in a book.

We can never be *real.*

So, I choose to be Love a little while longer.

And decline the call.

Love: Z, we can't. It's too risky for you to hear my voice.

Zac: Then don't say anything. Just listen.

He calls again.

I hang up a second time.

He calls right back.

Zac: Take a chance, L.

My throat bobbing, I clutch my phone against my chest and accept the call. I guide the phone to my ear, tensing up like my feelings for the guy on the other end are a time bomb waiting to blow up in my face. Not a sound is uttered down the line.

But I can hear him breathing.

Fuck's sake, even his breathing is hot.

Until he breaks the silence.

"Hey," a hushed, deep, ridiculously sexy voice says, and that simple sound sends shivers scurrying down my spine. I don't say a word, which doesn't seem to surprise him because he cuts to the chase immediately.

"See that glass of ice water on your nightstand?"

I glance at the glass in question.

How does he know about that?

Right. He must've seen it in the background of my first picture.

"Pick it up," he commands.

Confused as to where he's going with this, I stretch out my arm to grab the stone-cold glass I filled up in the kitchen earlier.

He gives me a few seconds before resuming.

"Reach inside the glass and pull out an ice cube for me, will you?" I know from his tone that he's not asking.

That voice.

I heard it so many times in real life, but Xav on the phone… I can't even explain what this guy is doing to me. The clearer his intentions become, the faster my pulse climbs. I oblige, dipping my fingers inside the freezing water and wincing at the temperature.

"Run it down your neck."

Bending to his every will, I press the melting ice to the soft spot behind my ear and drag it down my neck, grazing my collarbone with a small gasp.

Shit, that's cold.

Xavier releases a low grunt at the noise that just spilled from my mouth, and the thought of him grasping at any little scraps I'll give him sets my heart ablaze. He's just as desperate for me as I am for him.

Fuck, I wish this was real.

I wish we *were real.*

"Your chest," he instructs.

The ice cube trails from my collarbone to my breasts, nearing the fabric of my thin bralette, and I chew down on my lip to drown out my unsteady breathing.

"Take it off, L," he orders and my insides practically liquify at my nickname on his lips. Feels so good to hear him say it out loud. I tug the bralette down my chest on cue, the cold air like a sharp whip to my painfully hard nipples.

"Good girl," he rasps, and those two words alone make way for the strong, maddening pulse between my legs. "You're probably still sore. Why don't you go ahead and give those new piercings some ice?"

I swallow hard, my hand skirting down my chest to rest the ice cubes flat against my stiff, puckered nipples. I let out a loud, embarrassing gasp at the sensation and clamp my mouth shut. I figured they'd still be sensitive from last night, but there is no pain, no discomfort as I twirl the ice cube around the piercings. Only this infernal heat. Zapping through my entire body like thunder.

It feels like Xavier's here.

In my bed.

Touching me.

As though he's reading my mind, he grits out a pained, irritated "Fuck, it should be me."

I squeeze my thighs together to relieve the pressure between my legs. *Sorry. Better luck next time.* The pulse only grows stronger, and I know there is no stopping my unraveling.

"Why the fuck isn't it me, L?" His voice has this carnal edge to it. "Why am I not the one touching you right now? Fucking *why*?"

I visualize it.

Imagine it.

See his tongue teasing my pierced nipple, and a soft moan shoots out of my mouth before I can stop it. This seems to trigger him because he groans a low, desperate "Christ, just tell me who you are. Fuck the pact. Fuck the secrets. Fuck it all. Just tell me who are you, L. Please. *Let this be real.*"

The sentiment fractures my heart into a billion tiny pieces.

I want it to be real, too.

More than I've ever wanted anything in my life, but "real" is the scariest place a fragile, damaged heart could go. And mine's as fragile as they come.

I don't reply, breathing heavily down the line, but he doesn't take offense to it, venturing down a dangerous path.

"Take it off. *Everything.*"

The ice has now completely melted, leaving but a puddle dripping down my chest, but it doesn't stop me from complying. I suck in a quivery breath, tug on the waistband of my leggings, and slide the fabric down my thighs.

"Ashley, honey? Are you upstairs?"

Shiiiit.

Hurried footsteps come booming up the stairs.

My mom is home.

The footsteps increase in volume, and it dawns on me that I have three minutes tops before my mom swings my bedroom door open and catches me half-naked on my bed.

To ask me where her precious Ashley is, no doubt.

Ash's been acting out since she broke up with Logan the loser—don't ask. She won't tell us why. She comes home later and later every night, won't tell Mom where she is, skips two singing lessons out of three. I've been covering for her as much as I can, but there are only so many places my superstar sister could be in our small town.

"Ashley?" Mom shouts again.

Panicked, I hang up on Xavier without a goodbye and jolt off my bed, rummaging through my room for my clothes. My leggings aren't too much trouble to put back on, but I can't find my shirt.

Where the fuck is my shirt?

By some unknown miracle, I spot an oversized hoodie I left on my dresser a week back and sling it over my head barely two seconds before Mom swings the door open.

Xavier

Xavier: Hey, asshole.

Xavier: You forgot our Friday workout. Again.

Every muscle and bone in my body aching like a bitch, I hop out of my truck, eyes drilled to the text I just sent my best friend. Finn's been slacking lately, ditching our workouts, to hell with his six-pack. Dude's so hyperfocused on Dia these days, I'd be lucky to see him outside of school.

Can't blame him, though.

Given the choice between getting some ass or busting *my* ass, I'd skip the gym, too. I notice my dad's Jeep missing from the lot as I make my way to the front door, but I don't think much of it. He did mention he was going out for a beer with Hank and the guys tonight. I probably missed him by a few.

I'm breezing inside my house the next minute, tossing my

gym bag onto the tiled floor, and treading to the kitchen to fill up my water bottle.

"Hey, kid."

The familiar voice gives me a pause, and I spin to find the last fucking person I wanted to see tonight. He's braced against the kitchen counter, an unlit cigarette clutched between two fingers.

"Don." I don't bother pretending like I'm happy to see this parasite here again. "Twice in one week, huh?" I arch an eyebrow.

Last week it was the shower drain that needed unclogging. Monday it was the bathtub, but one more unexplained visit and my mom just might have to start breaking shit around the house to justify her fuck buddy coming over so much.

My life-giver ambles into the room the next minute, dressed in a knee-length silk nightgown she definitely shouldn't be wearing in front of anyone *but* her husband.

She stops dead when she sees me, her skin paling as she pats down her messy, tangled hair to make it seem as though she didn't just get banged to the moon and back. I shiver at the thought, the urge to vomit scratching at the back of my throat.

"Xavier, sweetie, y-you're home early," she stutters.

"It's 8:00 p.m.," I say blatantly.

"I thought you were hanging out with Finn tonight." She cracks the most unnatural giggle I've ever heard, and my entire body—my whole fucking soul—cringes.

"Change of plans," I spit and divert my attention to the loser in our kitchen.

"Right." She picks up on my judgmental glare. "Funny story, I asked Don to come over to, hm…" She smacks her lips together, running low on excuses, and I think, I *know*, watching her struggle to keep her head above water shouldn't feel this good. Her lies are like quicksand she can't escape. And at the risk of sounding like a terrible son…

I want her to keep sinking.

"Your mom needed me to clean some pipes," Don finishes for her, the cigarette in his mouth dangling off smirking lips.

I almost laugh in his face.

Clean some pipes

Clean some fucking *pipes*?

You cleaned her pipes, all right.

Don's been the family plumber for as long as I can remember. Dad met the low life through Hank when I was a kid. We needed the dishwasher installed, and he's been my dad's go to plumber ever since. Little did he know Mom would require his services in a *very* different way.

It's like clockwork. Mommy needs a plan B whenever my barely legal friend isn't available—or is the plumber plan *C*? I know Neal, our neighbor, used to be a regular, but he's been out of town for months on business. Maybe she had to improvise.

"Where's Dad?" I stare Mom dead in the eyes, refusing to entertain their pathetic excuse for an explanation a minute longer.

I wait for her to flinch.

Just once.

Recoil at the mention of her loving husband.

The same husband who booked her a five-star cruise for their vow renewal next month. Maybe have a wake-up call right then and there. Confess everything. Wishful thinking on my part, obviously, because she doesn't even bat an eye and says, "Out with Hank. Boys' night."

I want to scream in her face.

Tell her I know about Brody. That I know about her sleeping with Finn's brother for years. Tell her I know she's a fucking criminal who screwed a high school kid. I want to tell her I was there that day. That I came home from practice early and found her choking on Brody's…

I remember it all too well.

"Look, Brody, we… I… We can't do this anymore. I'm sorry."

"Funny. You said that my entire sophomore year, and it didn't stop us, did it?"

"I'm serious, I love my husband. We're renewing our vows soon. You and me… it's wrong, okay? You need to go back to college. Forget this ever happened."

"Come on, Del. You know you don't mean that. I'm in college now. You're not my principal anymore. We're good. Stop thinking so much."

I still can't stop seeing his hand pushing on the top of her head, her kneeling in front of him. I couldn't look after that, but

I heard everything.

The sound of his zipper.

The noises he made when she…

Hello, gag reflex, my old friend.

Then I ran like hell. I got back into my car and headed straight to Finn's. Infuriated by the memory, I walk off. Pretend like my mom isn't a colossal disappointment and I don't live every day of my life lugging her sins around.

I waltz into the bathroom connected to my room and shut the door, filling my lungs with the biggest gust of air I can muster. It's the lack of guilt in my mom's eyes… the absence of remorse on her face when I asked her about Dad.

Either she's completely deprived of a soul, or she thinks her son is a two-brain-cells dimwit.

Cleaning some pipes.

Can you believe this fucking asshole? *How about I throw some laxatives into your coffee and clean* your *pipes, motherfucker?* Sure did the trick on Brody. Finn said his big bro spent that whole weekend before he headed back to Duke shitting his organs out.

I straighten my arm out to yank the sliding shower doors open and flick the faucet on. Steam flocks to the ceiling, immersing the room in a thick fog, and I hook my thumbs inside the waistband of my sweats.

My phone pings with a text from the bedroom before I can strip out of my clothes, and I double back to my bed to grab it.

I half expected it to be Finn.

Or Brie, either asking me when we can fuck or threatening me—no in-between. She keeps saying she'll find out if I'm seeing someone else. Same old Brie. I'm not too worried about it, though. Girl's all talk.

Thankfully, the text on my screen isn't from her.

It's from Love.

I enlarge our conversation, my gaze thumbing through the messages she sent me last night after abandoning me with a massive boner mid-phone-sex.

Love: Hey, I'm so sorry I hung up on you.

Love: Remember when I said my mom constantly forgets that I exist? Well, she chose NOW to remember.

I didn't answer her last night.

Mostly because my dick was so big from her pictures I thought it was going to break in half if I didn't jerk off that very second. I always knew L was attractive. No chance in hell she would've made it to Theo's party if she wasn't, but that body…

The outline of her perfect tits, that cute stomach, the hint of a tattoo on her left shoulder. I couldn't see what the tattoo was, though. Who am I kidding? *It wasn't exactly my main focus.*

She knocked me on my ass.

The fact that I didn't really see anything isn't lost on me either. Her most revealing picture didn't even qualify as a "nude," for fuck's sake. It was all underwear, little skin action.

But, fuck, when I heard her…

Heard her gasp as she rubbed melting ice down her body. Her shy little moans down the line. Hottest shit I've ever heard in my life. To think we didn't even get to the good part, and I still had to beat off three fucking times *just* to function properly.

I scroll down our conversation, checking the text she sent me less than a minute ago.

Love: Z?? Everything okay?

She's worried.

I haven't answered her all day.

Good. She should be thinking about me. No, you know what? I hope she thinks about me so much she loses her fucking mind. Only seems fair since she's been taking up every inch of space in mine.

I reread her text.

Everything okay?

No, it's not.

The only girl I've ever given a shit about is the girl I can't have.

I didn't expect our phone call to rile me up the way it did. It's as though I'm eight times more on edge since I had a taste of the forbidden fruit. A sip of the holy elixir.

I know what I'm missing now.

And it stings like a…

Remind me again why I'm not trying to find her? This horseshit anonymity pact might've made sense once upon a time, but now? We've gone too far, dived into water too dark, too dangerous to remain strangers.

She has to know that.

Hell, sometimes I think she knows *me* better than my own best friend. In the heat of the moment, I let my anger takes the reins and send her an impulsive text.

Zac: Remember when I swore I'd never try to figure out who you are?

She texts back right away.

Love: Yeah…?

I don't think, don't hesitate, don't sugarcoat it.

I just draft out my warning and send it.

Zac: Sike.

I time her in my head, count backward to the panic I know is coming. *Freak-out in 3,2,1…*

My phone chimes once.

Love: What???

Then again a second later.

Love: Zac, what does that mean?

And again.

Love: You're kidding, right? Please say you're kidding.

Zac: Dead serious. I need to know, L. It's time.

Love: But you said you'd never try to find out who I am.

Zac: I know what I said.

Love: THAT'S IT? You're just going to break the pact? Find out who I am against my will?

She's right, Xav.

This isn't how it should be.

You can't take what she won't give you.

Zac: I didn't mean that. I'm just sick of this shit. This has to end.

Love: What? We can talk this out, Z. Nothing has to change.

Zac: Things did change.

Love: What? What's changed that's SO important you'd throw it all away?

Zac: What changed is I fucking like you.

Radio silence.

Zac: I know it's crazy. I know we agreed this would never be more, but I want to know you. Talk to you. I want all of you, L…

Zac: All or nothing.

The delay in her response reflects her shock.

Love: Z…

Zac: Tell me you don't feel it, too. I fucking dare you.

Love: I do. I feel everything.

Zac: Then what are you so afraid of?

I see her start to type a novel before erasing the whole thing. She repeats the process a few times, and it doesn't take a Nobel Prize to understand she's terrified to come clean. Five minutes later, the notification comes through.

Love: I can't, I'm sorry.

Love: You can't ever try to find out who I am, Z. Ever. It's bigger than us now.

This is it.

Last stop on the pen pal train.

End. Of. The. Fucking. Line.

Zac: I won't look for you, I promise.

Zac: But you can't text me anymore.

She doesn't waste a single second.

Love: What? Don't say that. Please.

Love: Zac, you're my best friend.

Zac: Goodbye, L.

* * *

Aveena

It's only been a day.

Twenty-four insufferable hours since Xavier put an end to… *whatever we were.* And I already feel lost not hearing from him every half hour. I'm like a lone sailor drifting at sea. No compass. No map. Just a fragile heart, sending out distress signals into the night.

Only question is, is Xavier Emery the lighthouse guiding me home… or the storm dragging me under?

Collapsing on Dia's single bed with a sigh, I revisit my last exchange with Xav while Dia's showering.

He said I was afraid.

And it kills me.

Because he's right.

I *am* afraid.

Afraid of letting him in. Afraid of loving him with all of my bruised little heart. Afraid that, one day, he'll walk away. Realize the same thing my mom did the day Ashley was born. The same thing my dad did the day he mixed painkillers with his oldest bottle of bourbon…

That I'm not enough.

I'll never be enough.

I find myself pacing around Dia's room to distract myself until my gaze darts to the red flyer my best friend dumped on her bedside table earlier.

I pick it up, suppressing a laugh.

Finn really went all out on this, didn't he?

Diamond's Birthday party,

Saturday Night

Richards' house

The basketball team spent most of last week handing out invites to Dia's birthday party, Finn's order. You could find the damn flyers all over the school. They were in the locker rooms, in the halls, the cafeteria. Poor janitor sure was in for a surprise.

What's Finn's reasoning?

It's not every day a girl turns eighteen.

Although something tells me Finn offering up his mansion to host the party has a lot more to do with said girl being the air in his lungs. Anyone familiar with their train wreck of a relationship knows the guy would rip the beating heart out of his chest and hand it to Dia if she just asked.

Oh, and did I mention these two are *still* not official?

It's laughable at this point.

My stomach grumbles, and I replay my best friend's promise to be out of the shower in five minutes—it's been thirty. We were supposed to get ready at her place, then grab dinner with her family before heading off to the party.

Fuck it, I think when my stomach growls at me one time too many and venture out of Dia's bedroom to meet Gaten and Dave down in the kitchen. The delicious smell of pasta alfredo tickles my nostrils as soon as I walk in, and I examine the empty kitchen.

Now that's not something you see every day.

On weekdays, Dia's house is crawling with noise, life, bickering—what else can you expect from a family of six?—but Catalina, Dia's older sister, spends every weekend at her boyfriend's now, and Jesse rarely ever makes it back home from college. As for Dia's baby brother, Charlie, she mentioned he was at his grandparents' for the night.

Gaten, Dia's dad, stands by the stove, a black-and-white apron branded with the name of the restaurant he owns around his waist. He's stirring the pasta with one hand, sipping on a glass of red wine with the other.

I'm guessing Dave got called away last minute for work. He's a firefighter. I'm taking a step forward, intending to greet him, when Gaten says, "Diamond, so help me God, you take one more shower this long and I'm charging you this month's water bill."

I crack out a laugh. "Will be sure to let her know."

Gaten jerks in surprise, spinning around.

"Oh, Aveena, darling, it's you. I'm sorry, I thought you were Dia." He opens his arms, and I march myself into his embrace without thinking.

I can't remember one time where I came over to the Mitchells' house and Gaten *didn't* give me a hug. This man is like a father to me. He's a warm, fuzzy, comforting papa bear. It's ironic considering he married grumpy Dave—*seriously. That's what people in town call him.* Dave barely ever smiles except when with Gaten and his kids.

"She still in the shower?" Gaten asks, exasperated, but I don't get the chance to answer before he adds, "Please say you're joining us for dinner. Dave had to step out, everybody's gone for the night, and I've got enough to feed a village. Help a man out, will you?"

"Happy to." I chuckle as he pulls away, large hands caging my shoulders as if to take a good look at me.

"Deary me." He gasps.

"What?" I worry.

"Your hair."

His reaction makes me question everything.

Did I make a mistake tagging along with Dia to the hair salon today? She's wanted blue, metallic highlights to accent her black hair for the longest time now, and with her birthday around the corner, I thought it'd be the perfect present for her.

But then the lady asked if I wanted something, too.

And next thing I knew, my brown, butt-length hair was a bold rose-gold color. I guess I just thought… I had nothing to lose? Mom can't possibly be more disappointed in me than she already is, and the only guy I've ever liked doesn't want anything to do with me anymore.

Plus, I used to dream of getting my hair dyed as a kid. Was always hounding my mom to get my whole head dyed red or blue or whatever color I liked that month. I'd just gotten the tips of my hair dyed the day I found Dad in the garage.

I remember feeling so helpless when I grabbed his hand.

He was so cold.

So… *dead.*

Then I never dyed my hair again.

Until now.

"Yeah." I flush. "Sort of did it on a whim. What do you think? Hit or miss?"

"Is that even a question? *Hit.*" Gaten twirls a strand of my pink hair around his index, nodding in approval. "Definitely a hit. You look absolutely stunning, sugar. Come. Take a seat." He points to the kitchen table. "Best to start without Diamond if we don't want to starve."

I laugh in agreement.

Sure enough, Dia is a no-show for the majority of dinner.

Gaten's food is out of this world, not that I expected any less. Gaten Mitchell isn't the best chef in Silver Springs for nothing. Halfway through dessert, my gaze drifts to the framed family pictures hung up on the dining room wall.

One in particular captures my attention.

Gaten and Dave's wedding picture.

I've heard the story once or twice over the years. How Gaten and Dave met at work years before Gaten branched out on his own and opened up a restaurant. How they were getting close, a bit *too* close, but Dave was still in the closet, and Gaten feared his feelings were one-sided.

Then Gaten made his move at the office Christmas party.

In front of everyone.

Talk about fearless.

"Okay. Who peed in your Cheerios this morning?" Gaten jolts me out of deep thoughts.

"What?" I play dumb, finishing my plate in one bite.

"None of that. Something's bothering you."

I've been off since Xavier cut me out of his life, but Mom hasn't noticed a thing. The irony of my best friend's father picking up on my emotional distress more than my own mother speaks volumes.

"It's nothing," I lie.

"Boy drama, maybe?" he keeps trying.

I nibble on my bottom lip, fidgeting with my fork.

"Boy drama it is." He nods. "Well… if you ever want to talk

about it, I happen to be quite the expert," he teases, and I smile at the accuracy. He has a point. Who better to talk about men than the guy who successfully married one?

"How did you know to take a chance on Dave?" I say beneath my breath. "Weren't you… I don't know, terrified?"

A deep, croaky laugh rips from the back of Gaten's throat.

"Are you kidding? I thought I was going to shit my pants."

I laugh quietly.

"But you did it anyway? Even knowing there was a chance he could reject you?"

He nods. "That's right."

"Why? I mean… *how*?" I can't seem to make sense of it.

"I'm not going to lie to you, I almost didn't," he admits. "Almost turned around and drove right back home that night. I couldn't cope with the possibility of him laughing in my face. Turning me down.

"And sure, the thought of never telling him felt good. Safe. Like I was protecting myself but then…" He pauses. "I realized that one day, years into the future—maybe one year, maybe twenty—I'd find myself lying awake. Wondering what could've happened. What could've been. And while I was scared of rejection, there was one thing that scared me more… *Regret*."

I get chills just from that.

"And well… it worked out pretty well for me, didn't it?" Gaten winks. His tale of love gives me hope. Hope that somewhere, somehow… there is a world, a scenario in which a happy ending is possible for Zac and Love.

Scratch that—*for Xavier and Aveena.*

"Take it from me, kid." Gaten maintains the eye contact as if to anchor the message deep inside my brain. "Biggest risk you could ever take in this life is not taking one."

My heart hurts just a pinch when he says it.

He's dead-on.

Dia winds up joining us a few minutes later, only to steal a plate of pasta away to her room and haul me back upstairs with her. The next few hours are a blur. Except maybe the nagging voice in my head. The one telling me what I don't want to hear.

Tell him, Vee.

Tell him or spend the rest of your life wondering.

A pit the size of my fist expanding in my throat, I climb inside my car with Dia before we leave for Finn's. Then I shoot Zac the text I can't come back from.

Love: Meet me in Finn Richards' bedroom at midnight.

Love: No more lying.

I wait and I wait, my mind running faster than my dad's race cars ever could. Is he ever going to answer? *Am I too late?*

Until finally, my phone pings with a reply.

A promise.

Zac: I'll be there.

Aveena

Parties always seem like a good idea… until you actually get to the party. It's always the same story, in my case, anyway. Getting ready, driving over to the rich-kid house, climbing out of the car, and…

Instantly missing your bed.

The urge to go home usually hits in the first hour for me. It turns out watching people getting shitfaced while sober isn't all that fun. This is especially true when the smell of alcohol makes you queasy. Just *one* whiff of alcohol and my stomach's doing cartwheels with last night's dinner.

But tonight will be different.

Tonight, I'll smile, store my social anxiety away, be a good best friend to Dia. I won't even get awkward or miserable.

At least, not before the cake.

Dia and I rolled up to Finn's palace a bit before eleven. I was secretly afraid the birthday girl would ditch me as soon as we stepped foot through the door, and while she *has* been getting birthday wishes left and right, she hasn't left my side once.

Not even for her "boyfriend."

Finn didn't seem to mind. Just kissed the breath out of her in front of everyone, wished her a happy birthday, then retreated to the kitchen to destroy Theo and Axel at beer pong. No sign of Xavier anywhere. And I've been looking.

It's almost like Dia gave Finn a heads-up that we'd be sticking together tonight. She did promise she was going to be a better friend from now on.

Looks like she meant it.

The clock reads 11:30 when I notice a sea of students rallying around Finn's kitchen island. There's yelling, laughing, chanting, but I can't make out what they're saying over the booming chorus of "Hot Girl Bummer" by blackbear.

"What's going on?" Dia takes notice of the frenzy and rises to her tiptoes, trying to see above the crowd, but it's too thick. We've got Finn's birthday flyers to thank for that. Pretty sure the entire senior class turned up to the party.

"No idea," I say.

"Let's go check it out." Dia clasps my arm, dragging me along as she shoulders her way through the mass of drunk seniors. A bunch of shoving later, we make it to the circle's center.

Four guys from the basketball team are lined up before Finn's kitchen island while an unidentified girl lies flat on the counter in a V-neck top that stops just below her ribs.

Three shots are scattered over her naked stomach with the last one nuzzled between her breasts. The crowd erupts in cheers as the first boy licks salt right off her skin, downs one of the shots, then eats the lime right out of the girl's mouth.

Then comes the second and third boy.

But it's when the fourth guy licks the salt in the navel of her breasts, takes the body shot, withdraws the lime from her mouth with his hand, and goes straight for the kiss that the crowd goes wild. The girl shoves the guy away with a laugh, sitting up on the counter, and I damn near go into respiratory arrest right then.

I couldn't see the party girl's face before.

But I can now.

"Ashley?" I shriek with such volume that everybody stops and stares. My sister's head whips in my direction, and I blink at her like I'm waiting—*praying*—to wake up from a bad dream.

But I don't.

The scene I'm witnessing is real.

She's really here.

Doing body shots on Finn Richards's kitchen island.

"Goodie, it's the fun police," Ash says with an eye roll, and hops off the counter. Then she walks away.

She. Just. Walks. Away.

Like she didn't get caught with a boy's tongue down her cleavage. Like she didn't just show up to an Easton High party when she promised Mom she'd never mix with public school kids.

"Ash? What the hell?" I chase after her, my elbows ramming into people's side as I try to get a hold of the stranger wearing my sister's face. She picks up the pace every time I get too close, but I still manage to grab her arm. "What the fuck are you doing here?"

At last, she spins to look at me, stares bullets into my skulls is more like it, then spits, "Same thing as you, sis. I'm here to party."

Who is this person?

And why does she look like Ashley?

"Does Mom know about this?"

She cackles at my question. "Are you crazy? Of course not. She thinks I'm at some late-night rehearsal for the school play."

That's what I mean when I said she'd gone off the deep end since her breakup with Logan. I don't even recognize her anymore.

"You can't be here right now. Mom will kill us."

"What *us*?" she spits. "There's no *us*. You told Mom you were sleeping at Dia's, didn't you?"

I nod.

"There. You've got your excuse. Now leave me alone."

"I'm just trying to help you!" I reach for her arm, ready to throw her ass in the trunk of my car and drive her home against her will if I have to.

"Fuck off, Vee. I'm not your responsibility." She flings her arm out of my grasp, turning to leave, and I almost laugh.

Not my responsibility?

Is that why I'm driving her to school every day? Picking her up from her singing lessons because Mom can't be bothered? Running to the fucking grocery store on a Saturday morning to buy Fiji Water? Because she's not my fucking responsibility?

She's been my responsibility since she was born.

She just never realized it.

"What's gotten into you?" I leap into her way before she runs away from me again.

"I just want one night!" she shouts at the top of her lungs, turning every head in the vicinity. Tears of rage well in her amber eyes. It's clear as fucking crystal that she's had enough.

"Just one night at a normal party," she hisses. "Drinking normal cheap beer. Talking to normal, boring boys. Like a normal fucking girl. Is that too much to ask?" She wobbles forward, nearly losing her balance. I hold her back so that she doesn't fall, but she rejects my help, shoving me away.

"Jesus, Ash. How much have you had to drink?"

"Stop. Just fucking stop." The tears pooling in her eyes begin streaming down her cheeks.

"Stop what?" I raise my voice.

I notice Dia approaching us from the corner of my eye. *Finally.* Some backup. I could use her help getting Ash into my car. She's at my side within seconds.

"Acting like a concerned sister. Just stop it," Ashley spits, wiping her face with the back of her hand.

"I'm not acting," I snap. "I've done *nothing* but cover for you these past few weeks. I'm on your side, Ash. I've always been on your side."

"Really?" She scoffs out a bitter laugh.

Then she daggers me in the heart with one question.

"Were you on my side when you were fucking Logan?"

I stumble back a step.

As though part of me wants to run.

And I *do*.

I've always known I'd have to tell her eventually. I just never thought Logan would pull the rug from under me. Ashley stares at Dia in expectation of a reaction. Probably thinks Dia should be disgusted by me, her own best friend, but Dia's known about me and Logan since the moment it happened. I called her bawling my eyes out afterward.

"Oh my God." Ashley's face collapses as it dawns on her. "Everybody knows, don't they?"

I wince at her betrayed expression. I should apologize, beg her to let me explain, tell her how much I regret it, but a high-pitched voice splits my ears in two before I can try and salvage what's left of my family.

"Babeees!" Arms are thrown around Dia's and my necks from behind. "I've been looking all over for you. I need a beer pong partner. Who's down?"

I flip my head back to see a wasted Lacey smiling at us. Her eyes are bloodshot and her breath reeks of liquor. I know what you're thinking—*Weren't we done with her?* I thought so, but she liked one of Dia's pictures on Instagram a few days back, and apparently that makes them friends again. I don't answer her, guiding my attention back to my sister.

Problem is, she's gone.

Damn it, Lacey.

I unlink Lacey's arm from my neck, exchanging glances with Dia, whose eyes say, "I've got this," and I nod, grateful when she starts making chitchat with the cheer captain. Conveniently, that's when my phone goes off in my pocket, and I pluck it out, convinced things can't possibly get any worse.

Until I read the alarm I set for 11:50 p.m.

Meet Zac in 10.

Fuck.

Can't believe I almost forgot about Xavier with the category four shit hurricane sweeping through my life. My phone pings again, this time, with a text.

Zac: I'm already here.

What do I do? Go meet up with my hotter-than-hell pen pal or chase my sister to the ends of the earth to apologize?

Another text from Xavier pops on my screen.

Zac: I can't fucking wait for this to be real, L.

His message settles it. I have the rest of my life to make it up to Ashley. Beg until my knees bruise. Pick up the pieces and earn her forgiveness.

But this…

This is *now.*

I check my phone again.

11:52 p.m.

"Hey, D, I'm not feeling too well," I tell Dia. "Mind if I go lay down in Finn's room or something?"

"What's wrong?" she worries, guiding her left palm to my forehead to check for a fever.

"I don't know, it's just… with everything that's happened with Ashley, I need a break," I improvise.

"Say no more." Dia cracks a sad smile, traps me into a hug, and whispers into my ear. "Third floor, last door at the end of the hall."

"Thanks." I nod as I pull away and set off for the staircase on the other side of the house.

I realize, while patting my jeans pockets halfway to the stairs, that I lost my keys somewhere in this circus—my house keys, car keys, work keys. *All gone.* This night just keeps getting better and better, doesn't it?

"Aveena? Holy shit, is that you?" a masculine voice asks before I can reach the stairs. I swivel to find Axel staring at me with ulterior motives and bad intentions glimmering in his eyes. I'm starting to think that's just this guy's default mode.

"Axel." I barely acknowledge him, checking my phone again.

11:55 p.m.

"Damn, Vee, I almost didn't recognize you with that hair." Axel smirks. "You look amazing."

"Thanks," I drone before attempting to walk around him, but he intercepts me, sidling into my way.

"Can I get you something to drink?" he asks.

"I'm good." I glance over his shoulders at the staircase barely a few feet away.

So close.

"Look, while I have you, there's this friend of mine I'd like you to meet. Said you're just his type."

"Thanks, but I'm not interested."

"You haven't even met him." He laughs.

One more peek at my phone.

11:57 p.m.

Jesus, this guy is harder to get rid of than a piece of gum under my shoe.

"I don't need to, I'm… seeing someone," I lie.

His eyes light up, and I mentally smack myself. Why did I have to say that? It's only going to lead to more questions.

"You are? *Bummer.* My buddy was really looking forward to it."

11:58 p.m.

I don't have time for this.

"So, who's the lucky fella—"

I interrupt him. "Sorry, I got to run."

"But you didn't even answer my question," he presses.

"Oh my God." I gasp. "Is that girl taking her shirt off?"

In typical Axel Fletcher style, he turns around immediately.

By the time he looks again, I'm gone.

A flock of giggling cheerleaders storm by me as I'm scurrying up the stairs, their captain leading the way. Bitch—I mean *Brie*—interrupts her chugging of the red cup in her hand to fire little old me the nastiest look she can muster. I take it she still hates me?

Feeling's mutual, honey.

My chest lifting up and down, I stop at the third floor's last step and grip the railing to keep myself from bailing. The only reason I'm not booking it back down the stairs and aborting the mission right now is my hand.

Tightly wrapped around this iron railing.

One more step, Vee.

Just one.

You've got this.

12:00.

My foot connects with the third floor.

I amble down the hall leading to Finn's bedroom and spot his closed door in the distance. My heart feels constricted into a suffocating lockbox, thank God for that. It's the only reason it's not bursting out of my chest right now.

I smooth down my clothes and free my pink hair from the tight bun squeezing my scalp. My long hair flows down my shoulders, past my belly button, and I take in the biggest breath my lungs allow.

I catch sight of myself in the mirror covering every inch of the ceiling—*because, of course, rich people need mirrored ceilings*—and think, "This is it."

This is *me.*

Me and my freckles, me and my unstable eyes that can never decide whether they're green or brown, me and my trauma.

This is me.

All of me.

Let's just hope it's enough.

I couldn't just catch a cyber crush on the average Joe, could I? A nice, normal-height, cute but not too far out of my league regular fella? *Nope.* I had to fall for the sinfully hot, over-six-foot Adonis who could score a hundred phone numbers in his sleep.

Finally, I halt before Finn's door.

Xavier's in there.

Waiting for you.

Let that sink in, Vee.

I reach for the knob but keep my hand still for a few seconds. Then I nudge the door open so slowly it doesn't so much as creak. I thought I'd find him sitting on the edge of Finn's bed. Playing with his fingers, hopefully as nervous as I am.

I thought he'd have his eyes fixed on the door, awaiting my

arrival. So, you can imagine my shock when I see her.

Them.

Together.

I must've gone over this moment a hundred times in my head.

Come up with a million scenarios. But none of them…

None of them included *her.*

Xavier is standing in the center of the room, his hands clutching her face, his tongue so deep down her throat it's a wonder she's still breathing. He *ravages* her mouth with his—plain and simple. Kisses the shit out of some girl as she moans in delight. His large, strong hands slip inside her hair, tugging her head forward for deeper access, and it feels like an invisible fist is compressing my lungs.

And it's only getting tighter.

And tighter.

The longer he gives her what I thought was mine.

Stupid, stupid girl.

Then comes the worst part.

The part where I recognize her.

Lacey.

My stealth must be out of this world because they still haven't noticed me. They're still going at it, completely clueless as to my presence, and frankly, I can't decide if it's a bad thing…

Or the big guy up there doing me a solid.

I might've been sneaky up until this point, but I don't hesitate to slam the door as hard as I can on my way out. I hate myself for shedding these ridiculous tears. Hate my dumb, foolish heart for thinking a relationship based off my darkest secrets could ever become real. And lastly…

More than anything,

I hate myself for thinking Xavier Emery actually cared.

Xavier

The door to Finn's bedroom closes with a bang, and I jerk in shock, moving away from my pen pal. My gaze streaks to the door, then around the room in search of an intruder.

No one.

I didn't even hear the door open.

How long has some weirdo been watching us?

My attention drifts back to the girl desperately trying to catch her breath in my arms. Her pink lips are swollen, her teal eyes glassy, and the smile on her face? It's a big, dopey giveaway as to the effect this kiss just had on her.

This is it.

The jig is up.

Love is Lacey Mattson.

It makes sense when you think about it. All the signs were there. Like bread crumbs, begging to be followed. I just didn't want to see them.

Runs in the same social circle as I do? *Check.*

Was invited to Theo's party that night? *Check.*

I mean, for fuck's sake, her name literally starts with *L*. How could I miss it? But mostly, why am I so bummed out? I should be happy. Lacey has it all: beautiful, slim, tight ass, good in bed—*especially with her tongue*—but she's… not what I expected.

Not that I know what that is.

All I know is *she* wasn't it.

I thought Love would be tortured. Figured she'd have this ridiculously sexy damaged look burning in the back of her eyes. I never, *ever* would've imagined, with all the shit L's been through, that she'd turn out to be Lacey, captain of the cheer squad, definition of a squeaky-clean, privileged person.

Truth is, the disappointment crept under my skin as soon as she came in, but it didn't stop me from making my move. I meant what I said in my last text. I couldn't wait another second for this to be real, so when she pushed the door open, her keys in her right hand, and offered me a shy smile, I went in for the kiss.

She kissed me back immediately, grasping at my clothes like an addict in need of a hit.

Dumbstruck, Love—I mean *Lacey*—clears her throat and lets out a breathless "Hi to you, too."

"I can't believe I missed it," I say, more to myself than her. "It was you all along."

I wait for those sharp eyes to light up in understanding, but the only thing I see in there…

Is plain confusion.

"What?" Lacey giggles.

"You were right under my nose. If I'd just fucking stopped to think," I lecture myself.

There's that confusion again.

Why does she look like she has no clue what I'm talking about?

"Take two—what?" she repeats.

My phone chimes with a text, and I pull it out of my pocket, typing in my password so fast I mess it up twice.

I have one new message.

From Love.

My stomach sinks like a rock.

Love: Lacey Mattson, really? Fuck you, Xavier. Fuck you.

It feels like a truck, two buses, and a wrecking ball just slammed into me all at once.

No, no, *fuck*.

The door…

It was her, wasn't it?

Love's the one who came in while we…

Fuuuuuuck.

Lacey isn't Love. She never was. She was just in the wrong place at the wrong time, and my dumb ass assumed…

Now that I think about it, Lacey doesn't even have a tattoo.

Dumb. Fucking. Idiot.

"What's wrong? Come here." Lacey takes my face in her hands for another kiss, but I dodge her lips and propel her hands off me. Operating on autopilot, I swing Finn's bedroom door open and bolt down the stairs without looking back.

I tear through the first floor in minutes, searching for Love, which, granted, is probably pointless seeing as I have no idea what she looks like.

My leading criteria is a sad girl.

Or an angry girl—*my* angry girl.

I just need one clue.

As expected, I come up empty-handed.

I text her back faster than my fingers allow.

Zac: Fuck. Love, you have to believe me, this is NOT what it looks like. I thought she was you.

Zac: Just tell me where you are. Please.

Zac: Love?

Ten minutes go by.

No answer.

The messages never deliver.

That's weird?

In a moment of panic, I tap her contact icon and give her a

call. If there's the tiniest chance that I can salvage this, I have to try. It doesn't even ring. Just goes directly to voicemail.

That's how I know I'm never going to get an answer, no matter how many times I apologize. I might not know Love in real life, but I know a thing or two about girls. And there isn't a single doubt in my mind…

Love just blocked me.

* * *

Aveena

"Where's Xav?" a familiar voice asks when I wander out of the second-floor bathroom after spending twenty minutes trying to fix my makeup—waterproof mascara, *my ass.*

"Probably upstairs getting a sloppy blowjob with too much teeth." A deep laugh makes my bone quiver with disgust.

I catch glimpse of Finn and Theo by the foosball table in the entertainment room and take cover in the reading nook by the door. If I were smart, I'd leave. Spare myself the glory details. After all, the whole point of blocking Xavier's number was to never hear from or *about* him again, but my legs keep me rooted in place.

"No way?" Theo sneers. "I thought he was done with Brie."

"Done dating her, maybe." Finn shrugs. "Never said

anything about fucking her."

My heart cracks.

"Wait, so Xav kept fucking Brie after dumping her?"

"You bet. Hell, he's probably doing it right now. He told me he was meeting some girl at midnight and planning to score. Who else would it be?"

Repulsion coils in my throat.

Is that what this was to him?

A booty call?

So, what? He got sick of waiting for me and launched himself at the first girl who walked through the door instead? Not to mention he's been sleeping with Brie this whole time? My bad for thinking he'd stop hooking up with girls because we were texting twenty-four seven and baring our souls in confessions. Guess Love was just a name on a screen to him.

Blinking back tears of rage, I walk off, beginning my search for my sister in Finn's dump of a mansion. The party's gotten completely out of control, not that it's anything his family's million maids can't fix. I'm well aware that trying to track down one person in a mansion this packed is the equivalent of looking for a needle in a haystack, but I can't leave this place knowing my drunk little sister might still be in here somewhere.

I know she hates me.

But I'd prefer she hates me from the safety of her bedroom.

I'm careful to avoid anyone I know for the next forty-five minutes. I skirt around Dia once or twice. The last thing I want is for her to see my teary eyes and drop everything until I tell her what's wrong.

I even hide from Xavier's make-out buddy at some point.

I'll admit I was surprised to see Lacey out and about so soon.

Guess Finn was right about the "*quickie*" part.

I don't see Xavier anywhere, to my great relief. Five bucks says he hit up Brie, since Love didn't show up. An hour of triple-checking every room later, I'm left to wonder if Ashley already went home. Then I remember there's one room I haven't checked yet.

The garage.

Definitely a long shot, but I'm desperate enough not to care.

I pad down the dark, deserted hallway I *think* leads to the garage that's interconnected with the house, trying to summon distant memories of the only time Dia gave me a tour of Finn's palace.

I exhale in relief when I spot the double doors in the distance.

Please be there, Ash.

Eager to get this garbage party over with, I grip the knob and burst into the well-lit garage like I own the place.

Then I see him.

And everything falls apart.

Starting with the protective barrier I built around my heart.

He's just sitting there, on the concrete floor.

He has his back against the furthest wall of the heated garage as he throws a small ball against the opposite wall, catching it over and over. There must be over five luxury cars parked in here, but I pay them no mind, gawking at my pen pal.

The stranger I spilled my darkest secrets to.

The boy I came *so close* to falling in love with.

I almost fell for a boy who still wants his ex. What kind of fool does that make me? I'm itching to scream in his face. Tell him what a huge disappointment he turned out to be. Tell him I wish he'd been the Zac I imagined in my head.

But I can't.

He still has no idea who I really am.

Xavier looks up at me through thick eyelashes. He seems sad—no, he seems *miserable*. He doesn't acknowledge me in the slightest, throwing the ball against the wall once more and catching it effortlessly.

I drum up an excuse. "Sorry, I was just… looking for some quiet. I'll go."

I spin on my heels, but I've barely opened the door an inch before he says, "You don't have to."

My hand still clutching the knob, I cast a dubious glance in his direction.

"Got plenty of quiet to go around." He gestures to the empty garage. I should go and never look back. Bandage up my bruised ego and walk the hell away, but against all expectations, I shut the door and ask him a very dangerous question.

"Are you… okay?"

Why is it dangerous?

Because it means I still care.

"Peachy." He releases a weak scoff.

It's his eyes.

Those sad, tug-at-your-heartstrings puppy eyes.

"What's wrong?"

"Nothing's wrong." He picks up the bottle of Fireball at his feet, swipes a huge sip, and wipes his mouth with the back of his hand. "I'm just a fucking moron, that's all."

I hesitantly cut across the garage to his side.

"Care to elaborate?"

"Sure. Once upon a time, I royally fucked up the only good thing in my life. *The end.*" He can't even muster a smile at his own joke. That's how I know something is seriously wrong.

"I assume we're talking about a girl here?"

"Not just any girl, Harper." He pitches the ball harder against the wall as if to channel his frustration. "*The* girl."

Brie?

Lacey?

Who fucking knows at this point?

"I'm sorry" is all I can think to say.

"Meh. Don't be." Xavier gives an unconvincing shrug before dragging another sip of alcohol. "It was always going to end this way. Any other story I fed myself was a load of shit."

I wish I had a sensible excuse to justify what I do next, but I don't. All I have is this insufferable need to give him the benefit of the doubt. I plop down by his side on the concrete floor.

Silence swallows us whole.

"I never apologized." Xavier fills the void.

"For what?" I nestle my knees to my chest.

"Being a dick to you that first time at Theo's."

His admission of regret takes me back to the start. This seems like a million years ago. Dia had invited me to hang out at Theo's, and I'd gotten there to find the lot of them in the pool. This was also the first time Xav and I had spoken since he'd stolen my first kiss at the park ten years prior.

He was such a scumbag to me that day. I remember Finn promising it wasn't personal and Xav was just going through a rough patch. Now I know there's a very good chance he'd just found out about his mom sleeping with his friend, hence his raining hell down on anybody within a five-mile radius.

And can you blame him?

"It's fine," I assure him.

"It's not fucking fine, Vee." Remorseful eyes lift to mine. "I was horrible to you. You didn't deserve that shit."

"I'm sure you had your reasons."

He stifles a deep, irritated scoff. "Can you stop being so damn understanding for one second and just accept my apology?"

I chuckle quietly.

"Fine. Apology accepted. Happy now?"

"Ecstatic," he says with a small grin.

There's a beat of silence.

"Dig the new hair, by the way." He lightly pokes me with his elbow. "Pink looks good on you, Harper."

"Thanks, dork."

It's like a switch.

From the second the words trickle out of my mouth, Xavier pulls back, his smile slipping away. He stares at me as though I just slapped him across the face with a pan, the shock in his eyes indecipherable.

"What did you just call me?" he asks.

Realization crushes me like a pile of bricks.

I just called him a dork, didn't I?

"Did you just call me a dork?" he urges when I don't reply.

No, it can't be.

It's just one stupid nickname.

He *can't* be thinking what I'm thinking.

He's about to speak again when my loud ringtone slashes through the air. Saved by the phone, I check the caller ID in a haste. *Mom.*

"I'm sorry, I-I have to take this," I babble, pushing to my feet and distancing myself from him before I guide the phone to my ear. "Hello?"

"What the hell did you do to your sister?" Mom screeches as soon as I pick up.

"Hi, Mother. I'm great, thanks for asking. *How are you*?"

"Do not start with me, Aveena. I just called one of Ashley's cast mates, since rehearsal was supposed to end hours ago. Turns out there was never a play rehearsal scheduled tonight."

Busted.

"Have you tried calling her?"

"What do you think?" she yells. "I put a tracker on her phone last week, and you know where it led me tonight? To the Richards' house. On a Saturday night. I'm not stupid, Aveena. I'm well aware of what kids like to do on Saturday nights, and I know your trollop friend Diamond is seeing this Richards kid. I was willing to turn a blind eye when you asked for nights out, but you're completely out of control! I can't believe you'd coerce your underage sister into getting drunk at some party!"

Of course she'd assume it's my fault.

God forbid Ashley actually made her own decisions.

"What? I wouldn't do that. She came all on her own. I tried to get her to leave, but I lost her in the crowd and now I can't find her."

"And you expect me to believe that?" A bitter laugh echoes down the line. "*My* Ashley would never be so reckless. She'd never mix with…" She pauses. "Your kind of people."

My kind of people?

Call us peasants, why don't you?

"Well, maybe you don't know your precious Ashley as well as you think you do." I erupt, shocked by my own audacity. This night has been a killer headache, and my bullshit meter is nearing its limit.

"Aveena Harper D'Amour, are you talking back at me?" Mom cranks the yelling up five notches, and I flinch, driving the phone away from my ear. I'm *this* close to losing my temper and going crazy town on her when I remember I have an audience.

"No, of course not." I exhale a gusty breath. "I'm just saying I had nothing to do with it. She's seventeen, Mom. I can't control what she does all the time."

"You have thirty minutes to find your sister and get her home. If you're even one minute late, I'm calling the police on this drugfest for underage drinking, am I making myself clear?" She spits out empty threats. Well, I *hope* they're empty.

"Yes, ma'am." I grumble and end the call before squeezing my phone in my jeans pocket.

Then comes the moment I dreaded the most. The moment where Xav and I finish a conversation I'm not prepared for.

I swivel to face him, my cheeks tinted with shame. My backstabbing crush just witnessed my mom chewing my head off over the phone. No big deal. If I thought he seemed shocked before, I was way off. This was *nothing* compared to the way he's looking at me now. His jaw goes slack, his mouth hanging open as he stares down my face, eerily quiet.

He looks like he's seen a ghost.

"Sorry you had to hear that." I shuffle my feet, playing with my fingers nervously. A million emotions blend together in his eyes, but his lips remain sealed. He looks like he's processing something. Assembling pieces of a puzzle he was never able to complete.

Until now.

"Anyway." I clear my throat. "I-I should get going."

He still doesn't make a sound, dissecting my every move as I speed-walk to the door, but right as I'm about to make a run for it, he does the last thing I expected.

He laughs.

It's a chest laugh.

Deep, and raw, and real. But don't think I miss the bitterness bubbling beneath the surface.

"I'm so fucking stupid," he mutters to himself, so quietly I almost don't hear him. I'm tempted to pretend I didn't catch that and haul ass out of there, but something tells me he wouldn't let me go that easy.

What he says next proves me right.

"It's you."

He said it to my back, but it paralyzes me from head to toe.

"*Of course it's you.*" He scoffs. "Jesus, Xav, be slower, will you?"

It takes me a few seconds to regain control of my body and spin myself around. *Play dumb*, a voice in the back of my head advises. *Only way you'll get out of here with your heart in one piece.*

"Huh, okay?" I mock, knowing damn well the only ridiculous person here is me. "How much have you had to drink?"

"Don't fucking do that, Vee," he growls, his patience wearing thin. He talks like it's a done deal. Like there's no point in denying it anymore. But I'm not going down without a fight.

I'm not ready to be vulnerable.

I'm not ready for this to be real.

Not when he chose Lacey over me.

Not when he's still *choosing Brie over me.*

"Stay here. I'll go get Finn so he can put your ass in a cab or something." I turn to leave, but Xavier rises off the concrete before I can even *think* of storming out. He makes his way over to me in two big strides, and my heart's fight or flight kicks in, begging me to run.

Before he ruins me.

He stops inches away from me, his eyes level with mine, and his breath fanning my lips. My throat bobs at the proximity, the inside coated in fear, but Xav? He's a cold, unaffected riddle I'd sell my soul to solve.

I can tell he's doing this on purpose. Crowding my space. Getting close to me in the hope of seeing me break.

"Admit it." It comes out as a bone-chilling order.

"Admit what?" I put on the performance of my life.

If I don't admit it, he can't rip my heart to shreds. *If I don't admit it, I can hold on to Love a little longer.* Irritated by my stubbornness, he grits his teeth together. It isn't long before he realizes he needs to find something I can't argue with.

And that's exactly what he does.

Without a warning, Xavier yanks my left sleeve down my shoulder, denuding my skin and leaving a trail of goose bumps in his wake. That's how I know I'm screwed.

He exposed me—*literally*.

More exactly my caterpillar tattoo.

If that's not a dead giveaway, I don't know what is. I told Xav about the ink on my left shoulder once, a long time ago. I was sure he'd have forgotten, but here we are. In Finn's garage, surrounded by Lamborghinis and custom Teslas, staring each other dead in the eyes.

Xavier's mouth drops at the caterpillar under my collarbone. The guy talks a good game, but the look on his face suggests he wasn't one hundred percent sure until now.

"Admit it," Xav repeats once he's regained his composure.

I chew down on my bottom lip.

"L, I know it's you. Just say it." He pauses. "*Please.*"

He's begging now. Backed into a corner, I lower my gaze to my feet, surrendering with a croaky, barely audible,

"*It's me.*"

Xavier stumbles back a step.

He doesn't react for several seconds.

"But… You… I…" He blathers, trying to settle on an emotion. Finally, he comes to a decision. "*This whole fucking time*?" He snarls. "You just let me ramble on about how I messed things up between us when you… you were sitting right next to me?"

Anger it is.

I look up at him, my brain looping images of him eating

Lacey's face off. Taking Brie from behind while I was pouring my heart out to him in confessions, dumb enough to let him in.

Xav drives a restless hand through his hair and barks out an angry "Jesus, I can't believe this shit!"

I can't believe I still want you.

"Oh, I'm sorry, was that before or after you shoved your tongue down Lacey's throat?" I fire back.

My comment blows him out of the water. He clenches his jaw, confronted with the facts.

"I knew you blocked my number," he surprises me by saying.

How the hell did he find out?

"I never meant to kiss her. You'd know that if you'd read just *one* of my billion fucking texts!"

"Right." I snort. "So, you accidentally tripped and landed on her mouth. Got it."

Why am I even bothering?

We were a mistake. A. Rookie. Fucking. Mistake. All that's left for me to do is find Ashley, get the hell out of this house, and forget about this pen pal disaster once and for all. I reach for the knob, opening the door an inch, but Xav smacks his palm against the wood, slamming it closed.

"Get out of my way, Xavier," I warn.

"No," he says bluntly.

"I said move!" I bump my shoulder against his hard chest.

He doesn't waver an inch. "You're not fucking leaving until we talk!"

"What's there to talk about?" I shriek. "You were right. It was always going to end this way. With you sucking face with a cheerleader while I—"

"I thought she was you."

I backtrack, needing to put some space between us.

"You… what?" I choke.

"It's true." He steps closer. "You have to believe me, Vee. First thing I did when she walked in was kiss her—no, fuck that, first thing I did when she walked in was kiss *you*."

My stomach churns at the thought of Xavier gripping my face and kissing me instead of her, slow and hard, liberating us from weeks of built-up tension.

My phone chimes with two texts from Dia.

Dia: Did Lacey get to you? She found your keys. Went up to Finn's room to give them back to you.

Dia: Never mind, I just talked to her. She said she didn't find you. I've got your keys. Text me before you leave xo

Holy shit.

Is *that* why Lacey wound up in Finn's bedroom? To give me back my keys? Axel kept getting in my way, trying to set me up with one of his friends, which would have allowed Lacey to get there before me.

Xavier's telling the truth, isn't he?

"Say that was even two percent true, it doesn't change the fact that you didn't notice she wasn't m…" I stop myself. That's not fair. He couldn't have known she wasn't me. He'd never seen me before, but I can't stomach the thought of him confusing "Love" with Lacey fucking Mattson.

Does he not know me at all?

After all our texts?

All our confessions?

"Oh, and let's not forget the fact that you were, how did he put it—" I make air quotes with my fingers. "*—planning to score?*"

Guilt sweeps across Xavier's face, and disappointment claws at whatever's left of that thing in my chest. Finn wasn't lying.

Xav cringes. "Who told you that?"

"Does it matter?"

"Aveena, who the *fuck* is it?" he hounds.

"I heard Finn talking to Theo."

Please tell me I'm wrong, I silently beg, *tell me Love was more than a conquest. More than a shiny trophy to add to your shelf.*

His silence is my cue.

"Copy that." I nod and set out toward the door, but his hand flies out to catch my wrist.

"Vee, wait. Just… let me explain."

"Save your explanation for someone who gives a shit." I retrieve my wrist. "Oh, I know. Why don't you try Brie? She's the one you're fucking and leading on, isn't she?"

I expect him to feel ashamed, but he knocks the breath out of me with his unapologetic answer.

"*Was* fucking."

"What?" is all I can say.

"You heard me." He steps dangerously close. "I ended it weeks ago. Something you'd know if you gave me one fucking minute to explain myself. But you obviously know everything already. So, why bother, right?"

Xavier starts closing in on me, and I step back without thinking, my pulse climbing to worrying rates.

"Don't pretend like Love was anything more to you than a booty call," I spit. "I heard Finn—"

He scoffs. "What you heard, that was just Finn spewing his usual bullshit. He read your text asking to meet up over my shoulder earlier. He didn't even see the sender. Just assumed we were meeting to hook up. My only mistake was not correcting him."

Oh.

"Strike that. My mistake was continuing to sleep with Brie to convince myself I didn't give a shit about you."

I swallow hard.

Don't fall for it.

He'll say anything right now.

"Wow." I shake my head. "You're good, Emery. *Ten out of ten.* Almost fell for it."

"I'm not fucking lying!"

"So, what? I'm supposed to believe you gave up your side piece because of me?" I force a careless cackle, but it sounds fake. *Painful.* "Your perfect cheerleader girlfriend with the perfect body? By all means, Xav, go back to her. Don't let me stop you."

"You did stop me!" he snaps, his outburst catching me off guard. "For fuck's sake, Vee, don't you get it? You stopped me before I even knew who you were."

His admission shakes me to my core.

It feels like the air has been sucked out of my lungs as he stalks toward me like he's the king of the jungle. And he's coming to claim his prey. A gasp sneaks past my lips when the back of my thighs hits something.

Finn's dad's white Tesla.

Xavier cages me against the parked car, propping his hand flat against the hood behind me, and I stiffen up, my heaving chest robbing me of any pretense of indifference.

There's no escaping him, heart.

I'm sorry, I tried.

"I don't fucking want her," he hisses. "What's it going to take for you to get that?"

"Why?" I blurt. "Why wouldn't you want her? Or Lacey? Or any of the million girls who'd sell an organ for five minutes alone with you?"

Why should I believe he ever cared about Love?

About *me*?

Why should I believe anything he says?

"I don't want them because they don't have a caterpillar tattoo on their shoulder." Xav clutches my face with both hands. "I don't want them because they're not the only ones who get me in a world of fucking idiots." He gives a breathy laugh, the garage's fluorescent lights shimmering in his eyes. "They don't drive me completely insane, keep me on my toes with everything they do. So, yes, I ended it with Brie. And *yes*, I figured out Lacey wasn't you."

Then he sets my expectations for any future guy way too high.

"Because none of them are, Vee. *Fucking none of them.*"

That's what does it.

I might've taken a major risk answering the troll who corrected my grammar all these weeks ago, but the move I make next will either go down as one of the best decisions I've ever made…

Or the worst.

I suck in a breath, trap Xavier's varsity jacket's collar into my fists, and smash our lips together. That's right, I, Aveena *Chicken* Harper, take the plunge for once in my life.

A guttural noise of satisfaction rips from Xavier's throat as soon as our mouths connect. He immediately tilts my chin forward, kissing me back with an intensity you'd go to the end of the world to experience *once.*

His lips are soft, but nothing about his kiss is gentle. Nothing about the way he claims me is *sweet.* Xavier kisses me with a need, a hunger I'm afraid even the best of me can't satisfy. I feel clumsy, inexperienced as my fingers slide into his hair, and I arch my back off the Tesla to slam our bodies together.

Am I doing this wrong?

Am I making a fool of myself?

Who does she think she is?

Kissing the captain of the basketball team?

I have no idea what I'm doing. My first contact with a man was with Logan—actually, I doubt he qualifies as a man. More like a human dumpster—and our kiss was nothing like this.

It was rushed.

Sloppy.

But Xav… he tastes like desperation, like I just found the last drop of water in a worldwide drought. And I might not know jack shit about anything, but I know this.

I'm not sharing this oasis.

I turn full control over to my body and press my hips flush to his, never once disrupting our rough, heated kiss. My cheeks blaze when I feel his rock-hard erection pressing against my thigh.

I take it I'm not so ridiculous after all?

His fingers travel to the nape of my neck, and he traps a handful of my pink hair into his fist, inching my head backward to deepen our connection. His tongue pries my teeth apart, and all the text messages in the world, all the nights I spent dreaming about what it would be like…

None of it could've ever prepared me for the real thing.

For his tongue dancing with mine.

The heavenly sensations prickling down my spine when he bites on my bottom lip and abandons my mouth. The thrill I feel when he bands his hands around the back of my thighs to plant me on the hood of the car.

Parting my legs slightly, I reach for the small chain he always wears around his neck and give it a yank, luring him closer. Xavier's lips crash back against mine as he settles between my opened thighs.

His large hand falls to my lower back as we shamelessly make out on top of Mr. Richards's car. We disconnect a minute later, gasping for air, but Xav doesn't return to my mouth.

This time, he goes straight for my neck.

He works my collarbone like a pro, sucking on my tattooed skin until I'm boneless, and I can't help moaning at the pressure of his mouth. I waste no time brushing my dyed hair off my shoulder and offering more of myself to him. He smirks at my wordless request, more than willing to deliver. It's all fun and games until I guide his lips back to mine, my hands creeping inside his opened jacket, while his slink up my rib cage over my shirt.

"Xav," I moan into his mouth, but it comes out as a warning.

Translation: this is getting out of control.

"I know," he agrees, his breathing ragged.

We're on the same page, but neither of us stop chasing the next kiss, the next touch. I don't recognize the person this boy has made of me. All bets are off when his fingers land on my pierced nipples over the fabric of my clothes, and he slowly flicks them with his thumbs, my thin bralette giving way to every sensation.

We fall backward onto the hood of the car, and I'm shocked by my own actions when I start playing with the buckle of his jeans. *What. Are. You. Doing?* He grunts at my initiative. I'm about to unbuckle his belt when the universe slams the brakes with a signal we couldn't ignore if we tried. The loudest, most deafening noise rings throughout the garage.

We just set off the car alarm system.

Chill, Universe, I hear you.

The alarm is so aggressive it shouldn't be long before Finn, and possibly the whole party, comes rushing into the garage to investigate. Breathless, Xavier and I unglue ourselves from each other, and my phone pings in my pocket.

It's my mom again.

Mom: Fifteen minutes. Tick-tock.

Her previous threats to unleash the cops on Dia's birthday party flash in my mind, and I plummet back down to earth. I can't believe I'm about to leave Xav hanging, but I'd rather my best friend *not* get charged with underage drinking on her birthday.

"Shit, I have to—"

"Go," Xavier cuts me off. "Find your sister before your mom rats us out to the sheriff."

How much of that phone call did he hear?

I slide off the white car, whose alarm is still pounding in our ears, and dash to the door to swing it open. My feet halt at the threshold, stopping me from running away.

I feel like I should say something.

Acknowledge the most memorable kiss of my life. So, I cast a glance toward Xav, slapping on an apologetic smile and giving him a squeaky "Xavier, I… I'm so sorry."

And I really am, for leaving him stranded like this.

But he seems to peg my apology as me regretting what just happened because the last thing he says before I storm out is…

"*I'm not.*"

Aveena

I've spent my entire life thinking I was worthy of the "big sister" title. Believed being someone's big sister made me a bigger person in general. I was the wise one, the experienced one, the one in charge of protecting my younger sibling from harm. Then I walked in on Ashley making out with a shirtless basketball player in Finn's bathtub, and suddenly…

I didn't feel so big anymore. I felt pretty damn small, actually.

She ended up in that bathtub, straddling Easton's ultimate player, moaning in his ear while his mouth bruised her neck because she's hurting. Because *I* betrayed her.

I'm in no position to blame her for trying to forget. We all need an escape sometimes.

I just wish she hadn't found it in Theodore Cox's mouth.

"Theo? *Really*?" I wince after five minutes of driving in utter silence. Ash hasn't said a word since I practically manhandled her out of the bathtub and into my passenger seat. She might not care if Mom calls the cops on Dia's party, but *I do.*

Heaving a childish laugh, she says, "Is that what his name is?"

"What would you have done if I hadn't showed up, huh? Slept with him?" I hound her, the images of Theo shoving his tongue down her throat too fresh to erase.

I sure hope this was a onetime thing. Theo wouldn't be caught *dead* in a serious relationship, and Ashley doesn't need another heartbreaker wreaking havoc in her life.

She shrugs. "Probably."

"Ash, you're better than this, the body shots, making out with some jock in a bathtub. I know you're hurting, but this isn't going to help."

I could smack myself for lecturing her. I'm aware I sound like Mom right now, but I'm embarrassingly clueless as to what I should say. How do you talk to your sister knowing you lost your virginity to her ex-boyfriend?

How do you even *look* her in the eyes?

We go minutes without speaking. I tie my hair into a ponytail when we come across a red light. I can't stand my hair getting in my eyes when I'm driving.

The moment the light turns green, Ashley blurts an indignant "Are you fucking kidding me?"

Caught off guard, I almost swerve off the road.

"What?" I yell, matching her tone.

"You're going to lecture me about making out with some guy when you were doing the same fucking thing?"

My cheeks ignite with embarrassment.

If anyone finds my jaw, I'd like it back, *thanks.*

I swallow hard. "What are you talking about?"

"Do you think I'm blind? You have a hickey the size of my fucking fist, Vee."

"I do?" I blurt, lifting a hand to my neck.

Damn it, Xavier.

"You're unbelievable!" Ash huffs, propping her dirty heels on my dashboard, just to piss me off. She knows I hate when she does that. Flushed, I let my hair back down pronto.

"You're avoiding the question," I say, well aware that I've lost all credibility. "I know you, Ash. This isn't you."

A hoarse, hateful laugh vibrates in the back of her throat.

"Oh, you know me, huh? Well, I got news for you, sissy. We never really know anyone. *That's a myth.* Take me, for example. Every time I think I know someone, they turn out to be cheating, abusive pieces of shit or a boyfriend-stealing traitor."

I flinch at the last part.

"Wait." I stiffen. "Abusive? W-What do you mean?" I grip the wheel so hard my joints ache. If Logan laid a hand on her, I'll break his neck like a twig.

She plays deaf.

"Ash, did Logan touch you?" I urge.

She responds by leaning her head against the headrest and staring out the window.

I'm about to pester her some more when she decides she has

more to say. "You're such a hypocrite, Vee. Telling me not to sleep with some random guy when you literally jumped into bed with my ex!"

Guilt clogs my throat. "I've been meaning to talk to you about that."

"Fine, then talk. How was Logan's dick? Good? How did he feel? Did you come? Did he make you feel *special*?"

Her cruel questions are my breaking point.

I slam the brakes so hard Ashley shrieks in shock. I pull over to the side of the road, battling tears with all my might. I've spent years biting my tongue about the way she and Mom treat me, but I can't take another second of this.

"Is that what you think? That I felt *good*?" I shout. "That I didn't throw up in the bathroom as soon as it was over? That I didn't hate every second of it?" Salty tears soak my mouth. "I slept with him because I was sad, Ash. And miserable. And lonely. You and Mom had been gone for days on some vacation *without me.* Then Logan showed up with a box of stuff you left at his place, and he was nice. He noticed my misery and pretended to care. He listened, and for the first time since Dad died, I felt like I mattered. So, when he kissed me, *I let him.* And no, it wasn't good. He was inconsiderate and brutal during…" I can't complete my sentence. "And no, I didn't feel special. I felt like garbage, Ashley. But you wouldn't know what that's like, do you? *Of course not.* People have been listening to you since you were born," I spit.

Drowning in tears and mucus, I grant myself a moment to still my anger before meeting her eyes. Her mouth hangs open, shock pasted on her face.

"I made a mistake, Ash. And I'll spend the rest of my life regretting it." I sniffle. "But don't think for a second that it felt *good*."

Silence submerges the car.

That's when tears begin to form in my sister's eyes.

"I… I had no idea," Ashley croaks.

I don't say a word, wiping my cheeks.

"We always assumed you wouldn't want to come. Our trips were always about music, and business meetings and… God, Vee, how long have you felt this away?"

Breaking into a thousand pieces, I whisper, "Only since I was born."

Ash chews on her lower lip, shedding a tear.

"And I'm not trying to make excuses for what I did, Ash. I know it's unforgivable, but I just can't stand you thinking I did it for fun, or… because I was trying to steal your boyfriend. It wasn't about him. It was about needing someone to choose *me*. Just once." I sound pathetic. Like an attention deprived little girl still waiting for her daddy to swoop in and make it all okay.

Tell her she's important, too.

But Daddy isn't coming home anytime soon.

It's time I accept it.

"Jesus, I'm so self-centered." Ashley cringes.

"You're not," I disagree.

She cocks an eyebrow.

"Okay, you are a little, but you try your best not to be."

A small laugh trickles from her lips.

"How could you not be focused on your own shit? Mom's been putting you under the spotlight since you could talk."

Ashley drags a deep sigh. "Still. You're my sister and I hurt you and I'm sorry."

Am I crazy or did she just…

She's apologizing to *me*?

After what I did?

I cry twice as hard at her admission of regret.

"I'm the one who's sorry. God, I'm so, *so* sorry, Ash," I mutter through the sobs.

"Come here." She stretches her arms in my direction, and I unbuckle my seat belt to give in to her embrace. I squeeze her a little harder before pulling away, and she winces, a groan of pain slipping from her lips.

"Shit, did I hurt you?" I worry as I lean back into the driver's seat. I must be one hell of a hugger.

"No, I… it's not you." Ashley clears her throat.

I understand immediately.

"I knew it. He *did* hurt you."

She doesn't confirm my suspicions, but the way she shifts in her seat to alleviate the pain tells me everything I need to know.

"That's why you broke up, isn't it?" I figure.

Her eyes are pinned to the dashboard as she gives a weak nod.

"What happened?" I say through gritted teeth, marinating in fury.

Ashley sighs. "He took my phone and checked my DMs when I was in the bathroom. He saw I was talking with some guy about music, and he lost his shit. Called me a cheating whore. That's when I knew he'd gone too far and I had to break up with him. I told him it was over, and he…" She flinches, reliving the attack. "He pushed me into the bookcase in my room. I fell to the ground. Then, he pulled me up by my hair and told me you'd slept together. I don't know what would've happened if Rob hadn't gotten there the next minute."

I can barely think straight, every muscle in my body tensing up in anticipation of a fight.

"I'm still a little bit sore in my back, but it's getting better," she tries to reassure me.

"Ash, you have to report him to the police."

"Rob said I shouldn't." She fidgets with her fingers.

"Fuck Rob! Your manager doesn't know shit. Logan hurt you. You can't let him get away with this."

"No, he's right, Vee. I'm just starting out in the industry. I don't need a police investigation right now. I just want to move on, never see the bastard again, and focus on my career."

I disagree.

I'd love nothing more than to drag Logan's reputation

through the mud and expose him for the lying, abusive scumbag that he is, but at the end of the day, it's up to her.

Ashley pauses for a moment as if to replay the words she just said and laughs. "If you can even call it *my* career."

"What do you mean?" I question.

"I don't know… It's just… Mom's pushing me so hard lately I wonder if I'd be pursuing a future in music if it weren't for her. I love singing more than anything, but I'd also love to have a life, you know? Away from the academy's preppy assholes and the unbearable pressure."

Unable to pinpoint the words to make her feel better, I pluck a page out of her handbook and open my arms for a hug. Ashley welcomes the hug, resting her head on my shoulder for comfort.

"God, in moments like this, I wish Dad was still here. He would've never let me date fucking Logan in the first place," Ashley confesses. "And he could remind Mom to let me breathe every once in a while."

My heart skips a beat.

This is the first time Ashley has acknowledged our father in years. At least, in front of me.

"If he was, he'd run Logan over with his race car and make it look like an accident," I point out, and we laugh.

"I miss him so much," she admits.

"Do you?" I can't fend off the curiosity. "Don't get me wrong, it's just… you never talk about him. Not on the anniversary of his death, not on his birthday. I kind of thought you didn't remember him."

Still in my arms, she says, "I used to… talk about him, I mean. Back when we were kids, but Mom would get *so* weird whenever I mentioned him. She'd look at me like I was—"

"A four-legged monster?" I finish.

She chuckles. "Something like that."

"I know the feeling." I withdraw from the hug.

"I still go see him, though. I visit his grave every month when Mom thinks I'm having dinner with Rob."

"You do?" The tears are back in my eyes in an instant.

She nods.

"Me too," I confide.

"Are you serious?" she chortles. "You're telling me we've both been going to see him in that creepy-ass cemetery *alone* when we could've gone together all this time?"

I laugh at how ridiculous it sounds when spoken out loud.

"Looks like it."

"Jesus, Vee. Why have we never talked like this?" She exhales and grabs my hand.

"You mean aside from the fact that you're always at some photoshoot? Or at an early lesson? Or making out with basketball players in a bathtub? *Beats me*," I tease, and my sister grins.

"Let's promise to never drift apart again, okay?" She offers me her pinky, because everybody knows a promise isn't valid unless it involves a pinky swear. Joy flowing out of me profusely,

I nod and lace my pinky around hers.

"*Okay.*"

* * *

"Where the hell have you been?" Mom blusters when we pad into the house twenty minutes later. We got carried away talking about Dad and Mom's selective amnesia. She's sitting at the kitchen island in the darkness, her stern features obscured by worry and her lack of sleep.

I almost didn't see her, as the only source of light in the room emanates from the kitchen hood. Mom leaps off the swivel stool before I can blink and thuds toward us. She's in her black satin nightgown, her short hair less tidy than usual.

"Out," Ashley says without a thought for her survival.

Brave.

Stupid but brave.

"What the hell did you say to her?" Mom turns to me. "How did you convince your sister to lie and go to this delinquent party—"

"She didn't *make* me do anything, Mom," Ashley interrupts. "I went all on my own."

Mom's gaze shifts between Ashley and me for a moment as if she's waiting for one of us to say "*Psych.*"

"But… Ashley, honey, why would you want to—"

"Live? Enjoy my youth? Experience new things? Gee, I don't know, Mother, maybe because I'm human?" Ashley exposes how toxic this "momager" situation of theirs truly is. Mom's lips part for a fleeting second before she slaps her poker face back on.

"Ashley, sweetie, why are you acting out? When we're so close to our goal."

"My goal, Mom. *Mine*," Ashley corrects. "Not yours. This is my life. My future. My dreams. Sometimes, I think you forget that."

"After everything I've done for you, quitting my job and working for you, you want to pretend like this has *nothing* to do with me? You are way out of line here, young lady."

"Me? How about you? Weren't *you* out of line the night you burned Dad's letter?" Ashley knocks me on my ass with her comeback.

I wish I were like her.

Courageous, ballsy enough to speak my mind.

Mom shuts down the second the word "Dad" echoes through the room. She schools her expression, chasing the emotions off her face until the blossoming love inside her heart is swapped with dead, infertile soil.

"I don't want to talk about this," Mom says, her expression blank and lifeless.

"That's too bad," Ashley insists. "Because we do. Vee and I had a talk, and we can't keep living like this. When are we going to talk about Dad? It's like you just erased him, Mom."

"I did not. I sent you to therapy so we could all move on."

I see a wave of pain roll through her eyes as she says it.

We're getting through to her.

"What if we don't want to move on?" I flare. Ashley rubbed off on me, apparently. "What if we just wanted to *learn* to live without him rather than pretend he never existed? Did you ever think about that?"

"Girl, that's enough," Mom orders, her jaw tight.

"No, it's not enough, Mom." I stand my ground. "We've been keeping quiet for nine years. Nine years acting like we don't miss him every single day. We can't forget him just because *you* did!"

Then she bursts out crying.

You read that right.

My mother, who hasn't shown an ounce of emotion since the day she peeled me off my father's body, bursts out crying in the middle of our kitchen.

"You think I forgot him?" she all but yells.

I feel lost, unprepared. Like my mom's breakdown is a job I'm not qualified for. Without a word, she takes off toward the stairs. Running on instinct, I grab Ashley's wrist and follow after her. We take the steps two at a time and reach the second floor to find Mom rushing in the direction of my dad's trophy room.

I mean, *her office.*

She drives the key in her hand through the door she's kept locked since Dad committed an irreversible act. Ash and I always assumed she just didn't want our noses in her business.

"You think I don't care?" Mom sobs as she fumbles with the lock. Then she pushes the door open, walks in, and gestures for us to do the same. I've barely stepped foot inside her office before my heart decomposes into a pile of dust. Mom doesn't utter a sound, simply pointing at the walls, ceilings, and furniture.

Every square inch of the walls and ceiling are covered in pictures of him, and us before the accident.

Every. Square. Inch.

Some are Polaroids, some developed photos, all of them telling a story. The first photo I spot was taken the day of my birth. Mom went into labor during one of Dad's most important races. He showed up to the hospital as fast as he could, but he was too late.

I was already here.

He's still wearing his racing suit as he stands by Mom's hospital bed, sporting a thumbs-up. She's holding me in her arms, looking exhausted.

Happy.

The next picture is the day Dad took Ashley and me on a fishing trip when I was seven. There were no fish all weekend, and Ashley fell into the water trying to chase a butterfly. Oh, and I got stung by bees so many times I couldn't move without crying for a week straight. I remember he insisted we take a picture of the one and only fish we'd caught before we left. It was small.

And we ended up letting it go right after the picture.

In the photograph, Ashley is soaked from head to toe, I look like a strawberry field, thanks to the swarm of angry bees, and Dad is holding the tiny fish up in the air.

Worst trip of all time, right?

And yet… this is my favorite memory with him.

My gaze sweeps around the room. There isn't one item in this place that isn't my dad's. She's kept his old desk, the hideous leopard-print computer chair Dad found on the street when he was a broke eighteen-year-old.

She's kept everything down to our last memory of him.

The last picture.

Mom took it ten minutes before the accident. He's holding us up in the air, Ash in one arm and me in the other. We're laughing like there's no tomorrow. Little did we know, because of this exact moment, there *would* be no tomorrow.

For Dad, anyway.

"Does this look like forgetting him to you?" Mom's voice is so weak, so fragile, I wonder how the tragically broken woman in front of me could appear whole for all these years.

But when she sinks to the floor, knees against the hardwood floor, crying into her hands, I understand…

That's just it.

She was never whole.

She just *appeared* this way.

I'd never related to Mom before. Could barely believe we

shared DNA for a while, but right now, looking at her, I see myself. Crying in my car alone at the springs while writing a letter.

I want to hug her, but Ashley beats me to it, plopping down on the floor and snaking her arms around her. Mom reaches for Ashley's clothes, fisting the fabric for reassurance. Ashley looks up at me, gesturing to join them with her chin.

My hands shaky, I settle by my mom's side, until her daughters flank her. From the moment I enfold her right side with my arms, she begins to howl with sobs.

"I'm so sorry, girls. I thought…" *Sniffle.* "I thought I was protecting you." She draws her hands away from her face, staring at me through teary eyes. "Especially you, Aveena. I didn't know what to say to you after you… Jesus, you were so tiny." She covers her mouth with her palm as though she can't bear the thought. "When I found you crying on his lap… My baby girl, lying on her daddy's body, I just… felt like I'd failed you as a mother. I was supposed to protect you." She breaks into sobs again.

The only difference is, *I'm crying, too.*

I grip her hand and intertwine our fingers.

"I wanted to make you forget. I tried to go on like nothing happened so that you wouldn't be haunted by Curt's death for the rest of your life, like I was, but I ended up branding you with the memory, instead. By forbidding you to talk about it, I made you think about it more. And I couldn't even touch you or hug you without falling apart and crying like a baby myself. God, I'm so sorry."

"It's okay, Mom," I whisper, the words aching in my throat like a handful of rose thorns.

"No, it's not okay, honey. I knew you needed help the most, and I pushed you away because I… I couldn't even begin to help *myself*." Her fingers dart out to cup my face, and my breath jumps at the affectionate gesture. I can't recall the last time she touched me like this. "I was so wrapped up in losing the love of my life, I didn't realize my girls were mourning the loss of their father, and I'm sorry. To the both of you."

I could never see it before…

But I can now. Parents aren't superheroes. Superhumans. They're just *humans*, doing their best, making mistakes, getting knocked on their ass and crawling until they can get back up again. My sister and I make eye contact, a single look the vessel of a thousand words. Ash nods, giving me the green light to bury the hatchet, and I relieve myself of the burden I've been lugging around for eons.

"We forgive you, Mom," I croak, throwing myself into her arms. Ash, Mom, and I stay on the floor, group hugging for five minutes. We cry, apologize, and cry some more.

"I love you. My beautiful girls," Mom whispers.

Ash is crying too hard to form an answer, so I take over and utter the three little words we haven't exchanged in nine years.

"I love you, Mom."

19

Aveena

Xavier didn't text me again after our kiss.

In his defense, I *did* bail on him to go find Ashley, not to mention blocked, then unblocked his number in a span of hours, but the anxiety monster feeding off my insecurities just couldn't resist screwing with my head.

What if I'm a horrible kisser?

What if he realized I'm not his type after all?

What if we never speak again after this?

Suffice to say, it took a serious pep talk and every ounce of bravery in my system to text him first the next day.

I was sitting in my car, parked mere minutes away from Duke University, waiting for my scholarship interview. Now, I'm not going to pretend like I didn't suspect they'd give me a shot when I first applied. I busted my ass for the perfect GPA all throughout high school for this specific reason, but I also knew better than to assume good grades would earn me a full ride. So, I used the only advantage I have, the only thing that could ever come *close* to making me stand out in this life—make me special.

My sister.

The admissions lady seemed particularly interested in Ashley's celebrity status over the phone, constantly bringing up Ash's wild success at such a young age.

Granted, I might've embellished the story a bit, including the part I play in Ashley's musical endeavors and the responsibilities I have "managing" her career. What can I say? I spent so much of high school playing personal assistant to my sister it left little time for extracurricular activities. You can bet I'm going to make the billion errands I've been running for the past six years count for something.

I skim over the messages Xav and I exchanged on Sunday. I figured I should change his name in my phone to Xavier after he had his tongue down my throat and branded me with the biggest hickey of all time.

Aveena: Hey. About yesterday, I'm sorry.

Thirty minutes later, he still hadn't replied, and I was growing worried that he never would.

Until my phone lit up with his answer.

Xavier: For?

Aveena: Running out on you like that.

Xavier: Don't apologize.

Aveena: I want to.

Xavier: You saved all of us from getting busted. If anything, I should be thanking you.

Aveena: Still. We were kind of in the middle of something.

Xavier: Fuck, Vee… Don't remind me. I'm getting a semi just thinking about it.

To say I didn't squeal like a pig at his admission would be a lie.

Xavier: What are you doing later? I need to see you.

Guess that settles the question of him regretting it.

My heart gave a jolt. I'd been obsessing over Xavier's skilled mouth, his tempting hands all over my body since the moment I'd fled Finn's mansion the day before.

Aveena: Ugh. I can't today. Just drove all the way to Duke for my scholarship interview. I'm so nervous.

Xavier: Don't be. You're going to kill it.

A question as obvious as it was unexpected popped into my brain. I'd never given much thought to the possibility of a future between Xav and I before, but now? I had to ask.

Aveena: What about you? Any schools in mind?

His reply made my smile that much wider.

Xavier: Hoping for a full ride at Duke, too. Rumor is, there'll be a scout at the next game.

Xavier: It's on Friday. You should come.

I couldn't picture it.

Not by any stretch of my imagination. Little old me showing up at every game from now on, cheering on the most popular guy in school from the stands, but I still let myself dream.

Buy into the fairy tale.

Aveena: I'd love to.

Then I spotted the time on my dashboard.

Aveena: Crap, I have to run. Wish me luck.

Xavier: Go get 'em.

We stopped texting after that.

Well, until now.

A new message from Xavier pops on my screen as I'm pulling into the school's parking lot.

Xavier: Fun fact about me: I fucking hate Mondays.

Xavier: Another fun fact about me: the thought of seeing you today makes me hate Mondays a little less.

You'd think I won the lottery judging by the dopey grin growing on my face. And, crazy enough, I think maybe *I did*? Sure feels an awful lot like I scored the guy of my dreams right now. Could it be… that things are finally going my way?

Tossing my phone into my opened backpack, I climb out of my car and head straight for the school's entrance. I wasted over ten minutes just sitting in my car and rereading Xavier's texts. I push the heavy glass doors open and waltz in, painfully clueless as to the nightmare awaiting me on the other side.

Everything seems normal at first.

The halls are lively, the students chatty.

I do notice teachers and school staff running around looking a bit distressed but don't overthink it.

Just another day at Easton.

I turn the corner and spot the thick crowd by the locker section. The hallway is crawling with what I'm sure is Easton High's entire student body. Kids are talking, laughing, whispering in each other's ears. I'm pushing to the tip of my toes, fishing around for a feasible explanation, when a tan hand wraps around my wrist.

"Vee, you're here." Dia materializes by my side. "Come on, you have *got* to see this." My best friend guides me through the masses, and my pulse accelerates when I spot Finn, Theo, Axel, and Xavier in the distance.

That's when I see it.

They're everywhere.

Printed by the thousands.

Stuck to each locker.

Covering every inch of the floors.

My darkest secrets.

Our darkest secrets.

I can feel the air thinning, my ability to speak dying on my tongue when Xavier and I lock eyes across the room, invisible strings tethering us together like chains. I must black out for a bit because by the time my brain reconnects with my body, Dia and I are part of the guys' circle, smack in the middle of the hysteria.

I can feel him staring at me.

I feel the weight of Xavier's gaze crushing my shoulders, every bone, every atom in my body imploring me to return his glances, but I can't bring myself to face him.

My confessions might not portray me in the best light, but *his* confessions, especially the one about his mom, could lead to criminal charges. They can't *ever* trace it back to Xav.

How is this even possible? We were so careful. Made sure to take the confessions out of the book as we went to prevent this exact situation.

"It's all everybody's talking about." Dia gestures to the pieces of my bleeding heart scattered all over school. "A bunch of anonymous confessions were found hidden in some book at the library."

That's not true, I want to scream.

They weren't found.

This is a setup!

I zero in on the copies dispersed down the hall. These are *pictures* of the sticky notes. It makes sense. The only way someone could have printed them out on such a massive scale was if they'd photographed each confession after we stashed them into the book.

But… *how*?

Was someone watching us this whole time? Lurking around the corner? Waiting for the right moment to get to the book? *Who could be so cruel?* That's when I notice the bold, black letters printed at the top of each copy.

WHO WROTE THE CONFESSIONS?
#FindZacAndLove

What. The. Hell?

As if it wasn't bad enough that they exposed our deepest, darkest secrets, now they want to expose *us*, too?

"Dude, check this one out." Axel elbows Finn, showing him one of our most painful memories.

"Man, I almost feel bad for this Zac fella." Finn guides his fist to his mouth to contain his laughter. "Guess the '*I fucked your mom*' jokes really do apply to him, huh?"

Axel and Theo burst out laughing. I feel so bad for Xavier. I can picture him standing there, taking his friends' slander like a champ, but I still lack the strength to look at him.

I just… can't.

"Guys, knock it off," Dia snaps, swiping the piece of paper from Axel's hands and crumpling it up into a ball. "That's an awful thing to do, air out someone's dirty laundry for the whole world to see. Fuck whoever did this."

"Maybe they should've thought of that before sharing their *dirty laundry* in a book anyone could find." Axel shrugs, picking another confession off the floor. "Someone's been a naughty girl."

"Let me see." Theo snatches the confession out of Axel's fingers to see for himself. "Damn, Love. Fucking your sister's boyfriend. Now that's *harsh*."

"What a whore," Axel sneers, ripping another sliver of my trauma off a random locker, and my stomach twists with shame. "Jesus, this is some dark shit," he chimes after reading the confession. "This one is about some guy offing himself."

I think I'm about to collapse for a second there.

The ground feels like it's caving in.

Slipping under my feet.

Tears start pooling in my eyes.

"I-I have to go the bathroom," I tell Dia, who's too busy scolding Axel for his latest remark to hear me, and spin on my heels, maneuvering around the crowd of gossipy students.

It feels like my world is ending at an excruciatingly slow pace. I'm watching my universe implode into a thousand fragments one frame at a time, leaving nothing but embers and destruction behind. I think I hear someone call my name, but I don't stop, making a beeline for the exit. I'm halfway to the door when a warm hand clamps around mine, holding me back.

"Aveena, wait!" a husky voice blurts.

I pivot to see Xav staring at me, blue eyes gleaming with a mix of rage and pain I've never seen before. I study the vicinity. Students of all grades are fully immersed in the confessions, passing the copies amongst themselves like it's Hollywood gossip.

Laughing at the absolute worst moments of my life.

No one is looking our way, not that Xavier seems to give a

flying fuck about people catching us holding hands. Seeing him standing there with his eyes full of regret…

I can't keep the floodgates closed any longer.

Yesterday, I was living a fairy tale. This morning, I was a girl who'd finally gotten the guts to kiss the guy she likes. A lone tear rolls down my cheek, and Xavier winces, dabbing the tear away with his thumb.

"Vee, I…" He opens his mouth to speak, his voice breaking, but no apology could ever make up for what's befallen us.

The damage is done.

We both know it.

So, I give him one last look, take back my hand, and do what I should've done from the first time he answered my letter…

Run.

Aveena

I was hoping the next few days would get easier.

Hint: *they didn't.*

I've barely stepped out of my room since I phoned my mom two days ago, faking the worst headache of my life. After I abandoned Xavier by the school exit, I drove myself home, turned off the lights *and* my phone, then crawled into bed.

I haven't left it since.

I couldn't bear the thought of opening social media and seeing mentions of our confessions all over my feed. I've spent the last forty-eight hours praying for this mess to miraculously go away. For people to stop talking about us, and move on to the next juicy gossip.

Problem is, in a town as small as Silver Springs, the "juicy" gossip is never *that* juicy. There's a fat chance any of them will top our dirty little secrets. I'm not senseless. I know there's no way Zac and Love will be ancient history by the time I go back to school, which will have to be soon, to my great misery.

I doubt Mom will buy the headache act much longer.

Reaching for my phone tucked away in my bottom drawer, I draw a long, shaky breath before turning it back on. The screen flashes white for a minute. Then it all comes rushing back—an unwelcomed reminder that just because I stopped living in the world doesn't mean it stopped turning.

I have five unopened messages from Xavier.

And six from Dia.

Xavier: Are you okay?

Xavier: Vee?

Xavier: Please talk to me.

Xavier: I'm so fucking sorry about what happened.

Xavier: Vee, at least tell me you're okay, I'm going crazy.

I tap out of the conversation without answering. Two days have passed and I *still* don't have it in me to face him.

Dia: Vee? What's going on?

Dia: Why haven't you been at school?

Dia: Are you ok?

Dia: Vee, please, call me back. I'm worried about you.

Dia: Look, I hate to tell you this over text, but people have been talking. I don't know what to think.

Dia: You should take a look at this.

Dia attached four screenshots.

I suspected the students at Easton would be curious about Zac and Love, but the images in front of my eyes call me blind.

Naïve.

This isn't healthy curiosity.

This is a witch hunt.

The first picture shows a recently created, private Facebook group called "WHO WROTE THE CONFESSIONS? #FindZacAndLove" with, believe it or not, two hundred and ninety-seven members.

What the…

That's like half the school.

There's also a Twitter account dedicated to anonymous tip-offs. Its username? @FindZacAndLoveTips. The third screenshot

Dia sent me displays a post in the Facebook group. It hoards speculations about Zac and Love's identities, lengthy paragraphs packed with insults detailing why we're the worst people on earth. Especially Love.

Well, *me.*

My throat tightens painfully as I skim over the comments.

"Love is such a whore. Think she's taking clients?"

"Backstabbing bitch. She should be ashamed of herself."

"Slut. No wonder someone close to her killed himself."

Don't cry.

They don't know the whole story.

They don't know you.

Names of potential candidates for Zac and Love keep piling up in the comment section, but none of them are accurate…

Except for one comment.

Brie's comment.

Brielle Randall: My money is on Aveena Harper for Love. Didn't her dad commit suicide? Also, anyone else notice she conveniently stopped showing up at school when the confessions came out? And why isn't she in this group? That's kind of suspicious. Just saying…

But the real horror? Her comment racked up a hundred and

sixty likes. The majority agrees. The third picture Dia sent me exposes other people's replies to Brie's accusation.

Theodore Cox: No way. Aveena would never do shit like sleep with her sister's boyfriend. Have you met her? She's as close as you can get to a saint.

Axel Fletcher: I wouldn't be surprised if she had tbh. Girl always came across like she was hungry for dick.

Finley Richards: @AxelFletcher, @BrielleRandall Will you two shut the fuck up? Aveena isn't Love.

Lacey Mattson: I'm with Brie on this one. Aveena's looking REAL shady here. Omg, can you imagine? Miss Goody Two Shoes screwing her sister's man? TEAAA.

Diamond Mitchell: @AxelFletcher You're a fucking pig. And @BrielleRandall, @LaceyMattson, the only reason Aveena isn't in this group is because she's at home RESTING. She's sick. Stop reaching.

I don't even get the chance to appreciate Dia sticking up for me before a hurricane of questions traps me in its eye. *How does Brie know about my dad?* Very few people at school know about that night. I was nine when it happened, years away from enrolling into Easton, and it's not like I went around school blabbing about my childhood trauma.

Did she look into me?

My phone chimes with a new text, snapping me back to reality. It's Dia again.

Dia: Vee, I have to ask... Is it true? Are you Love?

I wrestle with the idea of telling her for five minutes and come to the conclusion that I can't navigate this storm alone. I need to tell *someone.* And I can't think of a better person than my oldest friend.

Aveena: Yes, I am.

Dia starts typing out a reply immediately, and I cradle my knees against my chest, awaiting her answer.

"Vee?" A loud succession of knocks rattles my bedroom door. I recognize Ashley's voice. Mom isn't home yet, which is weird considering she's usually downstairs ordering dinner by now. She doesn't cook, remember?

"Yeah?" I yawn.

"You have a visitor."

What?

"Who is it?"

"A boy from your school," she says.

I sit up straight, my mind racing.

Xavier?

"Says he's here to drop off your homework," she adds.

What on earth is he doing here?

He *can't* be here.

Not when I look like I haven't slept in a century, am not wearing a bra *or* underwear under my pj's, my room is a condemned trash can, and my hair is a wet, tangled disaster from just getting out of the shower.

"T-tell him I don't feel like seeing anyone," I stammer.

My sister chortles on the other side, and my door opens a crack. Ashley pops her head into the small gap, a disconcerting smirk on her face, and says, "Tell him yourself." She nudges the door open fully, and I damn near yelp when I see him standing in the doorway.

My confidant.

My secret pen pal who's not a secret anymore.

Xavier. Fucking. Emery.

He ventures into my bedroom the next second, his tousled brown hair an intentionally perfect mess and his stunning eyes rimmed with dark circles. Even tired as shit, the boy puts Greek gods to shame.

He's wearing sweats and an opened zip-up hoodie over his basketball jersey, a sign that he came directly from practice. I peek at the time on my phone.

Wait…

He didn't come from practice.

He should be at practice *right now.* I would know. Dia's always talking my ears off about how impatient she is for Finn to sneak into her bedroom afterward. From where I'm standing, it looks like Xav got dressed, made it halfway to practice, then did a full 180.

Did he seriously ditch basketball practice to show up at my house? Knowing the most important game of his life is coming up on Friday? This game is his one-way ticket to Duke, for fuck's sake. Is he insane?

"I'll leave you to your *homework*," Ashley says with a smug grin, her voice crammed with innuendos, and closes the door.

As soon as her footsteps fade into oblivion, I spring off my bed, too irritated to mind my indecent outfit. Let's just say this tank top leaves very little to the imagination and my pierced nipples have been on high alert from the moment Xav walked into the room, but I couldn't care less.

Someone has to talk some sense into this dumbass.

"Are you crazy? What the hell are you doing here?" I scold him. "You should be at practice, getting ready for the game on Friday." I grip his forearm, attempting to drag his six-foot-three ass out the door.

If he leaves now, he can still make it.

He doesn't move an inch, cemented in place.

"Xav, you can't be here. You—"

"*Wrong*." He shuts me up. "Here is the only fucking place I should be." His voice is husky, tired, but his resolve is an impenetrable fortress. I know from his tone that he's made up his mind, and there's no changing it.

Shaking my head, I tug on his hand. "You have to go back. What about the scout coming to the gam—"

I don't get the chance to finish lecturing him before he's yanking on my hand and trapping me into his arms. I stop breathing instantly. I could barely breathe when he was just standing in front of me, so a hug?

I'd like white lilies at my funeral, thank you.

He smells infuriatingly good, and I sag into his embrace without realizing it. It's just a hug, but fuck, I could get used to this. I could get used to him, and it scares me shitless. He doesn't speak for long seconds, just hugging the hell out of me with his nose buried in the crook of my neck. His deep breathing prickles my skin, and shivers shoot down my spine like electricity.

There, in his arms, I finally feel them. All the emotions I've been repressing since I found our confessions hung to every locker in school. They claw their way back to the surface, ghosting my heart's desperate protests.

"I'm so fucking sorry, Vee, I…" Xavier whispers, his face nestled in my hair. "All the shit people are saying, the Facebook group, I… I can't fucking live with myself."

"It's fine," I lie, sinking my teeth into my bottom lip as a last resort not to cry. Truth is, no one is suspecting him, thanks to his unattainable guy persona. There wasn't even one mention of Xavier's name in the group. No one at Easton would ever *dream* of taking a jab at the Stallions' star player.

It's *me* people are targeting, *me* that people are tearing apart. My denial seems to trigger him because he draws back before taking my face with both hands, his grip almost bruising.

He presses his forehead to mine.

"Don't lie to me, Harper," he rasps.

With that said, I break down. Fifty bucks to any girl who can keep her walls up with Xavier's eyes piercing through her soul. Tears coat my cheeks, and I let it all in.

"Whore."

"Backstabbing bitch."

"Slut."

"No wonder he killed himself."

They're right.

They're all right.

"Who would do such a thing?" I crumble, eyes brimming with tears, and Xavier winces, the same way he did when he first saw me cry at school two days prior. He leads me back into his embrace, holding me closer.

Tighter.

"I don't know yet," he admits, never letting go. "But I'm going to find out. I promise, Vee. I'm going to make the son of a bitch pay, okay?"

I sniffle in response, bunching up the fabric of his hoodie between my fingers.

"Okay?" Xav urges.

"Okay," I barely say.

Takes me a few minutes to get the waterworks under control and peel my body off his. I'd stay there my whole life if he let me.

"So…" I dry my tear-slicked cheeks with the heel of my hand. "You bringing me my homework, huh?"

He smirks. "Only excuse I could think of."

"We don't even have a class together."

He shrugs. "Yeah, but she doesn't know that."

He draws a small laugh out of me.

A thick silence descends over us, and if this were any other conversation, any other guy, I'd hate this silence. Call it awkward. Uncomfortable. But with Xavier, it's…

Actually kind of *hot*?

For the first time since he burst into my room, Xav gives me a full body scan, drinking in my bloodshot eyes, wet pink hair, my pajamas shorts and the thin tank top putting my pierced nipples on display. Desire smolders in his eyes, and I'm positive our minds just traveled back to the hood of Mr. Richards's car.

The tension is so thick even the sharpest blade couldn't cut through it, and I feel the need to speak before one of us does something stupid like pick up where we left off.

Because we wouldn't want that, right?

Fine. Maybe I want to kiss him again—okay, maybe I want to do a *lot* more than kiss him, but I can't stop wondering where the confession debacle leaves us. Does he still see me the same way? Even with people saying all these things about me? With the world calling me a backstabbing slut?

If he were smart, he'd cut all ties with me. It's only a matter of times before people find out I'm Love. He should run while nobody suspects him. He can still save his future, his mom's reputation, and himself.

But he has to do it now.

"Is that why you came over?" I fail to clear the pit in my throat. "To apologize?"

Or to say goodbye?

"Why the fuck would I do that?" Xav shocks me by saying.

I can't speak.

"Aveena, why would I be saying goodbye?" he insists.

Damn it, Vee.

Ever heard of using your inside voice?

I open my mouth to speak, but nothing comes out. Xavier's eyes light up in understanding.

"Did you… Did you think I was going to *abandon you*?" He sounds pained by the very little faith I have in him. "Right when shit is hitting the fan?"

"It's just… You have an out," I explain. "They already think it's me, but you still have a chance to save yourse—"

Xavier lifts my chin up with his finger, letting our eyes meet. "Vee, do you remember the night we got pulled over?"

His question comes as surprise.

How could I forget?

Xav helped me navigate an anxiety attack, calmed me down in a way no one else could.

"Of course I do."

"So, you remember what I said to you? During your anxiety attack?" he questions. Events unravel before my eyes like a movie I've memorized scene by scene. I was hyperventilating. Xav grabbed my hand and said, "*I'm here, Vee. You're not alone.*"

I recall his reassuring words aloud.

Xav nods.

"I meant it then." He leans forward. "And I mean it now."

My heart swells in my chest, and I fill just enough of the space between us to tempt him. Our lips are inches apart, but I don't want to be the one to make the first move. Xavier's finger outlines the curve of my jaw before stopping at my mouth.

Breathe, damn it.

He looks like he's devouring me with his eyes.

But I want—*crave*—the real thing.

Still, I wait.

Until he proves he wants it just as much as I do.

Until I can taste his promises for myself.

"I'm never fucking deserting you, Harper." His voice is so low I can hear my own heart pounding. "Deal with it."

Then he crashes his lips against mine.

But Xavier Emery doesn't just kiss you.

Xavier Emery *owns* you.

I thought I'd feel more confident the second time around. I

thought I'd be more prepared having been there once with him, but his lips still taste like little drops of heaven, and I'm still a flustered, inexperienced girl from the moment his tongue slips into my mouth.

He's such a good kisser my knees fumble. His fingers fist my wet hair, taking all I have to offer, and I tug on his opened hoodie until the fabric skids down to the hardwood floor. He's only in his Stallions jersey now, and those bulging, basketball player arms…

Good Lord.

He's backing me up against my bedroom wall before I know it, grunting in my mouth when I suck his bottom lip between my teeth. Xavier slams his palm to the wall, right next to my head, and pries my legs apart with his knees, wedging his own leg between mine.

"I've been fantasizing—" Xav plants another rough, hungry kiss upon my lips. "—about this moment for days."

Me.

Fucking.

Too.

His lips trail to my neck again, his toned body towering over mine, but he's careful to avoid the already marked spot near my collarbone. I want to tell him not to give me another hickey, but the only sound that leaves my mouth when he starts nibbling on my sensitive skin is a surprised gasp.

My attention drifts to his knee lodged between my thighs. I

didn't bother throwing on underwear after stepping out of the shower, and right now? With the way Xavier's knee feels against my shorts? I think it may be one of the best decisions I've ever made.

Xavier's lips graze my earlobe, his knee shifting *right there*, and I let out a loud, mortifying moan at the friction. I'm shocked by the noise that just spilled out of my mouth. Appalled by the streak of pleasure tearing through my body.

I didn't even know it could react like that. Granted, I've never really been touched by a guy before. Logan couldn't have given less of a damn about giving back.

Xav immediately parts from me, and I'm so embarrassed by my loud moan I could cry. *Did I just turn him off?* Xavier seems confused at first. Until he glances down at his knee trapped between my legs, and realization fills his gaze.

Wait…

That wasn't even intentional?

Jesus, I don't even want to think about what it would feel like if he was actually trying. Xavier doesn't comment, the wicked smile on his lips informing me that he's pretty damn happy about this turn of events. His mouth slants over mine again, his knee teasing my clit with ten times more precision and determination. The feeling is… indescribable. Feels like too much and not enough all at once.

The pressure sends me to uncharted territories, and I flush, thinking about how ridiculous I must look. That's his knee, his fucking *knee*, and he's got me panting like I just ran a marathon.

"Fucking hell, Vee, you're killing me." Xav clenches his teeth, and I gaze downward, my breath hitching at the tent protruding from his pants.

He's straining against the fabric, and I mean *straining*. The thought of little old me doing this to him is an incomparable turn on. "Please say I can touch you," he growls, his breath flush with my cheek. "If you don't, I might die, I'm serious."

And I know he doesn't mean with his knee.

"Please." I'm the one begging now.

His fingers immediately snake down my stomach as I drop my head back against the wall, preparing myself for—

"*Oh, God.*" I can't keep quiet when he begins rubbing me through my shorts. Thanks to my commando situation, I feel everything. It takes Xavier little to no time to catch on, and I squirm when he slows down his strong circles.

"Shit, are you not wearing…"

Flustered, I shake my head.

His eyes pop open.

"Fuck this shit."

Xav yanks my shorts down to my ankles in one move, and I gasp. His hot mouth trails down my legs, kissing my thighs at a torturous pace.

Oh my… *I'm naked.*

Well, almost naked.

And somehow, I don't even care?

“Xavier,” I whimper, overly aware of how exposed I am, and Xav stops to stare at the sweet spot between my legs, chewing on his bottom lip. *Looks like waxing yesterday was a good move.* His mouth is back on mine in an instant, his fingers dropping to my center and rotating hard and fast against my clit.

If I’d known how talented Xavier Emery was with his fingers, I’d have told him who I was eons ago. His hand dips to my slit, and he pulls away an inch, staring me dead in the eyes to watch my expression as he slides a finger inside me.

My mouth falls open, my insides melting at the sustained eye contact. I’m guessing my face doesn’t disappoint because he smashes his lips back to mine with a groan, picking up the tempo as he adds his middle finger into the mix and starts finger-fucking me to another realm.

His thumb retreats to my clit at the same time, twirling it relentlessly and implanting a few concerns into my brain. *Serious question:* Can the human body sustain this much pleasure?

“So fucking wet.” He grunts inside my mouth, and I nearly fall apart. So, *that’s* what having intercourse with a guy who’s not a selfish scumbag feels like?

Lust pulsing through my veins, I drop my hand to his sweats and curve my fist around his length before I can second-guess myself. He sucks in a breath, his jaw clenching as he watches me palm him, squeeze him, jerk him off clumsily over his clothes.

I’m not courageous enough to sneak a hand inside his briefs and cross the line, but judging by the ecstasy fogging up his gaze, over-the-clothes action will do just fine.

Neither of us stop.

Or slow down.

The sight of Xav and me torturing each other, his fingers speeding in and out of me, his thumb stroking every single nerve in my clit, and my frankly awkward hand job, quickly become too much for me. Pressure explodes in my stomach, and my eyes roll back on their own.

Oh. My. God.

"Xav, I think I'm…"

His expression morphs with pleasure.

"Fuck, Vee. S-Stop," he grits out, his teeth chattering. "I can't come in my sweats."

I withdraw my hand without blinking, expecting him to remove his fingers as well, but he doesn't, his lips plastering hot kisses all over my neck as he doubles his efforts.

Then I hear the front door slam downstairs.

"Girls?" my mom shouts.

Shit.

Not again.

"Ashley?" she calls.

Xav and I trade glances, but my mom's arrival doesn't put him off for a second. On the contrary, he picks up the tempo, working my clit twice as fast.

"Aveena?" my mother yells from the kitchen. "Girls, I need your help with the groceries."

Footsteps.

She's approaching the stairs.

"Xav, she's close," I pant, certain he's going to admit defeat and sneak out my window before she catches us.

He doesn't budge.

If anything, his circles only grow rougher.

Then he smirks, guides his mouth to my ear, and whispers, "*So are you.*"

That's what sends me over the edge.

The feeling ignites in my toes, climbing up my legs in a flash. My orgasm is so intense I just *can't* keep quiet. Xavier instantly smacks his palm against my mouth as he continues to work my clit, which only makes my climax more intense. The second I stop shaking, my mother's footsteps roar up the stairs.

My room is closest to the staircase.

She's definitely coming to check on me first.

"Aveena?"

I'm. So. Dead.

Xav draws his fingers out of me, his parting gift a sharp thrust, and I respond with a full-body shudder.

"Hide," I mouth, my head foggy from coming so hard. Xav gives me a satisfied, cocky grin and throws the closet open before disappearing into a pile of clean clothes I didn't put away. I bend forward to pluck my shorts off the ground and stuff my legs into each hole. Xavier's barely shut my closet door when Mom waltzes into my room.

"Aveena, I've been calling you, did you not hear me?" Mom critiques as soon as she comes in. Here I am, with my back still pressed to the wall, my breathing erratic, and my shorts-covered thighs coated with my own arousal. I smile at her, acting like she didn't almost walk in on the captain of the basketball team getting me off.

"Is everything okay?" Mom worries. "Why are you breathing so hard?"

"Oh, I just… finished working out," I lie.

"Honey, that's great," she rejoices. "I assume that means your migraines have cleared up and you'll be going back to school tomorrow?"

Man, I didn't think this through.

"Sure." I cringe.

"Will you come help me with the groceries for dinner?"

"Of course." I pause. "Wait… you're not ordering in?"

Mom gives a shy smile. "Not tonight. I thought it'd be nice if we got together and cooked your dad's favorite. What do you think?"

Joy washes over me like a tide.

"I think that's a great idea, Mom. I'll be down in a minute."

"All right," Mom says and stops seconds before exiting the room. "Pick this up, will you? You know I hate when you leave your clothes on the floor."

I glance at the clothes she's referring to.

Xavier's black hoodie.

If she only knew.

My instinct when she jogs down the stairs is to laugh. Yes, *laugh.* I laugh at how surreal this situation is. Xavier just gave me the biggest orgasm of my life, then hid in my closet from my mom, and by some unknown miracle, we didn't get caught.

"Coast's clear," I inform him. "You're going to have to sneak out the back door when we're getting the groceries, though."

Xav stumbles out of my closet, a red top that fell on him while he was hiding amongst my clothes dangling down his shoulder.

"I think that belongs to you." He hands it to me.

"Thanks." I flush, tossing the tee onto my bed.

"Thanks?" Xav sports a sly smile. "I just hid into your closet like a ninja. I think that earns me more than *thanks*, Harper."

His hand knots around my wrist, and he jerks me closer for another deep, breathtaking kiss. It would be perfect if it weren't for the fact that we both can't stop smiling. It's not that easy making out while smiling like an idiot.

"I can't believe we just did that." I crack a giggle once we pull away, lacing my arms around his neck.

"Can't believe we didn't do it sooner," Xav replies, and I swat his arm, so happy my chest, my heart, my whole body hurts. I didn't know happiness could be this painful. Or… is it the prospect of *losing* said happiness?

"Go out with me tonight." Xav extends both arms around my waist. "I'll pick you up once everyone's passed out."

"Like a date?" I'm hesitant to ask.

"You're damn right like a date." He pecks the tip of my nose.

I inwardly swoon at the gesture and debate on sneaking out of the house in the middle of the night to meet the guy who wields the power to ruin me.

Sounds like a terrible idea.

"What time are you picking me up?"

Aveena

The springs used to be my favorite place in town.

It was the only place where I could breathe without the oxygen stalling in my lungs. The only place where I could just *be* without feeling like a fat man was sitting on my chest. The stream by the springs practically became my new home the weeks after my papa's funeral.

I'd sit on the grass for hours and listen to the water, the birds, and the quiet.

Mom didn't know what to do with me. She couldn't possibly comprehend why I'd flip my shit at the mention of driving back home. For a little while, visiting our spot helped me cope with the world continuing to spin without him.

Then I got sick of missing him, and it ruined our spot.

Like a song you listen to so much you eventually start to hate it.

Now I only ever come here on the anniversary of his death and visit him at the cemetery every few weeks.

When Xav's truck pulled up in front of my house at 1:00 a.m., I had no idea where he intended to take me for our "date." I was nervous It's hard not to be after he had his fingers deep inside me, but never in a million years would I have expected to wind up in the deserted parking lot by the springs.

Xav backed into a parking space in reverse to give us a clear shot of the water, grabbed a few blankets and pillows off the back seat and said, "You coming, Harper?"

We've been lying in the bed of Xavier's truck with the tailgate open, watching the sky, laughing and discussing everything but important matters for over an hour now.

We didn't bring up the confessions, or my reputation being dragged through the mud.

We've just been talking on a bed of blankets, munching on the three-week-old Jolly Ranchers Xav had lying around in his car. Pretending like the hunt for Zac and Love isn't still raging and the entire school isn't out to get us.

"Fucking clouds," Xavier huffs when the sea of stars above our heads disappear behind a thick layer of fog.

"Didn't check the weather for tonight, did we?" I tease.

A devilish smirk tugging at his lips, Xav whisks his head to look at me and sets my skin on fire with one question.

"You seriously think I was able to think about the *weather* after finger-fucking you against the wall?"

My cheeks heat up to intolerable degrees.

"So… Duke, huh?" I clear my throat, my sudden topic

change fueling the sexy smirk on his face. "I'm guessing that basketball scholarship is a lifelong dream of yours?"

"You bet." He shifts his attention back to the sky. "My pops and I have been talking about it since I was a five. Can't see myself doing anything else."

"I envy that," I confess. "Having a passion, a *purpose.* I wish I had one of those."

"You expect me to believe that the girl who knows *everything* doesn't know what to do with the rest of her life?" Xav taunts.

"I'm serious." I nudge him with my elbow. "I've never really had the chance to figure out what my thing was, you know?" My eyes widen. "Oh, God, what if I don't have a thing?"

Xav laughs a deep laugh that makes my pulse fall out of step.

"We all have a thing, Harper." He looks at me through the darkness. "Just takes some of us longer to find it."

I nod, a shy smile forming on my lips.

I want nothing more than to believe him.

"What about you?" Xavier revives the conversation. "What's the deal with your scholarship? I've seen your house, Vee. Your folks are clearly comfortable."

"Their money, not mine." I shrug. "I've known from the day we found out my sister could sing that I'd have to fend for myself."

"Ashley, is it?" Xavier asks.

I arch an eyebrow, questioning his knowledge of my sister's name. Xavier never even met Ashley. She was never at our play dates when we were kids, too busy getting yelled at by her singing coaches.

Xav never saw my dad, either. Curtis D'Amour would've preferred peeling off his own skin than attending a "Sunday brunch." He'd always stay back to train for his next race.

Xavier quickly picks up on my interrogations.

He grins. "I asked around about you. *Sue me.*"

My stomach flutters.

"Did you, now?" I chuckle. "Who'd you ask?"

"Theo." He scoffs. "Huge mistake, by the way. He just wouldn't shut up about your sister."

I half smile, and half cringe at the image of Ash and Theo devouring each other in Finn's bathtub. I have no idea how I feel about these two, not that it matters.

Even if something else *did* happen between them, it'd never be anything more than physical. There's no way Ashley will let Theo get close enough for anything real to sprout. Especially now that she's *this* close to leaving town with her manager Rob and taking over the music industry.

"That's her." I nod.

"Not to be too forward, but… isn't the whole point of having a famous sister that you don't have to worry about money?"

I snort out a laugh.

He sure doesn't know Esther Harper.

"In a normal family, maybe. *My* mom thinks it's pointless for me to get a job. If it were up to her, I'd stay Ashley's errand girl for the rest of my life."

Xavier cringes. "I take it this scholarship is your ticket to freedom, then?"

"Ding, ding, ding!" I confirm, and he laughs.

We don't speak again for a short moment, staring up at the sky and the million stars masked by dense clouds. If it weren't for the few lampposts casting light upon the area, we wouldn't be able to see shit. I feel calm. Peaceful. Until I sneak a peek in Xavier's direction, and guilt gnaws at me.

"There's something you should know," I feel compelled to say. He deserves the truth, to hell with the consequences.

His eyes jump to mine.

"I wasn't entirely honest with you before…" I need a breather to get a hold of my nerves. "I broke the pact. I figured out who you were long before we agreed to meet in Finn's bedroom."

Xavier sits up, his features darkened by shock and anger.

"You what?" he spits.

"I'm so sorry," I word vomit. "I know I should've told you, but it was an accident. I never meant to find out, I swear."

My apology doesn't ease his anger in the slightest.

"Xav, say something, please."

Stiff as a board, he inhales a long, steadying breath.

Then he dies laughing.

What the hell?

"I'm just fucking with you, Vee," he says, breathless from laughing too hard. "I've known for a while."

"What?" I blurt out. "*How*?"

"After I kissed you in Finn's garage, I started thinking of all the times your identity was right in my fucking face, and I realized you had to know. It was the only thing that made sense. Take senior prank night, for example, after we got stuck together. *Love*—" he uses air quotes, "—conveniently started asking me about the girl I was with. If she was pretty and if I liked her. You're probably the least subtle person on earth, Harper, you know that?"

"Says the guy who didn't figure it out until the last second!"

He laughs. "Hey, in my defense, you were misdirecting me left and right. Pretending like you didn't go to senior prank night to confuse me and shit. I still can't understand how you found out about me in the first place."

"Easy, I went to work."

His confused gaze flicks to me.

"I work at the school library." I elaborate.

"Shit, really?" He's stunned.

"Really."

"I'm guessing you saw me looking for the book, then?"

"No, my coworker did. I only work night-shifts," I explain. "She ended up telling me you showed up looking for a poetry book and, well… the rest is history."

He doesn't say another word for a few seconds, seemingly

lost in deep thoughts.

"What are you thinking about?" I question.

"I'm thinking you working at the library explains a lot. Like how you were able to answer my letters every single time."

"So, you're not mad?" I chew on my bottom lip. "About me breaking the pact?"

"Nah." He shrugs. "I told you some shit would happen and we'd find out without meaning to. And I was right, wasn't I?"

I nod.

Silence envelops us.

I seize the opportunity to sit up and undo the uncomfortably tight bun on top of my head. Xavier eyes me as I let my pink hair flow down my shoulders. I find myself assessing my surroundings for a moment. The tranquil stream and famous springs.

"Something wrong?" Xavier notices.

"No, it's just…" I exhale, embracing the nostalgia rather than dreading it. "My dad and I used to come here all the time."

Xavier's face crumbles.

"Your dad… He's the one you were talking about in your confession, isn't he?"

My heart squeezes in my chest.

"Yes, he is," I admit after a few seconds. "He killed himself when I was nine."

Xavier's skin pales. "I'm so fucking sorry, Vee. I had no idea. Do you want to leave?" His hot hand closes around mine, making me overly aware of how icy my hands are, but I wouldn't change a thing.

I want to stay here, in the empty parking lot next to the springs, with Xavier Emery holding my cold hand.

"Nah, this is perfect." I shake my head. "I didn't think I'd ever smile in this place again. Thanks for proving me wrong, dork."

"Don't call me that." He smothers a grin.

Xavier intertwines our fingers, squeezing my hand and lying flat on the bed of blankets. Except, he yanks on my hand to take me down with him and gestures to come closer with a flick of his chin.

My pulse shooting up, I rest my head on his torso, relishing in the sound of his beating heart and the delicious smell of his cologne. Xav stretches his arm out around my shoulders, hugging me to his chest.

"Do you regret it?" I ask the question that's been eating at me.

"Regret what?" He runs his fingers through my hair.

"The confessions. Love, Zac—*everything*."

"Honestly?"

A beat of silence.

"Yes."

I didn't expect the confirmation to hurt this much.

Of course he regrets it.

It could ruin his life.

I *could ruin his life.*

"I regret writing that fucking confession about my mom. If word gets out that I'm Zac, she could..." He can't bring himself to say it, but he doesn't need to. We're talking about possible jail time for Principal Emery if Xavier gets exposed. "Anyway, do *you* regret it?"

"I definitely regret not being more careful." I scoff a bitter laugh. "I keep thinking if we'd just kept an eye out, none of this would be happening and we—"

"Don't." He stops my spiraling. "It's not your fault. There's no way we could've known."

"It just doesn't make any sense! Whoever leaked the confessions had to know we were talking from the beginning. They had to follow us around like some crazy stalker. Learn our schedule to know when to access the book."

"Yeah, but that would mean they know exactly who we are," Xavier points out. "Why bother with this bullshit campaign to find Zac and Love instead of just outing us and being done with it?"

It hits me.

I look up at him. "To torture us, why else?"

"You think this is about revenge?" He meets my eyes.

"You got a better explanation, All Star?"

He nods, forced to admit I have a point.

"Let's say you're right. We still don't have any suspects."

"That's because we haven't looked for one. So... pissed

anyone off lately?"

Xavier smirks. "How much time you got?"

I laugh. "It can't be *that* bad."

"Well... let's see. There's the guy who slept with my mom. I made his life a pile of shit, *literally*. There's Lacey, who I slept with at my lowest point and completely ghosted."

The reminder cuts me to the bone.

I can't seem to wipe the disappointment off my face, severing the eye contact. I almost forgot for a minute there that Lacey has been with him... in that way. *He's an amazing fuck. I came four times.* Her bragging returns to my mind, and I flinch, pulling away.

Xav's arms grow tighter around my shoulders.

"Vee..." He winces in guilt, reading me loud and clear.

I anticipate an apology of some sort, but instead, he curses beneath his breath, flicks my chin up with one hand, and kisses the shit out of me.

It comes out of nowhere, but I immediately kiss him back, moving closer to him until my leg is sprawled over his body. I know damn well what this kiss entails. He's proving a point, and when he captures my face, sucking my bottom lip between his teeth, my skin morphs into a bundle of goose bumps.

Point made.

He doesn't care about Lacey.

He doesn't stop there, his hand darting to my leg draped across his stomach. He squeezes my thigh, marking my skin.

He's two seconds away from pulling me on top of him when I call him to order.

"Way to investigate, Emery," I mock.

"Fuck them, I'd rather investigate you." Xavier's lips are back on mine in a heartbeat, and I laugh through the kiss. I can't get enough, and it takes everything I have to withdraw.

"Xav, seriously. We need a suspect." I'm breathless with need.

"Fine." He pecks my mouth with a grin. "Only other person I can think of is Brie. I broke it off with her as soon as I realized I was a fucking idiot falling for his pen pal." He tucks a piece of hair that fell in front of my eye behind my ear. "Do we have any Jolly Ranchers left?"

I'm completely baffled, thrown off by his ability to change the topic as though he didn't drop a massive bombshell on me.

"What did you just say?" I'm staggered.

Xav arches an eyebrow. "Do we have any Jolly Ranchers left?"

"No, the other thing."

"I broke it off with Brie?" He plays dumb.

Irritated, I huff. "No, the other thing."

Xavier dazzles me with a stunning, boyish smile.

"Oh, you mean the part where I tell you I'm falling for you?"

My brain takes its sweet time deciphering the information.

Did that just happen?

I'm sure any other girl would be overjoyed to hear him say

that, euphoric at the thought of possessing Xavier Emery's heart.

But me?

I'm mad—*furious*, even. I stiffen up, detaching myself from him and sitting up in the bed of his truck.

"Don't do that," I warn.

His smile withers away.

"Do what?" Xavier frowns. "Tell the truth?"

"Xav, stop. It's not funny."

I need him to knock it off before he inflicts damage that can't be reversed. I'm afraid my heart wouldn't recover.

"Do you see me laughing?" he says with a straight face.

His obstinate behavior sets me off.

"I said stop!" I snap. "You can't just… say these things."

I jolt to my feet on an impulse and hop off the truck using the retractable tailgate step.

"Where are you going?" Xavier calls behind me, but I don't stop, walking with no specific direction in mind. All I know is I need to run the hell away from him before I make the mistake of believing him.

The whole town wants our heads on a pike, and here he is, digging himself in even deeper with me. Nobody suspects that he's Zac. That Xavier Emery could *ever* harbor secrets this dark. His untouchable, popular guy status has got him covered for now, but loving me will ruin him, get him exposed.

When they find out that I'm Love, and they *will*, I don't want him anywhere near the crossfire.

Footsteps erupt behind me.

He's following me.

"Why can't I say it?" Xavier hollers.

Shit, he's fast.

Stupid tall guy legs.

"Because you just can't, okay?" I blurt as I speed walk. "Not unless you—"

"Unless I mean it?" he finishes.

I swallow hard, willing myself to keep going.

I can still save him—I *have* to.

"What if I do mean it?" he shouts to my back.

I can't take another step.

Xavier, on the other hand, has no issue crossing the parking lot to reach me. He's barely a few steps behind me now, and my brain screams to escape, but it's as if my feet are embedded into ice blocks.

"What if you're the only thing that makes sense anymore?" He sounds pained, broken. "What if, when everything went to shit, all I could think about was making sure you were okay?" I hear him step forward but don't turn around. "What if I've never felt this way about anyone in my entire fucking life, Vee?"

I yelp when he grabs my arm and spins me around to face him. He doesn't waste a single second taking my face into his hands, aligning his gaze with mine as he whispers, "*Can I say it then?*"

A river of tears pools in my eyes, and anger overrides the warmth welling in my chest. I push him off me and slap him with a strength I didn't even know I had.

Xav stumbles back in shock, his jaw locked and his cheek a deep shade of red. Guilt and regret crush me, but I still bleat, "I told you not to go there!"

Xavier feels his jaw with a wince.

Then he steps closer, towering over me like I didn't just swing at him two seconds prior.

"Well, that's too fucking bad… Because I think I'm—"

"Don't you dare!" I bark.

"I think I'm falling in love with you, Aveena Harper."

My mouth falls open.

Instantly, my hand goes flying, but this time, Xav anticipates the slap, snatching my wrist midair and jerking me to his chest without batting an eye. Neither of us move, or speak, for several seconds. We stare at each other in the dark, quiet parking lot like it's a staring contest.

Then Xavier's lips rain down on mine.

And I come undone.

No better way to put it.

I fall apart in every way that matters, bombarded with the million emotions I've been covering up with anger. Desire, the fear of destroying his shiny little future… Love.

God, I love him.

My childhood bully turned pen pal. The only guy I've opened

up to since the day I lost my dad. I'm in *love* with him, and right now, I want to let myself love him.

Dropping the act, I push to my tiptoes and grasp at his branded clothes like a lifeline. I kiss him back with an unmatched intensity, and Xavier groans in satisfaction. I open for him, allowing his tongue to find mine, and slam our bodies together, my hips flush with his. Xav grunts at my clear intentions, looping his hands around the back of my thighs.

He lifts me up into his arms without breaking a sweat. I can feel his length trying to burst out of his pants as he carries me back to the truck, his palms gripping my ass firmly.

I just about gasp when he throws me into the bed of his truck and hoists himself up on top of me. Xavier's mouth clashes back with mine as soon as he's got me pinned down under him. He tastes like cherry Jolly Ranchers, bad decisions, and a vulnerability I could spend my whole life trying to outrun.

His fingers curl at the hem of my cropped sweater top, and he stops, disconnecting from me. His fiery gaze fused to mine, he expels a low "Tell me you want this."

My consent is immediate.

"I want *you*." My voice breaks.

Xav grins wickedly, squeezing my throat and granting my wish as his experienced mouth collides with mine. Every last drop of fear is drained out of my system when he jerks my sweater over my head and tosses it to the side.

His blue eyes rake down my body with a yearning so carnal

it's enough to make a girl dizzy. Xavier takes it all in, my bare stomach, my thin bra highlighting my pierced, puckered nipples, although I doubt he can see much in the darkness of the parking lot.

Wait, we're still in a parking lot.

My eyes pop open.

"Xav, s-someone could see us," I remind him, strangely aroused by the possibility of getting caught.

His deep, careless laugh makes me tingle everywhere. "*So*?"

I'm about to argue when he yanks my bralette down my chest, the sound of tearing fabric drawing a gasp out of me. I don't get a chance to scold him for ruining my clothes before his mouth latches onto my sensitive nipples one by one, his big hands cupping each of my breasts as he gets down to business.

I can't help moaning at the sensation of his tongue teasing my barbell piercings. Xavier works my painfully stiff nipples until I'm clenching my thighs together, needing more of that love *downstairs.*

You'd think I said it out loud by how fast his lips snake down my stomach, planting slow, torturous kisses all over my skin. Shy Aveena threatens to come out when he hooks his fingers into the waistband of my leggings, tugging them down my legs in a haste and exposing my lilac panties.

It's one thing to have him finger me, it's another to have him bury his face in my slit. No guy has ever been this close to me. Not even Logan.

I swallow hard.

Xavier catches on immediately.

"Are you okay?" he asks. "I can stop."

His voice is thick with need, repressed urges, but I know he means it, no matter how lustful he is.

"Don't," I reassure him and myself. "I want this."

Xavier smiles like the beautiful little devil that he is and slides my underwear off before jerking my thighs apart. He spreads my legs as far and wide as they go and I see him trap his bottom lip between his teeth at the close-up.

Then he goes to town.

Xavier eats me out like a starving man enjoying his last meal. His persistent tongue twirls around my clit. Fast. Slow. *Fast again.* This is nothing like I'd imagined. It's better. My head falls back when his palms slink under me. He grips my ass, sucking my clit into his mouth so hard my back arches off the truck.

Good God, did he take a class or something?

I take a fistful of his hair. One more flick of my clit and I forget all about the possibility of someone pulling into the lot and catching us. Because he's determined to rob me of my sanity, Xav comes to the conclusion that his tongue isn't enough.

I'm so wet he easily slides two fingers inside me, and grunts in appreciation when a moan trickles from my lips. His fingers curling in and out of me, and the pressure of his tongue combined are unbearable. I've never experienced this kind of ecstasy in my life, and I'm almost *embarrassed* by how fast I start to shake. How fast my eyes roll back.

I squeeze my thighs together to prevent my unraveling, crushing Xav's head, and he responds by forcing my legs apart again and continuing to finger-fuck me to high heaven.

"We're not done, Harper," he says in a gruff voice and presses his mouth back to my center. I'm at his mercy. Defenseless, but it's his tongue that disarms me completely.

His fast, powerful strokes.

My orgasm pours over me like sheeting rain, and my hips buck as I finally accept my fate and the heart-stopping pleasure that comes with it. I know there is no silencing my moans when I reach the pinnacle.

I have no words.

Except maybe "*Fuck*."

Xavier gives me a moment to catch my breath before climbing back up my body and tearing me apart with a kiss that tastes like me. His erection presses up against me, and I find injustice in the amount of clothes he's wearing while I'm butt naked in a public parking lot.

I'm hauling his T-shirt over his head before I know it. My fingers mold his smooth skin, his pecs, his shoulders, his six-pack. I drag slow kisses across his muscled chest and realize I want to kiss an entirely *different* part of him.

I surprise Xav by spinning us around and kneeling by his side. I unbuckle his belt so fast he can barely keep up.

"Vee…" he whispers when I yank his pants down his lap. He's only in his briefs now, and I'm quick to remove them to even the score. His length bobs between us, thick and hard, and I try my best not to gawk.

Not my fault he's much bigger than Logan.

Not nearly as confident as I look, I settle between his legs and grab him at the base, gazing up at him through my eyelashes.

"Jesus Christ, Vee." He clenches his teeth. "Don't look at me like that, I'm going to blow."

I blink at him, stunned.

"But I haven't even touched you."

"I know." He groans in annoyance, and I understand he's the one embarrassed now. The thought of him being unable to contain himself drives me wild.

I want more control over him.

More of that look on his face.

I set out on a quest to torture him and lean forward until my mouth is inches away from his tip, and his fists roll up into white-knuckled balls. I stick my tongue out to test the waters and wrap my lips around the head of his cock. I haven't even started sucking when he snaps.

"*Nope, I can't.*"

He's on top of me before I can blink, his hot, straining flesh throbbing between my legs.

"Why did you do that?"

"I can't come before I feel you." The desperation in his voice tangles me up in a whirlwind of emotions. I rope him closer to me, needing to feel him as much—*if not more*—than he does me. I inhale a big gust of air, unable to wrap my mind about what's about to happen, and rub myself up against him, allowing my body to do the talking.

"Wait," Xav grits out, like he hates himself for saying it, and grabs his pants next to us. He plucks something out of his pocket.

A condom.

I don't let it bother me. At least, *I try*. I would've brought up protection myself if he hadn't. So, he carries condoms everywhere he goes. What else did I expect from the captain of the basketball team?

His mouth finds mine as soon as he's sheathed himself, and he positions his size at my entrance, twisting my rose-gold hair around his fist. He's mere seconds away from filling me when it hits me.

We're about to have sex.

Me.

Xavier.

Sex.

This is a big deal.

We can't do this unless we're on the same page.

"Xav…" I yelp, and he plunges his gaze into mine, cupping my face with his hand and running his thumb across my lower lip. "No going back," I croak through the pit in my throat.

Catching my drift, Xav kisses the breath out of me before murmuring into my mouth. "*Never.*"

Pretty sure I go blind when he thrusts into me. It's just for a second, but it heightens all of my senses. He's big—*duh*, I knew that just by looking at him, but feeling him stretch me to the limit is enough to cut off my air supply.

I dig my nails into his back, my parted lips and widened eyes making his jaw flex. Pure bliss spreads over his face, and when he inches himself deeper inside me, we gasp in harmony.

Xavier stills himself, burying his face in my neck.

"Fuck, baby." He breathes heavily. "Stop clenching."

"I'm not," I whimper between moans. He hasn't moved since he pushed inside me, and I have a feeling the sting cutting through my stomach won't dissolve until he does. Xav pulls back, his eyes growing in size as he soaks up in realization.

Disbelief floods his gaze.

"Fucking hell, Vee… You're so…" He hisses, all the more annoyed with himself. "I'm going to last five fucking seconds."

"Best five seconds of my life," I assure him, and he laughs, kissing me so deeply I actually *do* clench around him. "Move. Please," I beg against his lips, his size too much to handle. He sucks my bottom lip into his mouth and thrusts into me once.

Twice.

Picking up speed each time.

Until he's full on fucking the pain out of me.

My insides liquefy at the uninterrupted eye contact. We both have our mouths open, entirely consumed by this moment, the unreal connection between us, the heavenly friction of our bodies slamming together.

I can't seem to do *anything* but moan as his slow thrusting gradually becomes faster. But it's when he slings my right leg over his shoulder and starts pounding into me with all he has that I go from discreet moaning to…

Let's just say I cover my own mouth.

My eyes shutter closed, but Xav isn't having it. He rips my hand off my mouth without a care, demanding the liberation of my raw moans and grabbing my throat as he fucks me harder.

"Look at me," he grits out, inches away from my face.

I'm shocked by how turned on I am by his dominant side and cry out in delight when his thumb drops to my clit, swirling it in rough circles as he rams himself inside me without restraint.

Then a drop of water trickles down his beautiful face. We're both sweaty, horny animals at this point, but this… it's not sweat.

It's rain.

"Are you shitting me?" A laugh slips past Xavier's lips when a second raindrop rolls down his shoulder.

"That's what happens when you don't check the weather, hotshot," I tease in between gasps, and he flashes a smug grin, crashing his mouth back to mine.

The light drizzle evolves into pouring rain in a matter of minutes, but Xav pays Mother Nature no mind, never slowing down his vigorous thrusting.

Xavier's slick brown hair drips down his forehead as our slippery bodies rock against one another. Our tongues join the moment thunder roars in the distance, almost in perfect timing with the electricity stirring in my toes. I bite down on my lip, drawing a pinch of blood and preparing myself for the mind-blowing orgasm creeping up my legs.

Xav shields me from the downpour with his body, twirling my clit with such relentlessness that I fall victim to the heat in my lower stomach.

"X-Xavier," I moan, clawing at his back.

"Fuck, say that again," he growls, flexing his hips into me over and over. I'm convulsing beneath him when my back rises off the bed of his truck.

"*Xavier*!" I cry out when my climax reaches its apex. And I'm not alone. Xav clamps his eyes shut, his reckless pounding becoming jerky, uneven. Knowing he's about to unload, I do precisely what he told me *not* to do.

I clench him.

I pour all I have into it, contracting around him until I have him right where I want him. His clear blue eyes snap open, his jaw flexing as he calls *my* name, his hot, damp body shuddering with spasms. He spills inside the latex a second later, drawing out this precious moment for as long as he possibly can.

We're completely soaked now, two lovesick kids naked in the rain. The second we reconnect with reality, our eyes lock and this paralyzing fear wraps me up. It was perfect.

We were perfect.

So perfect it's almost troubling.

I let Xavier Emery go down on me, then fuck me in the bed of his truck in the middle of the night in a public parking lot. I gave him the best of me tonight without the slightest concern as to what *tomorrow* would look like.

And it terrifies me.

As though my emotions are stamped across my forehead, Xav tilts my chin up, smacks a thousandth kiss on my lips, and looks into my eyes so deeply I wonder if he can see my walls disintegrating.

"No going back, Harper," he rasps, recycling my line.

All my doubts and worries vanish into thin air.

My heart swelling in my chest, I kiss him again, clutch his face and manage a shaky "*Never.*"

Aveena

Aveena: Hey, are you okay? You weren't at school.

Wednesday

Aveena: Xavier?

Wednesday

Aveena: It's been two days. I'm worried about you.

Thursday

Aveena: Are you mad at me or something?

Thursday

Did you know it was possible to be irritated by your own breathing? To feel so irked, so aggravated by the faintest sound you wish you could turn it all off?

Just for a moment?

A second?

I didn't.

Didn't know how painful silence could be until silence was all I had left. My life's full of it lately. It's roaming the halls, bouncing off the ceilings, lurking at every corner.

Reminding me of what I want to hear.

Like my phone buzzing with a reply from Xav.

Slumping against the couch and resting my phone on my lap, I contemplate how *awful* the past two days have been. Whispers and laughter have been shadowing me down the halls since I stepped foot into Easton on Wednesday morning.

I knew people suspected me of being Love by Brie's comment in the **"Find Zac and Love"** group, which I had to join to alleviate suspicions, but I was far from prepared to become the school's pariah.

Only people who deign talk to me anymore are Dia and the guys. I still eat lunch with the jocks, and while Finn and Theo turned out to be very supportive, Axel and Lacey are more than happy to test the shit out of me.

They keep trying to get a rise out of me by bringing up my dad's suicide and how I slept with my sister's man to see if they can get me to flinch.

Cry.

Get mad.

Anything.

They want nothing more than to see me break, and it's taken superhuman strength for me not to bat an eye at their cruel "jokes." Thankfully, that's as far as it's gone. No one's had the guts to confront me about the rumors yet.

I heard Finn and Theo asking each other what the fuck was up with Xavier once or twice. They haven't heard from him in a while either, but I can't rid myself of the pit in my stomach. This gnawing voice in my head telling me the world is about to end.

If it hasn't already.

The day after I gave Xav all of me, Dia came by my house with two pounds of pistachio ice cream, asking for an explanation, and I bared my heart to her.

Told her about the confessions and pretended I didn't even know who Zac was myself. That's not my secret to tell. I cried, she cried. Then I told her I slept with Xavier, and she freaked out, squealing that she knew something was going on between us since the night he gave me a ride.

She swore on her dads' lives that she wouldn't tell a soul about my secret identity, and I believe her. She also tried reassuring me about Xavier's disappearing act. Said he had to have a good reason since he's also been ghosting his friends.

As much as I'd love to believe her, his silence doesn't sit right with me. My messages all bare the dreaded "**Read**" receipt.

He saw my texts…

He's *choosing* not to answer me.

I'm scrolling through the private group, that gained over a hundred new members this week alone, with a cringe when my phone buzzes with a new text.

My hopes crash and burn at the sender.

Dia.

Dia: WHAT THE FUCK? HAVE YOU SEEN THIS?

I notice she attached the URL to an Instagram post, and anxiety blankets me from head to toe. I'm convinced the picture on the other side is going to wreck me before I've even clicked the link. Emptying my lungs with one exhale, I tap the URL.

Then I die inside.

The link displays Brie's new Instagram picture.

Xavier is there.

Sitting on Finn's couch in a dark T-shirt, his muscled, bulging arms knotted around Brie's waist. Dia said the gang was meeting up at Finn's tonight, but she couldn't make it. He's painfully gorgeous. With his natural tan, light brown hair slicked back, his square, masculine jaw sharper than a knife. He's like a beautiful dream I never saw coming.

But boy, did I notice when he left.

Brie is sitting on his lap in a white skirt and pink tube top, her arms wrapped around his neck as they lose themselves into a deep, passionate kiss.

They look so happy.

So… *in love.*

My gaze travels to the caption below Brie's post, and my heart cracks open at the four little words on my screen.

"Back where he belongs."

* * *

By the time Friday rolls around, I'm over it.

Over *him.*

Well… kind of.

Fine, I'm lying, but I didn't lash out and burn down his house yet, so I'd say… all things considered… I'm doing fairly well. I spent all night after seeing Brie's Instagram picture wallowing in bed, trying not to cry until I was in physical pain, but I didn't text Xavier once.

Didn't curse him out.

Didn't tell him I never should've trusted him.

Don't get me wrong, *I want to.*

I've been itching to call him a heartless monster, but confronting him would make me seem weak. Show him how much I cared. How much he hurt me. And I promised myself I'd *never* let myself be this vulnerable again after my dad. I've lived through a hell of a lot worse than the captain of the basketball team sleeping with me, then going back to his ex.

Who cares that he said he loved me in a scene worthy of a romance movie?

I'm okay.

Really.

I don't care.

Did I mention I'm okay?

"Vee, open the door. My hands are full," Dia requests from outside my bedroom, and I drag myself out of bed to let her in.

A smiling Dia stands in my doorway, a mountain of unhealthy snacks huddled up in her arms. She insisted we have a slumber party after tonight's basketball game, more than willing to skip the party at Theo's place.

Translation: she's worried about me.

"That was quick." I give a small chuckle as we plop down onto my bed. "Did you fly here?"

"Came as soon as the game ended." Dia laughs, snatching a bag of Jolly Ranchers off the pile and tearing the bag open. I wince at her flavor or choice.

Cherry.

You better not have ruined Jolly Ranchers for me, asshole.

Dia props her head against the decorative pillow on my bed and sighs. "The game was a fucking disaster. Xav-the-scumbag played like shit all first half."

I grin at her new nickname for him. Got to love the best friend solidarity.

"No, you know what? Saying he played like shit would be an insult to shit. I don't know what the hell was up with him. Good thing Finn came through. He carried the game on his back."

There was a scout from Duke in the crowd.

Did Xavier blow his chance?

"What about the second half? Did Xav recover?" I ask, more

curious than I can bear. I hate myself for giving a damn.

"I'm guessing Coach Diaz threatened to make him swallow his balls or something because he killed the second half. He ended up scoring the winning shot."

Thank God.

Did I just think that? What part doesn't register, heart? We hate him now. *Catch up.*

Dia nibbles at her lip when she takes a good look at me, her expression morphing into a mix of guilt and pity.

"Shit, Vee, I'm such an idiot. Going on about that crap bag after what he did to you, I'm sorry."

"What are you talking about? I'm fine." I'm shocked by the weak, broken sound coming out of my mouth. I freeze when I taste something salty.

Wait…

Am I crying?

"Come here." Dia sits up, opening her arms for a hug.

"I'm fine, I promise." I shake my head, rejecting her embrace.

"Vee." She arches an eyebrow.

"I-I'm fine." I'm sobbing now.

What. The. Fuck.

It's like my brain and heart are in disagreement, battling each other to death. My brain screams that I shouldn't care about Xav, but my heart is a pain in the ass I wish I could unfriend on all socials.

Dia ignores my miserable attempts at keeping a straight face and wraps me into a hug so tight I feel myself crumble to pieces. Neither of us say a word for the next two minutes. Dia just lets me cry in her arms the way she once did in mine, and I toss my pride to the side, admitting what I've known from the start.

He broke me.

I opened up to him, and he broke me.

For fuck's sake, I *slept* with him. I fell for his lies like one of his brainless groupies. And the worst part is, when he said he loved me… I believed him.

"Please tell me you talked to him," Dia whispers.

"What's the point?" I sniffle, pulling away and sweeping the tears off my cheeks. "Brie's picture told me everything I need to know."

"Fuck Brie! He slept with you and told you he loved you when he never said it to Brie *once* in a whole fucking year of dating!"

I blink at her. "How do you know that?"

"Lacey has a big mouth." Dia holds her hands up, and I smile. "This is fucked up, Vee. You can't let him disrespect you like that."

I don't reply, her words laying the foundations of an uprising in me, and grab my phone. I log on to Instagram, type Brie's name into the search bar, and click on her story.

The two first stories are videos of Theo's party. A game of beer pong and a Boomerang of Lacey and Brie downing shots.

But the third slide…

It shows a video of Xavier and Brie making out in the pool with "Bitter" by Fletcher and Kito booming in the background.

I'm bitter, all right.

I replay the video. Brie is smiling wide as she smashes her lips to Xav's, clasping his wet hair with her manicured hand. The clip cuts too soon to tell if he responds to the kiss, but I have no doubt he most likely kissed the breath out of her the next second.

Bastard chose her for a reason.

"*Vomit*," Dia comments, and I jump, twisting my neck to see her staring at Brielle's story over my shoulder. "What's the plan?" she questions. "Mission Movie or Mission Fuckboy?"

I pause.

She had it right the first time.

I inhale a deep breath and rise off my bed.

"Let's go."

* * *

"I can't do this." I sag into my driver's seat, assessing Theo's house across the street. Dia and I have been sitting in my car for twenty minutes now. Throwing on a dress, doing my makeup, and driving to the party was the easy part.

It's getting out of the car that's hard.

"Yes, you can. Worst-case scenario, he's the piece of shit you thought he was and you never have to speak to his clown ass again." Dia unbuckles my seat belt for me. "*On three.*"

She has to restart the countdown five times before I agree to drag myself out of the car. Dia tangles her arm with mine as we walk to the door, and I muster a grateful smile.

We're bursting into Theo's kitchen uninvited ten seconds later. The party is at its height, the house crawling with drunk, judgmental kids. All eyes are on me from the moment we amble past the threshold.

I'm almost thankful for the deafening music.

The loud bass.

The hammering beat.

This way, I don't hear the whispers, the laughs, the nasty names and insults following me everywhere I go. *"Whore," "Bitch," "Boyfriend thief,"* just to name a few. I pretend like I don't notice the glares pointed at me, cruising through the crowd with Dia on my arm. We've barely stepped foot into the living room when a masculine voice yells my best friend's name.

I flip my head to the left, and sure enough, Finn is tearing through the crowd to reach his girl. His yelling earns us the attention of most people in the living room.

Thanks, Finn.

"Missed me already?" He flashes a dimpled smirk, and Dia releases my arm. Finn's lips descend over hers in a split second, and Dia stumbles back, gripping his collar for balance. "I thought you said you weren't coming," Finn rasps against her mouth.

"I-I'm not staying." She clears her throat, backing away. "Vee needs to speak with Xavier. If you could just…"

Finn nods in understanding, and his eyes flick to me. He offers me an apologetic smile that reeks of pity and spins on his axis.

"The fuck you all looking at?" he barks at the nosey party people, and they quickly disperse into the crowd. Must be nice having the whole world either love or fear you.

"Where's Xavier?" Dia asks in my place. I seriously don't know what I'd do without her.

"Over there." Finn gestures with his chin.

I spot him instantly.

He's sitting on Theo's leather couch with Brie, Lacey, Axel, and Theo. He's got his arm tied around Brie's neck, his hair still damp from the pool, but he's all dressed now. Lacey and Brie are giggling, whispering into each other's ears as they stare at us.

At *me.*

Meanwhile, Theo pities me, and Xavier stares blankly at me.

Like I'm see-through.

An old, broken toy he swapped out for a newer model.

"Come on." Dia tugs on my forearm, but I stiffen up.

"D, let's just go. This was a mistake." I choke out.

"The only mistake here is his lying-ass. Time for the truth." Dia drags me toward the couch, while Finn trails after his girl friend, *notice the space.* I wish the ground would swallow me whole when Dia comes to a stop before the couch. I can barely look at Xavier, let alone talk to him. Theo shocks me by speaking up.

"Looking good, Vee."

I search for a hint of sarcasm in his voice, but weirdly enough, he seems genuine.

"Uh… thanks." I fidget with the hem of my dress.

I usually don't do dresses—like ever. But Dia convinced me that looking great would make me *feel* great, and I was dumb enough to let her pick my outfit. This dress shows way more cleavage and legs than I'm comfortable with.

"He's right. Nice dress," Finn chimes in.

I'm well aware they're pity compliments, but I'll take the confidence boost.

"Thanks." I crack a shy smile.

"Dia." Brie changes the subject. "How nice of you to join us. Although… you probably should've let the trash outside."

Believe it or not, it's not the insult that hurts.

It's his laugh.

Xavier actually *laughs* at his girlfriend ripping me apart.

As though he wasn't kissing me in the rain three days ago.

As though we haven't been talking nonstop for months.

As though I never ripped a part of my soul and gave it to him.

"Shut the fuck up, Brie," Dia snaps. "Tell him, Vee." My best friend elbows me, and I feel like an embarrassed kid at recess about to confess her crush.

I look Xavier dead in the eyes, ready to call him out on his bullshit, but no words come out.

"I…"

Brie and Lacey laugh, enjoying every bit of my struggle.

"Something wrong, Aveena? Why don't you go cry to Zac about it?" Brie mocks, her words piercing my flesh like a hot poker. I can't help glancing at Xavier. Not because I expect him to defend me, but because *he's* Zac. He's just as responsible for the confession debacle as I am.

Yet… Here he is.

Laughing with them.

"Oh, I'm sorry, are we still pretending like you're not Love?" Brie cackles.

Dia swoops in with a change of subject. "Get your ass off the couch, Emery. Vee needs to talk to you."

"Careful, Dia," Brie warns. "Girl betrayed her own sister. What's to say she won't steal *your* boyfriend, next? Oh, wait, that's right. You don't have the title. Must suck. Being good enough to fuck but not to date."

Finn's fists roll into firm balls. "Brie, you say one more fucking word—"

"Xavier. Talk. Now," Dia presses.

Xav rolls his eyes.

"Jesus Christ, fine," he huffs and pushes to his feet.

Ouch.

Dia shoots me an encouraging look, and I lead the way to an

isolated corner by the bathroom. Xavier's tall frame towers over me, his face an emotionless blank.

"What do you want?" he drawls.

Who is this guy?

Where did my pen pal go?

"Why?" I barely say.

"Why what?" He scans the area as if to find something worthy of his attention.

"Why did you sleep with me? If you knew you were going to go back to Brie."

"I didn't know I was going to get back with Brie. It just happened." He tops it off with a shrug.

"And you couldn't tell me that yourself?" I want to sound angry, but my pain melts through every word. "I had to find out on Instagram?"

"I did tell you, kind of. If you want to get technical about it, I *wrote* you. Left you another confession in the book. I was hoping you'd take the hint." He cringes. "Clearly, I was wrong."

He won't even spare me a look as he talks, drilling his focus into everything in the room but me.

"Gee, forgive me for expecting a text."

Xav sighs, driving a hand through his wet hair. "Look, it was fun, but I warned you I lost interest after sex. You can't honestly tell me you didn't see this coming."

Flashes of his confession way back then pop into my brain. He's right. He *did* tell me from the start.

"And what you said…" I croak. "About loving me? It was all bullshit? You didn't mean it?"

That's Xavier's cue to finish me off.

"I did until I pulled out."

There's a hemorrhage where my heart used to be now.

And I can't stop the bleeding.

I slap him for the third time in a matter of weeks. Difference is, this slap emanates from a place of hate. Xavier seems unfazed, his eyes still set on something in the distance.

"Go to hell," I hiss before booking it to the door.

Once upon a time, I had a dream the boy with the pretty blue eyes chose the nerd over the cheerleader…

Then I woke up.

* * *

I'm on my knees in aisle six less than thirty minutes later.

I drove straight to the library after Xavier mentioned his confession. Had to feed Dia some excuse about having forgotten something at work and left her waiting in the car. Thank God I can sneak into the library whenever I want. There's no way I could've survived waiting until tomorrow.

On edge, I yank the poetry book off the shelf and flip through the pages until I find it.

The confession.

Strangely, the sticky note isn't what catches my eye.

It's the name of the poem above it.

I had no time to hate.

I analyzed this very poem in my paper for Ms. Callahan's class. The whole poem basically revolves around how "hating" is a royal waste of time. Emily Dickinson, the author, inspires the reader to live a life full of love because said life is too short. There's a cruel irony to Xavier leaving his confession on this specific page.

Why?

Because it says the opposite.

Aveena

A week has gone by since Xavier carved my heart out of my chest, tossed it in the wringer, and smeared it all over the sidewalk. I've spent the last seven days thinking it would all blow over. That kids at school would eventually grow bored of the Zac and Love drama.

I was wrong.

Every time I think I've hit rock bottom…

I keep falling.

I knew it was just starting when I was removed from the **"Find Zac and Love"** Facebook group by the admin. I guess they weren't comfortable with Love witnessing their savage bullying up close.

Whispers I could handle. I could even accept the name-calling, but the cheer squad opting for a more direct approach… that I *can't* handle. Brie and her bimbos have been having a field day making my life a living hell.

Tripping me in the halls.

Slipping nasty notes into my locker.

Slapping my books out of my hands.

Any petty, mean-girl shit you can think of, they've done.

It's like middle school all over again.

Dia assured me Finn would keep the basketball team on a leash, and Mr. Popular strayed true to his word. Thank God for that. I can't imagine having to deal with Regina George the Second on top of Axel and his goons.

As much as I appreciate Finn looking out for me at Dia's request, I couldn't stomach the thought of continuing to eat with the jocks. And when I say jocks, I mean *Xavier.*

Dia and I eat just the two of us now, and while it's helped me avoid *Scumbag Emery*, I still run into him in the halls every now and again. The real kicker is, when we cross paths, he doesn't ignore me like any decent fuckboy would.

He *stares* until the last moment.

Maybe he gets a kick out of watching me suffer. Knowing he took everything from me. Maybe he feels powerful. Whatever it is, that single encounter is enough to ruin my day.

"Sorry to interrupt, ladies."

My head snaps up, and I find myself back in the crowded cafeteria in a nanosecond. I've been in my head since lunch started. Dia's sitting across from me, her dark, angry eyes staring bullets into Axel's forehead.

He's standing by our table, a cocky smirk plastered to his face. It takes me a second to realize he's talking to me. Finn didn't show up at school today. I'm guessing this makes today "Torture Aveena" day.

Gather around, everybody.

Tickets on sale, limited time only.

"What do you want, Fletcher?" Dia grits through her teeth.

"From you? Nothing." Axel's gaze flicks to me. "From Love, however…"

I don't react to his usage of my alias.

Everybody knows, no point in denying it anymore.

He presses the heels of his hands flat against the table, leaning forward as if to tell me a secret. I notice the room's gone quiet all of a sudden. As expected, the majority of the cafeteria is looking in our direction. It's crazy how human beings tend to be drawn to chaos. Not that I can blame them. Any kid who says they hate gossip and drama is lying.

We all live for that shit.

Until it happens to us.

"Think it's about time you fess up, don't you?"

I don't grace him with a reply, my throat so full of rage I couldn't form a sentence if I wanted to. The bullying doesn't make me sad anymore. It makes me *livid.*

"Come on, you can trust me. Who's Zac? I won't tell." He flashes a mischievous grin.

I'm convinced some higher power comes into play when I randomly lock eyes with Xavier sitting at the jocks' table. Like the rest of the school, he, Theo, Brie, and a few basketball players are watching the events unfold. Only… unlike the night where he broke my heart, there's emotion in his eyes.

Fear.

He's scared.

They still don't have any suspects for Zac, and the "Find Zac and Love" army is getting restless. I could wreck his life, future, and reputation with one word if I just felt like it.

Who's powerful now?

"Back off, Axel," Dia shrieks.

"Not talking to you, dickbag," Axel spits.

Dia's eyes flare with shock.

"Nice nickname, isn't it? Finn came up with it," he adds.

Dia smacks her mouth shut, a small glimmer of pain streaking through her almond eyes. *She can't seriously believe him.*

"Aveena, baby, you're just delaying the inevitable." Axel tilts my chin up with one finger, and I slap his hand away. "Why won't you tell me, huh? Are you really *that* ashamed to admit that you're Love? Is it because you fucked your sister's boyfriend?"

I don't so much as flinch.

I'm used to it by now.

"For what it's worth, Logan said you were *hella* tight."

Pretty sure my jaw falls into my food tray.

Axel cracks a laugh at my reaction. "Shit, did I forget to mention he's a friend of mine?"

The memories crash into me at a million miles per hour. Axel said he wanted to set me up with his buddy the night I agreed to meet Zac in Finn's bedroom.

He stressed that I was exactly his friend's type.

It was him, wasn't it?

Logan?

"He was super disappointed about you not wanting to see him at Finn's party, by the way." Axel confirms my doubts.

I deny him the satisfaction of an answer, boiling on the inside.

"Oh, well… Guess you were too busy sucking Zac's cock."

That's it, my brain thunders.

I can't control my body as I leap off my seat and knee Axel in the balls so hard a few guys at the next table audibly groan for him. He falls to the floor like dead weight, wailing like a little girl as he grips his crotch.

"You speak to me again, I'll rip them off," I bark, purposefully raising my voice for more students to hear me and bolt out of the cafeteria. Dia follows my lead, trailing behind me. I'm done letting them push me around.

And I want the world to know.

From now on… I'm fighting back.

***

My "fighting back" earned me two days of detention.

On the bright side, no one looked my way for the rest of the afternoon. I never thought I'd be this happy to be ignored. I felt like pre-confession Aveena for a second there. Normal. *Invisible.* Like I was in control of my life again. So much that I let Dia convince me to attend Theo's neon party on Saturday.

She was certain no one would dare annoy me after my public showdown with Axel in the cafeteria. And I thought, *What better way to show them that I'm not afraid?*

But now that Dia and I are ambling into Theo's kitchen with glow-stick bracelets on our wrists, I'm wondering if showing up at the jocks' party isn't just *asking* for trouble.

The Coxes' house is illuminated by black lights, engulfed into the smell of weed and strong liquor. Every guest carries some sort of glow stick, whether it be a necklace or a bracelet like us. A handful of seniors greet Dia when we come in, heads turning left and right as we venture deeper into the house.

Big surprise, they're looking at me.

Whatever.

As long as they leave me alone, I can handle a little staring. Finn meets us in the dining room less than five minutes later, a large tequila bottle in each hand. Dia's barely said a word before he's kissing her senseless. I divert my attention to, well… *anything* other than Dia exchanging saliva with Finn Richards.

That's when I see him.

Xavier.

He has his back propped against the wall, his eyes glued to his phone. He's jaw-droppingly hot, as usual, his white T-shirt fitting his muscled body to a T. My heart aches a pinch, and I let it happen without a drop of resistance.

I let myself hurt.

I let myself break.

Comforted by the prospect of the distant day where I'll look him in the eyes and feel nothing.

I spot Brie stalking toward him in a body-tight gray dress and cringe at her flawlessness. Stopping by his side, she runs her neon nails down Xavier's arm to get his attention. He doesn't give her the time of day, scrolling on his phone with a bored look stamped across his face.

Boyfriend of the year.

Vexed, Brielle glares around the kitchen, and, because the universe is not done torturing me yet, we make eye contact across the room.

She catches me staring at Xav and smirks, wasting no time in clutching his face and kissing him forcefully. Xavier doesn't return her enthusiasm, shocked by the suddenness of it all. Call me weak, pathetic, fragile, but I can't stand to look at them a second longer, so I turn my back on the happy couple. The first person I see on the opposite side is…

Wait… Axel?

What the hell happened to his face?

The tall basketball player is sporting not one but *two* black eyes, a busted lip, and a cut above his cheekbone. Why does he look like someone played High Striker on his face?

"Jesus, what happened to Axel?" I turn to Finn, who's busy

admiring my best friend like she's the only girl in existence.

"He and Xav got into it last night at practice," Finn replies, never peeling his eyes away from Dia.

"Good Lord," Dia gasps when she drinks in Axel's gruesome appearance. "What did Axel do?"

"Hell if I know." Finn shrugs. "Xav just threw himself at him out of fucking nowhere. I think Axel said something to his girl."

Dia's eyebrows shoot up to her hairline, a wicked grin twitching at the corner of her lips as she sets her eyes on me.

"*Which* girl?" Her voice is dripping with innuendos.

I know exactly what she's hinting at, but I refuse to consider the possibility for a single moment. So, Xav happened to pummel Axel on the exact same day he harassed me at lunch.

Doesn't mean anything.

And it definitely doesn't mean that he did it for me.

Well, to be fair, he did *place a confession that said "I hate you" smack on top of a poem named "I had no time to hate,"* my subconscious pesters. *What if that was code for something?*

The thought restores my capacity to hope. Then I steal a glance toward Xavier and Brie. He's holding her close, strong arms enveloping her thin waist.

The hopeful glimmer in my chest dies instantly.

"Would you look at that? It's *get fucked-up* o'clock," I hear Finn say before he swipes a sip of tequila right out of the bottle. "Ladies?" he offers, driving the tequila bottle closer to us.

"You know Vee doesn't drink," Dia reminds him, grabbing

the bottle of liquor and drawing a small sip.

Against my better judgment, I steal another glance at Xav and his girlfriend. *Terrible decision.* Just like that, all the promises I made myself since the night I lost my dad disappear down the drain.

"Actually, I'll have some," I surprise them by saying.

Dia's eyes snap open. "A-Are you sure?"

I snatch the bottle from her hands, the sound of my heart disintegrating in my rib cage echoing in my ears.

"Damn sure."

* * *

"Are you okay?" Dia asks me for the thousandth time in two hours, breaking the world record for most worried friend. I really *was* okay the first hundred times she asked.

And the second.

And the third.

But… it all went downhill from there.

It might have something to do with me finishing Finn's tequila bottle, then playing four games of beer pong. My head is spinning, my speech slurred and my vision blurry, but I feel good.

Well… *better.*

"I'm fine, D. Stop worrying."

Dia nods unconvincingly, focusing on the beer pong game at play. I'd be lying if I said I didn't gag my way through Finn's tequila bottle, but no matter how painful my throat felt, no matter how intense the burning got, I kept going.

Bit by bit, the clouds over my head cleared up, along with the feeling of having been stabbed in the chest repeatedly.

I get it, Dad.

I get why you liked it.

"Drink up, Vee," Theo laughs when the ball lands into our last red cup. He and Finn high-five each other, celebrating their victory, while Dia and I wallow in defeat. The boys have been owning our asses since game number one.

"Want to go again?" Finn smirks at Dia, and she shakes her head, gripping my arm.

"Nope, we've had enough."

It doesn't take a degree to figure out she's talking about me.

"We're next!" a high-pitched voice squeals on my left. I whisk my head to find Brie and Xavier standing by the beer pong table. Brie is holding on to Xav's bicep for balance, drunk as a skunk. The dazed smile slips off her lips the moment she sees me. "Why the fuck is *she* still here?"

"Don't fucking start, Brie," Finn growls.

Paying Finn no mind, Brie releases her grasp on Xavier's arm and staggers over to me. She stops inches away from me, looking me up and down with a hatred that makes my skin crawl.

"No one wants you here, freak. Actually, allow me to rephrase: no one wants you *period.* Not me, not my boyfriend—" She strikes me in the shoulder, and I stumble back in shock.

"—not even your own damn father."

As soon as the words leave her mouth, I see red.

And I don't mean metaphorically.

The sound of Brie's nose cracking under my fist is my first hint. The second is the loud gasps erupting around the room. The third is the blood gushing down Brie's face and into her mouth.

I just punched her.

I. Punched. Brie.

"Call me a whore, a boyfriend thief, whatever the fuck you want, but don't *ever* talk about my dad!" I scream in her face.

Brie's hand flies to her nose, and she bleats at the state of her bloody dress. She takes in her surroundings, her face twisting in horror at the whole party staring at her, and runs off. Theo turns down the music as she elbows her way through the mass. People swing their attention from her to me, shocked by the previous events. Astounded by the fact that I just proved them right.

It's not speculation anymore.

My punching Brie sealed the deal.

I'm Love.

Always have been.

Well… now that I have their attention. I have no idea how my drunk, clumsy self manages to climb on one of the kitchen chairs, but next thing I know, I'm standing above the crowd of seniors.

"That's right, people, *I'm Love*," I blurt shamelessly.

"Congrats, you heartless bastards, you caught me. I wrote the confessions. You're welcome for making your senior year interesting, by the way."

There isn't a single sound to be heard.

"I know you're all eager to find out who Zac is, so let me put you out of your misery."

My gaze shifts to Xavier, stiff as a board in the middle of the crowd, staring at me with familiar fear in his eyes.

I should expose you.

Let them tear you apart.

Show you how it feels.

"Joke's on you, idiots. He doesn't even go to Easton," I lie.

Xavier's shoulders sink with relief.

"He's older. Works at the library on the weekends. That's how we met. Although, I do appreciate you dumbasses racking your brains trying to figure it out. You're wasting your time. You'll never know who Zac is. Now, can we please move the fuck on with our lives?" I stare Xavier dead in the eyes, speaking to him and him only as I take back my heart, "*I sure am going to.*"

I'm off the kitchen chair in a heartbeat. I pick up my drink that's filled to the brim and walk away with the little dignity I have left. By the time I reach Xavier's side, he's staring at his feet in shame. I scoff under my breath, making sure to ram my elbow into his arm as I tear through the crowd.

"Vee!" Dia calls, but I don't stop until I've locked myself inside Theo's bathroom. My lungs release all the air they've been stocking when my back hits the closed door with a thud.

I just did that.

I told everybody.

I took back my power.

So, why am I crying?

Maybe it's the booze messing with my emotions. Maybe it's the last of my broken heart reminding me of its existence, but I stay in there for thirty minutes, crying Xavier Emery out of my system. Running my fist that's stained with Brie's blood under freezing water to soothe my painful knuckles.

Turns out punching someone hurts like a motherf…

By the time I totter out of the bathroom, the music is back and louder than ever. I can feel my phone buzzing with texts from Dia, but I'm too far gone to answer.

"Sorry," I slur when I bump into someone on my way out.

The stranger cracks a throaty laugh in response.

"Don't worry about it, *Vee-card.*"

I stop dead, panic suffocating me, and swivel around.

"L-Logan?"

24

Xavier

"Hey, asswipe. Who's that?" I stab Theo in the ribs with my elbow, earning a groan of pain. He blatantly ignores me, his eyes nailed to his phone. He's probably sexting Ashley.

Again.

That's all the guy does these days. I don't know what the deal is with those two, but Vee's sister seems to have become Theo's new obsession. I can't stop staring at Aveena and the rando chatting her up outside the bathroom. I don't know this dude. I've never seen him before, but judging by the hostility on Vee's face, *she's* seen him plenty.

My eyes roam her body, and repressed urges burn beneath my skin. I'm not surprised some loser would hit on her. I mean, look at her. She's wearing a tight little dress again—no doubt I have Dia to thank for that.

Those legs.

Those curves.

That perfect little ass.

Fuck.

I thought I was going to hurl all over the hardwood floor when Vee stood up on that chair, holding the power to rip my life to shreds in the palm of her hands. The worst part is, if she had chosen to expose me, I couldn't have blamed her.

But she didn't.

She lied to everyone.

Protected me when she had no reason to.

I never, ever thought I could be happy *and* feel like the biggest piece of shit to walk the earth at the same time.

"Cox, who the fuck is that?" I insist, smacking the back of Theo's head to get his attention. Finally, he looks up, tracking my stare to Vee and mystery guy.

"That's Logan, Axel's douchebag friend." Theo shrugs and tips his drink back, finishing it in one go.

"What's wrong with him?" I question.

"You mean aside from the fact that he's a world-class asshole?" Theo scoffs. "He's an abusive, worthless piece of shit, *that's* what's wrong with him. He hit Vee's sister when they were dating."

My jaw goes slack.

"Wait. You mean that's the guy from—"

"From the confessions, yep," Theo says with a nod. "Ladies and gentlemen, I give you, the guy who popped Vee's cherry."

My grip tightens around my beer bottle, my knuckles so tense I'm afraid my fingers might fall off.

He was her first?

Him?

That fucking nobody?

They're still talking, and by talking, I mean arguing. Vee is obviously disgusted by every stupid word coming out of his stupid mouth. Just as I'm wondering if he can feel my eyes boring holes through his skull, he twists his head to the side and notices me glaring at him.

I don't budge, my jaw twitching.

Fuck you.

Fuck you.

Fuck you.

You didn't deserve what she gave you.

You didn't deserve her.

Neither did you, the devil on my shoulder reminds me.

This Logan guy flicks his gaze back to Vee, leaning way too close to her for my liking and whispering something in her ear. Right away, she glances in my direction and catches me staring.

Bastard snitched on me.

I should pretend I wasn't looking, but I can't fucking tear my eyes away. I stare hard, mentally concocting a handful of ways to murder the guy. Then I see him slip something in her drink.

He. Slips. Something. In. Her. Drink.

It was fast.

Two seconds at most.

Anyone who wasn't paying close attention would've missed it. I beat up Axel for talking shit to her *once*. This guy has no idea he just signed his death warrant. Rage churns in my chest when Vee shoots me a bitter look that's tainted with sadness and zeroes in on Logan again.

She didn't see a thing. Logan offers her a predatory smile, topping it off with a comment Vee definitely doesn't like because she responds by pushing him away and scampering off.

Fuck, she can't drink that.

I have to stop her.

I'm dissolving into the crowd the next second, terrified to lose her in this clusterfuck of a neon party. Here I am, chasing after the girl I promised to leave behind.

The girl I promised to break.

And I did.

I broke her heart.

Little did I know I'd be breaking mine, too.

* * *

Aveena

I thought I was having a terrible night.

Then I ran into the worst mistake I ever made and realized I hadn't even begun to approach "terrible."

The night was bad, yes.

But I only achieved *terrible* when Logan cornered me by the bathroom. He started by complimenting my body in a repulsive way before point-blank telling me to have sex with him again.

After he laid hands on my sister, hurt her, pulled her hair.

The nerves on this guy.

I told him to fuck off and booked it. Partly because Xavier was glaring at Logan with a raw edge of… dare I say, *jealousy* in his eyes, and it made me a hair too happy.

Stretching my legs out on the lounge chair by the pool, I inhale deeply. Theo's backyard is pitch-black, the only source of light the faint patio lamp. Could hardly see myself showing my face inside after that speech, but I don't want to leave without Dia.

She's been skipping every party since the confessions were exposed. She stuck by my side through and through, coming over to my house daily, and she deserves this time with Finn. She'd die before admitting it, but I know she misses her "regular" life, eating and hanging out with the jocks, meeting Finn at his locker between classes.

I texted her and promised that I was okay. Figured I'd just hide out here and give her a few more hours of normality before I burst her bubble. I wince at the weird, salty taste of my drink as I finish it.

Jesus, what's the deal with my taste buds tonight?

The second I put my drink down, a nausea so brutal I almost puke rolls through my stomach, followed by a dizziness unlike anything I've ever known. I feel weak, disoriented, like my senses are deserting me one by one.

What the fuck is wrong with me?

It takes every ounce of energy in my body to push to my feet and—

"Going somewhere?"

I don't need to see him to recognize his voice.

Drained, I force my eyes open, barely discerning Logan and Axel advancing toward me in the darkness of Theo's backyard.

"W-What do you want?" I slur.

"What every teenage boy wants, baby." Logan smirks. "*Fun.*"

Time seems to slow down.

My eyes filling with tears, I glance at the red cup in my hand.

I know instantly.

No.

No.

God, please, no.

"Something wrong with your drink, Vee?" Axel taunts.

The red cup slips from my hands onto the cement, and I fall backward onto the lounge chair against my will.

So… Freaking… Weak.

How did I not see him slip me something?

When?

A tear streams down my face as the realization crushes me. It had to be when I glanced at Xavier. *Had to.* The boys continue to close in on me, and I don't even have the necessary energy to panic. I can feel myself fading.

"No" is all I can say.

Logan snorts. "Trust me, you'll be begging me to fuck you in a minute."

"*Why me?*" My eyelids weigh a thousand pounds.

"I thought it was about time we revisit that threesome idea." Logan pushes me flat against the lounge chair, climbing on top of me and pinning me down under his body. I can't fight back. All I can do is scream inwardly.

I scream and I scream.

But no one hears me.

"*Here?* Are you fucking crazy?" Axel scolds.

"Shut up and keep watch," Logan snarls.

"Keep watch?" Axel hisses. "Why do you get to be the one who fucks her?"

This is real.

This is happening.

I'm going to get raped in Theo's backyard by my sister's ex with my best friend just a few steps away. The last thing I see is Logan's hands fiddling with the straps of my dress.

The last thing I hear is the sound of his jeans' zipper as he shoves his pants down his hips.

The last things I feel are his nails digging into my thighs and his mouth tracing down my neck.

Then *nothing.*

25

Aveena

I thought it was a dream at first.

I just lay there with my eyes closed, trying to convince myself it was all in my head. That I'd wake up in my own bed. Between the turquoise walls Dad painted when I was eight.

Please let it be a dream.

Please.

I prayed and I prayed, but the stabbing pain in my skull, the fog consuming my every thought, and the weakness in my limbs demolished my illusions one by one.

Last night wasn't a dream.

I'm shivering and sweating like a pig when I sit up straight, blinking my senses back to life. This bed isn't mine. Neither is this bedroom. For starters, my bedroom's *never* been that clean. The door is closed, and the curtains are drawn, soaking the strange room in darkness.

My head hurts to the point of making it hard to keep my eyes open, and my body is *begging* me to succumb to slumber. I'm dying to let the comfortable mattress swallow me whole, but the memories anchored in my brain won't allow it.

I tense up, reliving the fear, the helplessness. Witnessing the scene like a movie I can't fast-forward. I feel Logan's nails digging into my thighs, his mouth robbing me of a choice.

The rest is a big black hole.

In a frenzy, I peel the blanket off me and blow out a breath of relief. I'm wearing a large T-shirt and oversized shorts.

That's good.

Better than being naked.

At first sight, I'd say this is a boy's room.

It is Logan's?

Maybe it's Axel's?

God, did they bring me back to their place for round two?

Nausea rolls through my stomach at the thought. I spot my phone on the nightstand and think, *What kind of stupid rapist gives their victim a way to call for help?* but I don't waste a single second overthinking it and trap it into my fist.

It's at ten percent battery.

Shit, I left the internet on all night.

This is going to rack me up a ridiculous phone bill.

I have around fifteen messages from Dia, asking me what happened, why I didn't sleep at her place, and as much as I want to answer her, I don't have a clue myself.

Her tenth message steals my breath.

Dia: Finn just told me you're with Xav. Call me as soon

as he drives you home.

Xavier did this?

He took me back to his house?

But… *why*?

Makes sense that I don't recognize the place, though. I've never been in Xavier's bedroom before.

I'm quick to decide that, while Xavier Emery *did* leave my heart in shambles, he's not a disgusting rapist, therefore, things could be worse. I'm considering my escape routes, debating on sneaking out his window when a new email pops on my screen.

Duke University, the sender reads.

I flatline for a second, unlock my phone with a slide of my thumb and open the email without checking the subject.

I shriek at the first line.

Dear Aveena,

It is a great pleasure for me to inform you that you have been selected…

My mouth falls open.

Holy shit.

I got it.

I got a scholarship!

I don't have the chance to fully relish in my hard work paying off before I make out the sound of footsteps in the distance. Someone's coming.

I clutch the blanket to my chest as if to protect myself from imminent danger. The footsteps grow closer. And closer. Until they halt at the door. I hold my breath, waiting for whoever is on the other side to make their move.

At last, the knob twists open.

And he materializes in the doorway.

Xavier.

He's shirtless, his black sweats hanging low on his hip and defining the V lines pointing at his crotch. Normally, I'd be drooling over his glorious body and cut abs, but my focus clings to the scar carving into his abdomen instead.

It's faded but deep.

Curving around his lower stomach.

I've never seen Xavier shirtless in the light before. He was shirtless on his Snapchat picture and at the springs, *sure*, but both times were too dark and conditions for a body scan weren't exactly optimal.

I remember my mom telling me Xav had been injured in the boating accident that stole Nora Richards's life, Finn's mom. I just never realized Xavier had to carry the traumatic memories of watching her die on his *skin.*

Xav holds a large glass of ice water in one hand, and the biggest painkiller bottle I've ever seen in the other. We make eye contact, and his lips twitch into a barely there smile.

"Morning," he says, his voice raspy.

I can tell he just woke up by his small, tired blue eyes and his untidy brown hair. I'm guessing he rolled out of bed mere minutes before I came to.

I stare at him blankly.

Morning?

Is that all he has to say to me?

Morning?

"Got you some water." Xavier sets the glass down on the nightstand and takes a seat at the foot of the bed.

I immediately rain down my concerns on him.

"What happened? How long have I been out? Why did you bring me here? What did you—"

"Easy." Xavier stops me. "I'll tell you everything you want to know."

Irritated, I inhale a long, shaky breath.

"What happened?" I start at the beginning.

Xav goes cold with fury, his jaw twitching.

Oh, this can't be good.

"Logan roofied you last night. Axel was in on it. They wanted to…" He can't bring himself to say it.

"Rape me," I complete.

I understand how uncomfortable he is with the term, but it's time we say things as they are. It wasn't just "teenagers having fun." Or a "drunken mistake."

It was rape.

Sexual assault.

Xavier nods, his gaze skirting mine as though he's sickened, *infuriated,* by our conversation. That's how I know he's about to tell me the one thing I'm terrified to hear. The boy made it clear he couldn't care less about me in his last confession, but fuck, the look in his eyes… The only reason you'd ever look at someone like that was if you cared about them.

Or the unthinkable happened.

My stomach flips, tears covering my cheeks as I sweep Xavier's blanket off my legs and examine my marked thigh. Logan's fingernails are imprinted on my skin.

I jerk my palm to my mouth, my voice breaking as I choke. "He… He did it, didn't he?"

My body begins to tremble with the aftereffects of being drugged and used like a blow-up doll. I can't discern a thing through my glassy eyes, and when the first sob rips from my throat, I wonder if he used protection.

If he gave me an STD.

God, what if I'm pregn—

"Vee!" Xavier's hand swaddles mine, and I fling my arm out of his reach, staring into empty space.

"He did it," I repeat, my voice so weak I barely hear it. Images of Logan violating a drugged, unconscious Aveena disconnect me from reality. It's like I'm floating out of my own body.

Staring down at the flesh I thought was mine.

"Vee, look at me." Xavier grips my face, reeling me back onto solid ground. "Look at me," he urges until I comply.

I plunge my gaze into his.

"*He didn't.*"

I expected the waterworks to stop, but I only cry harder.

"W-what?" I sniffle.

"He didn't," Xavier assures me. "Axel came to his fucking senses before anything happened. Bastard ran inside to get Theo and me. You were out cold by the time we got there, but we stopped him, Vee. *Nothing happened,*" he stresses, his fingers caressing the side of my face delicately. For the first time since the night we drove to the springs, I recognize the boy in front of me.

For a brief moment, he's my Xavier again.

My *Zac.*

Until he snaps out of it, as though he's just realized what he's doing, and unclasps his fingers from my cheek.

"What happened to Logan?"

"We took care of him" is all he says.

"Meaning?"

Xavier expels a long sigh. "He left in an ambulance."

"What? Why?" I blurt.

"I might've given him a tiny concussion, but it was an accident, *kind of.*" Xavier bites back a grin, and my traitorous heart flutters.

I can tell he's not sorry.

Not even a little.

And I like it more than I should.

"Aren't you scared he'll tell on you?"

"Nah." Xav shrugs. "Bastard wouldn't risk it. Ratting me out would only lead to what he did to you. There's four of us and one of him."

He's right. I have enough witnesses to open a summer camp.

"Well… Thank you." It comes out as a whisper.

He cringes. "Don't ever thank me for that, Vee. *Ever.*"

I nod in understanding. He was just doing what any decent human being would.

"Why did you bring me here?" I ask with a wince, feeling like a sledgehammer is swinging at my skull.

"Didn't have much of a choice." Xavier pushes off the bed. "Dia was wasted, and I could hardly see myself dumping you on your mom's doorstep half-dead."

"Good call." I rub my temples vigorously as if to diffuse my headache and pat the king bed beneath me. My hazy brain connects the dots at a turtle's pace.

Wait, I woke up in his bed.

Does that mean we…

Xavier reads my mind, sticking his hand up. "I stayed on my side, Scout's honor."

I crack a small smile.

"I'm sure Brie will be thrilled about us sleeping together."

Xavier's eyes grow at my comment.

That came out wrong.

"I-I meant sleeping in the same bed. Not like… the other thing," I squeak and snatch the glass of water on the nightstand. I chug the whole thing before I can embarrass myself further. "Anyway, I should get going."

I fling my legs over the edge of the bed and rise to my feet.

"Take it easy," Xav suggests. "You're probably still—"

My knees give out instantly, my energy levels dropping to an all-time low. Strong arms knot around my waist before I collapse.

"Weak," Xavier finishes, his breath fanning my cheek.

I swallow hard at the proximity.

"I'm okay. Just dizzy." I squint my eyes to regain focus.

Being roofied will do that you.

Oh, and don't forget the killer hangover.

"I need to go home." I wriggle out of his hold, bracing myself on furniture as I stumble to his bedroom door. Xavier extends his arm out in front of me, blocking my access to the knob.

"What you need is to eat and chug like five gallons of water. Let me make you breakfast."

We're closer than should be allowed, especially considering he's a taken guy, but I don't withdraw, staring up at him. I get he was just being a decent person last night, but blocking the door?

Why is he acting like he gives a shit all of a sudden?

"But your parents—"

He cuts me off. "Are out for the day."

I try to unlock my phone.

"It's fine, really, I'll just ask Dia to pick me up."

My phone screen flashes with an empty battery sign.

Damn it.

"Come on, Vee. It's the least I can do after…"

Breaking my heart?

Shitting all over our promises?

Going back to your ex?

"I'll just walk or something." I round him, anger soaring in my stomach, and swing the door open—who cares that I don't know my way around this house?

I catch my reflection in the mirror in the hall and cringe. My makeup is smeared everywhere, my pink hair a big bundle of knots. I already know trying to explain my homeless appearance to Mom is going to be a *blast.*

My head is killing me, I'm scared I might puke at any moment, and I'm wearing nothing but basketball shorts and a T-shirt, but I still tumble toward the stairs.

He's too nice right now.

Too… Zac.

Why can't he be mean?

Why can't he the asshole who loved me until he "pulled out"?

It would make hating him so much easier.

Unfortunately for me, Xavier's parents just had to be fancy and opt for a spiral staircase—in other words, I'm going to break something *for sure*—but it doesn't deter me one bit.

"For fuck's sake, Vee, you can barely walk," Xav growls when I sway down the stairs without a care. He's at my side in seconds, gripping my waist and helping me to the first floor one step at a time. I shiver at his touch, his bare torso flush with my back, but I blame it on the nausea.

"I didn't need your help," I grumble once downstairs.

I almost trip over my own feet the next second.

Fuck you, too, Universe.

Xavier scoffs. "I can see that."

"Can I have my dress back?"

"Kitchen's this way." He flat-out ignores me, gesturing to the closest room with his chin. "How do you like your eggs?"

Stunned, I watch him stroll to the kitchen.

Pretend like he didn't ruin me—ruin *us*.

Something tells me I could argue with him for hours and his stubborn ass still wouldn't let me leave until he gets his way. Takes me a minute to accept defeat. It's just one meal. One meal and he'll drive me home. One meal and I'll go right back to hating him. It's not the end of the world…

Right?

* * *

One awkward, silent breakfast and a much-needed shower later, I'm padding out of the bathroom with wet hair and a refreshed mind. As much as I hate to admit it, Xavier was right.

Rushing back home to my mom looking like a hobo would've been a dumb move. Might as well beg her to disown me while I'm at it.

It must've taken me over five glasses of water and two plates of scrambled eggs before I could even *begin* to feel like a human again. Extra-strength pain killers also came in handy. Good thing Xavier was nice enough to lend me a spare toothbrush. I couldn't bear the taste of cheap beer and tequila a minute longer.

Xavier looked like he wanted to say something multiple times throughout breakfast but never did. He seemed at war with himself. Like he was debating on a life-or-death situation.

He's holding back.

Withholding something.

I just don't know *what.*

Tugging at the hem of Xavier's T-shirt and pulling the baggy sweatpants he loaned me above my waist, I meet him in the living room. He stands off the couch when he sees me, squeezing his phone in his back pocket. He's still shirtless. And I still can't stop eyeing his scar. I make my way over to him before my staring becomes obvious.

"Okay, Mom, I ate, showered. Can I get my dress back now?"

He doesn't laugh.

Or smile.

Instead, he cringes, rubbing at the back of his neck. "I doubt you'd have much use for what's left of it."

I pull back.

"What does that mean?" I ask.

Pity plagues his gaze.

"Logan sort of…"

He doesn't elaborate, but I know exactly what he's getting at.

Logan ripped it apart, didn't he?

"Oh," I croak. "So… when you found me, I was…"

"I covered you with my jacket. No one saw shit."

My stomach sinks.

So, not only was I was passed out, I was also half-naked for the world to see. Got any more good news for me, Emery?

"Thanks… *Again*," I mutter.

"What did I say about thanking me?" Xavier scolds me, but he's smiling. I nod, swallowing a grin. "Let me put a shirt on. Then I'll drive you home," he says before taking the stairs two at a time toward his bedroom.

I wander around the living room while he's gone. To think Principal Emery and my nightmare of a PE teacher live here. A large picture hangs above the L-shaped couch. Principal Emery has her arm wrapped around her son's shoulders, kissing him on the cheek. Little Xavier is smiling wide.

I notice he's not wearing his silver chain.

It's the first time I've ever seen him without it.

"Creeping on my family photos, Harper?" Xavier's breath tickles my cheek, and I jump.

When the hell did he come in?

"What? No, I just…" I ramble, adding to the distance between us. I can't stand being this close to him. "Fine, I was creeping."

He laughs.

"Can't blame you. I'd do the same thing."

"You two seemed close," I point out, and Xavier's eyes dart to the framed picture on the wall.

"We were." A twinge of pain melts through his voice.

"I almost didn't recognize you without that chain you wear around your neck," I admit.

"I was seven then. Finn's mom hadn't made it yet."

"Oh… she made jewelry?" I question.

"Yep. Made Finn and I matching chains when we were eight."

That was a decade ago.

"Ten years, huh? You must really like it."

"I could never bring myself to take it off after she… *after the accident*," he rephrases.

Nora Richards's tragic death crosses my mind, and I feel awful for twisting the knife into a wound that will never heal.

"Anyway, you ready to go?" Xav dangles the keys to his truck.

"You bet." I nod.

Xav gestures for me to lead the way, which I do without a second thought. I'm halfway to the front door when my heart slams the brakes. I stop dead in my tracks, the maddening voice in my head daring me to take one more chance.

One *last* chance.

It's been bothering me since this morning. The way he says something, then does the opposite. His cryptic confession in the book, his convenient fight with Axel the day after he bullied me in the cafeteria. *Don't even get me started on his hero moment last night and how nice he was this morning.*

It just doesn't seem right. I might make a fool of myself, he might laugh in my face, but I have to try. My pulse throbbing in my throat, I make a beeline for him. I stop a little too close, but he doesn't back away, or warn me to keep my distance.

Instead… *he moves closer.*

I don't think he meant to do it. In fact, I don't even think he's aware that he did it, but his responsiveness sets my heart on fire. I clutch his face with both hands, crane my neck to let our eyes meet, and deep dive into his Caribbean Sea colored gaze in search for an answer.

A weak link.

Any sign of the boy I fell in love with.

"What are you doing?" he says bluntly.

"Testing a theory," I whisper.

Desperate times call for desperate measures.

I move closer, shifting my hips into his and slinging my arms around his neck. Our bodies are one now, but it's not enough. Determined to see him break, I push to the tips of my toes, aiming for his mouth.

Only, I don't kiss him.

Not yet.

I just hover near his mouth, dangling the possibility of a kiss in his face, praying that he'll take the bait.

His throat bobs.

I smile.

Score.

"Look, Vee…" he warns. "What happened last night doesn't change shit, I still don't want you."

His lies fail to pierce through my armor. I don't feel the burn, the sting of his rejection. But what I do feel… is his length digging into my stomach.

"Really?" I whisper an inch away from his lips, my fingers crawling up his chest slowly. I lay a hand flat against his pec, refusing to break the eye contact.

I can feel his heart pounding under my palm.

Rattling his rib cage like a machine gun.

"Then why is your heart beating so fast?" I call his bluff, keeping my hand fixed to his chest. He doesn't answer, but I catch his eyes gravitating to my lips.

"You're confusing your dreams with reality, Harper." He clenches his jaw. I almost give up right then, but a force inside of me wills me to keep fighting.

Just a little longer.

"So… if I kiss you right now, you'll push me away?" My fingers disperse into his hair, and I graze his lips with mine teasingly, careful not to go all the way.

His throat bobs again.

"Last chance, Z," I beg, my voice breaking.

He knows exactly what I mean by that.

I know you're still in there.

But you have to come back.

Come back before you lose me.

In response… he says nothing.

Absolutely nothing.

That's my cue to cut my losses.

"As you wish." I swallow my pride.

I start to pull away, unknotting my arms from his neck.

Only, *he won't let me.*

I gasp when Xav jerks me back to his chest and crashes his lips against mine almost violently. His mouth is bruising, vindictive, but I kiss him back like it's all I know how to do. There's no apology, no restraint in the way he devours me. Only this boiling mix of pain, lust, and resentment.

He slips his tongue inside my mouth with a feral, irritated groan I feel deep in my bones, and I come to understand…

It's not me he's mad at.

He's mad at himself.

We're grasping at each other's clothes for dear life, his need for me sticking out between us. I'm disappointed in myself. Disappointed that all it took was one decent gesture for me to crawl back to him. I'm disappointed in how much I love this asshole, but I love him all the same.

Loving Xavier Zachary Emery is a life sentence…

And I plead guilty.

"God, I missed you." He drops the act, grunting in between kisses, "I missed you so fucking much, Vee."

The mask he wore all week combusts, the chips flying in every direction, and tears scratch at the back of my eyelids. The confirmation that his whole "bad guy" persona was a lie is just as much a relief as it is devastating. I have to tap into every drop of self-control in my body to break away from him.

"Then why did you break my heart?" I choke out.

He flinches at my teary eyes, the way he always does, and drags a long sigh, resting his forehead against mine.

"*Because I had to.*"

With that said, he claims my mouth again, and I lurch forward, gripping his shirt. I lose myself into another heated kiss. Anger festers in me, and I curse my body's intolerable yearning for him. I hate how every fiber of my being needs his lips more than an explanation.

"That's not an answer," I insist through the kiss.

"It's the only answer I can give you." He bites my lower lip.

I'm deeply wounded by his reply, but I kiss him again.

And again.

And again.

Stop, Vee.

Fucking stop.

"No." I come to my senses, shoving him off me and backing away. "I don't accept that. You don't get to trample my heart and refuse to tell me why. Fuck that. Fuck *you*."

My chest is heaving up and down rapidly.

So is Xavier's.

He dares a step forward, and I move further away.

"Tell me," I all but shout. "Or lose me."

He clamps his mouth shut, this heart-wrenching sadness gleaming in his eyes. It's like he wants to tell me.

But he can't.

"Fine." I wipe my cheeks and turn away.

The closer I get to the door, the faster the pit brewing in my stomach expands.

Please don't let me go.

Don't lose me.

I grip the handle and begin to rotate—

"Wait," Xavier blurts at the last second.

I spin, pain throbbing in me like a drumbeat.

"Give me one good reason why I should," I plead.

I'm hanging on to him… to *us* by a thread at this point.

Then he says it.

"Because I love you."

That's all it takes for my walls to hit the ground.

I heard the words, but they don't register.

"You… what?"

"You heard me." He closes in on me. "*I love you.* I've loved you since the day I barbecued your babies and pushed you down the jungle gym just so I could kiss you." He pauses, pain lacing his voice. "I fucking love you, Vee… *And I'm paying for it.*"

His speech pulverizes what's left of my armor. Tears batter down my face, my throat aching beyond belief.

"But you… you said you hated me."

"I didn't mean it," he blurts. "Not for a fucking second. I thought you'd get it. I thought…"

"I'm sorry, is there a better way to interpret *I hate you* that I don't know of?" I snap.

"Remember what I said to you on senior prank night?"

His question sears the memories into my brain. We were stuck in the Chem lab together at 3:00 a.m. I told him I hated him, and Xav argued girls only said "I hate you" to the guys they liked.

"So, what? I hate you means I love you now, is that it?"

"Pretty much, yeah."

"So, according to your theory, I just told you I loved you?"

"Sure did. You see, whenever you tell me I hate you from now on, it'll mean the opposite."

Holy shit.

Of course.

How could I miss this?

"Still doesn't explain why you did it," I accuse.

"I didn't know what else to fucking do, Vee, I… Brie was watching my every move. It was the only way I could think of to get you the message."

"Brie?" I arch an eyebrow. "What the fuck does she have to do with anything?"

Realization sucks me into a vortex of shock.

I gasp. "Oh my God… is she—"

"Admin of the Facebook group? That she is." Xav nods.

The bombshell shakes me to my core.

"She's also the one who released the confessions. Bitch has been following us around for a while now," Xavier adds.

"So, you're saying *Brie* forced you to do all this shit? Rejecting me? Treating me like I meant nothing?" I spit.

Guilt obscures his features. "I'm so fucking sorry, Vee."

It sounds so good coming from him, so simple.

It'd be so easy to pin the blame on his crazy cheerleader ex, but he lost my trust. And he'll need a lot more than pretty blue eyes and botched apologies to win it back.

I wince. "I want to believe you, Xav, I do, but…"

"But you don't." He zooms in on the tiled floor.

A beat of silence.

His heard jerks up. "Fine, then believe *this*."

Xavier meets me by the front door, unlocking his phone and scrolling through his camera roll. He flips the screen around to give me a good look and presses Play on a video. The footage shows Xavier sneaking to aisle six before pulling the poetry book off the shelf. The video was shot in between bookshelves so he wouldn't notice. He scans his surroundings.

Then he slips a confession inside the book.

Crap.

Talk about damning.

"Brie sent me this the day after we went to the springs," Xav continues. "Girl's never been rejected in her life, and she didn't take it well. She promised she wouldn't rat me out as long as I remained her little bitch. Her only conditions were that I stay away from you and get back with her. She's been acting like a delusional psycho. It's like she thinks we're really together or some shit."

I stumble back a step, taking it all in.

"I know it's a lot, but you have to understand. I didn't have a choice. My mom… She…" Xavier bites his inner cheek, the right words slipping through his fingers.

His bloodshot eyes stab me straight in the gut.

He's falling apart.

Crumbling to pieces in front of me.

Right now, Easton High's god is but a mere mortal. A fallen king who gave up his crown and abandoned his kingdom.

For a short, fleeting moment, he's one of us.

He hurts.

He bleeds.

And he's scared.

Just like me.

"My mom could go to jail, Vee," Xavier croaks and plops down on one of the kitchen chairs. He props his elbows on his spread legs, nestling his head in his hands as strands of his brown hair fall between us like a curtain.

I sit on the chair in front of him.

"I thought I was doing the right thing. Protecting my family, but then last night…" He clenches his fists. "When I saw this Logan motherfucker on top of you… Your torn dress. *Fuck*, I thought I was going to kill someone. I didn't give a shit about my mom, or Brie, or anyone. All I cared about was you. The bastard never would've laid a hand on you if I…"

I can't imagine the pressure he's been under. I can't imagine having to decide between throwing your own mother to the wolves or breaking a heart. I get why he did it, as horrible and cruel as his methods were.

Frankly, I would've done the same thing.

"I don't fucking know how to choose, Vee." He looks up at me, overwhelmed in every sense of the word. "I… I *can't*."

A lone tear escapes his puppy dog eyes and drizzles down his perfect face, coming to die on his lips.

My heart shatters.

He's *crying*.

Instinctively, I seize his face into my palms, the magnetic pull between us too strong to withstand. I clean the tear off his bottom lip with my thumb and mesh my mouth with his so hard you'd think I'm trying to suck him dry, and I *am*. I want to take his suffering, the criminal mother, the broken family.

All of it.

No doubt.

No hesitation.

I'd sink my own ship to keep him afloat.

But I can't. So, instead… I give him all of me, and hope like hell that it's enough. The kiss is messy, raw, wet from all the crying. A low grunt sounds from somewhere deep in his throat, and Xav grips my wrist, guiding me onto his lap.

I settle on top of him, straddling him, and his arms box me in. His tongue darts out to licks the seam of my mouth, and I part my lips for him. Our tongues tangle in a tango the greatest dancers couldn't match, and I watch my window of opportunity shrink to oblivion. *There goes my chance to save myself.*

This is temporary.

We are temporary.

But "temporary" feels too damn good to give up, so I throw myself headfirst into a story with no tomorrow.

I'm not sure how we wind up in his bedroom. All I know is, as soon as Xavier slams the door, his mouth ravaging mine, the need to wipe that pained expression off his face trumps my insecurities. I can practically hear him gulp when I drop to my knees, blinking up at him.

He sinks his teeth into his bottom lip, watching as I loop my fingers into the waistband of his black sweats and yank everything down at once—underwear included. His hard length pops out between us. He looks… *majestic* like this.

Tall.

Naked.

Intimidating.

I'm the one gulping now.

I clasp my hand around his shaft, and he sucks in a sharp, rasping breath at my inexperienced touch. I drag my other hand down his toned body, smoothing over every curve, every muscle, until the tip of my index grazes the outline of his scar. A dark shade of pink, the scar stops just a bit above his crotch.

It looks like it was always meant to be there.

Jesus, even his trauma is beautiful.

It pains me to imagine how he got it.

Kills me to imagine little Xavier getting impaled in a boating accident. I'm aware the scenarios I'm drumming up in my head are most likely ten times worse than the real thing, but it doesn't stop my spiraling. I certainly wouldn't win the "queen of subtlety" award because he notices and sweeps hair off my forehead.

"Don't pity me, Vee. I left with a scar that day. Big fucking deal. *Finn left without a mother.*"

I nod, snapping out of it, and lead his tip between my lips. Xav immediately clamps his eyes shut, gripping my hair as I twirl my tongue around him, my tempo unstable.

Undecisive.

The pressure of my mouth, however, remains constant. I decide to test how far I can go, taking him deeper, and Xavier throws his head back with a noise so carnal my thighs clench together. I feel the head of his cock hit the back of my throat and curl my fist up and down his shaft quickly, letting my hand and tongue join forces.

"*Fuuuck, Vee,*" he grits out, opening his eyes to stare down my face, but I don't slow down. Unable to take it any longer, I slide my fingers down my stomach inside my borrowed sweatpants and start rubbing myself in small circles.

His eyes flare at my initiative and I feel him jerk inside my mouth.

"Get up," he orders in a bone-chilling, gruff voice and pulls out of my mouth. Xav traps my hand into his to help me off the hardwood floor and walks me to the bed without a word.

I've barely climbed on the bed before he smacks his palm between my shoulder blades and pushes my body flush with the mattress. He's yanked my sweatpants and panties down my legs in a heartbeat.

My face squashed against the duvet, I can picture his eyes roaming my body, drinking in every inch of me. I feel so exposed yet so ridiculously turned on I bet he could use my skin as a match striker.

"Spread your legs," he commands.

Goose bumps erupting all over my body, I obey.

His fingers slide across my crease, and I gasp when he smacks his palms against my ass cheeks and stretches me for a better look. Embarrassment stokes my speeding heart, but the self-conscious voice in my head is drowned out by the sound of angels singing as soon as Xavier's mouth closes on my clit.

He licks me up and down, eating me so hard and fast I'm almost scared the pressure will leave me numb once this is over. He's got me moaning into the bedsheet, fisting the blanket in a matter of minutes.

He comes to a screeching halt a minute later, pulling back, and I'm about to complain, but his dick replacing his mouth shuts me up. He rubs my clit restlessly, sliding back and forth against my slit, driving me fucking insane.

"Xav…" I whine, my body a bundle of spasms and fireworks. "*Please.*"

"What do you want, Vee? Show me." He teases me, stretching my entrance with his tip and pulling away repeatedly. Drunk on him, I twist my head back, stretch out my arm behind me to grab him…

And steer him inside me.

Bare.

We gasp in unison at the sudden sensation, Xavier's grasp on my ass cheeks tightening to the point of leaving a mark. By the time I realize I'm operating on crazy, it's too late.

"*Aveena.*" My name sounds like poetry on his lips.

I know how unsafe we're being.

He does, too.

But neither of us pull the panic cord.

"Fuck, we can't," Xav says as he plunges deeper inside me. "Shit, you feel so *fucking* good." He slaps my ass and I lose my mind.

"This is a bad idea." I moan, backing into his pelvis for more. He pumps his hips into me in response.

"Terrible idea," he agrees, twisting my hair around his fist as he moves inside me. "Fuck, Vee… we *really* can't." He manages to think straight for a moment, slowing down the pace. "Are you even on the pill?"

"I am." I nod. "Are you clean?"

Might've been a good idea to have this conversation before shoving his dick inside you, dumbass.

"Yeah. You're the only girl I've slept with since I got checked," Xav assures me, his teeth tugging at my earlobe. "You?"

"I got checked after Logan, and you're the only one I've been with since… well, ever," I admit shamefully.

That's what seals the deal.

His chest blanketing my back, Xav smacks a long kiss over my mouth, gathering speed with each thrust. It isn't long before he's fucking me senseless. Our first time was amazing, but nothing compares to this. To feeling him—*all of him*—without a barrier.

I squirm left and right when he curls his arm under my body and starts rubbing me in vigorous circles. He doesn't stand down until my clit is swollen under his finger. A million sparks ignite in my toes, zapping to the sensitive spot between my legs.

I yelp when he spins us around in a sudden move and lays

me down on my back. Xavier climbs on top of me and positions himself just right before plowing inside me again. I cry out when one of his hand finds my throat and the other finds my clit. This time, he doesn't kiss me, revelling in my reactions as our bodies lock together. Doggy style was better.

For my heart, at least.

It meant I didn't have to look into his eyes.

In doggy style, I didn't have to break.

But in missionary, I'm a splintered, glued-together china vase. Pleasure pulses through my body, and I squeeze my eyes shut.

"I'm close," I bleat, muffling my unraveling to the best of my ability, and Xav jerks my chin forward for a hot, messy kiss.

Close to giving you up.

Close to missing you until my heart bleeds.

Close to making the choice you *can't.*

His pounding loses momentum, becoming jerkier.

"I love you," Xavier rasps in my ear, and I kiss him before I do something stupid like say it back.

"Don't stop," I beg as the pleasure reaches its apex. My mouth drops open as I come undone for the last time. I'm trembling under him, and I know from Xav's heavy breathing that he's next in line.

"I fucking love you, Vee," he repeats, staring me dead in the eyes. Like he *knows* what I'm about to do.

Like he *knows* I have to leave him.

Spasms overtake him, and his jaw flexes as he spills deep inside me without a condom. I witness his climax, finding so much beauty and perfection in the way he comes apart.

"I love you." I slip up, and my heart fractures in two.

In four.

In six.

In a thousand fucking pieces.

Idiot. Why did you say it back?

Why would you make it sound like there's hope for you two? Why would you make him think you'll ever say a word to him again after this?

Sweaty and exhausted, Xavier and I collapse into each other's arms, and as I blink back tears, I find comfort in knowing the greatest love stories all have an expiration date…

I just wish ours didn't have to be today.

Xavier

At what point does a guy accept their new wuss status?

How many unanswered texts does it take before you *officially* declare yourself a whipped little bitch? According to my calculations, I should be falling to Aveena's feet, begging for scraps of her attention any day now.

She was still naked in my bed, with her perfect, pierced tit in my palm when I passed out. She was still there—still mine.

Until… she wasn't.

She left.

She gave me the best sex of my entire fucking life and took off.

I don't know what I was expecting to happen. I didn't think she'd go from moaning my name and coming on my cock to treating me like a complete stranger, that's for sure. She hasn't answered my texts in days. She won't even *look* at me, staring right through me in the halls.

It's like I never had her facedown, ass up on my bed.

Like I never poured out my whole fucking heart to her.

Sleeping with her again settled it.

I need her. End of story. The girl's become my best friend, the only person I trust, the only real thing in my life. She sees me for me. Sees *Zac* where everybody sees Xavier. She sees the guy behind the walls of useless popularity, title, and reputation.

I need Aveena Harper.

Any fucking way I can get her.

I figured I'd start texting her in secret. Sneak out every night to see her. Then she gave me a taste of my own medicine and ghosted *me*. Seeing her at school every day looking damn good, her long pink hair swinging from side to side as she walks away from me… *Definition of torture.*

That shit feels like falling to a slow, never-ending death. The real kicker is, I bet she thinks she's successfully pushed me away. That I'll forget all about her and abstain from going after what I want.

Oh, Harper… I don't play to play.

I play to win.

Eyes glued to my phone, I slam my locker shut and lob my gym bag strap over my shoulder while Finn and Theo wrestle each other like professional dimwits. Practice was rough today, and believe it or not, Coach Diaz had nothing to do with it.

It was Vee.

All Vee.

Fucking with my mind.

I couldn't stop glaring at Brie and her pom-poms across the gym. Caught myself wishing Brie would fall when tossed in the air by her squad of wannabes.

Break something.

Hit her head, maybe.

Grow a fucking conscience in the process.

"Xav?" Theo pesters. "Did you hear me?"

"He's been distracted all fucking week," Finn comments.

"Hm?" I glance at the assholes I call my best friends.

"Where's your head at, dude?" Theo snorts.

Back between Vee's legs.

"You haven't heard from Duke yet, huh?" Theo fishes for a reason to justify my behavior.

"Nah," I lie.

"It'll come, man." Theo shakes my shoulder. "I got the call just a few days back."

The truth is, my call came days ago. More specifically when I went up to my bedroom to throw a T-shirt on before driving Vee home. I'd like to say I couldn't believe it, but at this point, I felt almost *entitled* to that damn scholarship.

Before Vee, ball was my whole life. I hate to admit it, but Brie was nothing but a convenient piece of ass. I spent years killing myself for that five-minute phone call.

I haven't told a soul.

Theo was bummed because he hadn't heard back at the time, and I didn't want to rub it in his face. I also don't need Dad on my ass during the playoffs. I can already hear his speech about showing Duke they made the right call.

Proving myself worthy.

"Still waiting for my call," Finn jokes, and I scoff. Finn's dad is so loaded it'd be a fucking joke for him to get a scholarship.

He wouldn't need one in a million years.

Plus, just because I'm dying to turn pro doesn't mean Finn does. He loves ball, sure, but he's admitted to seeing a big black hole when thinking about the future. He said he'd take a year off after high school to figure shit out.

Finn, Theo, and I saunter out of the locker room together, the guys raving about some party I couldn't give less of a shit about. I just want to head home. Maybe pull up to Vee's house and beg like a pussy until she takes me back, not that we ever really dated, but fuck, if it was up to me, we would. I'm thinking she won't have a choice to talk to me if I show up on her doorstep.

If you're thinking that sounds desperate as hell…

It's because I am.

Disgust tickles my throat when we turn the corner and I spot Brie by the drinking fountain next to the gym. She's in her cheer uniform, her red hair pulled in a high ponytail, her nose still bruised from Vee's punch. There isn't a single doubt in my mind that she's waiting for me. Sure enough, her head jerks up as soon as I come into her line of vision.

She smirks. "Hey, sexy."

The guys take notice and snort out a laugh, certain I'm about to get some after-practice action. I almost laugh at the thought. I might play along in public, let her kiss me—while wishing she was someone else—but she's fucking insane if she thinks I'd ever touch her again willingly.

"We'll leave you two," Theo quips.

"See you, man." Finn gives me a quick handshake.

He and Theo trail off, leaving me alone with my egomaniac ex. I don't waste calories acknowledging her and carry down the hall. Brie trails after me, following me around like a lost puppy. I check my text conversation with Vee as I walk.

Still no answer.

Xavier: When can I see you?

Xavier: I don't give a shit what I have to do, Vee, we'll figure it out.

Xavier: I can't fucking stop thinking about last week.

Xavier: Jesus, Vee. If it's over, just put me out of my misery and tell me.

Then the one I sent her just before practice.

Xavier: I miss you, dork...

"Lacey's having a get-together tonight, want to go?" Brie asks, picking up speed to catch up with me. "She said the goods are... well, *good.* Might take the edge off before the playoffs."

"Let me see... Getting high with my manipulative ex-girlfriend? I'd rather rip off my balls and play mini-golf."

Axel turns up down the hall the next minute, but I know he's not staying long. Bastard runs away scared whenever we make eye contact these days. I made it clear he was dead to me, and his last-minute change of heart about raping Vee doesn't mean he's off the hook for one fucking minute.

I tolerate him at practice, but he hasn't dared show his face at lunch in a week. As expected, the trash bag turns the other way from the moment he sees me.

I'm halfway to the exit when Brie pulls out the big guns.

"You know, I heard orange is *the* color this season." Brie grips my forearm, digging her red acrylic nails into my arm. "Bet your mom would look great in it."

Her prison jumpsuit reference paralyzes me. She does it every time I wander too far. Tug on my leash like I'm her fucking property. Dangle my mother's sins over my head.

Remind me where my place is.

Screaming inside, I dive my hands into my pockets, curl my fists into tight balls of rage, and accept defeat.

"What time is this *get-together*?"

* * *

Aveena

I just wanted to eat lunch in peace.

Watching Brie straddle Xavier in her Instagram story is the *opposite* of peace. To be fair, I'm the one constantly checking her profile. What can I say?

I must love getting my heart stamped on.

Just because I cut all ties with Xav doesn't mean it's not killing me to know he went to some party with her yesterday, on a school night, at that. Because I removed myself from the equation doesn't mean I don't turn into a pathetic, broken mess whenever I see them holding hands in the halls.

I know their "love" is a load of shit.

But… part of me dreads the day where it's *not.* The day Xavier forgets it was ever a lie to begin with.

In a moment of weakness, I allow myself to glance toward the jocks' table and lock eyes with the devil himself.

Turns out he was already staring.

I maintain the eye contact like I'm compelled to. Like I *physically* can't look away. If eyes could speak, we'd be writing a whole damn novel. Shit, I've been so good this week. Delivered an Oscar-worthy performance, if I say so myself. I never once looked his way, no matter how much I wanted to.

Until now…

Brie is sitting on his lap, her arm knotted around his neck as she chats with Lacey. I wince when she kisses him hard, jumps off his lap, and walks away with Lacey. I peel my eyes off the picture-perfect couple and shift my attention back to Dia sipping on a water bottle. That's when my phone pings with a new message.

From him.

I skim his text, my heart beating double time.

Xavier: I wish it could be you.

I look up, meeting his eyes. Xavier won't budge, staring at me so hard my skin prickles. Pain wraps me up like a hug I can't escape. It's too tight.

Too strong.

I wish it was me, too.

It hurts so bad I pretend I didn't see his text and shove my phone into my back pocket. I should be happy. My drunk speech at the party seems to have done the trick.

All signs point to people buying my story about Zac not being a student at Easton. The confessions are slowly becoming old news, along with the whispers in the hall.

The name-calling has also gone extinct.

So, why do I feel like I'm dying?

I'm close to finishing my lunch when a loud voice echoes from the intercom on the ceiling, reverberating through the cafeteria.

"Aveena Harper, please report to the principal's office immediately."

The chatter dies down right away, and every single head turns in my direction. To think I used to wish I could be the center of attention, virtuoso sister and all. I must've been out of my fucking mind because this is my worst nightmare.

What could Xavier's mom possibly want with me?

I glance at Dia.

Worry gleams in her eyes. "Tell me after?"

I nod in agreement and pick up my tray. I throw the rest of my food away before heading out of the cafeteria under the entire school's scrutiny. I plop down on one of the stackable chairs outside of Principal Emery's office a few minutes later.

Not a single sound can be heard inside.

I play with my fingers nervously, shifting in my seat until the soundproof door creaks open. Easton's vice principal, Mr. Hall, comes into view, acknowledging me with a nod.

"Come on in, Aveena."

Wait… *he* asked me here?

I falter into the room to find Xavier's mom standing into the corner of the office, a blend of shame and guilt plaguing her delicate face. Mr. Hall gestures for me to take a seat at Mrs. Emery's desk. I do so without question. I've been here once before. After I kneed Axel in the balls and Xavier's mom gave me detention.

The office is a boring shade of gray, two large windows illuminating the small space. Mr. Hall sits at the desk, a clear indicator of who's in charge today.

Why are they looking at me like I committed a crime?

"You're probably wondering why you're here, so I'll just cut to the chase," Mr. Hall says firmly. "Do you know what this is?"

Mr. Hall angles the old computer on the desk toward me.

I swallow hard at the texts on the screen.

"Who wrote the confessions? #FindZacAndLove"

The private group.

"Pretty hard not to. Everybody in school does," I say.

Mr. Hall nods. "You see, it's been brought to our attention that you're rumored to be one of the writers of the leaked confessions."

Fuck.

I knew this would come back to bite me in the ass. I just didn't know when. The school did everything in its power to bury what happened. I ran back home in pieces the day Brie spread the confessions everywhere, but Dia said there wasn't so much as *one* copy left in the entire school by lunchtime.

Of course it was too late by then.

Students were already intrigued.

Invested in our fucked-up secrets.

"Is that true? Are you Love?" Mr. Hall asks.

I don't answer, biting the inside of my cheek and peeking at

Principal Emery hiding in the corner like a coward.

"As I'm sure you can understand, parents are not happy with us. Many are accusing us of having lost control of our students. They say this *Zac and Love* nonsense has distracted their kids from their studies. We're under fire here, Miss Harper."

I still don't say a word.

"People want names. They want whoever's responsible for this to take accountability."

"And you think *I'm* responsible?" I question.

Mr. Hall sighs a discouraged sigh.

"We know, Aveena. Drop the act."

I frown. "What act?"

"We know you released the confessions. And we know you made the Facebook group."

My jaw plummets to my feet.

"You think *I* did this?" I shriek.

The worst part is, even if I wanted to prove to them I wasn't the admin by bringing up the group settings, Brie was smart enough to make a fake account so that no one could trace it back to her.

Mr. Hall pauses for a long moment.

"Brielle Randall came clean. She told us she overheard you talking and you almost broke her nose to keep her quiet."

I'm smoking with rage.

Of course they'd believe that Malibu Barbie over me. They'd believe a *talking monkey* if he said the right thing, anything to save their own ass and please the angry parents.

"Why would I ever do that?" I snap. "The confessions were humiliating. They ruined my life."

"Did they? To me, it looks an awful lot like they—what's the expression—*put you on the map*," Mr. Hall counters.

I'm completely baffled.

"You think I did this for attention?" Tears fill my eyes.

"Miss Randall pointed out you've always been quite the loner and you don't have many friends."

"If I wanted to make friends, I'd talk to people. Not destroy my own reputation. You're wrong. Brielle did this. *She* released the confessions. *She* made the Facebook group."

"Look, Aveena… High school is messy, life is hard—*I get it.* Our intention is not to punish you here. You're an excellent student. Maybe even one of our best. After all, only the best get a scholarship to Duke."

My jaw tightens, a tear rolling down my cheek slowly.

They're going to blackmail me, aren't they?

"Wipe your tears, kid. We have a proposition for you."

Yup, blackmail coming right up.

"People already know it's you, but Zac… He's been difficult to pinpoint. His confessions are… well, you know how bad they make us look. Parents are furious. All you have to do is tell us who he is."

I steal a glance at Xavier's mom.

She avoids my gaze by every means possible. She seems

tortured. Terrified. She knows Zac is her son. *She has to.* That's why she's not doing the talking. Why she dumped this on Mr. Hall.

I bet she never wanted to find the responsible students in the first place. She knew it'd be like digging her own grave. She probably ignored the parents' backlash until she had no choice, which would explain why their blackmail didn't come sooner.

"Give us Zac, and I promise we'll make this go away *quietly*. No punishment, no consequence. Duke never has to know about the havoc you wreaked here."

"I told everyone Zac is an employee at—"

"At the library?" Mr. Hall laughs. "Yes, we heard. Too bad we haven't had a male employee working at the library in years."

Shit.

"Sorry to say this deal only applies to the *real* Zac."

"And if I don't tell you?" My voice trembles.

"Well, then, I think Duke deserves to know exactly what kind of person they're letting into their institution, don't you?"

I'm full-on crying now.

Choking on my sobs in the principal's office.

"So, what's it going to be? Choose wisely." Mr. Hall rests his forearms on the desk, joining his hands together.

I don't bother answering.

Why?

Because it's already over.

No matter what he says next, I'm doomed.

"Tell you what, I'm going to give you the weekend to make up your mind. Come see us on Monday with your answer."

I'm dead silent.

"Okay?" he urges.

I give a small nod and drag my feet to the exit. I know damn well I don't need the weekend to know what my answer is.

I can't do it. I'll never tell on Zac.

On Xavier.

Ever.

Feeling like Mr. Hall stapled my heart to his dull gray walls, I rush down the hall toward my locker. I need to get the hell out of here. It's Friday. I doubt Mom will mind if I skip the afternoon. I'll just tell her I wasn't feeling well. It's not like I can tell her I lost my scholarship—she doesn't even know I got one yet. Guess it's a good thing I didn't tell her…

Since there's nothing to tell anymore.

A text from Dia sits on my phone screen.

Dia: What happened?

I text her back as I push through the crowd.

Aveena: Nothing much. Just lost my scholarship.

Her reply comes through instantly.

Dia: WHAT??? Where are you?

Dia: I'll meet you.

Aveena: I'm going home. Talk later?

I reach my locker the next minute. I pack my things in record time and dash down the hall, hell-bent on booking it to my car before I run into anyon—

"Vee?"

My head snaps up.

It's a miracle I manage to recognize him through the tears.

Xavier.

Of fucking course.

I attempt to swab my face dry but end up smudging my mascara everywhere. His lips trickle open as he drinks me in. To say I'm a mess would be the understatement of the century.

A marriage of pain, regret, and guilt simmers in his blue eyes.

He opens his mouth to speak. "I—"

"Baby?" a familiar voice says behind us. Brie pops up by his side, locking a possessive hand around his bicep. "There you are." She smacks a loud kiss on his cheek.

Normally, this would break my heart.

Problem is, there's nothing left to break.

"Aveena, hey. Didn't see you there." Brie flashes me her best backstabbing slut smile. I don't have it in me to pretend, so I opt for my best and only option: run for the hills. Blowing off Brie, I stare Xavier dead in the eyes.

The boy I sacrificed my dreams for.

Then I storm out of the school.

* * *

I've never liked Theodore Cox's car.

It's bright red and flashy in a cocky way.

I think I heard him say it was his dad's car once and he didn't get a say in it, but I still hate it. And right now… I hate *him.* To be fair, I hate anyone on earth who's sort of happy.

I thought I'd be home alone when I decided to ditch school, and technically, I *am.* If only my driveway wasn't occupied with Theo's car… The fogged-up windows and bouncing movement left very little to the imagination.

It didn't take a degree to know my sister was in there, screwing Easton High's player in the back seat. "Still Don't Know My Name" by Labrinth was booming from inside the vehicle, but the deafening music wasn't enough to cover up Ashley's moans, her calling of Theo's name over and over.

Fed up with my day, I parked in the street and bolted inside the house. They were so busy tearing each other apart that they didn't even see me.

I hope you know what you're doing, Ash.

You're leaving soon.

You're leaving and he's staying.

Do the math.

I expel a sigh as I slam my bedroom door and collapse to the ground, back against the wooden surface. I'm so sick of crying. So sick of watching everything I love get ripped away from me.

I still can't believe I lost it.

I lost my scholarship.

I wish I'd never written these stupid confessions.

I cry until the tears soak my shirt. Until my makeup is no more and I look like a depressed racoon. My phone pings in my pocket five times before I check the screen.

I have one text from Xavier and four from Dia.

Xavier: Who was it? They're fucking dead.

A bitter laugh cuts through my pain. I must be delirious because I actually text him back for the first time in a week.

Aveena: Ask your mom.

The three dots pop on the screen, informing me that he's answering, but I select my conversation with Dia so that I'm not tempted to text him again.

Dia: Are you okay? Xav said you left crying?

Dia: I'm worried.

Dia: This is about the confessions, isn't it?

Dia: Vee, I want to help, but I can't do that unless you tell me what's going on.

I type a quick reply.

Aveena: They asked me to tell them Zac's identity or I'd lose my scholarship.

Dia: Why didn't you tell them? He's just some guy you met at the library.

I sniffle and cradle my knees to my chest.

I can't keep lying anymore.

She shoots me another text before I can reply.

It's time, a voice in my head whispers.

Dia: He's just some rando. Right??

Aveena: Wrong.

Xavier

"I'm not wearing a suit." Theo snorts, giving Finn the finger as he throws himself onto the cloud couch in the home theater. We hang out in here whenever Theo and Finn want to smoke a blunt inside and Finn's pops is home—this room is the furthest from Hank's office, so he can't smell squat.

Hank would chop us into pieces if he found out. And he just might if Dia keeps coughing at the smoke.

"Like hell you're not." Finn drags a long hit from the blunt between his fingers. "My dad poured a shit ton of money into this thing, so either you wear a suit or a black-eye, Cox. *Your choice.*"

They've been talking about tomorrow's cocktail party for hours. Finn's dad hosts this "varsity" thing in his backyard every year at the end of the basketball season. Easton's entire personnel is invited, along with the basketball team and cheer squad. It mainly consists of praising the Stallions and blowing smoke up Coach Diaz's ass.

Welcome to Silver Springs, town of basketball-obsessed people.

Did I mention we love basketball?

Can't wait for my annual nap during Coach's speech.

"Heard they're announcing player of the season before the appetizers this year," Finn relays.

"I do love those mini egg rolls," Theo reminisces. "Fuck, and the cheesy bread sticks."

Dia chuckles. "Is it just me or are you guys really invested in the food?"

"It's not just you," I say.

Dia glares at me in response, like she's mentally subjecting me to a painful death. She's been giving me the evil eye since she got here. No doubt her newfound hatred of me has something to do with Vee. I've been bombarding Aveena with texts since she stormed out of the school in tears yesterday.

She only answered me once.

And it wasn't even a definite answer.

It only raised more questions.

Ask your mom.

What the fuck does that mean?

I haven't slept a wink since. I tried everything. Meditation—doesn't work for shit, by the way. A good wank, while I thought of Vee's mouth wrapped around my cock. Her gasps and the little noises she makes when I go down on her.

Nada.

"Oh, and he hired some old-people band again. Bring

earplugs," Finn scoffs, tightening his hold around Dia's waist, who's sitting on his lap.

This party's been the talk of the town all week. Finn's dad does *not* mess around when it comes to making everybody feel poor. He hires servers to walk around handing out food and booze on silver platters and shit.

"Who do you think's going to get player of the season this year?" Finn coughs my name into his fist. "*Xavier.*"

I stifle a laugh.

I get their silly player of the season plaque every year.

"Gee, I wonder." Theo scoops a handful of the popcorn bag on his lap and lobs it at me.

I duck his assault.

"You got your speech ready, dickhead?" Finn asks me.

"Nah." I slump against the couch. "I'll just say the same shit I always say. *Thank you, goodbye.*"

"At least tell me there'll be alcohol, Richards," Theo groans.

Finn cocks an eyebrow, shooting Theo a look that says "*Is that even a question*?" It's not Finn's first rodeo. The guy could sneak booze into rehab if he wanted to.

"If anyone asks, we're not drinking champagne but sparkling apple juice, got it?" Finn smirks, drawing another hit and puffing out a thick cloud of smoke. I can tell Dia strongly disapproves of his substance abuse, but she doesn't comment.

"I'm going to go call my dad real quick." Dia smacks a small kiss on the corner of Finn's mouth and exits the room.

Light bulbs go off in my head.

I wait a few minutes so that I'm not too obvious.

"I need to take a leak." I leap off the couch and chase after Dia—*what? I know an opportunity when I see one.* I wander around the third floor for a bit before finding her in Hank's library.

She's on the phone when I come in, arguing with someone.

She sounds emotional.

Distressed.

"You're kidding, right?" Dia tries reasoning with her dad. "Tell me you're kidding."

Something is definitely wrong.

"No, Vee, listen to me. This isn't going to fix anything."

My breath hitches.

Vee.

She's not talking to her dad.

"I'm coming over, okay? I'll be there as soon as I can. Don't move." Dia curses under her breath and ends the call.

I don't waste a second. "What's going on with Vee?"

Dia shrieks in surprise, spinning to face me.

"Jesus, Xavier. Ever heard of privacy?" Dia scolds.

"What's going on with Vee?" I repeat without a fuck given.

"Wouldn't you like to know, *Zac*?" Dia stresses.

My jaw goes slack.

"She told you?"

Stupid fucking question.

Of course she told her.

"What do you think?" Dia fumes.

I don't even care at this point. I just need to know she's okay.

"How is she?" I try.

"Like you care," Dia scoffs, skirting around me, ready to leave.

I step into her way.

"I do! Dia, I care so fucking much I'm losing my mind… I have to know, I… *Please.*"

She doesn't speak for long seconds, not entirely convinced.

"You want to know how she is, huh?" Dia cocks her head to the side, analyzing me like she's debating on whether or not I'm worthy. "Okay. *She's terrible.* I've never seen her so sad in my entire life. Happy?" She tries to walk around me again.

"Why?" I stop her once more.

I'm that guy now, huh? I'm the stalker, pestering a girl's best friend just to get a sliver of information about her?

"Because of you." She doesn't sugarcoat it.

I wish I was shocked, but I'm not.

"Remember when she got called to the principal's office yesterday?"

I nod.

"Mr. Hall asked her to give up your identity or they'd call Duke and tell them all about the confessions Vee—" she creates air quotes with her fingers,—"*allegedly released.* They ruined her chance at a scholarship, Xav. She's devastated."

Her words are like a slap in the face.

That's why Vee told me to ask my mom.

Because she and Mr. Hall shattered her dreams.

"Wait, they think *Vee* released the confession?" I'm enraged.

"Yep. And made the Facebook group."

"Why the fuck would they think that?" I hiss.

"Because that's what your girlfriend told them. Brie played the victim to a T. Said she heard Vee talking and that she almost broke her nose to shut her up."

Uncontrollable anger swirls in my gut.

Fucking bitch.

Her parents should pay an annual fine for making her.

"She should've told them it was me," I mutter.

"I told her that, *repeatedly*, but she's stubborn. For some unknown fucking reason, she loves you. And she'd rather lose everything than snitch on you." Dia cracks a hateful scoff, glaring at me to death. "Frankly, I don't even see what's worth saving."

With that said, Dia maneuvers around me and ambles to the door. That still doesn't tell me what that call was about.

"What were you talking about on the phone?" I nag.

"Dream on. I've told you too much already." Dia keeps walking and curls a hand around the doorknob.

"Dia, I… I fucking love her." I'm almost embarrassed by how pathetic I sound. How fragile. How *needy*. Dia stops short, considering her next move carefully, and swivels around.

"It's a shame you won't get to tell her that."

Fear grips me.

"What the hell does that mean?"

Dia sighs. "She's leaving, Xav."

It feels like she just shoved a hunting knife into my gut and tore me apart organ by organ.

"*What?*" I snap.

I heard that wrong.

I had to.

Vee *can't* be leaving.

"She just told me she and her mom are moving to LA with Ashley. Ash was supposed to stay in Silver Springs for one more year, but apparently, she got some huge opportunity, and they're leaving early."

"But… how is Vee going to graduate?"

"Either she'll enroll into another school, or maybe she'll do online class, I don't know. Hell, if I'm honest, I doubt she'll graduate at all."

"Why the hell not?" I bark.

"She told her mom about losing her scholarship, and, well… Now that she's not going to Duke, she's let her mom convince her that her best option is to become Ashley's assistant full-time."

I want to break shit.

Tear every damn book in this library to shreds.

This is everything she *didn't* want. Everything she worked so hard to avoid. She told me how much she wanted to have her own life, a shot at discovering who she is away from Ashley's shadow.

To live for *her.*

"When are they leaving?" I say through gritted teeth.

"Monday morning." Dia sets the countdown. "They might travel back and forth to get some affairs in order, but her mom wants to sell the house."

This is bullshit.

Complete. And. Utter. Bullshit.

This can't be how our story ends. With Vee boarding a plane toward a life she doesn't want. There's no way that I'll never see her again.

No way.

Dia swings the door open and casts a glance at me over her shoulder. "Congrats, All Star, you saved your reputation..."

Then she twists the knife into my wound.

"*But you lost the girl.*"

* * *

"Everything okay, honey?"

Every hair on my body stands on end at my mom's croaky voice. On edge, I twist my head to see her leaning against the bathroom's doorframe. I haven't spoken a word to her since I found out about her and Mr. Hall's stunt to ruin Vee's life.

Struggling with my tie, I pretend she's background noise.

Hank and Finn are expecting Dad and me to pull up at their house two hours early to help set up for the party, and we won't be coming back home, so I have to change now.

"Look at you. So handsome." My mom compliments my suit.

I ignore her, continuing to wrestle with this fucking tie.

She laughs at my complete lack of skills.

"Let me take care of that for you." She passes the threshold and takes over for me. I stiffen up at her touch.

Jesus… what happened to us, Mom?

I used to love you to death.

Now I can't even look *at you.*

"All done." She smiles, patting my chest.

I don't answer, or smile, or give her *any* reason to believe I'm enjoying her presence, but she still crowds my space, opening her arms for a hug. She laces her arms around my shoulders, resting her cheek flat against my torso. I don't return her embrace.

"I'm so proud of you, you know that?" she whispers and breaks away. I'm relieved when she turns to leave.

Until she stops at the door.

"Right, I almost forgot. What time do you think you'll be coming back home from the gym tomorrow?"

Anger rips me apart. I know exactly what she does when I'm at the gym.

"Why?" I spit defensively. "So you can squeeze in a quickie

with the plumber?"

Her mouth falls open.

She even stumbles back a step for effect.

Two points for efforts, zero points for the non-existent acting skills.

"W-What are you talking about?"

Oh, for fuck's sake.

"Save it… I know you're cheating on Dad."

She shuffles her feet, her gaze descending to the floor.

"Xavier, baby, you have to understand. After twenty years of marriage… the spark isn't what it used to be. I did what I had to do."

I scoff.

Is she seriously pulling the "I had no choice" card?

"You did what you had to do?" I lose my temper. "Are you even listening to yourself? I'm supposed to believe that you *had* to fuck a minor? *My* fucking friend? Finn's fucking brother?"

Her skin pales. "So you *are* Zac."

Why am I surprised that's all she got from my speech?

"Spare me the part where you act like you didn't know," I spit.

"I didn't!" she shrieks. "Well, I had my doubts, but I wasn't sure until now. I was still hoping it was a coincidence."

"News flash: you're the only person in town who fucked a minor."

Her cheeks flare, but instead of taking accountability, telling me she was out of her mind, how much she regrets it, she says,

"I should've known you were Zac when I came home and saw that pink-haired girl getting into her friend's car last week."

Like a lovesick fool, I take the bait.

"Don't fucking talk about her!"

Her eyes grow, and she nods as though she sees things clearly.

"You think you're in love with her, don't you?"

I don't entertain her, keeping my mouth shut.

Think I'm in love with her?

Woman, I *know* it in my fucking bones.

"I know that look." She laughs. "Hell, I had that look. Back when I first met your dad."

This nonsense has to stop. I have to try and appeal to the last shreds of her humanity.

"Mom, she doesn't deserve this," I breathe. "Vee's going to lose everything. Her dreams, everything she's worked for. All because you had to go and fuck a student."

"Me?" Her features twist in anger. "*You* wrote the confessions. I'm sorry, honey, but this is your doing. If you hadn't blabbed to this Harper girl, none of this would be happening."

Annnd she's trying to pin it on me.

Great.

"I never meant for the confessions to get out."

"It doesn't matter whether you meant to or not. They got out anyway. This is your fault, Xavier. Not mine."

A resentful laugh stirs in my throat. "Funny. Somehow, I doubt the police would feel the same way."

Only then does the fear take hold.

I see it in her eyes.

She's just realized I'm not messing around.

"Sweetie, y-you can't be serious." She pads over to me, capturing my face in her hands. "I know it seems like love because you're young, but this girl… She's nothing. A fling. We're family."

Her panic soars when I don't cave in to her manipulation.

"Baby, look at me." She forces our eyes to meet. "I'm your mother. I carried you, gave you life, tended to every fit. There are a million girls just like her out there, but there is only one of me."

She's wrong.

So fucking wrong.

There *aren't* a million Aveena Harpers out there.

My angry girl.

My pen pal.

My Love.

Just one.

And she's getting on a plane tomorrow.

"You can have any girl you want in college, Xavier."

"I don't want another fucking girl," I fire back.

"You also don't want to be responsible for destroying your family, do you?"

Shit, she got me with that one.

I tense up, my jaw twitching.

"Let her take the fall, Xav. Protect your blood. *Protect the people who would protect you.* They're your real family."

I laugh in her face. She has *no* idea how ironic this is. My phone pings in my suit pocket, and I peel my mom's hands off my face before checking the screen. I let myself hope Vee texted me back for a second, but *nope*, I'm not that lucky.

It's Finn.

Finn: Tell Brie to jerk you off quicker. You're late.

I cringe.

Finn's my oldest friend, but he's so oblivious it's almost unbearable. Still can't believe he thinks I got back with Brie by *choice.* In his defense, I'm the one keeping him out of the loop. Hard to talk to someone when you can't tell them the whole story without *also* telling them that your mother fucked their brother.

"I have to go," I tell my mom, cold as fucking Antarctica, and race downstairs to meet my dad in the kitchen. Just before I get into his car, I shoot Aveena a thousandth and final text.

Xavier: Look, I know you're leaving tomorrow and you have no fucking reason to listen to me, but please, just come to the party at Finn's house.

Then I'll never text you again.

P.S: I still hate you.

Aveena

In case you were wondering how my mother reacted to the caterpillar tattoo I've kept hidden for years…

The answer is *not well.*

I knew from the moment I squeezed into the black, spaghetti-strap dress Dia gave me for my birthday that I was tempting fate. My mom spent years in the dark about the memory stamped across her own daughter's skin, and she didn't hesitate to share her disapproval with me.

I jumped at the chance to remind her I'd basically given up my whole life to follow her and Ashley to LA.

Needless to say, *it shut her right up.*

I was lying in bed, drowning my sorrows in chocolate and ice cream when Xavier's text popped on my phone screen. I'd been careful not to check his messages in fear of falling victim to my feelings and texting him back, but for some reason…

I granted this text *one* peek.

Unfortunately, one was enough.

Xavier: Look, I know you're leaving tomorrow and you have no fucking reason to listen to me, but please, just come to the party at Finn's house.

Then I'll never text you again.

P.S: I still hate you.

I can't pinpoint when or *how* Xav found out about LA, but it didn't stop me from hopping in the shower, then texting Dia, who's been harassing me to come to the party all day, a quick "Changed my mind, I'll see you there."

I still hate you. I played his words in my head until my heart begged me to stop. The hidden meaning isn't lost on me.

I love him, too.

So much.

But Xav and I…

We're a game I can never win.

No matter how many times I play.

Edging my way through the crowd of teachers, parents, and basketball players gathered in Finn's backyard, I second-guess the hell out of my decision. Why did I show up again?

The reason comes to me in a flash.

Because Xavier asked you to.

And… because you secretly want to see him one last time, but you're too damn stubborn to admit it.

"Vee!" Dia's voice slashes through the ambient music, and I twist my head to see her cutting across the lawn in stiletto heels. Finn trails behind, his hand possessively wrapped around hers.

They look perfect.

Outrageously perfect.

Finn is sporting a navy-blue suit that probably cost more than the scholarship I lost, while Dia's wearing her dark hair up in a curly, messy bun, wearing a tan dress that complements her sun-kissed skin. I've barely greeted her before she's unlatching her hand from Finn's and flinging her arms around my neck.

"I'm so glad you came," she whispers, sadness bleeding through every word. I'm going to miss the shit out of her. How am I supposed to get through life without Diamond Mitchell?

"Me too, D." I pat her back.

"Are you… all packed?" She pulls away, her almond eyes glimmering with a pain I'm in no way prepared for.

"Not completely, but Mom said we'll be coming back in a few weeks to get the last of it," I explain, and she gives a small nod.

"I-I can't believe you're leaving." Her lower lip quivers, a clear sign that she's not doing much better than I am. She wipes a tear before it has a chance to fall, and I wince.

"Don't be like that, D. I'll visit every summer. And we'll FaceTime all the time. *This isn't goodbye.*" I reach for her hand, giving her fingers a gentle squeeze.

"Right." She sniffles, nowhere near as comforted by my promises as I was hoping she would be.

"Anyway, where are the guys?" I ask Finn, making quick work of studying the Richards's backyard. I saw Lacey flirting with one of the waiters on my way in, spotted Brie and a few cheerleaders taking selfies by the chocolate fountain, *yes, they have a chocolate fountain,* and ran into Axel in the driveway. His suit was messed up, and he looked terrified as he got into his sports car and bolted.

"Fuck if I know." Finn shrugs. "My guess is, Theo's raiding the wine cellar and Xav is—"

"Right here," a deep voice says behind me.

My heart propels itself forward, dead set on breaking out of my chest, and I spin, coming face-to-face with my biggest weakness. He looks so damn perfect I'm tempted to poke his cheek to make sure he's real. I analyze his attire from head to toe, memorizing every inch of him.

Brown hair slicked back.

Coal-black suit.

Hands tucked in his pockets.

This.

I want to remember him like this.

"Hey, man," Finn says, and Xavier acknowledges him with a quick flick of his chin before pinning me with a look that makes every nerve ending in my body tingle.

Dia clears her throat. "Baby, weren't you going to show me

something earlier?"

I turn to stare at Dia, my widened eyes screaming, *"Don't you dare,"* but she completely blows me off.

"What thing?" Finn doesn't follow.

"You know, the thing over there by the…" She pauses. "*Thing.*"

Xavier bites back a laugh at how obvious she's being.

Still confused as hell, Finn plays along, "Right… the thing."

"Catch you guys later." Dia traps me into a quick hug.

"I hate you," I half joke in her ear before she pulls away and she flashes me a satisfied *"You'll thank me one day"* grin. Finn whisks his head back seconds before they dissolve into the crowd. "Oh, and Vee, nice ink."

I offer him a smile. "Thanks."

As soon as they're gone, Xavier scoffs a mocking "And the award of subtlety goes to…"

I suck in a breath, meeting his eyes. I don't have an inkling of how to say goodbye to him.

It was nice falling in love with you.

Sorry we're a lost cause.

See ya?

Not sold on my previous ideas, I opt for a simple "Hi."

Xavier's lips pull into a sad smile. "Hey, Harper."

There's a beat of silence.

"So…" I start. "I… You wanted me to stop by?"

Just so we're clear, he's *still* melting my insides with a single look, and I'm *still* a babbling idiot who can't form a sentence. Xavier moves closer to me, a single whiff of his cologne enough to make my knees buckle.

"No," he shocks me by saying.

My jaw hangs limply.

"I wanted you to come and *stay*," he corrects, and a herd of murderous butterflies assault my stomach.

"Stay tonight?"

He moves closer again.

"*Forever*," he says unapologetically.

I avoid his gaze. "Xav, I—"

"Don't fucking go, Vee." He cuts to the chase, cupping my face in his hands without a single thought as to the possibility of people seeing us. "I know this is shitty, and complicated, and it'd be easier for you to get on that plane, but… I don't want easy—fuck easy. I want you. *I love you, Vee*," he croaks, pressing his forehead flush to mine. "Just… stay."

I should've known I'd end up here.

Rethinking everything because of one speech.

Wondering if I should stay because of those eyes.

That mouth.

This boy.

"There's nothing left for me here anymore," I whisper.

"Bullshit! You have me," he counters.

His beautiful illusions rip me apart. Burdened by my realistic mindset, I separate his hands from my face.

"*Do I*?" I confront him with the facts.

Xavier clamps his lips together, and I know, as much as he wants to argue, he can't.

Because I'm right.

I don't have him.

I never did.

He's about to speak when loud microphone feedback lacerates the air. My gaze darts to the elevated platform planted across the backyard. A man I recognize to be Xavier's coach is up on the center of the stage, tapping a microphone that's mounted on a stand as he prepares for a speech.

Theo pops up behind us. "Go sit your ass down, man. Coach is calling player of the season in a few." He shakes Xav's shoulder and saunters toward the rows of chairs reserved for the varsity team before the podium.

The cheer squad and most of the basketball team are already seated, the rest of the guests constrained to stand up as they wait for the "ceremony" to begin.

Sure enough, the next second, Coach Diaz says, "Calling all basketball players over here, please."

When he says all players, he means *Xav*. He's the only one still missing in action. I catch Brie staring jealousy-laced bullets at us from the third row.

Good.

Take a picture, bitch.

Xavier's eyes lock with mine, his aqua irises charged with

frustration, regret, fear.

"Shit, I have to go."

"Go kill it." I muster a weak smile.

I let out a small gasp when Xav takes my head into his hands and plants a kiss on my forehead. No hesitation. He just did that, in front of everyone, knowing damn well they were staring.

"This isn't over," Xav promises.

I nod, but inside, I'm thinking…

Yes, it is.

I watch as Xavier walks away from me and go join Dia in the crowd. She smiles when she sees me, but her joy fades as soon as she notices the water pooling in my eyes.

She has the good sense of *not* asking me about it, linking our arms together for emotional support. The speech kicks off with the guys' coach thanking everyone for being here and kissing Finn's father's ass for hosting the thing.

Coach Diaz rambles on about his career and what drove him to Easton and coaching the Stallions for twenty minutes straight before cutting to the point.

"Anyway, enough about me. I think it's time we acknowledge our brightest star, don't you?"

There isn't a single person in the backyard that doesn't clap.

Probably because they're glad he's done.

"I know we do this every year, but, let me tell you, this part never gets old." Coach Diaz grabs something on the table set up behind him and lifts a cheap looking, golden plaque in the air for the crowd to admire. "Many of our guys played well this season, but one player in particular carried us to victory."

Finn and Theo swat Xavier in the shoulder like two hyped-up kids, and I suppress a smile. Can't believe I'm about to say this, but… I'm going to miss these idiots.

"He was outstanding on the court, never missed practice… Well, except one, but nobody's perfect, eh?" Coach Diaz teases, and people's laughter blends as one.

I know exactly who he's referring to when I remember Xav's surprise visit at my house to bring me my "homework." You've got to appreciate the irony of him bringing me an earth-shattering orgasm instead.

Coach Diaz pauses for suspense and laughs a wheezy laugh. "Who am I kidding? Xavier Emery, get up here, son."

The crowd breaks into cheers.

And my heart breaks period.

Xavier rises off his seat, making his way over to the stage. Coach Diaz shakes his hand in a congratulatory way, pats him on the shoulder, and hands him the *Player of the Season* plaque.

"Hold on." Xav adjusts the mic to his height, seeing as Coach Diaz is much shorter than him, and the crowd snickers. "Man… I don't even know what to say."

Finn curls his hands around his mouth like a megaphone. "Try thank you!"

Parents, teachers, and athletes laugh again.

"That would be a good place to start, wouldn't it?" Xav grins, and I hate that even his *smile* hurts now. I hate that I can't stand seeing him like this.

Happy.

Not if it's the last time.

"Thank you." Xavier inspects the golden plaque up close. "I have to say I'm not sure how much I deserve this. I didn't carry us to victory this season. The team did. Great team, great friends, great coach. What else can a guy ask for?"

Yep, I can't do this.

I glance at Xav one last time and squeeze my eyes shut to snap a mental picture of him in his element, a moment in time where he was carefree. Then I tuck the picture away in a mind drawer. The one labeled, "Things I Loved and Lost."

Right next to my dad.

"I have to go, I… I'll call you later." I pull Dia into a parting hug before squeezing through the crowd at full speed. Faces pass me by as I bombard people with *I'm sorry*'s and *Excuse me*'s.

I see Xavier's mom.

His dad.

Finn's dad.

Mr. Hall.

They're all sipping on expensive champagne. They came here to celebrate their brightest stars…. but *I'm* in no mood to celebrate. Because Xavier Emery was meant to shine in somebody else's sky. And I'm not quite ready to watch him leave mine.

I'm halfway to the house when Xav stops speaking abruptly. I assume he just forgot what he wanted to say and keep walking.

Running.

Until a low curse echoes through the sound system.

"Fuck, I can't."

I halt my strides.

You could hear a pin drop.

"I'm sorry, I can't do this," Xavier admits, and I turn around, my anxiety shooting through an imaginary roof. "I'm full of shit," Xav declares after a few seconds of gathering his thoughts, slipping a hand through his slicked-back hair.

No.

Triple no.

What the hell is he doing?

"This year wasn't great," he breathes. "Far from it. If anything, it was the worst year of my entire fucking life. Everything went to hell. Everything. And the only good part—" his eyes find me in the crowd, "—was meeting a girl."

I swallow hard.

He's looking at me like I'm the only person at the party.

The only person in the whole damn universe.

"Technically, I didn't meet her. I've known her for a while. Since I was a hyper little boy playing tag in this very backyard. I just didn't know how much of an amazing human being she was until recently."

I give him a pleading look.

Don't do this.

There is nothing left to save.

Nothing worth ruining your life over.

I'm confident it can't get any worse until he calls me by name.

"You were right, Aveena."

Heads turn on cue, searching for me somewhere in the mass. People spot me in a matter of seconds, boring holes through my skull.

"I *am* a dork," Xavier admits, each word coated in guilt.

My throat starts aching like a motherfucker, and I welcome the thick layer of tears stealing my sight.

I can't watch this.

"I'm the biggest fucking dork on the planet for letting you suffer in my place. I might not have been strong enough before but…" Xavier shifts his focus back to the bewildered guests. "Someone once told me to protect the people who would protect me—" he steals a glance at his mother standing near the buffet with his dad, "—and I think it's time I listen."

His father looks flaming mad.

And his mom… she's as pale as a sheet.

Xavier doesn't speak again for the longest, most miserable wait of my life, keeping every person present on their toes.

That's when he says the one thing he can never take back.

"*I'm Zac.*"

Time stops.

No one moves.

Reacts.

Makes a sound.

And, for once in my life, I truly understand what my dad meant. For the first time since he left me, I experience one of those life-altering moments that'll either make you stronger…

Or kill you.

Here, gathered with half the town in Finn's backyard…

I experience my first slow-mo.

Until the first gasp reaches my ear.

Followed by the second.

And the third.

Before I know it, an amalgam of gasps and whispers ricochets throughout the spacious backyard.

He didn't.

Xav, tell me you didn't.

"That's right, I wrote the confessions. Oh, and Brie." Xavier looks Brie straight in the face. "Piece of advice, if you have to blackmail a guy into dating you, he's just not that into you."

The basketball team and cheer squad stare at Brie with their mouths hanging, failing to stifle their laughter as Brie's cheeks turn bright red. I study the vicinity, half expecting to find hidden cameras or a television crew of some sort…

I never do.

The sound of glass shattering manages to peel my attention away from Xav. A woman dropped her champagne glass against the concrete patio. Except, it's not just *any* woman.

It's Xavier's mom.

Realization finds every guest at once, her interruption resulting in a domino effect. Whispers soar around me, a wave of shock submerging the entire party.

"*It's her*," I hear a woman on my right say.

"*Principal Emery is the woman in the confession*," another chimes a hair too loud in her husband's ear.

"*She slept with a minor*?" his husband questions in horror.

So much for the confessions being a high school thing, huh?

Zac and Love didn't only take Easton High by storm.

They took over *all* of Silver Springs.

It all started with an anonymous letter…

And two small-town kids with secrets the size of a city.

Xavier's mom delivers the performance of a lifetime, a purposefully loud sob shooting from her throat as she makes a run for it, crocodile tears coursing down her face. Xav follows her lead, rushing off the stage without further explanation.

Everybody watches as Xavier shoulders his way toward the house. The mansion swallows him whole in an instant. No one chases after him, too shaken up to muster a reaction.

No one but me.

I've barely taken a step before I'm kicking my heels off, my toes smoothing over the grass as I run after the boy who set his own life on fire to extinguish the blaze ravaging mine.

The glass doors of Finn's square-shaped house close behind me the next second, my heart pulsing in my head to the point of giving me a migraine. Worried sick, I wander into the living room and call his name.

Once.

Twice.

Nothing.

Then I hear a car engine roar outside.

And panic tightens its hold on me.

Shit, did he leave?

He can't run.

He can't—

"What happened to your shoes?"

Every bone in my body unwinds at once. I spin on my axis, my chest heaving with my lack of cardio, and tears of relief hail down my face.

He's here.

He ditched his suit's black jacket, wearing nothing but the button-up shirt he had on underneath with the sleeves rolled up. I don't bother elucidating my shoe situation, struck by this intense need to kiss him.

So, I do.

I charge toward him, hurl my arms around his neck, and mesh our lips together before he can get a word in. Xavier immediately angles my chin for more, his large hand sneaking into my hair as he kisses the fear and adrenaline still pumping in my stomach goodbye. His mouth acts like a tranquilizer, his tongue tangling with mine soothing my worries. I'm still crying, and I'm not sure if it's because I'm happy, sad, terrified…

Or all of the above.

"What were you thinking?" I choke against his lips, my voice a quivering mess. "Your scholarship, your future. God, what if Duke finds out? Xavier, *what did you do*?"

Xavier grabs my face with one hand and squeezes my cheeks, staring into my eyes as if to engrave the words into my brain as he whispers, "I protected my family."

My crying picks up again, twice as hard this time, and Xavier's lips enclose mine, his thumbs swabbing my tear-soaked cheeks dry. He kisses me so hard I wonder how I could, for even a split second, consider moving 2,216 miles away from him.

I don't have the faintest idea of what this means for us, if I'm still getting on a plane tomorrow, if his coming clean to the entire party changed anything in the grand scheme of things, but I can't bring myself to care. Not when Xavier Emery is kissing me like it's the last thing he'll ever do.

I'm gripping his collar, squashing our bodies together, when I discern fast-moving footsteps heading straight for us. Next thing I know, the door to the living room is blown wide open, and Xav gets ripped away from me violently.

The following events unfold too fast to catch up.

I barely get the chance to see Mr. Emery, sorry, *Xavier's dad*, glaring at us like he's planning a homicide before he cocks his fist back and swings at his own son.

He strikes Xavier smack in the face with all his strength, and

I scream, my hand flying to my mouth in an involuntary impulse. Gobsmacked, Xav staggers backward, swaying like he's going to lose his balance and regaining control just in time. Royally pissed off, Xav jerks his head up and wipes the blood off his mouth with the back of his hand.

"Do you have any fucking idea what you've done?" Mr. Emery belts at the top of his lungs, nostrils flaring with rage. "You ruined our lives, son. We were perfectly happy this way."

Xavier's features twist in disgust, rage thrumming through the bulging vein in his neck.

"Wait… Are you saying… you fucking *knew*?" Xav yells.

Mr. Emery clenches his teeth together, debating on revealing a secret Xav will never be ready to hear.

Finally, he says, "Of course I knew."

The confirmation serves as a detonator to the explosive anger that's laid dormant in Xavier for far too long. Matching his father's violence, Xav grips Mr. Emery's suit into his fist and seethes inches from his face. "So, you knew all this time? You knew she was fucking a minor? *My friend*?"

Mr. Emery, who's a hair shorter and not nearly as muscular as his son, has no choice but to face his disadvantage.

"Jesus, no!" His dad sticks his hands up in surrender. "I knew about the plumber, and the neighbor, but I didn't know about the kid, I swear."

Far from convinced, Xav lets go of his dad's suit with a strong shove that leaves daddy dearest straining to restore his balance.

"So, what?" Xavier hisses. "You two had some fucked-up cheating arrangement? You knew she was screwing all these losers from the get-go and you were just *okay* with it?"

Mr. Emery releases a long sigh. "I found out two years ago. I came home one night and heard them going at it upstairs. At first, I was livid. Went out and returned the favor. I convinced myself it would make us even. I'd even planned on telling her before filing for divorce, but then… I just… *never stopped.*"

Xav looks like he was just force-fed a chunk of reality he can't digest. His mother cheating on his dad was one thing. *Both* his parents cheating on each other is a completely different story.

"Come on, son." Mr. Emery steps forward. "You didn't really think I was with Hank all these nights, did you?"

Xavier stumbles back, his lips parting for a moment.

"But… how could you stay with her?"

"Look." Mr. Emery steps closer. "When your mom got pregnant with you right out of high school, I stepped up. Married her. Learned to be a dad. It was a no-brainer. I wanted you, my boy, *my pride and joy.* But when she started screwing the help, I guess it made realize that…. Because I wanted the kid—" he pauses, "—doesn't mean I ever wanted the *wife.*"

Xavier's eyes are bloodshot, his fists clenched so tight his knuckles are as white as chalk.

"Plus, we have the house together. Jobs at the same school.

It was easy. Familiar. And I wasn't looking to start all over again with someone new. So, I played the perfect husband. Showered her with love so she wouldn't suspect a thing and we could go on as before. You'd be surprised how anxious the woman gets. She's always breathing down my neck, asking me where I'm going. Like she's projecting her misdeeds onto me."

His dad stifles a scoff. "Not that any of it matters anymore. There isn't a goddamn school on the planet that'll hire us after this. Not to mention your mom's going down. Say goodbye to Silver Springs, kid. It sure as hell ain't home anymore." Xavier's dad turns to walk away, but he stops two steps in, his hateful eyes raking over me. "*I sure hope she was worth it.*"

Mr. Emery slams the door on his way out, and silence retrieves its rightful place, descending over us.

But it doesn't last long.

"I'm so sorry." I mean it.

"Doesn't matter." Xav acts invincible, but I pick up on his pain. He grabs my waist with both hands, jerking my hips against his. "All that matters is you don't have to leave."

"Xav, I… That wasn't the deal. Mr. Hall said I had to tell him who you were or he'd pull the plug on my scholarship."

"And you did."

"What? No, I—"

He pecks my mouth to shut me up. "I pulled him aside before you got here. Told him you'd convinced me to come clean and he owed it all to you. We made a deal. I agreed to take the heat as long as they leave your name out of it. Duke never has to know shit."

I'm ugly crying at this point.

Partly because I've never been so relieved in my life.

But also… because I've never felt so guilty.

"You planned this? When?" I sniffle.

"As soon as Dia told me you were leaving."

Taken aback, I give myself a moment to let it sink in.

"They can do whatever the hell they want to me, Vee, but not you—*never you.*"

"But… What about you?" My voice cracks. "Your dreams? Your scholarship? You didn't have to do this, Xav. I was ready to leave. I was okay with it."

Xavier laughs and reels me into his arms, resting his chin on top of my head. "Well, that's too fucking bad, because I'm not."

Crying my eyes out, I sag into his embrace, bunching up the bloodstained fabric of his shirt between my fingers and inhaling his scent. His busted lip is looking rough, so I drop a small kiss on the non-bloody corner of his mouth.

He said it himself.

Everything went to hell.

And it's going to keep going to hell.

Tomorrow, next week, next month.

The difference is… I don't care.

Because I found someone worth walking through fire for.

"I love you, L," Xavier whispers, brushing his thumb across

my lower lip, and I laugh at the nickname.

"I love you, Z," I croak.

He smiles.

I smile.

Then I move Xavier from my "Things I Loved and Lost" mind drawer to a completely new drawer.

One I never had before.

My favorite drawer of all time.

Things I Loved and *Kept*.

Epilogue

Aveena

Duke University

Freshman Year

"You can still change your mind, you know? It's not too late." Dia trails after me, carrying a box labeled "FRAGILE" toward Xavier's truck parked out front.

"Shit, you're right. Let's move everything back to the dorm," I snark, hoisting the heavy box in my arms into the car's brimming trunk. I've barely shut the tailgate before Xavier, who's been on the phone with our landlord for ten minutes, ends the call and rounds the truck to meet us.

"We all set?" Xavier knots his arms around my waist from behind and jerks me flush to his chest. I crack a girlish giggle as he rains kisses all over my face.

"Got one box left," I whisk my head over my shoulder to kiss him, our mouths moving slow and hard in unparalleled sync.

"Oh, hell no," a chuckling Dia intervenes. "I still have her for a few more minutes. *Hands off, Emery.*"

Dia's about to peel us apart when her ringtone cuts through the empty campus, the perk of moving two weeks after summer break kicked off. Most students have cleared out already.

Xav and I come up for air just in time to see Dia pull out her phone and check the caller ID. A smile that doesn't quite reach her eyes stretches her lips.

It's that Chance guy.

Has to be.

"Never mind, keep sucking face. I'll be back," Dia teases, distancing herself from us before pinning the phone to her ear. I throw my head back against my boyfriend's shoulder, watching my best friend dig herself deeper into a hole of denial.

"Is that her new boyfriend?" Xav asks, his mouth flush with my ear. He seizes the opportunity to kiss my neck and suck the sensitive skin behind my ear between his teeth.

I shudder all over.

"More like a temporary fix to a permanent problem," I correct.

Dia might be semi-mad at me for moving out of our dorm and getting a place with Xav off campus, but we both know she could use having the room to herself—it was getting harder and harder to sneak Xavier in every time we got horny.

Also… bunk beds.

Not sex-proof.

Granted Xav and I aren't exactly gentle in bed, fine, we're

animals, but I'll never forget having to explain to Dia why the top bunk was broken. I paid for the damages, but she didn't let me hear the end of it for months. Even now, I'm convinced I'll never live it down. *Seriously*, she'll be telling the story at my wedding one day.

"Have you told her he's back in town?" Xavier questions.

The thought makes my skin crawl.

"Nope. And I'm not going to," I reply.

The *last* thing Dia needs right now is Finn fucking Richards back in her life, especially considering all that's happening with her family. Finn is, and will always be, Dia's blind spot. Her epic, arguably toxic love. I don't care that he's back in Silver Springs after dropping off the face of the earth; it nearly killed her when he left.

God, that was almost a year ago.

It's crazy how things change.

Less than a year back, Xavier was on stage at the cocktail party, spilling his deepest secrets to the world. The events that followed ranked a solid ten out of ten on the *crazy shit* scale. Word spread through town like wildfire, and by Monday morning, every student at Easton knew Zac's identity.

Not that anyone risked confronting Xavier about it.

They wouldn't have lived to see graduation if they had.

The Stallions remained loyal to their captain through and through, more than happy to hand out broken jaws and black eyes to anyone who ran their mouth. But the best part? Brie was eventually exposed as admin of the Facebook group and "confessions spreader" by *Lacey* of all people. I think it was something about Brie saying Lacey looked fat in her cheer uniform.

One quick recording on Lacey's phone and it was over for Brie. Bright side is, Lacey's revenge scheme got Brie off our backs. The bitch landed so much detention she couldn't possibly fit another evil plan to ruin our lives into her schedule.

Xav's parents were fired from Easton High immediately, and as discussed, Mr. Hall rained hell down on Xavier for the confessions. Gave him a three weeks' suspension and cleaning duty every day until graduation. Xavier didn't complain *once*. He simply accepted things for what they were and waited for Duke to call and revoke his scholarship.

Only… they never did.

We later found out Finn's dad had meaningful connections at Duke and pulled some strings. To this day, I'm still unsure what Mr. Richards had to do to switch up the narrative. All I know is Xav got a call from someone high up in the selection process a day later, praising him for his courage and selflessness in delivering his own mother to the authorities.

As far as *my* mother is concerned, I came close to becoming an orphan when I bailed on my assistant job. That tends to happen when you nearly give your mom a heart attack.

She was beside herself at the news that I'd be staying in Silver Springs. She tried everything to talk me out of it, but with my scholarship to Duke back on the table, she knew she didn't stand a chance. Plus, Dia's dads had already agreed to take me in until graduation.

She and Ashley forged ahead with their plan to move to LA to chase some huge opportunity, only to return home with broken dreams a week later.

Long story short, *it didn't pan out.*

Mom, Ashley, and her manager Rob decided moving to LA was still the way to go, but they'd grant Ashley one last summer in Silver Springs before the big move.

You can imagine the situation it put her in with a certain dark-haired, green-eyed heartbreaker. Ash spent every spare second she had with Theo that summer, until September rolled around and an inevitable dilemma reared its ugly head.

Choose the boy…

Or her dreams.

So much has happened since then, but my most vivid memory is of the day Xavier got called to the police station for questioning. I tagged along for emotional support.

I can still picture the resentment, the pain, the sheer disgust in his blue eyes when they asked him to describe what he saw happen between Brody and his mom.

In detail.

The trial took forever to start, but we finally got into the Courtroom three months ago. It was the first time Xav had seen his mom since the day he'd exposed her crime to half the town.

He didn't want to see her before then, but it still destroyed him to watch his mother be put on the stand this way.

Brody, Finn's brother and the student she slept with, testified in her favor. Made it clear she had never raped him, and, as wrong as it was, whatever happened between these two was consensual.

Then the verdict came…

Five years in jail with the possibility of parole.

We were shocked—*astounded*—that something as small as confessions in a book could have such a massive ripple effect.

That's when Xavier stopped sleeping.

He drowned in guilt for weeks on end.

Drove himself mad.

I crashed with him at the frat house he rented a room in every night after that. Spent the next month reminding him his mom had only herself to blame. Delilah Emery made her bed when she chose to have sex with a sixteen-year-old boy.

Xavier and his dad paid her a visit a month ago.

After months of rejecting her family, she finally agreed to see them. Xav wasn't up for sharing when he came back, but he looked like the weight of the world had been lifted off his shoulders, so… safe to say it went relatively well?

Things started looking up from there.

Xavier was able to halt his free falling into bottomless pits of guilt and get his head back in the game. His plan is clear: get drafted in the NBA. And I have no doubt in his capacity to attain his goals.

He always does.

I got the proof of that last month, when he blurted a spontaneous "Move in with me" while squeezing in and out of me bareback in my bunk bed. He was making love to me so savagely, his thumb spinning around my clit so hard and fast, I thought he'd finally done it. Driven me crazy in the literal sense.

But I wasn't hallucinating.

He'd really said it.

"What?" I moaned, clawing at his back as toe-curling pleasure exploded in my stomach.

"You." *Thrust.* "Me." *Thrust.* "A place?" he simplified and kissed the breath out of me, slowing down his pounding in an effort not to spill inside me, an effort that turned out to be unsuccessful, in case you were wondering.

I had my doubts for a while, said we were not ready and he'd get sick of me if we lived together, but Xav wasn't going down without a fight. Many sneaky orgasms while Dia was asleep and conversations later, I said yes, and well, *here we are.* Packing our entire lives into the back of his truck, ready to drive across town and move in together.

"What are you thinking about?" Xavier's husky voice puts an end to my dirty thoughts.

"Us having sex," I say shamelessly. I lost my filter around this guy a long time ago.

"Funny. So am I. Should we go do that, then?" Xav smirks

and boxes me in against his truck's tailgate. He's got that mischievous look in his eyes. The one he sports whenever he's about to do something *very* dirty to me.

"Are you crazy? We're in a public parking space." I laugh.

Xavier scoffs, arching a mocking eyebrow, and I know what he's about to say before he opens his mouth.

"Never stopped us before," he teases, referring to the first time we had sex in the springs' parking lot and his lips find mine for a kiss I'd need superhuman strength to resist.

"Xav, seriously." I pull away with a chuckle. "We can't. Still waiting for my period after *someone* didn't pull out right after I switched pills. What if I'm late?"

"The risks are low, babe. Relax." Xavier smacks a kiss on my temple, and I wrap my arm around his torso, bracing my head against his chest. Silence hovers around us.

"Would it be so bad if you were?" Xavier shocks me by saying.

I pull away an inch, staring up at him.

"What do you mean?"

"I'm just saying it wouldn't be the worst thing if you *did* miss your period."

"Hold that thought." I examine him carefully, sweeping his tousled brown hair away from his eyes and skimming my fingertips over his forehead.

He frowns. "What are you doing?"

"I don't see the bruise. *Weird.*"

He catches on instantly.

"That's how it's going to be, huh?" He tickles me until I'm squirming like a worm in his arms.

"I'm kidding!" I laugh a breathless laugh.

"I didn't hit my head, smart-ass." He stops his tickling.

"So… hypothetically speaking, you'd be okay with me being pregnant?"

He stops to think about it. "Hypothetically speaking, I want to marry your ass and have babies with you. *How's that?*"

I'm smiling so wide I'm sure you can see it from outer-space. I respond the only way I can think of, by gripping his collar into my fists and crashing my lips to his for a long, heated kiss.

"Hypothetically speaking, *you're crazy*." I pant.

Xavier pouts. "Why?"

"For starters, we're nineteen and you'll change your mind."

"Okay, but what if—" Xavier pecks the tip of my nose. —*hypothetically speaking*, I ask you in a year or two once you understand how much I could never change my fucking mind about you even if I wanted to?"

My heart is beating so fast you'd think it's trying to go into cardiac arrest.

"Well, then, *hypothetically*, I'd say yes."

"Cool. So, *hypothetically*, can we go the fuck home now so I can strip you naked and—" he leans forward to whisper the rest in my ear.

Sweet Lord.

My eyes flare, his graphic description rousing my animal instincts.

"By home you mean our unfurnished apartment?" I remind him of our less-than-optimal living arrangements. We need to go furniture shopping as soon as possible.

Xav flashes an adorable grin. "Don't worry, I'll blow up an inflatable mattress or some shit to make you comfortable."

I snort. "And they say romance is dead."

I spot Dia ambling toward the truck with her phone in her hand before I can shower my boyfriend with kisses. She stops by our side a second later.

"Okay, pervs, make-out time over. We should get that last box before Chance gets here," she says and makes a beeline for the dorms. Xavier and I follow close behind.

My heart hurts from the moment Dia twists the door to the dorm open. A handful of memories linger in the air—move-in day, arguing with Dia, getting ready for our first college party. Dia's stuff is left untouched, but I was always the hoarder around here.

It's almost… unrecognizable like this.

Xavier picks the last box off the floor without breaking a sweat, and I dread the impending pain of saying goodbye.

"This is it," I tell Dia, a tear warning me of its descent.

"I can't believe you're leaving," Dia whines.

"Come on, D, I'm not moving to Canada," I chuckle. "I'll be a thirty-minute car ride away *tops*."

"Still, I'm going to miss you," she admits, opening her arms for a hug, which I welcome on cue. "Even though you're messy, and you steal my clothes, and you two broke the bed—*literally*."

All three of us laugh.

She's barely pulled away before she says, "Jesus, is it hot in here?"

"Is it? I can't tell anymore. Happens every time Vee walks into the room." Xav smirks, and I swat at his chest, topping it off with a fake gag. What? I can't have him knowing I'm a sucker for his lines.

"Before you guys go, can you give me a hand? I can never get the damn thing open," Dia asks, halfway to the window.

"Sure." I nod, following her lead.

Dia screams like she just saw a ghost the next second.

"What's wrong?" I ask.

Dia moves at least five feet away from the window, her palm squeezing her pounding heart.

I rush to the window myself, the biggest, stupidest, goofiest smile spreading across my face when I see an old friend crawling its way up the window frame.

Just like that, my fears vanish. One look and I'm not scared of anything anymore, not the future, not my missed period, not my decision to move in with Xav.

Nothing.

"What is it?" Xavier pops up behind me, craning his neck to see over my shoulder, and I smile.

Because I know everything's going to be okay.

"It's a caterpillar."

Thank you so much for reading Dear Love, I Hate you!

This is the part where I need your help!

If you would like me to write more books in the Easton Boys series, (Finn and Dia's story, Theo and Ashley's story) please make sure to leave a review for Dear Love, I Hate You on **Amazon!** It helps tremendously and lets me know this series is worth continuing :)

Connect with me:

Want to stay updated on my next releases?
www.eliahgreenwood.com/subscribe

Instagram: @eliahgreenwood

Private readers group: Eliah's Rule Breakers

Also by Eliah Greenwood

The Rules Series

Unwritten Rules (Haze & Winter, Book 1 in the Rules series)

Unspoken Rules (Haze & Winter, Book 2 in the Rules series)

Unbroken Rules (Haze & Winter, Book 3 in the Rules series)

Forgotten Rules (Will & Kass, Book 4 in the Rules series)

Forsaken Rules (Will & Kass, Book 5 in the Rules series) TO BE RELEASED.

About Eliah

Eliah Greenwood is a Canadian author, who started her writing journey on the internet at the age of fifteen. When her debut gathered 35,000,000 reads online, she decided to publish the series that set so many hearts, including hers, on fire. When she's not writing and screaming at her computer screen, you can find her binge-watching her favorite TV shows on repeat or reading in a warm blanket. She is currently working on her sixth book.

Helpful hotlines

National Suicide Prevention Lifeline:

1-800-273-8255

National Sexual Assault Hotline: 1-800-656-HOPE (4673)

National Domestic Violence Hotline:

1-800-799-SAFE (7233)

Acknowledgements

First and foremost, I want to thank Amanda Anderson (@allaboutthatromance) for being a great book friend slash the most amazing, unofficial PA I've ever had. You were the first to read this book, and I am forever grateful for your precious feedback and advice.

To Michelle Lancaster, (@lanefotograf): thank you so much for giving me the best Xavier. I can't possibly imagine our main boy having any other face.

To my editor, Sandra from One Love Editing, who always finds ways to squeeze me into her schedule at the last minute: thank you for not being sick of me yet and hyping me up along the way.

To my readers, new or from the OG Wattpad gang: a huge thank-you and a big hug. I know this book would be nothing if it weren't for your willingness to give it a chance. I'm able to live my dream because I have the most supportive readers to ever exist, and I'm eternally grateful for your time, support, and love.

To my street team for *Dear Love, I Hate You*: I couldn't do this without you. Amanda, Amy, Angelica, Jenifer, Lia, Amara, Rachel, Leslie, Dani. Selecting you is the best decision I ever made, and I hope we rock more releases together.

To my dad: thank you for caring when no one else does.

Printed in Great Britain
by Amazon

78085646R00308